THE GOD OF SMALL THINGS

A Saga of Lost Dreams

THE GOD OF SMALL THINGS

A Saga of Lost Dreams

K.V. SURENDRAN

Published by

ATLANTIC

PUBLISHERS & DISTRIBUTORS (P) LTD

7/22, Ansari Road, Darya Ganj,
New Delhi-110002
Phones : +91-11-40775252, 23273880, 23275880, 23280451
Fax : +91-11-23285873
Web : www.atlanticbooks.com
E-mail : orders@atlanticbooks.com

Branch Office
5, Nallathambi Street, Wallajah Road,
Chennai-600002
Phones : +91-44-64611085, 32413319
E-mail : chennai@atlanticbooks.com

Printed in India at Glorious Printers, A-13, D.S.I.D.C.,
Jhilmil Industrial Area, Delhi-110095

Dedicated to

THE MEMORY OF MY FATHER
K.V. KUNHIKANNAN NAIR
(Kadachira)

Teachers' Union Leader and Social Activist
(1918–1990)

PREFACE

Ms. Arundhati Roy has established herself as a novelist par excellence with her epoch making work *The God of Small Things*. Her novel is at the top of the best seller list in many countries and even before she won the Booker Prize it had attracted considerable attraction of the readers and reviewers across the world. The Booker Committee has described Roy as "an architect in literary circle moulding language in all shapes and sizes as was never done before at least in the Indian literary context." Roy herself has this to say about her work : "It tells a different story from the story the book is telling you. The book is not about what happened but about how what happened affected people."

The God of Small Things is about several things at the same time. It has a strong political undercurrent or rather it is a political satire at a certain level. It is also a protest novel which is radical and unconventional. The novel is the story of a family too. Religion is another point of interest. Also, an anti-establishment dimension can be attached to it if one wants to. Untouchability as a canker is dealt with in the novel at some depth. To crown it all, the novel is about certain people we come across in our day to day life and who have their own private worries and concerns. Of course, the novel is remarkable for the linguistic innovations also and Shomit Miller has observed that the book "uses language in a way that is rare... very rarely do you get someone who can tear apart the rules and give you something that is fresh and not pretentious."

The present book *The God of Small Things : A Saga of Lost Dreams* is an attempt to analyze Roy's novel giving focus to some of the important characters. In a novel where the writer draws a large canvas characters belonging to five generations make their appearance. Each one of these characters has a story of lost dream to tell and hence the significance of the title. Apart from delineating the characters the book also concentrates on some of the salient aspects for which the novel has carved out a place of its own. Thus, the novel is considered as a social satire where the contemporary society is portrayed in a disinterested way. The technical innovations are discussed at some length followed by the narrative technique adopted by the novelist. It is interesting to note that the author herself makes her appearance to offer her own comments. The significance of the title is discussed towards the end which is followed by an Epilogue which has in it a discussion of the autobiographical elements.

Before closing these prefatory remarks let me place on record my heart-felt gratitude to Prof. Jaydipsinh Dodiya of Saurashtra University, Rajkot for his valuable help, guidance and unstinting support.

I should be grateful to my wife Jaya and children Vishnu and Gayathri who put up with me whole-heartedly in all possible ways during the preparation of this book. I am also grateful to Ms. Sugandhi for neatly typing the draft even under great pressure.

Finally, I put on record my sincere thanks to Dr. K.R. Gupta of M/s Atlantic Publishers and Distributors, New Delhi for bringing out this book in a most elegant way in a record time.

K.V. SURENDRAN

CONTENTS

	Preface	*vii*
1.	Introduction	1
2.	A Saga of Lost Dreams	10
3.	A Sunbeam Lent .... Too Briefly	33
4.	Esthapappychachen Kuttappan Peter Mon	42
5.	The Die-vorced and the Barren	60
6.	Receipt No. Q. 498673	74
7.	Rumbled Porcupine	88
8.	The Bushy Eyebrowed Waitress	100
9.	The Ex-Nun	108
10.	The Modalali or the Blind Mother Widow with a Violin	123
11.	The Imperial Entomologist	135
12.	The Untouchable	143
13.	The Chameleon	157
14.	Politeness, Obedience, Loyalty	169
15.	Unadulterated Effluents	175
16.	'Themmadykuzhi' and Other Stories	192
17.	Living Backwards	217
18.	What Happened to Our Man of the Masses?	230
19.	*The God of Small Things*	241
	Epilogue	247
	References	251

1

Introduction

I

"Woman? very simple, say the fanciers of simple formulas : She is a womb, an ovary; She is a female — this word is sufficient to define her. In the mouth of a man the epithet 'female' has the sound of an insult, yet he is not ashamed of his animal nature; on the contrary, he is proud if someone says of him : 'He is a male!' The term 'female' is derogatory not because it emphasizes women's animality, but because it imprisons her in her sex; and if this sex seems to man to be contemptible and inimical even in harmless dumb animals, it is evidently because of the uneasy hostility stirred up in him by women." These are the opening sentences of Simone de Beauvoir's *The Second Sex*.

Now there is a different picture that is unfolded before us. More and more women are learning to know and discover themselves. There are enough indications that imaginatively they have become important, perhaps more important than ever before. They have started questioning patriarchal constructs like marriage and family. No longer is the subject of their novels love and romance; instead it is sex and respectability and also social and political issues.

A work that can undoubtedly be called the book of the decade is the much discussed *The God of Small Things* by Arundhati Roy. The Booker citation describes the novel as one written with extra ordinary linguistic inventiveness. Roy reveals a child's vision of the adult world in this novel in one sense, she herself being an "unprotected child in some ways" (as it was reported in an interview).

The novel can be said to be about several other things. Those interested in politics can claim that it is a satire on politics — communist establishment, to be more specific. One can call it a protest novel which is radical, subversive and taboo-breaking. Still another way may be that it tells the story of a family. Those worried about religion can certainly give a religious tone to it. An anti-establishment dimension can also be given to the novel if one wishes to do so. The book has in it a strong position taken against the way the 'untouchables' are treated in the society.

New York Times has made the following comments on Salman Rushdie's novel *Midnight's Children* which won the prestigious Booker Prize in 1981 : "The literary map of India is about to be redrawn...*Midnight's Children* sounds like a continent finding its voice, an author to welcome to world company." Seventeen years later Arundhati Roy has brought the honour again, this time to a small state in the South of the country and, of course, to the country at large. Roy joins the company of Rushdie "to welcome to world company." As Jain (1996) observes in her Introduction to *Women's Writing : Text and Context*, "with all its variety, timidity and marginality it (Women's Writing) has been moving through self-expression and self questioning towards self-assertion and redefinitions. It has projected alternative structures and meanings, and transformed disorder and chaos into enabling structures. It has attempted to dissolve polarities and move towards pluralistic meanings" (p. XVI).

A word should be said about the use of time and space in the novel. A huge general shift in perception and in consciousness for the western world heralded the modern century. As Hughes (1958) has observed "nearly all students of the last years of the nineteenth century have sensed in some form or another a profound psychological change" (p. 34). It meant rejection of positivism, and abandoning the notion of "Objectivity". But one of the most striking features of the period was a fascination with time, space and their relationship. Randall Stevenson has pointed out that during the 1920's, time and space became fashionable terminology and a conscious theme among artists and intellectuals. In Roy's novel also these become conscious themes and we can see certain characteristic modernist techniques, such as the frequent use of allusion and of verbal collage, as a result of attempting a radical compression of time within narrative. In fact, as Bergson (1971) rightly puts it "time, conceived under the form of a homogeneous medium, is some spurious concept, due to the trespassing of the idea of space upon the field of pure consciousness" (p. 98).

The terms "modernism" and "post-modernism" are becoming increasingly fashionable and the readers of the novel will be curious to know which label fits Roy's novel best. It may not be absurd if one says that much will depend on how one defines these terms. Perhaps post-modernism may be more a way of reading than a way of writing. Virtually any work can be said to have post-modern characteristics if we read it in the right spirit. Barth (1990) has rightly pointed out that however we draw our definitions, few writers are consistently anyone thing : "Joyce Carol Oates writes all over the aesthetical map...My own novels seem to me to have both modernist and post modernist attributes : my short story series, *Lost in the Funhouse*, strikes me as mainly late-modernist, though some critics have praised or damned it as conspicuously post-modernist" (p. 66). Similarly Mc Hale (1987) has argued that modernism deals with epistemological concerns, post-moderns with ontological ones, so there is a "shift of dominant from problems of *knowing* to the problems of *modes of being*" (p. 10).

Thus, it will be better to leave the whole thing to the reader to make his own interpretations. One fails to miss the characteristics of both these labels in the novel under consideration. What matters is how we read it out. But the fact remains that in whatever way one wants to read the novel, its enjoyment will never be affected.

II

This Volume is a collection of essays containing eighteen chapters in which a serious attempt is made to have a close look at the main theme of the novel followed by an analysis of the main characters. The government departments come under attack and the contemporary society with all its pitfalls is unfolded before us in the novel. A couple of essays deal with these issues. Essays on the structure of the novel and the narrative technique adopted follow and in the concluding essay the title of the novel is taken up for discussion.

The opening chapter entitled 'Saga of Lost Dreams' considers the novel as one where almost all characters, both major and minor have shattered dreams. Ayemenem and Ayemenem house have lost their old glory and in a certain sense they also have lost their dreams. Rev. John Ipe's father is the oldest member of the Ayemenem family who makes his appearance in the novel. Then we have Rev. John Ipe himself and his wife Aleyooty Ammechi, both of whom disappointed for one reason or the other. Baby Kochamma, their daughter finds life an absurd drama and she continues to write love letters even at the age of eighty. Pappachi, her brother and Mammachi, her sister-in-law also follow the same pattern with their own despairs and unhappy plights for different reasons. Chacko, Pappachi's son and Margaret Kochamma, his daughter-in-law have almost the same story to tell. Ammu, Chacko's sister is the one who is made to suffer most. Estha and Rahel, Ammu's twin children attract our sympathy. The short life of Sophie Mol, Chacko's daughter also is eventful. We have also characters like Velutha, with whom Ammu establishes physical relations, Vellya Paapen, his father, Kuttappan his brother, Muraleedharan of the streets, Father Mulligan, the priest and several others who all have the same story to tell — the story of their lost dreams.

In the second chapter 'A Sunbeam Lent...Too Briefly' Sophie Mol's life and premature death is discussed. She is one of the very important characters who prove that "a few dozen hours can affect the outcome of whole life times" (p. 32). She comes to Ayemenem from London to recover from the shock of her father (of course, not the real one) only to know that greater shocks are in store. But fortunately for her, life does not become a burden. She has her playmates with whom she spends her time quite joyfully. She becomes the pet of the entire household. But somehow she fails to love Chacko, her 'real father'. The advances of Baby Kochamma also she resists. She dies in a boat tragedy when along with Estha and Rahel she is on her way to Velutha's house. Her death marks an important turning point in the novel and it leads to the total disintegration of the Ayemenem family which was known for its past glory.

Estha, another important character is discussed in some detail in the third chapter, 'Esthapappychachen Kuttappan Peter Mon.' He is one who begins to suffer even before he was born. He is made to pay the prize for the premature death of Sophie Mol. He was also in the boat which capsized on the way to Velutha's house. He is a deprived child who always longs for his mother's love. He believes in the theory that anything can happen to anyone. He is not young and not old and never runs short of pragmatism. He is comfortable in the company of his sister and the relationship turns incestuous. It is Baby Kochamma who is most impatient with Estha and she plays an important role in returning him to his father after the Sophie Mol incident.

'The Divorced and the Barren' is the title of the fourth chapter. Rahel, the twin sister of Estha is discussed in this chapter. Like Estha she also is destined to suffer. Her mother gets separated from her husband at a very young age and this makes life miserable for the whole family. She returns to Ayemenem house with her mother and brother as an unwelcome guest. It is the death of Sophie Mol which becomes a turning point in her life. She is sent to a convent and from there to a College of Architecture. Her love affair culminates into marriage which turns out to be a failure. Thus, she becomes a divorcee and there are people who consider her to be a divorced and the barren for the simple reason that she gets separated from her husband and does not give birth to a child. Her return to Ayemenem house after a gap of twenty-three years does not change her life in anyway.

In chapter five ('Receipt No. Q. 498673'), we discuss how Ammu a dreamy young girl becomes a mere receipt in the crematorium. She is uncared for and escapes to Calcutta to lead a new life. She gets married only to realize very soon that it is a wrong person to whom she is married. She gives birth to the twins Rahel and Estha and returns to Ayemenem. It is a hostile world where she does not have many to share her concerns. She is drawn to Velutha which turns out to be something that spoils her whole life. She is sent out of the house to do odd jobs. She is made to suffer in all possible ways and finally dies uncared for even by her own children.

The next chapter is 'Rumbled Porcupine' where Chacko,

Ammu's brother is discussed. He is one who takes pride in being a Rhodes Scholar at Oxford once upon a time. He fails in his life miserably and his dreams remain unfulfilled. He has his own ways with women and in such affairs he gets full support from his mother. His love affair and married life ultimately do not bear fruit. For the same reason he continues to lead the life of a disappointed man. Probably one thing that should be mentioned here is that he is able to establish a good relationship with the twins. But he fails before his own daughter who does not love him. He considers himself to be a prisoner of war and in a certain sense his whole life is one that is spent in 'prison'.

Margaret Kochamma, Chacko's wife is discussed in some detail in the chapter 'The Bushy Eyebrowed Waitress'. She gets disillusioned after her marriage and chooses to live with Joe. But she loses him very soon as he dies in an accident. Chacko invites her to Ayemenem and she arrives there with her daughter Sophie Mol. But life continues to be a tragedy for her. Her daughter is drowned and that makes her hysteric. In such a state of mind she even slaps Estha a couple of times as she believes that he is responsible for Sophie Mol's death.

Chapter eight ('The Ex-Nun') is devoted to delineate the unique character Baby Kochamma. She is one who lives backwards in the novel. Her love affair with Father Mulligan fails to click. She goes abroad for studies but returns to Ayemenem with disappointment as her constant companion. Ammu and her children bring discomfort to her and she makes use of every opportunity to humiliate her arch enemy Ammu. It is she who joins hands with Mammachi to show Ammu the door. Even at a very old age she lives the life of a young woman. As fate would have it she is made to live alone in the Ayemenem house with only the servant girl. But even at that age she is not ready to change. Estha and Rahel returning to Ayemenem is a torment to her and she is very eager to see that they leave Ayemenem at the earliest.

In the next chapter ('The Modalali or The Blind Mother Widow with a Violin') the focus shifts to Mammachi, another important character in the novel. She has weakness for her son Chacko, whereas, she is not fair either to her own daughter Ammu or her daughter-in-law Margaret Kochamma. Her major concern has been her Paradise Pickles and Preserves factory. When Ammu is involved in the scandal she mercilessly joins hands with Baby Kochamma to send her away from Ayemenem house. She is rather cruel to Vellya Paapen, the Paravan for no fault of his. Her attack on Velutha also goes beyond the limit. On the whole she plays a very important role in the disintegration of the Ayemenem family.

The tenth chapter has the title 'The Imperial Entomologist' where Pappachi, Mammachi's husband is discussed. He is one who is disappointed for more reasons than one. His wife brings misery and he can never adjust to the fact that he is old and his wife is young. To 'compensate' he beats her regularly. He has bought a car which he never allows others even to touch. The nightmare that continues to haunt him is the moth that he has discovered. By sheer ill-luck he loses the glory. He is one who will be remembered as a great academician and researcher destined to be a disappointed man.

Velutha, the Paravan is the centre of discussion in chapter eleven ('The Untouchable'). He can perhaps be called the hero of the novel and he is the 'God' in *The God of Small Things*. He is a carpenter, a rebel, a trade unionist. The society makes him a scapegoat and he dies in police custody for no convincing reason. He represents the down trodden and the attitude of some of the characters in the novel to him exposes the society where human qualities take a back seat. His death marks a turning point in the novel and some of the characters never recover from the shock.

K.N.M. Pillai is 'The Chameleon' who makes his appearance in the next chapter. He is a true politician who has nothing to lose but power. He plays a very important role in the novel and is instrumental in making life miserable at least for some of the characters. He is a master plotter who does everything for his own benefits. He never has any prick of conscience to betray Velutha who has ever been loyal to the party. He organizes the workers of Paradise Pickles Factory in his favour which ultimately presents sleepless nights to Chacko, its owner. On the whole he is presented as a typical politician in the contemporary society who has absolutely no regard for ethics in public life.

The chapter with the title 'Politeness, Obedience, Loyalty...'

has in it a discussion of the working of some of the government departments of our times. 'Politeness', 'Obedience', 'Loyalty', etc. are certain qualities that should go with the police. But they are neither polite nor obedient. They are not loyal either to those who approach them seeking help. The PWD, Airport Authority, Education department etc., are some of the agencies which are sharply criticized by the novelist. An attempt is made to examine some of these issues.

Contemporary society is further put to scrutiny in the following chapter ('Unadulterated Effluents') where we get a clear idea of the life of the middle class people. The ecological problems, marginalization of women, untouchability, the influence of Gulf money are some of the issues highlighted. Cultural decadence and some of the problems to do with religion are also discussed. Family relation is another area which is also focussed. Sexuality which is an important theme is also examined in some detail. On the whole, the novel is remarkable for its portrayal of the contemporary society and the novelist is successful in her attempt to expose what is undesirable.

'Themmadykuzhy' (Pauper's pit) and other stories' discusses the innovations in language that Roy makes use of in the novel. The novel is remarkable for the different techniques that are made use of. Some of these are her use of Malayalam words, italicization, use of brackets, 'one-word sentences', use of clusters of adjectives, verbs etc., coinages, compounding, changing word class, topicalization, words running into another, repetition of negatives and also a series of others. The novel will certainly stand out for the unique experiments Roy makes in her treatment of language.

'Living Backwards' is the chapter where the structure of the novel is taken up for discussion. The novel is unique for the way the plot develops. The technique is one of narrating almost the whole story in the first chapter and going into the details in the following chapters. She even makes use of cinematic techniques. The plot does not simply involve the journey and trial of the hero. Instead the role of the major and minor characters is given equal importance. Alongwith that some other issues are also highlighted which all contribute to make the novel an interesting one to read.

The narrative technique is the theme of Chapter seventeen

('What Happened to Our Man of the Masses'). The story is mainly narrated in third person but there are interesting techniques which are made use of in the novel. For example, the novelist sometimes makes use of authorial comments with very specific purpose in her mind. This method, which is sometimes referred to as interior monologue becomes an effective tool in her hands while she narrates the story.

The last chapter 'The God of Small Things' examines the effectiveness of the title of the novel. The novelist makes it out that Velutha, the Paravan is 'The God of Small things'. The interesting thing is that the three important words 'God', 'Small' and 'Things' are repeated in the novel several times and she has her own motives behind such repetitions. In short, one can very well say that there cannot be a better title for the novel than the present one which is notable for the use of irony especially in the use of 'small things' which is a major theme which recurs in the novel.

In the Epilogue an attempt is made to show how the novel caught the attention of the world. The views of some of the reviewers and members of the Booker Prize committee have been quoted. Since the novel has by and large an autobiographical element woven in it, it is shown how Rahel and Ammu are none but Roy and her mother Mary Roy. The turbulence in their life has been beautifully portrayed in the novel which ultimately adds to its greatness.

2

A Saga of Lost Dreams

I

The God of Small Things is a saga of lost dreams from several points of view. Almost all the characters in the novel have something to say about their loss. Even the minor characters are not an exception to this rule. Roy draws a large canvas and the novel unfolds the story of five generations beginning from Rev. E. John Ipe's father. Rev. Ipe is the great grandfather of Sophie Mol whose arrival to Ayemenem becomes a turning point in the novel.

Rev. Ipe's father was one who could make his son a little blessed one. But Rev. Ipe did not take much time to realize that his daughter was going to be a 'constant lover.' His wife also was not destined to lead a peaceful life. Baby Kochamma their daughter had to live life backwards! Her brother Pappachi and his wife Mammachi also had a tale to tell of lost dreams. Their son Chacko also had serious problems. Ammu, Chacko's sister was the worst affected and her children Estha and Rahel too were born to suffer. Sophie Mol, the youngest member of the family who had a premature death had the same story to tell. Velutha, Vellya Paapen, Kuttappan, Muraleedharan all had their own sad plight which makes the novel "a saga of lost dreams."

II

Sophie Mol came to Ayemenem with her mother Margaret Kochamma to join her real father Chacko. But things took an entirely unexpected turn within a few days : "Perhaps it's true that things can change in a day. That a few dozen hours can affect the outcome of whole life times. And then when they do, those few dozen hours, like the salvaged remains of a burned house — the charred clock, the signed photograph, the scorched furniture — must be resurrected from the ruins and examined. Preserved, Accounted for" (p. 32).

It is not the characters alone who 'suffer' in the novel. When Faulkner wrote his *The Sound and the Fury*, there was a critical assumption (perhaps incorrect) that "Faulkner was trying to write a sociological study of the American South but did not know how to go about it" (see Carvel Collins p. 156). For Roy it is Ayemenem which has a story to tell of its old glory.

Even the opening sentences of the novel are about Ayemenem where we get a description of the summer in Ayemenem. "May in Ayemenem is a hot, brooding month. The days are long and humid. The river shrinks and black crows gorge on bright mangoes in still, dustgreen trees. Red bananas ripen. Jack-fruits burst. Dissolute bluebottles hum vacuously in the fruity air. Then they stun themselves against clear windowpanes and die, fatly baffled in the sun" (p. 1).

There was a time when Ayemenem was known for its freshness, an unpolluted river and matchless greenery which made life pleasant for the people there. But when the characters in the novel started losing their dreams Ayemenem did not stand a mute witness. It also started changing, changing for the worse to match perhaps the unscrupulousness of some of the characters in the novel.

Ayemenem which boasted of a typical countryside in Kerala gradually got urbanized. The Gulf culture took its toll and lifestyles in the village changed drastically. Small fish "appear in the puddles that fill the PWD potholes on the highways" (p. 1) to add to the misery of the people who lived there! Now the banks of the river "smelled of shit, and pesticides brought with world Bank loans" (p. 13). Around Ayemenem one could only see the new, freshly baked, iced, Gulfmoney houses built by nurses, masons, wire-benders and bank clerks who worked hard and unhappily in far away places. There was exploitation everywhere.

The honest ration buyers were tempted by "cheap soft-porn magazines about fictitious South Indian sex friends" with "glimpses of ripe, naked woman lying in pools of fake blood" (p. 13). The houses nestled under trees and unmotorable narrow paths which branched off the main road gave Ayemenem the semblance of rural quietness. However, the population had swelled to the size of a little town.

The people in general also were not quite different. They could gather at a moment's notice. They were capable of beating to death a careless bus driver. Without an iota of hesitation they could smash the windscreen of a car that dared to venture out on the day of an opposition *bandh* (which naturally would paralyse normal life). Police officers who were expected to protect the life and property of the people had eyes which were 'sly' and 'greedy' and stared at their victim's breasts as they spoke and openly called a woman 'veshya' which means 'prostitute' (Maybe, this is not something peculiar to Ayemenem).

A saltwater barrage had been built down river in exchange for votes from the influential paddy-lobby. "The barrage regulated the inflow of saltwater from the backwaters that opened into the Arabian sea. So now they had two harvests a year instead of one. More rice, for the price of a river" (p. 124). Once it had the power to evoke fear and to change lives. Now "its teeth were drawn, its spirit spent. It was just a slow, sludging green ribbon lawn that ferried fetid garbage to the sea. Bright plastic bags blew across its viscous weedy surface like subtropical flying-flowers" (p. 124). Children defecated directly onto the riverbed and by evening "the river would rouse itself to accept the day's offerings and sludge off to the sea, leaving wavy lines of thick white scum in its wake. Upstream clean mothers washed clothes and pots in unadulterated factory effluents" (p. 125). (Factory effluents are described as 'unadulterated'!).

The assault of Ayemenem did not end there. Further inland, there was a fivestar hotel chain. The view form the hotel was beautiful, but the water was thick and toxic. *No Swimming* signs had been put up in stylish calligraphy. In all sense it was a smelly paradise. In their brochures the hotel people called it 'God's own country.' But "that smelliness, like other people's poverty was merely a matter of getting used to" (p. 126).

In short, Ayemenem had changed unbelievably. The river which was polluted beyond words, the swelling population, the people who had lost their innocence, the chain of fivestar hotels all told of its lost glory. Ayemenem could never dream of going back to what it was earlier.

III

We get enough indication in the novel that it was not Ayemenem alone that had a tale to tell of its decadence. This was also true of Ayemenem house which saw the rise and fall of five generations who occupied it. Ayemenem house which had been a good old house was gone to the dogs. It was aloof looking although "it had little to do with people that lived in it" (p. 165). The old house on the hill stood there "like an old man with rheumy eyes watching children play, seeing only transience in their shrill elation and their whole hearted commitment to life" (p. 165).

The house and the people who occupied it were known for their grandeur. But no more. The house had not two, but four shutters of panelled teak. In the old days ladies could keep the bottom half closed, lean their elbows on the ledge and bargain with visiting vendors "without betraying themselves below the waist" (p. 165). There were nine steps which led from the drive way up to the front verandah. It overlooked a beautiful ornamental garden.

That was an old story now. There was an old car which stood a silent witness to the fall of the house that boasted of its pristine glory. Ayemenem house which was dirty had near its 'mittam' (yard) the old Plymouth car (which again had a story to tell) which had started settling more firmly into the ground with every monsoon. It was "like an angular, arthritic hen settling stiffly on her clutch of eggs. With no intention of ever getting up" (p. 295) Obviously, the car was no more in use and grass grew around its flat tyres. What remained of 'The Paradise Pickles and Preserves' which once added glamour to the Ayemenem house was a signboard "rotted and fell inwards like a collapsed crown"

(p. 295). Roy also draws a picture of a sparrow lying dead on the back seat of the car which is symbolic of the Ayemenem house which had lost its life in all sense. The house was almost empty. The doors and windows remained locked. The front verandah was bare even though there was some trace of life inside as Baby Kochamma, who was originally Navomi Ipe, the daughter of Rev. E. John Ipe was still alive. "Filth had laid siege to the Ayemenem house like a medieval army advancing on an enemy castle" (p. 88). But Baby Kochamma had stopped noticing the sticky floor, white walls which had turned an uneven grey doorhands which had become greasy, plug-points clogged with grime and light bulbs with a film of oil on them.

To sum up, Ayemenem house which had a story to tell of five generations had fallen from its golden days fully in-keeping with the fate of its inmates. A dreamy house full of life was on its deathbed and it seemed to appear to wait for the last breath of its only legitimate inmate which would ultimately see its 'death' putting an end to decades of its eventful existence. Aymenem house had only a past and not even a meaningful present to boast of. All the hopes of a life 'full of sounds' had been shattered. The novel has several parallels in Faulkner's (1966) *The Sound and the Fury* which again tells the story of the decline of a family. Like *The God of Small Things*. it is also the history of an inward turning family living for the most part in the past.

IV

In this section we shall begin discussing how the novel is a chronicle of lost dreams from the point of view of the characters who are destined to play their respective roles. Van O' Connor (1964) has made the following observation as regards the task that is there before a good fiction writer : "We expect a fiction writer to know his craft, and to help us discover something about the world we did not know before or know in the same way, something we believe to be true and that has relevance to our own attitudes and conduct" (p. 9). In fact, beyond doubt Roy proves that she knows her craft and let us see further how she helps us discover a world (where we have a dozen or more characters) we did not know before.

The oldest member of the Ayemenem family that Roy tells us about in the novel is Rev. E. John Ipe's father. But we don't know much about him not even his name. We only know that in 1876 when his son Ipe was seven years old, he had taken him to see the Patriarch who was visiting the Syrian Christians of Kerala. The Patriarch had blessed Rev. Ipe, which might have brought ecstacy to his father because to get the personal blessing of the Patriarch of Antioch, the sovereign head of the Syrian Christian Church was something great. We don't know what other dreams he cherished and for the same reason do not know how many of them were shattered.

In the opening chapter of the novel ('Paradise Pickles & Preserves') itself Rev. Ipe is introduced. He was priest of the Mar Thoma Church, well known in the Christian Community. He continued to be known as *Punnyan Kunju* — Little Blessed One — and people came down to him to be blessed. He had the dubious distinction of starting a school for the untouchables. He grew up and became a priest. Rev. Ipe got the first shock of his life which ultimately shattered his dream when his daughter Baby Kochamma defied his wishes and became a Roman Catholic. Within a year of her joining the convent, he began to receive puzzling letters from her in the mail which made him go to Madras and withdraw her from the convent. Her insistence that she would not reconvert was a second shock to him. He started realizing that his daughter had developed a 'reputation' and was unlikely to find a husband. This made him think that since she couldn't have a husband he would send her abroad for studies. She attended a course of study at the University of Rochester in America. When she returned after two years he gave her charge of the front garden of the Ayemenem house, where she raised a fierce, bitter garden that people came all the way from Kottayam to see. Naturally, his daughter's fate might have made Rev. Ipe a disappointed man. A sad end should await him though in the portrait he "smiled his confident-ancestor smile out across the road instead of the river" (p. 30).

Aleyooty Ammachi is Baby Kochamma's mother. We know that it was she who realized that 'Koh-i-noor' in the letter that Baby Kochamma sent to her father was none other than Baby

Kochamma herself. Long ago she had shown Baby Kochamma a copy of her father's will in which he had written "I have seven jewels one of which is my Koh-i-noor." He was describing his grandchildren in these words. Baby Kochamma's mother realized that Baby Kochamma had assumed that he had meant her to be the Koh-i-noor. We don't know anything more about Rev. Ipe's wife except that she continued to live in an oil portrait which was put up in the front verandah. The portraits of Rev. Ipe and his wife hung on either side of the stuffed, mounted bison head. A contrast is drawn between the two photographs. While Rev. Ipe smiled, Aleyooty Ammachi looked more hesitant. There are enough indications in the whatever little descriptions the novel has about her that she also was not one who was happy with her life. The 'hesitant Aleyooty' "would have liked to turn around but couldn't. Perhaps it wasn't as easy for her to abandon the river" (p. 30). May be the cruel fate made her abandon the river rather forcefully, which might be the reason for her possible shattered dream.

V

The first member of the third generation for whom life was "a tale told by an idiot, full of sound and fury, signifying nothing" [see Shakespeare's Macbeth (1969-p. 219)] is Baby Kochamma. Conrad (1965) has made the following observation in his Preface to *The Nigger of the Narcissus* : "My task which I am trying to achieve is, by the power of the written word, to make you hear, to make you feel — it is, before all, to make you see" (p. 5). Roy makes us hear, feel and see Baby Kochamma in her novel.

For Baby Kochamma life was a crushing defeat. Fate was so cruel and unkind to her that she was made to live her life backwards. Her eventful life made the 'real beginning' when she was eighteen and fell in love with Father Mulligan a handsome young Irish Monk. He was in Kerala for a year on deputation from his Seminary in Madras. "He was studying Hindu scriptures, in order to be able to denounce them intelligently" (p. 22). More than anything she was sexually excited and made advances to the Irish Monk. Her father was not intelligent enough to notice this weakness in her. However, the Father was not a fool to miss the meaning of her hovering around the table long after lunch had been cleared away.

At first she tried to seduce him with weekly exhibitions of staged charity. "Every Thursday morning just when Father Mulligan was due to arrive Baby Kochamma force-bathed a poor village child at the well with hard red soap that hurt its protruding ribs" (p. 23). Father was more than merely flattered by the emotion he aroused in the attractive young girl who stood before him "with a trembling, kissable lips and blazing coal-black eyes." (p. 23). He was young too and sometimes the temptation was irresistible for him. Every Thursday, they would stand by the well in the midday sun. The young girl and the intrepid Jesuit, both quaking with un-Christian passion.

She entered a Convent in Madras after becoming a Roman Catholic with special dispensation from the Vatican. Her hope was that it would provide her opportunities to be with Father Mulligan. Somehow she wanted to be near him. "Close enough to smell his beard. To see the coarse weave of his cassock. To love him just by looking at him" (p. 24). To her disappointment (In fact, her dreams get smashed form this point onwards) she realized the futility of it all. She found that the senior sisters monopolized the priests and bishops with biblical doubts more sophisticated than hers would ever be. She grew restless and unhappy.

She was brought back, sent abroad for studies and two years later she returned with a diploma in Ornamental Gardening, but more in love with Father Mulligan than ever. Baby Kochamma creamed her feet every night with real cream and pushed back the cuticles on her toe-nails. After fifty years strangely enough, she abandoned the ornamental garden to fall in love with her new love. She had installed a dish antenna on the roof of the Ayemenem house. Wars, famines, football, sex, music, etc., began to arrive in her drawing room. Ironically, her ornamental garden wilted and died. She could outlive everybody else only to love the Ayemenem house and the furniture she had inherited. She did not have much faith in others. That was what made her lock even her fridge where she kept her week's supply of cream buns brought from Best bakery in Kottayam. She was fond of rice-water which she drank instead of ordinary water.

Baby Kochamma had managed to persuade herself over the years that her unconsummated love for Father Mulligan had been entirely due to her restraint and her determination to do the right thing. Her hypocrisy is revealed from this line of thought. She thought that "a married daughter had no position in her parent's home" (p. 45). She strongly believed in the theory that a divorced daughter had no position anywhere at all. A divorced daughter from a love marriage was "outrageous". A divorced daughter from an inter community love marriage was simply unbearable for her. That was why she never tolerated the presence of Ammu in her house. She also disliked the twins, daughters of Ammu. She very often eavesdropped relentlessly on the twin's private conversations and whenever she caught them speaking in Malayalam, she levied a small fine which was deducted from their pocket money. She also made them write "impositions". She was more than hurt when somebody in a trade-union procession at Cochin suggested 'Modalali Mariakkutty' as a name for her, made her hold a red flag, wave it and made to say 'Inquilab Zindabad.'

She was snobbish in all sense and pretended that she had great knowledge of literary works like *The Tempest*. She enjoyed the way Ammu was punished for her sins. But Ammu's affairs with Velutha, the untouchable surprised her quite a lot : "How could she stand the smell? Haven't you noticed? They have a particular smell, these Paravans" (p. 257). May be, only the smell of an Irish Monk is all right for her!

In some respects she was a changed woman. Her concerns included filling in a Listerine discount coupon that offered a two-rupee rebate on their new 500 ml. bottle and two thousand rupee gift vouchers to the lucky winners of their lottery! She never forgot to lie about her age when she filled in the applications.

We sympathise with Baby Kochamma at least in her weaker moments when she lived in her dreamy, lost world. There was a routine thing that she did. That was turning the pages of the diary and making a fresh entry "I love you, I love you." Every page in the diary had an identical entry. She had a case full of diaries with identical entries. The entries all began with the same words : " I love you I love you" (p. 297). Even the death of Father Mulligan did not alter the text of the entries in her diary. She was reduced to an ordinary woman whose mind was deranged. We don't need to go in search of further pieces of evidence to establish that Baby Kochamma expecially stands out in the novel as one who lost her dreams at a very young age and continued to be so even at the age of eighty-three.

VI

It is often said about the impressionistic tradition that "life does not narrate but makes impressions on our brains." *The God of Small Things* makes impressions on our brains and even a minor character who is not properly developed somehow does not disappear from our mind. Pappachi, who is the brother of Baby Kochamma is one such character. He is also one who suffers multiple shocks and lives a 'lost life'. He could never reconcile himself to the fact that Mammachi, his wife was seventeen years junior to him. It was a shock to him when the realization came to him that "he was an old man when his wife was still in her prime" (p. 47).

He was a self conscious man who took pride in the fact that he was a high-ranking ex-government official and never considered pickle-making a suitable job for such a person. He was jealous of his wife especially when she started getting attention suddenly. Perhaps this might be the reason why he took pleasure in beating his wife quite frequently, sometimes even mercilessly. It was Chacko, his son, who came from London who put a sudden end to this practice. Pappachi stopped beating Mammachi and also stopped talking to her. He always had the feeling that Mammachi was neglecting him, which was an added reason for making his life miserable. "To some small degree he did succeed in further corroding Ayemenem's view of working wives" (p. 48).

He bought a skyblue Plymouth from an old Englishman in Munnar. The snobbish man sweated freely inside his woollen suits. The Plymouth was Pappachi's revenge and he never allowed Mammachi or anyone else in the family to use it or even sit in it. This dream of driving away people from his car was smashed the moment he died when it passed on to Mammachi, his wife. But even when he lived misfortune continued to chase him. He had been an Imperial Entomologist at the Pusa Institute. The greatest setback in his life was not having had the moth he had discovered named after him. The moth which fell into his drink one day was identified as a slightly unusual race by the taxonomic experts after an anxious waiting for about six months. Then came the real blow. The experts discovered that Pappachi's moth was, in fact, a separate species and a genus unknown to science. By then he had retired. His moth was named after the acting director of the Department of Entomology, a junior officer whom he had disliked. The moth, ultimately "tormented him and his children and his children's children" (p. 49).

His children Ammu and Chacko had no good words to say about him. Ammu said he was a shit-wiper and Chacko liked to refer to him as Anglophile. He did have a double face. He donated money to orphanages and leprosy clinics. He liked the public to look at him as a sophisticated generous, moral man. But alone with his wife and children he turned monstrous and cunning. They were beaten up, humiliated, and then made to suffer the envy of friends and relations.

In short, Pappachi too died a disappointed man showing the world his Plymouth and never at peace with himself. Fame was his life's mission, which mercilessly evaded him even when it was at arm's length. Naturally, such a person cannot be blamed when he behaves unexpectedly. May be his near ones also are to be blamed if he made himself believe that he was being neglected. To be sure, Pappachi is a second member of the third generation who dreamed and dreamed and ultimately lost the love and respect of everyone including that of his wife and children.

VII

Mammachi, the unfortunate wife of Pappachi was destined to be beaten up rather frequently by her husband. She might have dreamed of a peaceful life. But fate had decided dismantling the whole thing. To add to the misery she was almost blind, which of course, is a second factor responsible for uprooting her tree of life. "Her own grief grieved her. His (Chacko's) devastated her" (p. 5).

She was not at all kind to her workers. When the accountant brought news about dissatisfaction among workers her reaction was : "Tell them to read the papers. There's a famine on. There are no jobs. People are starving to death. They should be grateful they have any work at all" (p. 122). Her responses were harsh, straightforward and predictable. Her mind often wandered back over the years to her first batch of professional pickles. How beautifully they had looked, she used to exclaim. That means, it continued to be an unfulfilled dream for her to think of perfect preservation of the pickles. This was a third factor which shook her.

Mammachi had a separate entrance built for Chacko's room so that the object of his 'needs' wouldn't have to go traipsing through the house. She was full of rage at Velutha who succeeded in having sexual relations with Ammu. She even imagined "a Paravan's coarse black hand on her daughter's breast. His mouth on hers. His black hips jerking between her parted legs" (p. 257). Mammachi thought about it and nearly vomitted. It was the thought of her naked, coupling in the mud with a man who was nothing but a filthy coolie which made her condemn Ammu. Her fury was, infact, unmanageable. She thought Ammu had defiled generations of breeding and brought the family to its knees.

She was at her cruellest when Velutha arrived before her. She spewed her blind venom and her insufferable insults at him. She "continued her tirade, her eyes empty, her face twisted and ugly, her anger propelling her towards Velutha until she was shouting right into his face and he could feel the spray of her spit and smell the stale tea on her breath" (p. 284). She threatened him saying that she would have him castrated like the pariah dog. She didn't stop there. She "spat into Velutha's face. Thick spit. It spattered across his skin. His mouth and eyes" (p. 284).

When we finish reading the novel Mammachi evokes no sympathy from us. One might even think that she did deserve all the beatings and it was good that she was almost blind. One would like the problem of preserving the pickles to be a continuous headache to her. At the sametime the argument is well-established. Mammachi is another character in the novel destined to lead a lost life. In this respect at least she is a perfect match to Pappachi.

VIII

Chacko was Mammachi's only son. He is first introduced in the novel as the biological father of Sophie Mol. He was a voracious reader and took pleasure in extensively quoting from books which were his favourites, of course for no apparent reason. He had been a Rhodes Scholar at Oxford and "was permitted excesses and eccentricities nobody else was" (p. 38). It is perhaps his eccentricity that made him claim that he was writing a Family Biography for which the family would have to pay him not to publish. In Ammu's words it was "biographical blackmail."

Chacko also did not and could not lead a life the way he wanted to. For him life brought misery and desperation. His own words substantiated the claim. "We're prisoners of war, our dreams have been doctored. We belong no where. We sail unanchored on troubled seas : we may never be allowed ashore. Our sorrows will never be sad enough. Our joys never happy. Our dreams never big enough. Our lives never important enough. To matter" (p. 53).

Mammachi often said that Chacko was easily one of the cleverest men in India. But Ammu had enough reasons to disagree with this point of view. Her conclusion was that all-Indian mothers are obsessed with their sons and are therefore, poor judges of their abilities. It was only after Pappachi died that Chacko resigned his job as lecturer at the Madras Christian college and came to Ayemenem. The first thing he did was to have the pickle factory registered as a partnership with Mammachi as the "sleeping partner." Though Ammu did as much work in the factory as Chacko, he always referred to it as "my factory, my pineapples, my pickles" (p. 57). He believed in the strange logic "what's yours is mine and what's mine is also mine" (p. 57). Comrade E.M.S. was Chacko's hero. His father even used to address him as "Karl Marx" ! He often said that his ambition was to die of over eating.

Chacko was a proud and happy man to have a wife like Margaret Kochamma. But things took an unexpected turn. She divorced him. For Chacko the worst punishment was when he reminisced about Margaret. "He spoke of her often and with a peculiar pride. As though he admired her for having divorced him... she traded me in for a better man" (p. 249) he would say to Mammachi.

To conclude, Chacko also had a sad tale to tell. Blows came to him one after the other, his daughter Sophie Mol's death being the one which caused him irreparable loss. He wanted to be happy and complacent. But far from being a happy man it was the absurdity of life that haunted him. He was not very kind even to his own sister who found him to be an active member of the "wonderful male Chauvinistic Society." His eccentricity was an outward manifestation of the complexities of his inner self and the interest he showed in reading was perhaps a good diversion from the psychological problems he confronted. Chacko very well would qualify to be the son of his father within the thematic pattern that is being discussed.

IX

Chacko's wife Margaret Kochamma was Sophie Mol's English Mother. She used to be Chacko's wife ! That was because she had got a second husband in Joe. Margaret also, we find, had to live a life which was in no way rosy. She was working as a waitress at a Cafe in Oxford when she met Chacko first. Her family lived in London. Her father owned a bakery. She was one who moved out of her parents' home just to assert youthful independence. "She clung nervously to old remembered rules, and had no one but herself to rebel against" (p. 241). Her meeting with Chacko turned out to be a turning point. She had never before met a man who spoke of the world of what it was, and how it came to be, or what he thought would become of it. She was too young to realize that what she assumed was her love for Chacko was actually tentative, timorous acceptance of herself. She was married to him and her father never attended the function as he disliked Indians. He thought of them as sly, dishonest people. He couldn't even believe that his daughter was marrying an Indian.

Within a year Margaret realized that Chacko was the wrong

person she had married. She could easily find fault with whatever he had done or not done : "That he didn't apologize for the cigarette burns in the new sofa. That he seemed incapable of buttoning up his shirt...." (p. 245). Meanwhile they moved to London. But Chacko and Margaret had to occupy smaller rooms. Margaret was pregnant and physically most attractive. "Pregnancy had put colour in her cheeks and bought a shine to her thick, dark hair" (p. 248). She met Joe a biologist. For Margaret he was everything that Chacko wasn't. Eventually the inevitable happened. By the time she gave birth to Sophie Mole, Margaret realized that for herself and her daughter's sake, she had to leave Chacko. She asked him for a divorce. He had to leave sadly, but quietly. Even after their parting they continued to write letters and over the years the friendship matured. For Chacko, it was keeping in touch with the mother of his child.

"Take everything", her colleagues had advised Margaret in concerned voices. "You never know." This was their way of saying to a colleague travelling to the Heart of Darkness :

> "(*a*) Anything can Happen to Anyone
>
> So
>
> (*b*) It's Best to be Prepared" (p. 267).

Several things had happened to her which made her life match that of Chacko's. For her it was not just a tragedy but a chain of misfortunes. She got a divorce (which of course materialized at her initiative), Joe died and to crown it all her dear daughter Sophie Mol also had an unexpected death. The last one in the series was certainly the most unbearable one. That was why she expressed her irrational rage at Rahel and Estha, Ammu's children who had for some reason been spared of death by drowning. But she did realize that she had no right to behave the way she did. She was terribly ashamed of her action which made her write to Ammu apologetically. To put it briefly, Margaret Kochamma also does not stand as an exception to the rule that almost all the characters in the novel have a story to tell — the story of a shattered dream.

X

Ammu is the tragic heroine of the novel. She is the most

conspicuous representative of the fourth generation who died at a very young age of thirty-one which is described as "not old, not young" and "viable die-able age."

Her suffering started at a very young age. She finished her schooling the same year that her father retired form his job in Delhi and moved to Ayemenem. He insisted that college education was unnecessary for a girl. So she had to leave Delhi. She had nothing to do at Ayemenem other than waiting for marriage proposals. But there again problems awaited her. Pappachi, her father did not have enough money to raise a suitable dowry. Naturally, no proposals came her way. She dreamed of escaping from Ayemenem, from her ill-tempered father and bitter, long-suffering mother. Finally, her father agreed to let her spend the summer with a distant aunt who lived in Calcutta. She met her future husband at someone else's wedding reception there.

She had an elaborate Calcutta wedding. But very soon things began to take a very bad shape. Her husband was a misfit in more ways than one. He lied outrageously when he didn't need to. He was an alcoholic and he made her smoke. Twins were born to her and by the time they were two years old drinking had driven him into an alcoholic stupor. Meanwhile, Mr. Hollick, the English manager summoned him to his bungalow to tell him that he should resign. He told him this also : "You're a very lucky man, you know, wonderful family, beautiful children, such an attractive wife.... An extremely attractive wife". (p. 41). Clearly the Manager had an eye on her. He suggested that Ammu be sent to his bungalow to be 'looked after.' The only choice left before her was to return, unwelcomed, to her parents in Ayemenem, which she did.

Somehow the well-built Velutha created ripples in her. While he had held her little daughter in his arms, she felt that he was not the only giver of gifts but had gifts to give him, too. The gift was her own body. "Her brownness against his blackness. Her softness against his hardness. Her nut-brown breasts (that wouldn't support a toothbrush) against his smooth ebony chest" (p. 335). This was, in fact, the beginning of the end. Vellya Paapen, Velutha's father was a mute witness to whatever went on near his house and he rushed to Ayemenem house to give a full factual report. Ammu was locked in a room and meanwhile as a coincidence Sophie Mol got drowned. Ammu was shown the door and soon we hear about her death. She died in a grimy room in the Bharat Lodge in Alleppey, where she had gone for a job interview as someone's secretary. She died alone.

The church refused to bury Ammu. So Chacko had to hire a van to transport the body to the electric crematorium. He had her wrapped in a dirty bedsheet and laid out on a stretcher. Finally, she became a number. Receipt No. Q. 498673. That was the number of the pink receipt the crematorium 'In-charge' gave them. That entitled Chacko and Rahel to collect Ammu's remains.

Ammu reminds one of *The Scarlet Letter*, which has been described as "the story of three sinners and the consequences of their acts" (see David Levin p. 12). In Roy's novel Ammu takes the role of Hester Prynne, the publicly known "sinner". Maybe we have two more sinners in Rahel and Estha! Ammu's is more than a tragedy. She is made to suffer even from a very young age and continues to suffer throughout her life. She is humiliated at the hands of the police, her near and dear ones and also the public at large. Even at her death bed she was left to herself. In short, Ammu, without her knowledge, becomes instrumental in precipitating the tragedy which confronts two generations of Ayemenem house.

XI

As has been pointed out earlier the novel resembles Faulkner's *The Sound and the Fury* in several respects. We have Rahel and Estha, the twins in Roy's novel who led lives of tragedy and waste as the children in Faulkner's novel. The youngest child, Benjy, who grew into a huge man with the mentality of a three year old and lived in emotional deprivation is very much like Estha in Roy's novel who was neither young nor old and who suffered from emotional deprivation through out. The chief tragedy of the son named Quentin in Faulkner's novel was that he was drawn to his sister but repelled from acting on this emotion by social convention. Estha also suffered from similar problems in Roy's novel.

"Estha and Rahel thought of themselves together as Me, and

separately, individually as We or Us. As though they were a rare breed of Siamese twins, physically separate, but with joint identities'' (p. 2). Their tragedy began the moment they were born. They were nearly born on a bus. For years the twins harboured a faint resentment against their parents for having diddled them out of a life time of free bus rides, for they thought if they were born on a bus they would get free bus rides for the rest of their lives.

The sense of loss is very much evident in the fact that Estha and Rahel had no surname. That was because Ammu, their mother was considering reverting to her maiden name. This itself is enough to create emotional crisis in young children. They were not privileged to learn what other children learned. ''While children of their age learned other things, Estha and Rahel learned how history negotiates its terms and collects its dues from those who break its laws'' (p. 55). Baby Kochamma had been put in-charge of their education and they found it a torture. They were fond of reading backwards and showed Miss Mitten, Baby Kochamma's Australian friend how it was possible to read both ''Malayalam'' and ''Madam I'm Adam'' backwards as well as forwards. The result was that they were punished. They were made to write ''(In future we will not read backwards. In future we will not read backwards). A hundred times'' (p. 60).

Ammu told them the story of Julius Caesar. The message that was given to them was that they ''can't trust anybody. Mother, father, brother, husband, best friend. Nobody'' (p. 60). Ammu's fear was that her son would grow up to be a ''Male Chauvinist pig'' like her brother Chacko. The children continued to remember their parent's anger and may be that also contributed to their emotional crisis in a non-trivial way. Their mother continued to pester them teaching them manners which they couldn't take kindly. Many a time they had to sing in English in obedient voices. The children were weighed down by Ammu's words : ''If it weren't for you I would be free. I should have dumped you in an orphanage the day you were born. You're the millstones round my neck'' (p. 292). The effect of these words could be tremendous. Perhaps these words might have echoed and re-echoed in the ears of the twins which ultimately might have contributed to their emotional crisis more than ever before.

There was a very special relation established between the twins. They always had a feeling of oneness and there were even physical relations between them. "She was lovely to him. Her hair. Her cheeks. Her small, clever-looking hands. His sister" (p. 299). They witnessed one of the greatest tragedies in their life one morning. Velutha was beaten to death by the police in front of them.

Estha had special problems too. He had a terrible experience at Abhilash Talkies which claimed to be the first cinema hall in Kerala with a 70 mm cinemascope screen. The Orangedrink Lemondrink Man in the Talkies had taken Estha to a private corner only to make him hold his penis. "He moved Estha's hand up and down. First slowly. Then fastly" (p. 103). This experience was something he could never cancel from his memory which considerably contributed to the emotional breakdown of Estha in his later life.

Again it was Estha who was taken to the police station only to tell a lie to say "yes" to the question asked by the Uncle with the big 'meeshas' (moustache). He was the chosen one because he was the more practical of the two. He was the more tractable, the more far-sighted and the more responsible. He was made to tell the police that Velutha had abducted them. He didn't know the full significance of why they wanted him to say like this. He only knew that it was to save his mother from being taken as a prisoner. Then he had no alternative other than obeying the elders.

Also it was Estha who was returned and re-returned. He was returned to his father after the incident in which Sophie Mol got drowned. He was re-returned twenty-three years later. "23 years later, Rahel, dark woman in a yellow T-shirt, turns to Estha in the dark.

> 'Esthapappychachen Kuttappen Peter Mon'
>
> she whispers...
>
> Estha...takes his fingers to it... His hand is held and kissed...
>
> Then she sat up and put her arms around him. Drew him down beside her.
>
> They lay like that for a long time. Awake in the

> dark. Quietness and Emptiness.
>
> Not old. Not young.
>
> But a viable die-able age.
>
> They were strangers who had met in a chance encounter. They had known each other before life began" (p. 327).
>
> What happened next?

Only that once again they broke the Love Laws. That lay down who should be loved. And how. And how much" (p. 328).

This sums up the life history of Rahel and Estha. For them it was darkness, absolute darkness even before they were born. They lived in quietness and emptiness fighting a losing battle. They were born together with a gap of a few minutes, eighteen minutes to be exact. But they were strangers who had met in a chance encounter. But they had known each other before life had begun also. Did they dream? Have they lost their dreams? Dream is a privilege which is allowed for those who live a life. But could Rahel and Estha lead a life, at least a dog's life? Barring a few golden moments like the ones they spent with Velutha, they were failing, failing miserably to live like their fellow children. In this sense the whole novel tells about their tragedy, the tragedy of Estha and Rahel.

XII

Sophie Mol is the next member of the Ayemenem family to whom also life was more than a tragedy. She along with Estha and Rahel belonged to the fifth generation of Ayemenem house.

Sophie Mol is introduced 'dead' in the opening chapter of the novel itself. "It is reported that the government never paid for Sophie Mole's funeral because she wasn't killed on a zebra crossing" (p. 4). That tells everything of Sophie Mol. She was destined to live only for a very brief spell of time. She was only nine when she died. But her presence continued to be felt through out the novel as the action progressed.

She had two fathers, one biological (in Chacko) and the other 'unreal' (in Joe). Her biological father was compelled to leave her early in her life and the other father got killed in a car accident when she was a young child. "She had Pappachi's nose waiting inside hers. An Imperial Entomologist's nose-within-a-nose. A moth-lover's nose". (p. 143). May be she carried within her mind her great grand parents' private worries also.

The biological father could never find his proper place in Sophie Mol's mind. When Rahel asked who she liked most in the world, even without a hesitation she told her that it was Joe. When Estha reminded her that Chacko was her dad her reply was "He's just real dad, Joe's my dad. He never hits. Hardly ever" (p. 151). so we find that her life was torn between two dads, one real and the other 'unreal'; one who hit and the other who never hit. She was frank enough to tell the twins that there was no love lost between them. Probably she never got a chance to be soft to others, even when they were children younger to her. But even within a week of her arrival at Ayemenem she underwent a sea change. She succeeded in confounding all the expectations of the twins. She had informed Chacko that even though he was her Real Father, she loved him less than Joe. She had turned down Mammachi's offer that she replace Estha and Rahel as the privileged plaiter of Mammachi's nightly rat's tail. Most importantly, she outrightly rejected Baby Kochamma's advances and small seductions.

But within another week Sophie Mol became a memory. It was a fisherman who saw "a wrinkled mermaid. A mer-child. A mere mer-child. With red-brown hair" (p. 258) in the river. He pulled her out of the water into his boat. She was already dead.

Sophie Mol's unfulfilled dream mainly lies in the fact that hers was a friendship that never circled around into a story. she became a memory too soon. She was "like a fruit in season" (p. 267). Everyone liked her though she had her own reservations in responding to their gesture. She had come to Ayemenem to escape from the pain caused by the death of Joe. But fate had stored a similar destiny to her also. It was a mere coincidence that Ammu was caught red handed the same day for her illicit relations with Velutha. The juxtaposition of the two events helps the novelist to make her readers 'feel' the intensity of the whole tragedy.

XIII

Life was a lost dream for some of the characters outside the Ayemenem house as well. This is true of some of the very minor characters also who are just introduced in the novel. The most important character who is not a member of the family but a very strong 'member' of the family in a certain sense is Velutha. Roy develops this character to the level of a tragic hero. His was a life full of hopes and aspirations. He represented the downtrodden who were the most underprivileged in the society. He was a self made man who was excellent in his own profession. He was a Communist follower and did take part in party activities rather seriously.

But when tragedy struck him in the form of Ammu everything went upside down. There was no one to help him, not even the party for which he had made sacrifices. He was mercilessly tortured to death by the police for no legitimate reason. The twins who he loved ardently remained mute witness to the torture.

He was called Velutha which means 'white' in Malayalam because he was so black. As a young boy, he would come with Vellya Paapen, his father to the back entrance of the Ayemenem house to deliver the coconuts they had plucked from the trees in the compound. The untouchables were not allowed to touch anything that Touchable touched. They were not even allowed to walk on public roads in Mammachi's time. They were not allowed to cover their upper bodies, not allowed to carry umbrellas.

Velutha thought that it was his life's mission to change the existing conditions. He became a rebel and very often he even declined to pay heed to what his father said. But events took an unexpected turn and he was stamped the real villain. The humiliation that he suffered at the hands of Mammachi was simply unbearable for him, perhaps worse than the torture to death at the hands of the police. In short, Velutha, the brave is one of the very well drawn out characters in the novel who lived to see that his dreams were smashed even before their fulfilment.

Vellya Paapen, his father was compelled to see whatever he was not supposed to see. His son going astray was something he could never put up with. His years of loyalty to the Ayemenem house collapsed by a single action of his son which was something beyond his comprehension. It was Vellya Paapen who ultimately became instrumental in the custody death of his own son. He had rushed to Ayemenem house to report whatever he had seen and that ultimately led to the whole tragedy. In short, Vellya Paapen also appears in the novel to be one whose dreams were broken.

Then there is his other son Kuttappan who lay paralyzed from his chest downwards, Muraleedharan, who lost his arm which was blown off in Singapore in 1942, with free first class Railway pass for life and also his mind. Father Mulligan, the Irish Monk who couldn't do justice to Baby Kochamma is another character who has a tale to tell of unfulfilled dreams. Another important character is comrade K.N.M. Pillai who believed in the theory "work is struggle; struggle is work." He was one who "merely slipped his ready fingers into History's waiting glove" (p. 281). He cherished the dream of becoming a member of the Legislative Assembly, one day.

XIV

To conclude, *The God of Small Things* is a chronicle of a society where we confront people of different types. All of them have their own problems and worries. There is failure of love within a family and absence of self-respect and mutual respect. "The deepest quality of a work of art," said Henry James, "will always be the quality of the mind of the producer ... No good novel will ever proceed from a superficial mind" (Quoted from Rene Welleck (1966 p. 220). *The God of Small Things* certainly doesn't come from a superficial mind because such an in depth study of human mind can never be a cup of tea of such a mind.

The dream world in the novel is slowly built up and we witness the collapse of this world. As we have seen some kind of unity is established among Ayemenem, Ayemenem house and almost all the characters in the novel in the sense that the "lost dreams" remain as a predominant motif.

3

A Sunbeam Lent ..... Too Briefly

I

"Modernism" according to Kershner (1997) unlike most other major literary movements, was represented not by a particular style and structure in literary works, but by the search for an individual style and structure" (p. 45). In this sense Roy is certainly a modernist novelist for what she attempts in the novel is an individual style and structure. Sophie Mol in the novel is one of her unique creations, created in her own individual style.

"Her funeral killed her. *Dus to dus to dus to dus to dus*. On her tombstone it said *A Sunbeam Lent To Us Too Briefly*" (p. 7). In a certain sense it all began when Sophie Mol came to Ayemenem. Sophie Mol was a sunbeam that was lent to the inmates of Ayemenem house for a very brief period. Her coming to Ayemenem and death after exactly two weeks marked the beginning of the total disintegration of the family. She lay in the coffin "in her yellow Crimplene bellbottoms with her hair in a ribbon and her Made-in-England go-go bag that she loved" (p. 4). Her face was pale and as wrinkled as a dhobi's thumb from being in water too long. She smelled of cologne and coffinwood. "The congregation gathered around the coffin, and the yellow church swelled like a throat with the sound of sad singing. The priests with curly beards swung pots of frankincense on chains and never smiled at babies the way they did on usual Sundays" (p. 4).

Sophie Mol was "the seeker of small wisdoms" and her loss stepped softly around the Ayemenem house like a quiet thing in socks. It hid in books and food, in Mammachi's violin case, in the scabs of the sores on Chacko's shins that he constantly worried and in his slack, womanish legs. She was the harbinger of harsh reality and the Ayemenem family had to accept her death also as a harsh reality. She was taller and bigger than Estha and her eyes were 'bluegrewblue'. Her pale skin was the colour of beach sand and her hatted hair was beautiful and deepred-brown. She had Pappachi's nose waiting inside hers. It was an Imperial Entomologist's nose-within-a-nose and a moth-lover's nose. Baby Kochamma said that Sophie Mol was so beautiful that she reminded her of Ariel, a 'wood-sprite' in Shakespeare's *The Tempest.*

II

By the time Sophie Mol was born Margaret Kochamma, her mother realized that for her own sake and for the sake of her daughter she had to leave Chacko. This made her ask him for a divorce. Consequently, Sophie Mol got a new father in Joe even before she was born. But she was not lucky enough to have him as father for a long time. For he died in a car accident at the most inopportune time. But somehow Margaret Kochamma ensured that Sophie Mole's school routine remained unchanged. Chacko, her father invited her and her mother to Ayemenem and her mother readily agreed to the idea.

Sophie Mol who was the *thimble-drinker* and *coffin-cart wheeler* arrived on the Bombay-Cochin flight "hatted, bell-bottomed and loved from the beginning". She walked down the runway, the smell of London in her hair. "Yellow bottoms of bells flapped backwards around her ankles. Long hair floated out from under her straw hat. One hand in her mother's. The other swinging like a soldier's (lef, lef, lefright lef)" (p. 141). As per a direction from her mother, Sophie Mol greeted everyone through the iron railing. Chacko introduced everyone to Sophie Mol. When he introduced Baby Kochamma as his aunt Baby, Sophie Mol was a little puzzled. She regarded Baby Kochamma with a beady-eyed interest. "She knew of cows babies and dog babies. Bear babies — yes. (She would soon point out to Rahel a bat baby). But *aunt* babies confounded her" (p. 144). Later Chacko picked Sophie Mol up and remarked that the last time he got a wet shirt for his pains when he did that. "He hugged her and hugged her and hugged her. He kissed her bluegreyblue eyes, her entomologist's nose, her hatted red brown hair" (p. 147). Sophie Mol felt a little uncomfortable and requested Chacko to put her down as she was not used to being carried.

When Estha greeted Sophie Mol asking 'How do you do?' Sophie Mol's reply was 'Just like a ladoo one pice two'. She had learned this in school from a Pakistani classmate. Estha looked at Ammu who said "Never Mind Her As Long As You've Done The Right Thing" (p. 150). When Rahel asked Sophie Mol who she loved most in the world her immediate reply was 'Joe'. She said that he had died two months ago and they had come to recover from the shock.

When Rahel said that she had love for her Sophie Mol asked her what she loved her for. Rahel had a simple answer that they were first cousins and so she had to love her. This did not impress Sophie Mol who found no logic in a person loving another who did not even know the other. She made it clear that she had no love for Rahel. But Rahel was confident that she would start loving her once she came to know her. When Estha remarked that Rahel was shorter than him Sophie Mol's comment was that he might be a midget that was taller than a dwarf and shorter than a human being.

Thus, Sophie Mol and her mother received a rousing welcome at the airport. Though she was in dejection following her 'father's' death the change of air helped quite a lot to make her feel relieved from the shock. Though Rahel and Estha were younger to her she never had blind faith in them. Her sense of humour was revealed though her comment on "ladoo". That she did not have much love for Chacko her real father was also made clear when she conversed with the children. A better reception awaited Sophie Mol at Ayemenem where Mammachi was eagerly waiting for her arrival. Of course Kochu Maria also was there with her "Welcome Home Our Sophie Mol" cake ready.

III

Sophie Mol was led to Mammachi and to her questions Sophie Mol replied that she was pretty and tall for her age. Kochu Maria took both Sophie's hands in hers, palms upward, raised them to her face and inhaled deeply. Sophie Mol was confused and wanted to know what she was doing. She didn't know who she was and why she was smelling her hands. Chacko made things clear for her telling her that she was the cook and that was her way of kissing her. Sophie Mol was unconvinced but she thought it to be interesting. Kochu Maria hoped that when Sophie Mol grew up, she would be her Kochamma and she would raise her salary and also give her *nylon saris* for Onam.

Within a week she had "performed unfalteringly under the twin's perspicacious scrutiny and had confounded all their expectations" (p. 189). She had informed Chacko that even though he was her Real Father, she loved him less than Joe. She turned down Mammachi's offer to replace Estha and Rahel as the privileged plaiter of Mammachi's nightly rat's tail and counter of moles. She also astutely gauged the prevailing temper and rejected all of Baby Kochamma's advances and small seductions. She also revealed herself to be human. One day the twins returned from a clandestine trip to Velutha only to find her in the garden in tears for not taking her with them and keeping her alone.

During her stay at Ayemenem, Chacko had taken a black and white photograph of Sophie Mol with Lenin (Pillai's son), Estha, Rahel and Margaret Kochamma. She had turned her eyelids inside out so that her eyes looked like pink-veined flesh petals in the photograph. She wore a set of protruding false teeth cut from the yellow rind of a sweetlime. "Her tongue pushed through the trap of teeth and had Mammachi's silver thimble fitted on the end of it. (she had hijacked it the day she arrived, and vowed to spend her holidays drinking only from a thimble). She held out a lit candle in each hand. One leg of her denim bellbottoms was rolled up to expose a white, bony knee on which a face had been drawn" (p. 135). Minutes before the photograph was taken, she had explained patiently to Estha and Rahel how there was a pretty good chance that they were bastards, and what bastard really meant.

Sophie Mol was able to establish a friendship with the twins soon after her arrival at Ayemenem. Sometimes she walked out to see what Rahel was doing. She walked when Rahel walked, stopped when she stopped. She would inspect "the smelly mayhem with clinical detachment" (p. 186). The fond smiles stayed on her, like a spot light "thinking perhaps, that the sweet cousins were playing hide-and-seek, like sweet cousins often do" (p. 186).

One afternoon Sophie Mol got out of bed and rummaged through her sleeping mother's purse. She found what she was looking for — the keys to the large, locked suitcase on the floor. She opened it and rooted through the contents with all the delicacy of a dog digging up a flowerbed. "She upset stacks of lingerie, ironed skirts and blouses, shampoos, creams, chocolate, Sellotape, umbrellas, soap (and other bottled London smells), quinine, aspirin, broad spectrum antibiotics" (pp. 266-67). Sophie Mol then found what she had been looking for. She wanted some presents for her cousins and now she knew what she was going to give them : "Triangular towers of Toblerone chocolate (soft and slanting in the heat). Socks with separate multi-coloured toes. And two ballpoint pens — the top halves filled with water in which a cut-out colleage of a London streetscape was suspended. Buckingham Palace and Big Ben. Shops and People. A red double-decker bus propelled by an air-bubble floated up and down the silent street. There was something sinister about the absence of noise on the busy ballpoint street" (p. 267). She put her presents into her bag and went forth into the world. The idea was to drive a hard bargain, and to negotiate a friendship. But this friendship was destined to be left dangling and incomplete. This friendship never circled around into a story.

But though for a very brief spell it was a friendship which was very strong in every sense of the word. One day all the three of them went to Velutha wearing *saris*. Estha was the draping expert who pleated Sophie Mol's pleats. They had red *bindis* on their foreheads and they looked like three raccoons trying to pass off as Hindu ladies. They visited Velutha and introduced themselves as Mrs. Pillai, Mrs. Eapen and Mrs. Rajagopalan.

In short, Sophie Mol left an indelible mark even within the very short period of her stay in Ayemenem before the tragedy. To begin with she was unsure about the attitude of her future companions but once she established a friendship with them it was as strong as a rock. On the other hand, she was not very kind to her real father Chacko or Baby Kochamma. She found pleasure in moving around with Estha and Rahel and it was on one of those secret trips that the tragedy struck her.

IV

"Three children on the river bank. A pair of twins and another whose mauve corduroy pinafore said *Holiday*! in a tilting, happy font" (p. 291). The "another" was Sophie Mol and for her it was a real holiday. Estha and Rahel dragged the boat out of the bushes where they usually hid it. They set it down in the water and held it steady for Sophie Mol to climb in. Sophie Mol was more tentative and a little frightened of what lurked in the shadows around her. She had a cloth bag with food purloined from the fridge slung across her chest. She had a stock of bread, cake and biscuits.

Sophie Mol had convinced Estha and Rahel that it was essential that they should take her also with them. She also told them that the absence of children would aggravate the adult's remorse. According to her it would make them truly sorry, like the grown-ups in Hamelin after the Pied Piper took away all their children. "They would search everywhere and just when they were sure that all three of them were dead, they would return home in triumph. Valued, loved and needed more than ever" (p. 292). Her argument was that if she were left behind she might be tortured and forced to reveal their hiding place.

They lurched into the deeper water and began to raw diagonally upstream, against the current, the way Velutha had taught them to. In the dark they couldn't see that they were in the wrong lane on a silent highway full of muffled traffic. They were past the really deep when they collided with a floating log and the little boat tipped over. They headed for the shore, surprised at how much effort it took them to cover that short distance. Estha and Rahel somehow managed out of the water.

Rahel said to Sophie Mol that all their food was spoiled. But Sophie Mol never heard what she said. She was missing. They ran along the bank calling out to her. But she was gone. It was "a river accepting the offering. One small life. A brief sunbeam. With a silver thimble clenched for luck in its little fist" (p. 293).

About four o'clock in the morning the twins made their way through the swamp and approached the History House exhausted. They were almost sure that Sophie Mol was dead. It was a fisherman who found something moving with the current, swiftly towards the sea. He sent out his bamboo pole to stop it and drew it towards him. "It's a wrinkled mermaid. A mer-child. A mere mer-child. With red-brown hair" (p. 258). He pulled her out of the water into his boat and put his thin cotton towel under her. She lay at the bottom of his boat with his silver haul of small fish. The body of Sophie Mol was brought to Ayemenem house and was laid out on the chaise longue.

That was how Sophie Mol lost her life. It was a death which shook the entire Ayemenem house. The twins were never able to bear the tragedy. In a way they were responsible for the series of incidents which culminated in the drowning of Sophie Mol. Her sojourn in Ayemenem house proved to be for a short period — just a fortnight. The journey of Sophie Mol to forget everything turned out to be an unforgettable one for the survivors.

V

The death of Sophie Mol was more than the death of a daughter for Margaret Kochamma who had earlier lost her second husband. She cursed herself and beat Estha who she thought was responsible for the tragic incident. She never allowed Chacko, Sophie Mol's biological father put his arm around her to comfort her.

Mammachi went out of the house and her tears trickled down and trembled along her jaw like raindrops on the edge of a roof Though Ammu, Estha and Rahel were allowed to attend the funeral, they were made to stand separately, not with the rest of the family. Nobody would look at them also. Estha stood close to Ammu "barely awake, his aching eyes glittering like glass, his burning cheek against the bare skin of Ammu's trembling, hymnbook-holding arm" (p. 5).

Rahel, on the other hand, was wide awake, fiercely vigilant and brittle with exhaustion from her battle against real life. She noticed that Sophie Mol was awake for her funeral. When they lowered Sophie Mol's coffin into the ground in the little cemetery behind the church, Rahel knew that she still wasn't dead. "She heard (on Sophie Mol's behalf), the softsounds of the red mud and the hardsounds of the orange laterite that spoiled the shining coffin polish. She heard the dullthudding through the polished coffin wood, through the satin coffin lining. The sad priests' voices muffled by mud and wood" (p. 7).

Sophie Mol's death made life untenable for Estha, Rahel and Ammu. Ammu was given marching orders in connection with the Velutha episode which coincided with Sophie Mol's death. Estha was sent back to his father and soon Rahel also had to leave the house. Even after her death Sophie Mol continued to live in Ayemenem house like a quiet thing in socks. "It hid in books and food. In Mammachi's violin case" (pp. 15-16). Over the years, as the memory of Sophie Mol slowly faded, the loss of Sophie Mol grew robust and alive.

This, in a nutshell is the story of Sophie Mol, the Sophie Mol who came to her real dad to recover from the shock of her dad. She was the little girl who led a successful life though for a very short while. She brought a lot of relief to her cousins Estha and Rahel, who had been suffering from depravation. Though she was a little unkind to the children she was inextricably drawn to them within no time.

In the Ayemenem house she was the pet for the older ladies also. Mammachi saw the Imperial Entomologist in her. Baby Kochamma and Kochu Maria also found her to be one who influenced them tremendously. For Chacko her arrival marked the beginning of a new life. Somehow he had the feeling that he had regained his lost daughter. Also he thought that Margaret Kochamma who was lost to him would be accessible to him again. But things took an unexpected turn with her death. He chose to leave for Canada than remaining in Ayemenem anymore.

At the same time it would be ironic that Sophie Mol immediately after her arrival at Ayemenem had revealed her inner feelings. She had told Chacko that she loved him less than her dad Joe. She also made it unambiguously clear that she did not want to take the position occupied by the twins. That is, she did not want to be privileged plaiter of Mammachi's hair. Baby Kochamma's advances also were rejected outright by her. Again it is ironic that she shared her love with those members of the family with whom the elders did not have any sympathy. Thus, Estha and Rahel were considered to be problem makers in the house whereas Sophie Mol found herself most comfortable in her house. It is again a cruel fate that she had to abandon her life when she was proceeding to Velutha's house to be away from the fault finders and "accusers."

The fact that death occurred when Sophie Mol was moving together in a boat with them made Rahel and Estha totally miserable. They could not even dream that such a tragedy would ever have happened. Ammu's affair with Velutha came as a second blow and ultimately the family itself got disintegrated which all could perhaps be described as a chain reaction of Sophie Mol's death. Thus, it would not be out of place if Sophie Mol be taken as the central character around which the whole action of the novel revolved.

4

Esthapappychachen Kuttappan Peter Mon

I

The long name 'Esthapappychachen Kuttappan Peter Mon' belongs to Estha who was 'short' and 'neither young nor old.' This name was presented to him as a whisper by his two egg twin sister Rahel in the penultimate chapter ('The Madras Mail') of the novel : ".... Rahel, dark woman in a yellow T-shirt, turns to Estha in the dark.

> 'Esthapappychachen Kuttappan Peter Mon,' She says.
>
> She whispers.
>
> She moves her mouth.
>
> Their beautiful mother's mouth.

Estha, sitting very straight, waiting to be arrested, takes his fingers to it. To touch the words it makes. To keep the whisper. His fingers follow the shape of it..." (p. 327). Dorothy Richardson's novel series *Pilgrimage* complains, "All that has been said and known in the world is in language, in words.... The meaning of words change with people's thoughts. Then no one knows anything for certain. Everything depends upon the way a thing is put, and that is a question of some particular civilization" (1967- p. 99). We find that the meaning of words change with Estha's thought. Sometimes one even fails to know anything for certain when he speaks.

There was a time when life was full of 'beginning and no end' for him. It was a time when he along with his sister Rahel thought that everything was for ever. But as he grew older he started realizing that everything was not for ever. He was singled out and made to pay the prize even for the 'crimes' committed by others. He was born to be 'returned' and 're-returned'. In a sense he was like a football which never reached the goal post. He did not know who it was to be blamed for the suffering which was bestowed upon him. He was born to fight a losing battle, born to suffer and suffer. He had always been a quiet child and without the knowledge of his dear ones and 'non dear' ones (and without even his own knowledge) he had stopped talking altogether. "It had been a gradual winding down and closing shop. A barely noticeable quietening. As though he had simply run out of conversation and had nothing left to say" (p. 10).

In a sense the whole novel is about Estha's silence. Silence reached out of his head and enfolded him in its swampy arms. Slowly he was withdrawing from the world around him. "He grew accustomed to the uneasy octopus that lived inside him and squirted its inky tranquillizer on his past. Gradually the reason for his silence was hidden away, entombed somewhere deep in the soothing folds of the fact of it" (p. 12).

In the following sections we shall consider in some detail what made Estha "a silent man" and also who were all responsible for his withdrawal symptoms which ultimately made him insensitive to the world around him. "Contemporary study of character has de-emphasized traditional humanist perspectives on the issue, just as much 'advanced' contemporary fiction, features characters with little apparent psychological depth" (p. 108), observes Kershner (1997). But Estha does not fit very well to this pattern. Estha is a character with great psychological depth.

II

Estha and Rahel were two-egg twins. The doctors called them 'dizygotic'. They were born from separate but simultaneously fertilized eggs. Estha or Esthappan was older by just eighteen minutes. "They never did look much like each other, Estha and Rahel, and even when they were thin-armed children, flat-chested, worm-ridden and Elvis Presley-puffed, there was none of the usual 'Who is who'? and 'Which is which?' from oversmiling relatives or the Syrian Orthodox Bishops who frequently visited the Ayemenem house for donations" (p. 2).

For Estha it was almost a humiliating birth. The car in which Baba, their father, was taking Ammu, their mother, to hospital in Shillong broke down on the winding tea estate road in Assam. They had to abandon the car and get into a crowded State Transport bus. The passengers saw "how hugely pregnant Ammu was." So they made room for the couple and for the rest of the journey "Estha and Rahel's father had to hold their mother's stomach (with them in it) to prevent it from wobbling". (p. 3). He was born in November, 1962 after a hair-raising bus ride to Shillong, at a time when there were rumours of Chinese occupation and India's impending defeat. He was born by candle light in a hospital. The twins emerged without much fuss. Their mother failed to notice the single Siamese soul. But she was glad to have them.

By the time Estha was two years old his father's drinking, aggravated by the loneliness of tea estate life, had reached a point of no return. One day Ammu had to take the extreme step of hitting him with the heaviest book that came her way. Mr. Hollick, the English manager of his company had an eye on her and he made it clear in unambiguous terms to Ammu's husband. But he couldn't react to it in a way a husband should. Ammu finally decided to return to Ayemenem, the place from where she had fled from only a few years ago.

Estha began a new life with his sister Rahel at Ayemenem house. He had slanting, sleepy eyes and his new front teeth were still uneven on the ends. On the other hand, "Rahel's new teeth were waiting inside her gums, like words in a pen. It puzzled everybody that an eighteen minute age difference could cause such a discrepancy in front-tooth timing" (p. 37).

Baby Kochamma who had been put in charge of the formal education of Estha and Rahel was rather unkind to them. For the same reason they never found themselves comfortable in her company. Her Australian missionary friend, Miss Mitten could only bring more problems to Estha and Rahel. When she visited Ayemenem she presented them a baby book — *The Adventures of Susie Squirrel* — which they first read forwards and then backwards. This naturally offended her. Reading forwards and backwards never amused her and she didn't even know what Malayalam was : "They told her it was the language everyone spoke in Kerala. She said she had been under the impression that it was called Keralese. Estha, who had by then taken an active dislike to Miss Mitten, told her that as far as he was concerned it was a Highly Stupid Impression" (p. 60). That was the stuff Estha was made of. He could never bear absurdities and he never waited to give vent to his inner feelings. When Miss Mitten complained to Baby Kochamma about Estha's rudeness they were made to write "impositions" which should certainly worsen their attitude to Mitten. By a sheer coincidence Mitten had a premature death in an accident. She was killed by a milk van in Hobart, across the road from a cricket oval. The 'hidden justice' for the twins was that the milk van had been "reversing."

In short, the childhood of Estha had nothing envious about it. Ever since he was born he was confronted with problems which were mainly psychological. That a child had to part from his father at a very young age of two is itself something painful and it should certainly take its toll. Things were not better for Estha when he came to Ayemenem along with his sister and mother. He was forced to be in the company of certain 'characters' with whom he couldn't some how adjust himself. The education he 'received' at Margaret Kochamma's hands fell, probably, far short of his expectations. But as far as he was concerned whatever he had experienced was simply insignificant as some of the later events in his life showed.

III

Estha had the first ever shock of his life in its true sense in the 'encounter' he had with the Orangedrink Lemondrink Man at Abhilash Talkies, Kottayam. It all happened when they went to the theatre to see *The Sound of Music*. Chacko, their uncle, Ammu and Baby Kochamma were there in the Plymouth car, which originally belonged to Pappachi, Chacko's father. Their plan was to stay at Hotel Sea Queen after the movie. The next day was very important especially for Chacko. Early next morning they would go to Cochin Airport to pick up Chacko's ex-wife — their English aunt, Margaret Kochamma and his daughter Sophie Mol, who were coming from London to spend Christmas at Ayemenem. Margaret Kochamma's second husband, Joe had been killed in a car accident. Chacko invited them to Ayemenem when he heard about the accident. He said that "he couldn't bear to think of them spending a lonely, desolate Christmas in England. In a house full of memories" (p. 36).

The previous week to that was one of torture for Estha and Rahel. That whole week Baby Kochamma insisted on the children to speak only in English. Whenever she caught them speaking in Malayalam, they paid the price in the form of writing "impositions" : "*I will always speak in English, I will always speak in English*. A hundred times each. When they were done, she scored them out with her red pen to make sure that old lines were not recycled for new punishments" (p. 36). She even made them practise an English car song for the way back. They had to form the words properly, and be particularly careful about their pronunciation. (For Baby Kochamma it was "Prer NUN sea ayshun") :

> Rej-Oice in the Lo-Ord Or-Orlways
> And again I say rej-Oice,
> Rej Oice,
> Rej Oice,
> And again I say rej-Oice.

Naturally Estha went to the theatre with a disturbed mind. The presence of Baby Kochamma should make his outing a more than miserable experience for him. But the real misery awaited him at the theatre.

Estha had multiple problems when he reached the theatre. To begin with he was the only male member in the group as Chacko had gone to see about the bookings at the hotel. His second problem was that he didn't have enough height "to piss onto naphthalene balls and cigarette stubs in the urinal. To piss in the pot would be Defeat. To piss in the urinal, he was too short. He needed Height". (p. 96). But on the whole he had an inner feeling that he was somewhat grown up even though he was just seven years old : "Estha Alone organized the rusty cans of nothing in front of the urinal. He stood on them, one foot on each, and pissed carefully, with minimal wobble. Like a Man..... (p. 96).

Since he was very short, Estha had to sit on the edge of his chair in the theatre. The film had already started. Suddenly the people in the audience started turning around to mutter "shhh! shh!". There was a voice from outside the picture cutting through the darkness. It was Estha who was singing. He couldn't help it. He was given marching orders by the audience. "Shutup or Getout. Getout or Shutup". That was what they said. "The Audience was a Big Man. Estha was a Little Man, with the tickets" (p. 100). Ammu also, among others, asked Estha to keep quiet and soon he did. He made a request to allow him to go out and sing which was eventually granted. He sat on the electric blue foam leather car-sofa, in the princess circle lobby, and sang in a nun's voice as clear as clean water. The man behind the Refreshment Counter, who had been asleep on a row of stools, waiting for the interval, woke up. He was the Orangedrink Lemondrink Man and the third and most dangerous problem for Estha came in the shape of this man.

The Orangedrink Lemondrink Man was a homosexual and the moment he found Estha alone and singing loudly oblivious of his surroundings he slowly pounced on a new prey. Initially Estha didn't even bother about the man when he interrupted. He continued to sing. The man who was almost a hairy bear ["His gold wrist watch was almost hidden by his curly forearm hair. His gold chain was almost hidden by his chest hair. His white Terylene shirt was unbuttoned to where the swell of his belly began. He looked like an unfriendly jewelled bear" (p. 102)] threatened Estha by telling him that he could file a written complaint against him for waking him up. With words filled with sarcasm the man successfully took Estha with him making him believe that he was going to provide him with a drink. Though Estha made an attempt to escape from his hands he was unsuccessful. The Man did not forget to ask a couple of vulgar questions about his grandmother like 'who does she sleep with?' Then he was made to do the unexpected : "His hand closed tighter over Estha's. Tight and sweaty. And faster still.

Fast faster fest
Never let it rest
Until the fast is faster,
And the faster's fest.

.....Then the gristly-bristly face contorted, and Estha's hand was wet and hot and sticky. It had egg white on it.... The lemon drink was cold and sweet. The penis was soft and shrivelled like an empty leather change purse. With his dirtcoloured rag, the man wiped Estha's other hand" (p. 104).

'The Orangedrink Lemondrink Man episode' was something more than what Estha could bear. It had its immediate effect on him. More than that, the episode continued to hover over his mind from which he never had an escape. Even when he heard the words of this man ["You're a lucky rich boy, with porketmunny (his version of 'pockẹt money') and a grandmother's factory to inherit. You should Thank God that you have no worries" (p. 105)] he was holding his sticky other hand away from his body. Inside the theatre also he continued to do so. The words and deed of the Man continued to echo and re-echo in Estha's mind. Ammu never knew what exactly had gone wrong with Estha. For the same reason she went on with her scolding him. But Estha had a burning sensation within him : "His stomach heaved. He had a greenwavy, thick-watery, lumpy, seaweedy, floaty, bottomless-bottomful feelings" (p. 107). He wanted to vomit. He was taken out but he convulsed and nothing came : "Just thoughts. And they floated out and floated back in. Ammu couldn't see them" (p. 108). The Orangedrink Lemondrink Man did not forget to offer a drink to Ammu, "the luminous woman with polished shoulders."

The Orangedrink Lemondrink Man made Estha think "Two Thoughts, and the Two Thoughts he thought, were these :

(*a*) *Anything can happen to Anyone*

And

(*b*) *It's best to be prepared*" (p. 194).

The incident made Estha wiser. But we find that he was not

prepared to face adversities in his life as is revealed from the steady disintegration of his personality.

IV

Though Ammu, Estha, and Rahel were allowed to attend the funeral, they were made to stand separately, not with the rest of the family. Nobody would even look at them. Meanwhile, Ammu's affairs with Velutha had been made known to the world. This made Ammu take the twins back to Kottayam police station. But things had already taken a different turn, that too for the worse. Kottayam police had already tortured Velutha to death in their custody.

Consequently, two weeks later Estha was "returned." Ammu was made to send him back to their father, who had by then resigned his lonely tea estate job in Assam and moved to Calcutta to work for a company that made carbon black. By then he had remarried, stopped drinking and suffered only occasional relapses.

Estha's father sent him to a boy's school in Calcutta. He was not a very good student, but neither was he backward, nor particularly bad at anything. "*An average student*, or *Satisfactory work* were the usual comments that his teachers wrote in his Annual Progress Reports. *Does not participate in Group Activities* was another recurring complaint. Though what exactly they meant by 'Group Activities' they never said (p. 11). He finished school with mediocre results, but refused to go to college. Instead he preferred to do housework : "He did the sweeping, swabbing and all the laundry. He learned to cook and shop for vegetables..... He never bargained. They never cheated him. When the vegetables had been weighed and paid for, they would transfer them to his red plastic shopping basket" (p. 11).

Very soon Estha developed into the 'silent man'. When Khubchand, his beloved, blind seventeen year old mongrel struggled with his life, Estha nursed him through his final ordeal as though his own life somehow depended on it. After his death, Estha started walking. He walked for hours on end. Initially he patrolled only the neighbourhood, but gradually went further and further afield : "A well-dressed man with a quiet walk. His face grew dark and outdoorsy. Rugged. Wrinkled by the sun. He began to look wiser than he really was. Like a fisherman in a city. With sea-secrets in him" (pp. 12-13). Then we hear about him twenty-three years later when his father "re-returned" him to Ayemenem.

Estha, we find, had been made to live a 'dogs life'. He was brought to Ayemenem at the age of two. For the next five years his life was rather uneventful. But at the age of seven he had to suffer misery of a life time. Tragic events chased him like a shadow. The Abhilash Talkies incident was only one among the chain of events. Sophie Mol's death added to his misery. His returning to his father was the last nail in his coffin. But what we find of him is that he is a young man with a mighty will. Even when he knew that he was being sidelined by people who were dear to him he never thought of ending his life. It was a fight against odds. Later, even when he became a mental wreck somehow we feel that the fate of a tragic hero will never wait him. In fact, he was born to fight.

V

It can be seen that the life that Estha led with Rahel was something unique and extraordinary. In a sense that was expected from monozygotic twins. Before Estha was returned to his father a Twin Expert was consulted. She wrote back to say that it was not advisable to separate such twins but that "two-egg twins were no different from ordinary siblings and that while they would certainly suffer a natural distress that children from broken homes underwent, it would be nothing more than that. Nothing out of the ordinary" (p. 32).

Estha certainly suffered a natural distress. But he was most comfortable in the company of Rahel. When they were alone, they pretended that they were clerks : "They would blow spit-bubbles and shiver their legs and gobble like turkeys" (p. 84). Their mother used to object to all the three of these actions, that is, shivering legs, spitting bubbles and gobbling. When they went to the movie at Abhilash Talkies, the questions arose in their minds :

"(a) *Did Captain von Clapp-Trapp shiver his leg*?

He did not.

(b) *Did Captain von Clapp-Trapp blow spit-bubbles?*

Did he?
He did most certainly not

(c) *Did he gobble*?
He did not" (p. 106).

The do's and don't's continued to pester them as is evident from this.

There are indications in the novel that they did have incestuous relations. In the hotel room they were almost two-in-one, two bodies and one soul : "On the next bed, his (Chacko's) niece and nephew slept with their arms around each other. A hot twin and a cold one. He and She" (p. 122). Again, in the following descriptions also this is indicated : "If they slept there, she and Estha curled together like foetuses in a shallow steel womb" (p. 188). Later on also we find them spending time together : "Rahel was lying on Estha's bed..... Her soft, sleeveless T-shirt was a glowing yellow in the dark. The bottom half of her, in blue jeans, melted into the darkness.... From where he sat....Estha... could see her. Fairly outlined. The sharp line of her jaw.. She turned her head and looked at him. He sat very straight. Waiting for the inspection.... She was lovely to him. Her hair. Her cheeks. Her small, clever-looking hands. His sister." (p. 299). Such descriptions we get elsewhere in the novel also. For example, in the chapter entitled 'Big Man the Laltain, Small Man the Mombatti' thus goes the narration : "Estha put on the tap and water drummed into a plastic bucket. He undressed in the gleaming bathroom. He stepped out of his sodden jeans... He didn't hear his sister at the door. Rahel watched his stomach suck inwards and his ribcage rise as his wet T-shirt peeled away from his skin, leaving it wet and honey-coloured .....

Now they were. Old enough
Old
A viable *die-able* age" (pp. 91-92).

Now they were not young. They were thirty years old and whatever they did at the young age of eight had a repetition at the "die-able age" : "Rahel searched her brother's nakedness for signs of herself.... Rahel watched Estha with the curiosity of a mother watch her wet child. A sister a brother. A woman a man.

A twin a twin.... He was a naked stranger met in a chance encounter. He was the one that she had known before Life began." (pp. 92-93).

In certain respects they were evenly matched. For example, when they had serious physical encounters "the fights went on for ever, and things that came in their way — table lamps, ashtrays and water jugs — were smashed or irreparably damaged" (p. 62). The twins were mostly "We and Us" and they even dreamed together. They dreamed of their river, of the coconut trees that bent into it and watched the boats slide up. Whenever their mother admonished them it was a very common sight to see the two heads nodding twice. They could swim like seals, and had crossed the river several times. Sometimes they even squatted on their haunches "like professional adult gossips in the Ayemenem market" (p. 209). The morning Sophie Mol drowned they lay down in the back verandah of the History House like a pair of dwarves, numb with fear, waiting for the world to end. Also, both of them witnessed the policemen beating Velutha to death : "In the back verandah of the History House, as the man they loved was smashed and broken, Mrs. Eapen and Mrs. Rajagopalan, Twin Ambassadors of God-knows-what, learned two new lessons.

Lesson Number One :

"Blood barely shows on a Black Man .....

And

Lesson Number Two :

It smells, though

Sicksweet" (pp. 309-310).

At the police station they received the same treatment. When Baby Kochamma told them that they would have to be sensible to ensure that their mother was never sent to jail we again see the two heads nodding. Later the two frightened voices whispered almost together: "Save Ammu." In the years to come also they would replay this scene in their heads, as children, as teenagers and as adults.

In short, what we find in the novel is something unusual and strange as regards the relation between Estha and Rahel. They liked to move together, stay together and even think together. Though Rahel hadn't been there she remembered what the Orangedrink Lemon-drink Man did to Estha in Abhilash Talkies. She even remembered the taste of the tomato sandwiches that Estha ate on the Madras Mail. She had a memory of walking up one night giggling at Estha's funny dream. Also, we find Estha walking out of his room (after vomiting) and standing quietly outside Rahel's door. Strangely enough, Rahel stood on a chair and unlatched the door for him : "Chacko didn't bother to wonder how she could possibly have known that Estha was at the door. He was used to their sometimes strangeness" (p. 119).

At the same time there are moments in the novel where the twins do not see eye to eye or are made to stand apart. Estha didn't like Rahel sporting in an airport frock. He told her to her face that she looked stupid in that dress. The response from Rahel came in the form of a slap and he slapped her back. Also, Rahel and Estha were separated when the crucial moment came in which only one of them was asked to say "yes" before the Inspector : " 'No need for both. One will serve the purpose,'... Thomas Mathew said. 'Anyone. Mon. Mol. Who wants to come with me?" (p. 319). Estha being the more practical was given the task by Baby Kochamma. More importantly, we find Estha being separated from Rahel when he was returned to his father after the incident in which Sophie Mol was drowned and Ammu's affairs with Velutha was made known and Velutha was tortured to death.

VI

Estha's relationship with his own mother also deserves a close study. It can be seen that her attitude to him is more or less ambivalent. On the one hand she felt immense love for him but on the other hand she took every opportunity to insult him. He never could think that his mother had deep love for him. That was perhaps because even when she had love for him in the heart of hearts, it never took a concrete shape apparently.

One instance where we get glimpses of Ammu's love for Estha is when he went to the urinals in the Abhilash theatre. After passing urine he came out and then "Ammu felt a sudden clutch of love for her reserved, dignified little son in his beige and pointy shoes, who had just completed his first adult assignment. She ran loving fingers through his hair. She spoiled his puff"

(p. 97). Another occasion where Ammu is best as a mother is when she "returns" Estha to his father. When the train was about to leave she reminded him to write. She told him that she would soon get him back. When Estha asked when exactly she would do it her reply was "Soon, sweetheart. As soon as I can... As soon as I get a job. As soon as I can go away from here and get a job" (p. 324). But, as we know that never happened. He couldn't even join Ammu's funeral when she died at a very young age. Probably he had a premonition that it was not going to happen. That might have made him say "but that will be never."

At the same time Ammu had been unkind to Estha and his sister very often. They remembered how angry Ammu was when their father gave them puffs from his cigarette and they sucked it and wet the filter with spit. They remembered being pushed around a room once, from Ammu to Baba like billiard balls. Ammu even pushed Estha away and said : "Here, you keep one of them. I can't look after them both" (p. 84).

On another occasion when Rahel had put on the sunglasses Ammu had scolded her which made Chacko ask Ammu not to be fascist in her dealings with children. Ammu had told the children that they "can't trust anybody. Mother, father, brother, husband, bestfriend. Nobody" (p. 83). She had also said that it was entirely possible "that Estha could grow up to be a Male Chauvinist Pig" (p. 83). When Ammu was really angry, she said Jolly Well. "Jolly Well was a deeply well with larfing dead people in it" (p. 148). She used to warn Estha and Rahel that if ever they disobeyed her in public, she would see to it that they were sent away to somewhere where they would well learn to behave. She wanted them to learn the difference between 'clean' and 'dirty' and also say 'Hello' properly. These warnings were most unwelcome to the twins. Again, she very often used to remind them that if it weren't for them, she would be free and that she should have dumped them in an orphanage the day they were born. At the same time Estha's longing for mother's love was nothing unexpected : "Estha knew that if Ammu found out about what he had done with Orangedrink Lemondrink Man, she'd love him less as well. Very much less. He felt the shaming churning heaving turning sickness in his stomach" (p. 113).

In sum, we find that Ammu had been kind and unkind to her son Estha. This also contributed to Estha's psychological problems. At the sametime the entire blame cannot be put on Ammu because she herself was one who was not free from emotional crisis. Naturally, it is quite logical that one behaves predictably and unpredictably depending on what goes on in one's mind. Certainly, we can say that it is all part of a pattern.

VII

It will not be out of place if an inquiry is made into the attitude of others to Estha. One of the characters who failed to show her kind face to Estha was Kochu Maria, the servant girl. Ammu had told Estha the story of Julius Caesar and how Caesar was stabbed by Brutus. This made him stand on his bed at night with his sheet wrapped around him and say. "*Et tu? Brute*? Then fall Caesar! and crash into bed without bending his knees, like a stabbed corpse" (p. 83). This was intolerable for Kochu Maria and she abused him quite sharply : "Tell your mother to take you to your father's house.... There you can break as many beds as you like. These aren't your beds. This isn't *your* house" (p. 83).

At the funeral of Sophie Mol Estha was to suffer humiliation along with Ammu and Rahel at the hands of the other members of the Ayemenem family. Inspector Thomas Mathew had referred to Estha and Rahel as "illegitimate" (though they did not know the meaning of the word then) when they were taken to the Kottayam police station by Ammu after Sophie Mol's funeral.

Baby Kochamma disliked Estha and Rahel. She considered them doomed, fatherless waifs. She was keen to remind them that they lived on sufferance in the Ayemenem house and that it was their maternal grandfather's house where they really had no right. What she expected from them was some token of unhappiness. The twins were never comfortable in the company of Baby Kochamma.

Velutha, the untouchable had been very kind to Estha. He had been very good to him and though he was forbidden from visiting his house he did visit the house even without waiting for permission. Chacko also had been careful to see that he did not hurt the feelings of the twins, Estha and Rahel.

On balance, we find that where as Baby Kochamma and her servant Kochu Maria continued to pester Estha and his sister, Chacko and Velutha brought some comfort to them.

VIII

Next we shall consider the "re-return" of Estha after twenty-three years of his return to his father who was at Calcutta. Estha came back to Ayemenem with a suitcase and a letter. The suitcase was full of new clothes. The letter was shown to Rahel by Baby Kochamma. The signature was that of the twin's father. The letter said that their father had retired and was emigrating to Australia where he had got a job as Chief Security at a ceramics factory, and that he couldn't take Estha with him. There was also a promise in the letter that he would look in on Estha if he ever came back to India, which he himself said, was a bit unlikely.

The most important thing that Estha did on reaching Ayemenem was walking all over Ayemenem. Some days he walked along the banks of the river that smelled of shit, and pesticides bought with World Bank loans. Other days he walked down the road past the new Gulf-money houses built by nurses, masons etc. He walked past the village school that his great-grandfather built for untouchable children also. Sometimes he walked past Sophie Mol's yellow church, Ayemenem Youth Kung Fu Club, the Tender Buds Nursery School, the rationshop and also Lucky Press, Old Comrade K.N.M. Pillai's printing press, once the Ayemenem office of the Communist party. Pillai would greet him and he would walk past, not rude, not polite but just quiet.

There was some visible change in Estha when Rahel came. She brought the sound of passing trains and the world which was locked out for years, suddenly flooded in. But the fact remained that he had become an altogether different person. This is made clear from the words of Baby Kochamma : "I told you, didn't I?' She said to Rahel. 'What did you expect? Special treatment? He's lost his mind, I'm telling you! He doesn't *recognize* people any more!" (p. 21). So Estha had already lost his mind and stopped recognizing people. But being one of the two-egg twins, Rahel could feel the rhythm of Estha's rocking, and the wetness of rain on his skin. She could also hear the raucous, scrambled world inside his head. It was Baby Kochamma who had written to Rahel about Estha's return. She even reminded Rahel to lock her bedroom door at night.

When Estha returned after his walking Baby Kochamma would observe " 'Here he comes'... 'Now watch. He won't say anything. He'll walk *straight* to his room. Just watch!'" (p. 90). She was saying this as if she were good at predicting the behaviour of others. The next thing Estha would do after going to his room was washing his cloth. "He's very over-clean .... he won't say a *word*!" (p. 90). We find Rahel following him to his room, which had kept his secrets. The floor was clean, the walls white, the cupboard closed, shoes arranged and the dustbin empty. There was an unwillingness on the part of Estha to subsist on scraps offered by others. One cannot say for certain whether he had seen Rahel, whether he was really mad and whether he knew that she was there. "They had never been shy of each other's bodies, but they had never been old enough (together) to know what shyness was" (p. 92). But later we find Estha not looking at her and retreating into further stillness. It was as though his body had the power to snatch its senses inwards away from the surface of his skin, into some deeper more inaccessible recess!

Estha who had always been a quiet child suddenly stopped talking and nobody could pinpoint when or why he stopped talking. In fact, it was a gradual process barely noticeable. Yet his silence was never awkward. It was neither intrusive nor noisy. It was also not an accusing or protesting silence. It usually took strangers sometime to notice him even when they were in the same room with him. On the whole, "Estha occupied very little space in the world" (p. 11).

IX

Thus Estha stands before us not as a grown up man but as a young boy who started suffering the moment he was born. He was practical minded and was common sensical even at a very young age. That he could rise to an occasion is made clear more than once in the novel. When Ammu was completely upset while returning from Kottayam police station after Velutha's death, it was Estha who could tell the conductor that they wanted a ticket to Ayemenem. He began to do housework including sweeping and swabbing. That he never liked to bring trouble to others is clear from these actions.

He was a kind hearted nurse also. When Khubchand, his beloved, blind, bald 17 year old mongrel "decided to stage a miserable, long-drawn-out death, Estha nursed him through his final ordeal as though his own life somehow depended on it" (p. 12). It was after the death of Khubchand that life became a totally meaningless affair for Estha. He walked for hours on end. Initially he patrolled only the neighbourhood, but gradually he went further and further and people got used to seeing him on the road. This was exactly what he continued to do when he was re-returned to Ayemenem after twenty-three years.

His expulsion from Ayemenem never made him impolite or rude. He continued to be quiet and polite to others. He was always curious and nobody was there to clear certain doubts that cropped up in him. For example, he had noticed that the hair on Muralidharan's head was curly grey, the hair in his windy armless armpits was wispy black, and the hair in his crotch was black and springy. Nobody told him how one man could have three kinds of hair.

Cleanliness was something that Estha never compromised with. He ensured that his room always remained clean. It was a sort of obsession for Estha to keep the room so. We also find that very often his reaction to his surroundings is rather spontaneous. That is what made him sing in the theatre quite oblivious of the people around him. Like a true 'child' he always longed for his mother's love. The important lessons that he had learned from his life also remains as something very significant. He had come to realize that anything could happen to anyone and it was best to be prepared. We also find that he was quite happy with his own bit of wisdom. The contrast that is drawn out can perhaps sum up his character. He was as clean as his clean room in the dirty Ayemenem house. Though he is described as not young and not old he never ran short of pragmatism. He was a stranger who met another stranger (his sister Rahel) in a chance encounter. They had known each other before life began and that was why he was most comfortable in the company of Rahel. But life was a 'big encounter' for Estha throughout.

5

The Die-vorced and the Barren

I

In his address to Japanese youth William Faulkner has observed that "man himself will prevail over all his anguishes, provided he will make the effort to; make the effort to believe in man and in hope to seek not for a mere crutch to lean on, but to stand erect on his own feet by believing in hope and in his own toughness and endurance" [Quoted from Edmond L. Volpe. (1964 — p. 288)]. 'The Die-vorced and the Barren' in Roy's novel is such a one who endured all kinds of assaults from all corners in her life and struggled against all kinds of adversities.

Comrade K.N.M. Pillai firmly believed that Estha's generation of Ayemenem Family was perhaps paying for its forefather's bourgeois decadence. He saw that one was mad and the other divorced, probably barren. Obviously Estha was the mad one and Rahel the barren one who was "die-vorced". The impression that we get of Rahel is that of a young imaginative girl. She was a deprived child who failed to receive love when she was a child and even later. She was often defiant and a rebel who never tolerated the snobs. Throughout her life she had to suffer neglect, neglect by her mother and everyone else. She always had the feeling that she had been uncared for and that was why she thought of escaping into a world which she thought, would take care of her. She was mostly alone and nobody took interest in her affairs. Sophie Mol's death was something that she could never reconcile herself to. Her relationship with the twin brother was something unusual and strange.

Rahel, at one point in the novel, is described as an excited mosquito on a leash. "Flying. Weightless. Up two steps. Down two. Up one. She climbed five flights of red stairs for Baby Kochamma's one" (p. 98). Somehow she was made to create an impression in her mother that she was good at hurting the feelings of others. That was what made Ammu remark "when you hurt people, they begin to love you less. That's what careless words do. They make people love you a little less" (p. 112). She was badly and madly in need of love and that is clear from what she asked Chacko : "Chacko, do you love Sophie Mol Most in the World?" (p. 118). She also wanted to know whether it was necessary that people had to love their children most in the world. Chacko had told her that anything was possible in human nature. The possibilities were love, madness, hope and infinite joy. Rahel thought that of the four things that were possible in human nature, "*Infinnate Joy*" was the saddest. Of course, 'joy' and 'sadness' are things that can never go together.

To the old generation Rahel was known only through their grandmother. Thus, Pillai introduced her to a man with a photograph as "The old Paradise Pickle Kochamma's daughter's daughter" (p. 129). But that 'Kochamma' also was known only through 'Punnyan Kunju'. She was one who increasingly looked at nature which gave her some relief whenever she suffered from mental depression : "Inside the curtain, Rahel closed her eyes and thought of the green river, of the quiet deep-swimming fish, and gossamer wings of the dragonflies... in the sun" (p. 148).

For Rahel it was all bleak — the past, present and future. She came back to Ayemenem after a gap of several years on hearing that Estha had come to Ayemenem. But she was unsure as to how long she was going to be in Ayemenem. Baby Kochamma had already asked her how much longer she planned to stay and what she planned to do about Estha. But the fact was that she didn't have immediate plans as to what she was going to do and what she was going to do with Estha. Probably when Baby Kochamma wrote to say that Estha had been re-returned, she might not have thought that Baby Kochamma would ask her when she would return. At least, she wouldn't have given up her job at the gas station in America if she had anticipated this.

II

Rahel who is introduced in the opening page of the novel itself did not have a life different from that of Estha till the 'Sophie Mol incident'. Though Rahel and Estha were twins, they never did look much like each other. Chacko had said that Rahel, like Estha was indecently healthy. Rahel was not sure what she suffered from, but occasionally she practised sad faces. Sighing in the mirror she would say "*It is a far, far better thing that I do, than I have ever done*" (p. 61).

Like Estha, Rahel also was very short. Her curiosity and imagination sometimes went on unexpected lines. In the Abhilash talkies when Baby Kochamma went to the urinals Rahel studied her baby grant aunt's enormous legs. "(Years later during a history lesson being read out in school — *The Emperor Babur had a wheatish complexion and pillar-like thighs* — this scene would flash before her. Baby Kochamma balanced like a big bird over a public pot. Blue veins like lumpy knitting running up her translucent shins. Fat knees dimpled. Hair on them. Poor little tiny feet to carry such a load!)" (p. 95).

Just as Estha had a terrible experience at the theatre in the hands of the Orangedrink Lemondrink Man Rahel too had a horrible time with the man though not as awful as the one Estha had. The man offered Rahel a sweet and as she approached him, "he smiled at her and something about that portable piano smile, something about the steady gaze in which he held her, made her shrink from him. It was the most hideous thing she had ever seen... she backed away form the hairy man" (p. 111). Ammu was impressed by the gesture of the 'Orangedrink' man and even remarked that he was a sweet chap. This irritated Rahel and she said to her mother's face that she could marry him. Ammu was angry like anything. Rahel was desperately sorry for what she had said. She didn't even know where those words had come from. Ammu cautioned her against uttering careless words. Rahel had to pay the price for what she had done. When they returned to the room in Hotel Sea Queen, Rahel was made to sleep with Chacko as against the original plan of sleeping with Ammu and Baby Kochamma : "But now that Estha wasn't well and love had been reapportioned (Ammu loved her a little less), Rahel would have to sleep with Chacko, and Estha with Ammu and Baby Kochamma" (p. 114).

Even little things would make Rahel sad. She had in her the sadness of Sophie Mol coming. Ammu's loving her a little less made her sad. Whatever the 'Orangedrink' man had done to Estha in Abhilash Talkies also made her sad. In her younger days she used to be blunt and sometimes she talked in such a way that she never bothered about the consequences. Once when she observed that she would be in Africa when she grew up Kochu Maria had replied that Africa was full of ugly black people and mosquitoes. Rahel's reaction to this comment was spontaneous. She said that Kochu Maria was the only one who was ugly and a 'stupid dwarf.' Kochu Maria stamped her jealous and said that jealous people would go straight to hell.

Sophie Mol's death had turned out to be a turning point in the life of both Rahel and Estha. Estha was immediately returned to his father. For Rahel something else was in store. After her mother's death Rahel drifted from school to school. She was largely ignored by Chacko and Mammachi. On the other hand, Baby Kochamma was ignored by Rahel. Chacko and Mammachi had provided her food, clothes and fees, otherwise called 'care'. But they never showed any concern for her.

The loss of Sophie Mol continued to be felt in the Ayemenem family like a fruit in season. It was as permanent as a Government job and "it ushered Rahel through childhood (from school to school) into womanhood" (p. 16). Even at a very young age of eleven, Rahel was blacklisted in Nazreth Convent. This was the first of the series of 'blacklistings' she had to confront with. She was caught outside her House mistress's garden gate decorating a knob of fresh cowdung with small flowers. "At Assembly the next morning she was made to look up *depravity* in the Oxford Dictionary and read aloud its meaning. '*The quality or condition of being depraved or corrupt*', Rahel read, with a row of stern-mouthed nuns behind her and a sea of sniggering schoolgirl faces in front" (p. 16).

She was expelled again after six months. This time it was a result of repeated complaints from senior girls. She was accused of hiding behind doors and deliberately colliding with her seniors. On persistent questioning (which included cajoling, caning and starving) she admitted that she had done it to find out whether breasts hurt! This was a big insult to a Christian institution because nobody acknowledged breasts in that institution. Since they were not there the question of hurting also didn't arise!

She was expelled from school two more times. The second one was for smoking and the last one for setting fire to her Housemistress's artificial hairbun which was stolen by Rahel. The teachers noted that she was an extremely polite child without any friends. The general impression was that she didn't know how to be a girl. On the whole, she was a neglected child everywhere. In certain respects she was like her mother Ammu. There was no one to arrange a marriage for her. She had to live "without anybody who would pay her a dowry and therefore without any obligatory husband looming on her horizon" (p. 17). This made her make her own inquiries into breasts, false hair buns and also into life and how it ought to be lived.

Once she finished her school, she won admission into a mediocre College of Architecture in Delhi. She happened to take the entrance examination and happened to get through. "The staff were impressed by the size (enormous), rather than the skill, of her charcoal still-life sketches. The careless, reckless lines were mistaken for artistic confidence, though in truth, their creator was no artist" (p. 17). For about eight years she was in the college without finishing her course and taking her degree. She very rarely went to classes and instead worked as a draughtsman in architectural firms. She was a lone woman there also. Her fellow students never invited her to their houses. Even the teachers were suspicious of her. It was her impractical building plans which were presented on cheap brown paper that made them wary. She occasionally wrote to Chacko and Mammachi but never returned to her native place not even when Mammachi died or when Chacko emigrated to Canada.

In short, Rahel's life as a child and also as a grown up girl was one of total depravation. She was isolated wherever she was at her own home, school and also college. She never received the concern a young child is expected to get at the hands of its elders. This eventually made her a rebel and the provocations for her suspension and expulsions from school have their root in this kind of an attitude from others. After all, Chacko and others in the family cannot be kind to her because indirectly she also was responsible for the death of Sophie Mol. The school authorities knew pretty well that she was an 'unwanted' child even in her own family. By the time she reached college her attitude to everything might have become cynical and naturally nobody was comfortable in her company. But this was not entirely true. There was someone who showed interest in her when she was at the School of Architecture.

III

While Rahel was at the School of Architecture she met Larry McCaslin who was in Delhi collecting material for his Ph.D. thesis on *Energy Efficiency in Vernacular Architecture*. He was attracted to Rahel almost at first sight : "He first noticed Rahel in the school library and then again, a few days later, in Khan Market. She was in jeans and a white T-shirt. Part of an old patchwork bedspread was buttoned around her neck and trailed behind her like a cape. Her wild hair was tied back to look straight though it wasn't. A tiny diamond gleamed in one nostril. She had absurdly beautiful collarbones and a nice athletic run" (p. 18). If the novel is an autobiographical one this is a description of Arundhati Roy herself. Just as she drifted from school to school she drifted into marriage only to return to Boston.

Larry liked her and he held her as though she was a gift given to him in love which was unbearably precious. But very soon problems started cropping up. When they made love he was offended by her eyes. They started behaving as though they belonged to someone else. He never knew the meaning of her look. He thought that she was indifferent if not desperate. "What Larry McCaslin saw in Rahel's eyes was not despair at all, but a sort of enforced optimism. And a hollow where Estha's words had been. He couldn't be expected to understand that. That the emptiness in one twin was only a version of the quietness in the other. That the two things fitted together. Like stacked spoons. Like familiar lovers' bodies" (pp. 19-20).

They were soon divorced. After that Rahel worked as a waitress in an Indian restaurant in New York for a few months. She worked as a night clerk at a gas station outside Washington for several years where pimps used to approach her with lucrative job offers. Stabbing and shooting incidents were very common there. "Twice she saw men being shot through their car windows. And once a man who had been stabbed, ejected from a moving car with a knife in his back" (p. 20).

Then Baby Kochamma informed her about Estha's re-return to Ayemenem house. She immediately gave up her job at Washington, left America gladly and returned to Ayemenem and to Estha. It was an altogether different Ayemenem that waited for Rahel when she reached there in the month of June.

IV

It was raining when Rahel came back to Ayemenem. "The old house on the hill wore its steep, gabled roof pulled over its ears like a low hat. The walls, streaked with moss, had grown soft, and bulged a little with dampness that seeped up from the ground.... The house itself looked empty. The doors and windows were locked. The front verandah bare. Unfurnished.... and inside, Baby Kochamma was still alive (pp. 1-2).

One important thing that Baby Kochamma did was to ask Rahel to keep the letter that the twin's father sent to Ayemenem with Estha. She put it back into its envelope. She had almost forgotten how damp the monsoon air in Ayemenem could be. "Swollen cupboards creaked. Locked windows burst open. Books got soft and wavy between their covers" (p. 9). Ayemenem also had changed considerably when she came back years later. The river "greeted her with a ghastly skull's name, with holes where teeth had been, and a limp hand raised from a hospital bed.... Downriver, a saltwater barrage had been built, in exchange for votes from the influential paddy-farmer lobby" (p. 124).

A band of children followed Rahel on her walk. They asked her : "Hello, hippie, ...what is your name?" (p. 127). Someone even threw a stone at her taking her to be a strange creature who was on a 'visitation'. On her way back she emerged into the main road. She found that Ayemenem had almost lost its rural quietness. Outside Lucky Press she was intercepted by Comrade K.N.M. Pillai. She had tried to walk past unnoticed though it was absurd of her to have imagined that she could.

"'*Aiyyo*, Rahel Mol! Comrade K.N.M. Pillai said, recognizing her instantly. '*Orkunnilley*? (Don't you remember?) Comrade Uncle?' " (p. 128). Rahel answered in the affirmative. She did remember him very well. Both she and he knew that there were things that could be forgotten, and things that couldn't be forgotten. Rahel sarcastically remarked that she was there when Pillai enquired whether she was in Ayemenem. She was introduced to a stranger with some photographs in his hand. He remembered vaguely a whiff of scandal. He had forgotten the details, but remembered that it had involved sex and death. It had been in the papers.

Once the stranger parted Pillai began to ask Rahel certain inconvenient questions. He wanted to know about her husband, name, issues and a host of other things. He even asked her whether she was in the planning stage or expecting a baby. When she told him that she was divorced he described it as most unfortunate and even pronounced the word as though it were a form of death. He also asked her about Estha. It was unclear for Rahel why he asked her these questions. She wondered what he gained by questioning her so closely and completely disregarding her answers.

The 'Wisdom Exercise Notebooks' in Pappachi's study helped Rahel to go back to her younger days with Estha. There were four tattered notebooks. Two had her name on them and two Estha's. Inside the back cover of one was written "*I Hate Miss Mitten and I Think her gnickers are TORN*" (p. 156). It was written by 'Esthappen Un-known' who never could bear Miss Mitten. The notebook also brought back to her memory the tragedy that struck Ayemenem house twenty-three years ago. "Rahel stood there with her tattered wisdom notebooks. In the front verandah of an old house, below a button-eyed bison head, where years ago, on the day that Sophie Mol came, *Welcome Home, Our Sophie Mol* was performed" (p. 164). One of the 'villains' of the tragic story, Estha, she saw, was disappearing through the gate exactly at that moment.

It was again a kind of reliving the old Ayemenem days for Rahel. The sound of the 'chenda' (drum) used to travel up to a kilometre from the Ayemenem temple, announcing a kathakali performance. Now she went to the temple drawn by the memory of steep roofs and white walls. "Of brass lamps lit and dark, oiled wood. She went in the hope of meeting an old elephant who wasn't electrocuted on the Kottayam — Cochin highway. She stopped by the kitchen for a coconut" (p. 192). On her way out, she noticed that one of the gauze doors of the factory had come off its hinges and was propped against the doorway.... The low cement pickle vats silhouetted in the gloom made the factory floor look like an indoor cemetery for the cylindrical dead" (p. 192). Again she remembered Sophie Mol's visit to Ayemenem and how things changed in a day.

With memories of the temple festival fresh in her mind, Rahel went to the temple where the sound of the chenda mushroomed all over. She found the thin priest asleep on a mat in the raised stone verandah. Kochu Thomban, the temple elephant was asleep, after having done his duty. She saw that he wasn't *Kochu* (means 'small') Thomban any more. His tusks had grown. He was *Vellya* ('big') Thomban or the big tusker. There was kathakali performance in the temple and the story was 'Karna shabadam' — Karna's oath. Rahel with her back against a pillar watched Karna praying on the banks of the Ganga. He was the abandoned child, the generous and the most revered warrior of all. To her utter dismay, Rahel found that Karna was stoned that night. Suddenly she knew that Estha had come. She didn't turn her head, but a glow spread insider her : "Estha settled against a distant pillar and they sat through the performance like this, separated by the breadth of the kuthambalam, but joined by a story. And the memory of another mother" (p. 234). The gap of twenty-three years had made tremendous change in them. They had become "Quietness and Emptiness, frozen two-egg fossils, with hornbumps that hadn't grown into horns... Trapped in the bog of a story that was and wasn't theirs" (p. 236). As they stepped through the temple gateway Comrade Pillai stepped in and remarked : "'Oho!' you are here!

'So still you are interested in your Indian culture? Goodgood. Very good." (p. 237). The twins didn't react to the comment. They were especially careful to see that they were neither rude nor polite. They just walked home together.

The twins had begun to make Baby Kochamma uneasy. A few mornings earlier she had opened her window and caught them red-handed in the act of returning from somewhere. She was at a loss to know where they had spent their night together and what they were doing sitting together in the dark for so long. The fact was that Rahel was lying on Estha's bed. "Her soft, sleeveless, T-shirt was a glowing yellow in the dark. The bottom half of her, in blue jeans, melted into the darkness. It was a little cold. A little wet. A little quiet" (p. 299). The obvious question is what happened next. "Only that there were tears. Only that Quietness and Emptiness fitted together like stacked spoons. Only that there was a snuffling in the hollows at the base of a lovely throat. Only that a hard honey-coloured shoulder had a semi-circle of teeth marks on it. Only that they held each other close, long after it was over. Only that what they shared that night was not happiness, but hideous grief. Only that once again they broke the Love Laws. That lay down who should be loved. And how. And how much" (p. 328).

This is the short life-history of Rahel ever since she came back to Ayemenem at the age of thirty-one. Life continued to be almost the same for her even at this age. Her relations with Estha also remained unchanged. The incestuous relation that they had when they were very young continued even when they grew up into a 'matured' man and woman. Ayemenem house was as hostile to her as it was years ago. Baby Kochamma, the sole heir of the family (as she believed it to be the case) never wanted Rahel to remain there for long. That was why she repeatedly asked her about her future plans. She deliberately made herself not rude to Comrade Pillai who in a sense was the villain who played a very important role in precipitating the tragedy that struck Velutha. The home-coming also helped Rahel to travel down memory lane where she was able to get flashes of incidents and also people who were once upon a time intimate to her.

V

What remains to be discussed is the kind of relations Rahel kept with those who were dear to her and also with those who were otherwise. Ammu and Estha being two egg twins any discussion should start with Estha. But now that enough has been said about the kind of life they led which includes their desperation, the incestuous relations and so on we shall pass on to some of the other characters who play major as well as minor roles in the novel.

As has already been seen in the case of Estha, Ammu's attitude to Rahel also was one of ambivalence. On the one hand she loved (or rather tried to love) her children and on the other hand she continued to create psychological problems for them. Rahel and Estha were obedient children at least before their mother. Ammu loved her children (of course), but their wide-eyed vulnerability, and their willingness to love people who didn't really love them, exasperated her and sometimes made her want to hurt them — just as an education, a protection....

"To Ammu her twins seemed like a pair of small bewildered frogs engrossed in each other's company, lolloping arm in down a highway full of hurtling traffic. Entirely oblivious of what trucks can do to frogs. Ammu watched over them fiercely. Her watchfulness stretched her, made her taut and tense. She was quick to reprimand her children, but even quicker to take offence on their behalf" (p. 43). So this was her general attitude to her own children, the children for whom practically she was both a father and a mother.

That Ammu had genuine love for Rahel was clear from the fact that on her last visit to Ayemenem she had brought presents for her daughter : "With the last of her meagre salary she had bought her daughter small presents wrapped in brown paper with coloured paper hearts pasted on. A packet of cigarette sweets, a tin Phantom pencil box and *Paul Bunyan* — a Junior Classics Illustrated comic" (p. 159). These were presents for a seven year old. Rahel was nearly eleven at that time. Ammu asked her a number of questions but never allowed her to answer them. She was terrified to think of the 'adult answers' that Rahel might give. But Rahel was in an entirely different mental make-up at that time. When Mammachi suggested that she visit Rahel as seldom as possible Ammu had no other way but to quit. Chacko wanted Rahel to see her off. But she pretended she hadn't heard him. The reason was that she hated her mother then. Ironically enough, Rahel never saw her again.

Probably Rahel continued to keep in her mind her mother's insistence on her afternoon nap which she hated. Of course she might not have forgotten the fact that Ammu had a role in the killing of Velutha. But the fact remained that there were moments when Ammu and Rahel were real mother and daughter. There was at least one evening when Ammu blessed her daughter after dinner which was followed by an observation by Rahel : "*We be of one blood, ye and I*" (p. 329). To put it briefly, Ammu was both good and bad to Rahel and much must have depended on her mental condition on different occasions.

Sophie Mol, was rather straight forward in her attitude to Rahel. She had told her to her face that she didn't love her. Rahel's response to this comment was that she would start loving her once. She came to know her. Rahel did prove right later. Sophie Mol and the twins became very good friends : "Sophie Mol, hatted, bellbottomed and Loved from the Beginning, walked out of the Play to see what Rahel was doing behind the well. But the Play went with her. Walked when she walked, stopped when she stopped. Fond smiles followed her" (p. 186). But as fate would have it Rahel had the lead role in 'leading' Sophie Mol to death.

Chacko, her legal uncle (she never called her 'uncle') was never a fascist. Not only that. He often used to advise his sister Ammu not to be a fascist when it came to the dealings with her children. There was a contrast drawn between Rahel and Chacko the evening they spent together at Hotel Sea Queen : "A dinnerless niece and her dinnerful uncle brushed their teeth together in the Hotel Sea Queen bathroom. She, a forlorn, stubby convict in striped *pyjamas* and a Fountain in a Love-in-Tokyo. He, in his cotton vest and underpants." (p. 116). On the whole, Rahel did not have any problems in her dealings with Chacko.

Margaret Kochamma, by and large, was never unkind to

Rahel. On their first meeting when Margaret greeted her she had felt that to be the voice of a kind school teacher. But when the tragic incident in which Sophie Mol was drowned, she also did join the other members of the family in isolating Rahel, her brother and mother. It was also Rahel who remained in Ayemenem who received Margaret Kochamma's apology to Ammu for being unkind to Estha. That was because Ammu had to pack her bags and leave and Estha was returned to his father.

Baby Kochamma never trusted Rahel and her brother. She thought that they were capable of anything. She feared that "*they might even steal their present back*" (p. 29). She took them as a single unit and in Rahel she noticed "the same eerie stealth, the ability to keep very still and very quiet that Estha seemed to have mastered" (p. 29). Rahel's quietness had disturbed her considerably. She didn't have anything pleasant to think of Baby Kochamma. Her making them speak in English and sing English songs were only some of the things that made Rahel and Estha hate her. Baby Kochamma "grudged them their moments of high happiness... But most of all, she grudged them the comfort they drew from each other. She expected from them some token unhappiness" (p. 46). She always thought that they were Half-Hindu Hybrids whom no self-respecting Syrian Christian would ever marry. In short, Rahel and Estha created moments of uneasiness for her and there was nothing in the relation between them to make Rahel or Estha feel comfortable with her.

Velutha, the untouchable was the most beloved friend of Rahel. He had carried her on his back more times than she could count. It was Velutha who had made her "the luckiest ever fishing rod" and taught her and Estha to fish. Very many times did she lung at him *ickilee ickilee ickilee*. To be sure, Velutha was the one with whom Rahel could easily establish an intimacy which was in a sense not possible even in her relations with her mother.

In short, the relations Rahel could establish with her near ones and some of the others in the novel do not have a pattern. On the whole it was a story of 'lovelessness' even though she did experience some flashes of love and care form some of them. Ammu was mostly a puzzle for her and Estha could not be treated as a person different from her. She was happy with Sophie Mol though at a later stage. Velutha was the one whom she liked most. Pillai and Inspector Thomas Mathew were people whom she hated though she was careful enough to see that she was never rude to them at least apparently. She disliked Baby Kochamma and also the servant girl Kochu Maria. She didn't have much problems with Mammachi. Chacko also was not unkind to her.

VI

Thus, we find that Rahel, the twin sister of Estha was destined to suffer. She had to suffer from fatherlessness at a very young age of two. Her mother who had her own problems, probably as a result of her separation from her husband expectedly was not a successful mother. She came to Ayemenem with her brother and mother as unwelcome 'guests' and she had to suffer ill-treatment especially at the hands of Baby Kochamma.

The death of Sophie Mol turned out to be a turning point in her life and her mother's 'sin' which coincided with this incident made her also an 'unadulterated sinner". She had to leave Ayemenem and in the school also only problems awaited her. She was stamped as a "deprived child" and all these might have a non-trivial influence on her which ultimately led to an emotional crisis. Her college days also was not satisfactory. A silver lining came in the form of a love affair. But that again was short lived. She tried to find pleasure in the odd jobs in which she was engaged abroad.

When she received the news of Estha's "re-return" to Ayemenem she thought that happy days had dawned upon her. She gave up her job only to return to Ayemenem. Here again disappointment awaited her. There were people who found pleasure in her being a divorcee. The people who believed that they were the legal heir to Ayemenem house started asking her when she was going to return. Ultimately a black world was opened before her which means she was one who was destined to suffer incessantly.

6

Receipt No. Q. 498673

I

"The crematorium 'In-charge' had gone down the road for a cup of tea and didn't come back for twenty minutes. That's how long Chacko and Rahel had to wait for the pink receipt.... Her ashes. The grit from her bones. The teeth from her smile. The whole of her crammed into a little clay pot. Receipt No. Q. 498673" (p. 163). Yes. Ammu had become a number, a receipt number.

Ammu's tragedy began even when she was very young. It followed her like a shadow right up to the last moment in her life. The people who were dear to her in one way or other made her lead a miserable life. She had a husband who she found was unfit to be called a husband. She was a mother but very often she took her children to be a liability. She had a brother who was nothing short of a "male chauvinistic pig." But she did get some consolation. But it was from a wrong person. That even lasted for a very short period, say, two weeks. She touched the untouchable or she tasted the 'untasteable'. The consequence was something that went beyond her anticipation. She was isolated. She was treated as a sinner and she was shown the door. This ultimately made her more lonely than she ever was. She had to part from her children and also from everything that was dear to her. Here is an attempt to 'feel' her life from her young days up to the moment she became a receipt. Many appeared and some disappeared from her life. The tragedy was something unique, far from the ordinary.

II

We don't know many things about Ammu's childhood from the novel. Her father Pappachi retired as the Joint Director, Entomology which was a rank equivalent to Director. When Ammu finished her schooling she had to move to Ayemenem. For Ammu college education was a luxury as her father had found it an unnecessary expense, she being a girl child. She idled away time at Ayemenem. Her eighteenth birthday came and went unnoticed and unremarked upon by her parents. She grew totally desperate and somehow wanted to run away from Ayemenem to some place or other. She conceived of her own little plans and eventually one worked. She received the green signal to go to Calcutta to join her aunt. Theodore Dreiser (1981) has made the following observation in his novel *Sister Carrie* : "When a girl leaves her home at eighteen, she does one of two things. Either she falls into saving hands and becomes better, or she rapidly assumes the cosmopolitan standard of virtue and becomes worse." In Ammu's case her leaving home at least for the time being was to fall into saving hands.

Ammu soon met her future husband. He was small, well-built and pleasant looking. He was on vacation from his job in Assam where he worked as an assistant manager of a tea-estate. He belonged to a once wealthy *Zamindar* family who had migrated to Calcutta from East Bengal after partition. He was twenty-five and had already been working on the tea estates for six years. Just like Ammu he also didn't have college education. He proposed to Ammu five days after their first meeting. She never pretended to be in love with him. Instead, she weighed the odds and accepted the proposal. She thought that "*anything*, anyone at all, would be better than returning to Ayemenem" (p. 39). Even though she wrote to her parents about her decision they never cared to respond to the letter.

Her father-in-law was Chairman of the Railway board and was the Secretary of the Bengal Amateur Boxing Association (BABA). The young couple were given a Fiat car as a present which after the wedding he drove off in himself, with all the jewellery and most of the other presents. But he did not survive long. He died before the twins were born to her. Death took place on the operating table while his gall bladder was being removed.

Ammu and her husband moved to Assam. She was beautiful, young and cheeky and was the toast of the planter's club. "She wore backless blouses with her saris and carried a silver lame purse on a chain. She smoked long cigarettes in a silver cigarette holder and learned to blow perfect smoke rings" (p. 40). At the same time her husband turned out to be "not just a heavy drinker but a full-blown alcoholic with all of an alcoholic's deviousness and tragic charm" (p. 40). He had strange ways. In a conversation with friends he would talk about how much he loved smoked salmon when Ammu knew he hated it. He would come home and tell Ammu that he saw *Meet Me in St. Louis* when they had actually screened *The Bronze Buckaroo*. He was never apologetic about this kind of a behaviour. When she questioned he would just giggle.

War broke out in 1962. Ammu was eight months pregnant and the planters' wives and children were evacuated from Assam. Being too weak to travel, Ammu chose to remain in the estate. She gave birth to two little ones, instead of one big one. "Twin seals, slick with their mother's juices. Wrinkled with the effort of being born" (p. 40). She found that the children were all right — four eyes, four ears, two mouths, two noses, twenty fingers and so on. But she also made a serious omission. She failed to notice that the twins had a single Siamese soul and that had its own consequences later.

Slowly life began to become unbearable to her. Whole days went by during which her husband lay in bed and didn't go to work. Soon he received a clear message from his manager that he was going to be sacked. But the English manager never forgot to tell him that his wife was most welcome to be looked after by him. Viewed practically it was a mutual benefit programme. But Ammu's husband took sometime to muster courage and tell her about the proposal. But eventually he was bold enough to tell Ammu that new ideas had struck Mr. Hollick, the manager.

("Already there were a number of ragged light-skinned children on the estate that Hollick had bequeathed on tea-pickers whom he fancied. This was his first incursion into management circles" (p. 42). Ammu remained silent for sometime which made her husband infuriated. Suddenly he "lunged at her, grabbed her hair, punched her and then passed out from the effort. Ammu took down the heaviest book she could find in the book shelf — *The Reader's Digest World Atlas* — and hit him with it as hard as she could. On his head. His legs. His back and shoulders" (p. 42). Drunken violence continued and she had no option but to return to her parents in Ayemenem. "To everything that she had fled from only a few years ago. Except that now she had two young children. And no more dreams" (p. 42).

Thus we see that Ammu's life at Ayemenem since she left Delhi was one of desperation and boredom. Somehow she wanted to escape from the dreary life with her parents and she did succeed in that. But life continued to be so even after she joined her aunt at Calcutta. If getting married was a problem when she turned eighteen married life turned out to be a problem for her later. Her husband's drunkenness was instrumental in making her more desperate than she ever was. Though she liked her children as any other mother, the same children began to become a liability for her very soon. Greater misery awaited her at Ayemenem on her arrival with her children there.

III

Pappachi, her father could never reconcile to the theory that an Englishman would covet another man's wife. As for Ammu, her world was confined to the front and back verandah of Ayemenem. She continued to love her children as she did earlier "but their wide-eyed vulnerability, and their willingness to love people, who didn't really love them, exasperated her and sometimes made her want to hurt them — just as an education, a protection" (p. 43). She knew that there would be no more chances. A parallel can perhaps be drawn between Ammu and Joseph, the central character in Saul Bellows novel *Dangling Man* where we find the quest going inward "...into his own private room, where the 'perspectives end in the walls" (see Bradbury

1985 p. 135). What is common between Joseph and Ammu is that both discover their existential dilemma, an existence without essence in a hostile world.

Within the first few months of her return to Ayemenem she found that there were people around her who were specialists in sympathising. But unfortunately for Ammu, she was one who never liked to be sympathised with. "She fought off the urge to slap them. Or twiddle their nipples. With a spanner. Like Chaplin in *Modern Times*" (p. 43). When she looked at herself in her wedding photographs she felt very sorry that she had permitted herself to be painstakingly decorated before being led to the "gallows". The whole thing was both absurd and futile. She thought it would be wiser on her part to see that her wedding ring was melted so that nothing of her wedding would remain on her. So she went to the village goldsmith and had her ring melted down to take a new shape — a thin bangle with snake-heads. She put that away for her daughter Rahel. She knew that weddings were not something that could be avoided altogether. But a late realization came to her mind that weddings could be *small* in *ordinary* clothes.

Slowly, without her knowledge, she was becoming restless. She would like to walk out of the world like a witch, to a better, happier place. "On days like this, there was something restless and untamed about her. As though she had temporarily set aside the morality of motherhood and divorceehood. Even her walk changed from a safe mother-walk to another wilder sort of walk. She wore flowers in her hair and carried magic secrets in her eyes. She spoke to no one. She spent hours on the riverbank with her little plastic transistor shaped like a tangerine. She smoked cigarettes and had midnight swims" (p. 44). A reckless rage of a suicide bomber was battling insider her. This eventually led her to love by night Velutha, the man her children loved by day. "To use by night the boat that her children used by day. The boat that Estha sat on, and Rahel found" (p. 44). People started avoiding her for they realized that it was best to leave her alone. Sometimes she was the most beautiful woman that Estha and Rahel had ever seen. At other times she wasn't so.

Meanwhile, Baby Kochamma was never at peace with Ammu.

She subscribed whole-heartedly to the commonly held view that a married daughter had no position in her parent's home. As for a *divorced* daughter.... she had no position anywhere at all. And as for a *divorced* daughter from a *love* marriage, well, words could not describe Baby Kochamma's outrage. As for a *divorced* daughter from a *intercommunity love* marriage — Baby Kochamma chose to remain quiveringly silent on the subject (pp. 45-46).

·Ammu did as much work in the pickle factory the family owned as Chacko. But he always referred to it as "*my* factory, *my* pineapples, *my* pickles". Legally, he was right because Ammu, as a daughter, had no claim to the property. Chacko told the twins that Ammu had no "Locusts Stand I." Ammu blamed it all on the wonderful male chauvinist society. To her face Chacko said : "What's yours is mine and what's mine is also mine" (p. 57).

Ammu used to see cruelty and as she grew older, she learned to live with this cold, calculating cruelty. She developed a lofty sense of injustice and the mulish, reckless streak that would develop in someone small who had been bullied all their lives by someone big. She never did anything to avoid quarrels and instead she sought them out and even enjoyed them.

In short, the period between her coming to Ayemenem from Calcutta and the arrival of Sophie Mol is not very eventful as is given in the novel. But there is enough hint that Ammu is slowly moving in a forbidden direction. She never got love from any of the members of the family and naturally she had been a little unkind to her own children. Chacko, her brother and Baby Kochamma, her aunt made use of every opportunity to sideline her creating an impression that she was an outsider in Ayemenem house. But we find a determined woman in Ammu who sheds her 'motherhood' and 'divorceehood' only to establish a connection with Velutha, the untouchable.

IV

Velutha, the Paravan carpenter was an inextricable part of the Ayemenem house. Even from a very young age he used to visit this house with his father Vellya Paapen. He was dear to everyone in the family more so because he was an expert in carpentry who could do other odd jobs also. As a little boy he used to help his father to count coconuts at Ayemenem. He used to hold out little gifts he had made for Ammu, flat on the palm of his hand so that she could take them without touching him, he being an untouchable. He called her Ammukutty (Little Ammu) and made boats, boxes, small windmills, etc., for her even though she was much less little than he was.

Both of them had grown up and Ammu slowly got drawn to Velutha. "In the dappled sunlight filtering through the dark green trees, Ammu watched Velutha lift her daughter effortlessly as though she was an inflatable child, made of air.... She saw the ridges of muscle on Velutha's stomach grow taught and rise under his skin like the divisions on a slab of chocolate. She wondered at how his body had changed — so quietly from a flatmuscled boy's body into a man's body. Conquered and hard. A swimmer's body" (p. 175). When she looked at him she thought that the man he had become bore so little resemblance to the boy he had been. Suddenly she found that her daughter had a sub-world that excluded her. She felt envious but was not sure whether the target of her envy was Rahel or Velutha.

Very soon this developed into physical relations which continued at least for a fortnight. It was Vellya Paapen who witnessed the "unholy alliance" one day. The matter was promptly reported to Ayemenem house and Velutha paid the price for it. Ammu became more desperate than ever before and she did not have anyone who showed her even a semblance of friendliness or concern. Her fate was almost sealed and like a true "sinner" she had to wait for the punishment that was in store for her. It was a series of punishments beginning from the custodial death of Velutha. Estha was returned to his father which came as the second punishment. Next she was given marching orders which separated her from her daughter.

This is yet another phase in the life of Ammu, which perhaps is the greatest turning point in her life. Ammu, a young woman of twenty-seven was separated from her husband at a young age. Being isolated everywhere, Ammu was badly in need of the company of someone who would bring her some consolation. Velutha being someone whom she knew rather intimately from her childhood became her natural choice. Velutha also appeared to be waiting for a breakthrough. This was again nothing unexpected as he had by then developed all the qualities of a rebel who wanted to deviate from the conventional life which was familiar to him. The affair Ammu had with Velutha naturally shocked Ayemenem and the consequence was disastrous more so for Velutha.

V

The real facts as to what went on between Velutha and Ammu were misrepresented. So immediately after the funeral of Sophie Mol Ammu took the twins to the Kottayam police station. The police station was a familiar place for them as they had already spent a good part of the previous day there. Ammu asked for the Station House Officer. She was sent to the officer where she told him that there had been a terrible mistake. She expressed her desire to make a statement and without knowing the fate of Velutha asked to see him.

Inspector Thomas Mathew with his sly and greedy eyes began with an initial remark that it was all too late. He spoke in coarse Kottayam dialect and as was his wont he stared at Ammu's breast as he spoke. He told to her face that the police knew all they needed to know and they didn't take statements from prostitutes and their illegitimate children. He even advised her to leave the place and did not forget to tap her breasts gently with his baton. She left the police station crying and it was the first time the twins had seen their mother cry.

Baby Kochamma was shocked to hear what Ammu had deposed before the police. Somehow she had the impression that Ammu, whatever else she did, and however angry she was would not publicly admit to her relationship with Velutha. For her that would amount to destroying herself and her children for ever. So she thought that somehow she should get Ammu out of Ayemenem as soon as possible. This she managed by convincing Chacko that it was Ammu and her two-egg twins who were directly responsible for Sophie Mol's death. Thus it was her idea that Ammu be made to pack her bags and leave and that Estha be returned to his father.

This is yet another critical phase in the life of Ammu. Things took an entirely different turn on the fourteenth day of her physical relationship with Velutha. She never anticipated that Vellya Paapen would be a witness to all that went between her and Velutha. She least expected that he would rush to Ayemenem house to report the matter. That Baby Kochamma would immediately report the matter to the police station and that she would misrepresent the facts there also was something that Ammu couldn't surmise.

The biggest damage, of course, was done by Baby Kochamma. She rushed to the police station and told the Inspector about the circumstances that had led to the sudden dismissal of a factory worker. She convincingly reported that he was a Paravan who had tried to force himself on her niece, a divorcee with two children a few days ago. Obviously she had in mind Velutha and Ammu. The misrepresentation of facts was done not for the sake of Ammu but to contain the scandal and salvage the family reputation in the eyes of the Inspector. But she never thought that Ammu would later invite shame upon herself by going to the police and setting the record straight. To the Inspector's question why the matter was not reported to the police she replied that their family was an old one with a reputation to boast of. She also told him that the molestee was at home and was frantic with worry about the children. She added that she wouldn't have let her go to the police station.

The story Baby Kochamma made to indict Velutha went like this. The previous evening at about seven o'clock when it was raining rather heavily, Velutha went to their house to threaten them. The light had gone out and the only male member of the house, Chacko was away in Cochin. Only three women were in the house. Velutha started off by saying that Ammu, the molestee had *consented* to share her bed with him. He argued that they had no ground to dismiss him and he couldn't be kicked around like dogs. She also told him that Velutha had Naxalite connections. He recorded Baby Kochamma's statement in the First Information Report and promised to take action against Velutha before the day was out.

As a precaution he sent a jeep to fetch Comrade Pillai to ascertain whether Velutha had any party connections. Like a true politician Pillai told the inspector that he was acquainted with Velutha but deliberately omitted to mention that Velutha was a member of the Communist Party or that he had knocked on his door the previous night, which made Pillai the last person to have seen Velutha before he disappeared. He assured the Inspector that Velutha did not have the patronage or the protection of the Communist Party which gave a free hand to the Inspector and his associates to deal with Velutha with an iron hand which they did.

Later, when the real story reached Inspector Thomas Mathew, the fact that "what the Paravan had taken from the Touchable Kingdom had not been snatched but *given*," (pp. 259-60) concerned him deeply. That was why he terrorized and humiliated Ammu as a premeditated gesture. This leads us to the last phase in the life of Ammu.

VI

Ammu had to leave Ayemenem house after the 'Velutha incident' which coincided with Sophie Mol's death because she had no "Locusts Stand I" and because Chacko had told her that she had destroyed enough already. As Karl (1972) has suggested, "in the serious novel, love should of course create conflicts, whether they be conflicts within one's own feelings or with society" (p. 45). Ammu does create a two way conflict and had to leave Ayemenem.

She came back to Ayemenem "with asthma and a rattle in her chest that sounded like a faraway man shouting" (p. 159). Since Estha was returned to his father he never saw her like that. When she made a visit to Ayemenem the last time Rahel had just been expelled from the Convent. Ammu had been working as a receptionist in a cheap hotel and this was one among a series of jobs she did. She had lost the job as she had been ill and had missed many days of work.

Ammu had brought a present to Rahel who was eleven years old then. "It was as though Ammu believed that if she refused to acknowledge the passage of time, if she willed it to stand still in the lives of her twins, it would. As though sheer willpower was enough to suspend her children's childhoods until she could afford to have them living with her" (p. 159). Ammu told Rahel that she had applied for a UN job and they would all live in The Hague with a Dutch ayah to look after them. She told her about the possibility of staying on in India and starting a school. She also reminded her that choosing between a career in Education and a UN job wasn't easy.

Ammu was swollen with cortisone, moonfaced and not the slender mother Rahel had known. "Her skin was stretched over her puffy cheeks like shiny scar tissue that covers old vaccination marks. When she smiled, her dimples looked as though they hurt. Her curly hair had lost its sheen and hung around her swollen face like a dull curtain" (p. 160). She breathed with great difficulty and "each breath she took was like a war won against the steely fist that was trying to squeeze the air from her lungs" (p. 160).

Ammu appeared to be nearing her end and over lunch she belched like a truck driver. She said to those around her that she felt like a road sign with birds sitting on her. Rahel didn't have any love left for her atleast at that time. Ammu went away without anyone there even to bid goodbye to her.

Then we hear about her death. She died in a grimy ro the Bharat Lodge in Alleppey, where she had gone for a job interview as a secretary. She was left for herself when she died. She was thirty-one on her death. "Not old, not young, but a viable, die-able age" (p. 161).

She had woken up at night to escape from a horrible dream in which the police approached her to hack off her hair, something they did to prostitutes caught in the *bazaar*. That night Ammu sat up "in the strange bed in the strange room in the strange town. She didn't know where she was, she recognised nothing around her. Only her fear was familiar. The faraway man inside her began to shout. This time the steely fist never loosened its grip. Shadows gathered like bats in the steep hollows near her collarbone." (pp. 161-62).

She was found dead in the morning by a sweeper. "A platoon of ants carried a dead cockroach sedately through the door, demonstrating what should be done with corpses." (p. 162). For more reasons than one the church refused to bury Ammu. Chacko carried her deadbody in a dirty bedsheet, laid out on a stretcher and hired a van to transport it to the electric crematorium. Ammu's body jiggled and slid off the stretcher over the jarring bumps and potholes in the road.

The crematorium bore a deserted look. Only beggars, derelicts and the dead in police custody were cremated there. When Ammu's turn came, Chacko held Rahel's hand tightly. The steel door of the incinerator went up. The heat lunged out at Chacko and Rahel like a famished beast. Rahel's Ammu was fed to it. "Her hair, her skin, her smile. Her voice" (p. 163). The door of the furnace clanged shut. There were no tears. And she became a mere receipt. Ammu's breath-taking story ends there. May be a few things should be said about the attitude of some of her fellow members in the Ayemenem family which ultimately led to a death most tragic.

VII

Chacko, Ammu's brother and Baby Kochamma, her aunt were far from kind to Ammu. The latter was especially cruel to her. She resented Ammu "because she saw her quarrelling with a fate that she, Baby Kochamma herself, felt she had graciously accepted. The fate of the wretched Man-less woman" (p. 45). She never reconciled herself to the presence of Ammu in Ayemenem house.

After it was known to the world that Ammu had done the "undreamable" thing it was Baby Kochamma who became the real performer. She concocted her own story and made the Police Inspector finish off Velutha. When it was found that Estha and Rahel were missing it was Baby Kochamma who sent her servant Kochu Maria to look for them. It was again Baby Kochamma who kept the keys when they locked Ammu into her room. She was locked away like the family lunatic in a medieval household. She was unlocked only after Sophie Mole's body was brought to Ayemenem. Even earlier it was Baby Kochamma who added fuel to fire when Mammachi insulted and threatened Velutha.

Very often Ammu had found Chacko and her mother Mammachi insufferable too. At the dinner table "the conversation used to circle like a moth around the white child and her mother as though they were the only source of light" (p. 329). Ammu found this unbearable and even felt that she would die, wither and die, if she heard another word. It was simply impossible for her to endure another minute of Chacko's proud, "tennis-trophy" smile. The undercurrent of Mammachi's sexual jealousy was also something that she couldn't tolerate. Baby Kochamma's conversation that was meant to exclude Ammu and her children, naturally was in tune with the attitude of the other two.

To put it briefly, the last phase of Ammu's life by itself is a tragedy in which more villains than one play a crucial role. She had to struggle for her survival once she was sent out of Ayemenem. There was no one who could bring some relief to her when she was suffering from multiple health problems. Naturally she had to die a lone death with no one to give a drop of water even at the last moment. There was a matching effect when the church refused to bury her dead body. The status that was assigned to her by the society was that of an urchin and even her own children who were once dear to her remained helpless — one of them even remaining in the dark about her death.

VIII

Among major modern British novelists, only C.P. Snow has sought realistic explanations of the social and political conflicts of the period and according to Karl (1972) "Snow has lost in intensity of characterization and situation what he has gained in range" (p. 6). *The God of Small Things* also has social and political conflicts of the period embedded in it. But in sharp contrast to the novels of C.P. Snow what we find here is that Roy is a total success in her characterization and development of situations. Perhaps one of the important characters that would come to one's mind significant for the realistic portrayal is Ammu.

She would have liked to study in a college if she had got a chance. But she was brought to Ayemenem without her approval. She did have the dreams of a young girl about marriage and married life. But the hope was belied when she came to know that nobody was there to provide her dowry to get her married off. Her escape to Calcutta invited fresh troubles. What she achieved, if at all it was an achievement, was only a married life which lasted for less than a couple of years. Hopes were once again shattered when she returned to Ayemenem to discover that nobody was interested in her. Later as fate would have it, she was drawn to Velutha and that marked the beginning of the ultimate tragedy. She was made to suffer in all possible ways and finally she became a receipt number with nobody even to shed a drop of tear for her, not even her own daughter Rahel though she was her Ammu and her Baba and she had loved her double. Unfortunately for Ammu, Estha, her son also was not there at the time of her cremation. But even if he were there he would only keep the receipt, he being known as the keeper of records — the natural custodian of bus tickets, cash memos, cheque book stubs and so on.

7

Rumbled Porcupine

I

"It was the summer of his final year at Oxford. He was alone. His rumpled shirt was buttoned up wrong. His shoelaces were untied. His hair, carefully brushed and slicked down in-front, stood up in a stiff halo of quills at the back. He looked like an untidy, beautified porcupine" (p. 241). The rumbled porcupine described here is Chacko, Ammu's lone brother and Mammachi's son. He was four years older than Ammu and was a Rhodes scholar. He wanted to write a Family Biography that the Family would have to pay him not to publish. He was known in the family for his "Reading Aloud Voice" and did not care whether anyone was listening to him or not. Even if someone were listening to him he would not care whether they had understood what he was saying.

That was the kind of man Chacko was. As Vernon Lee has observed one "can see a person, or an act, in one of several ways and connected with several other persons or acts" (Quoted from Halperin (1974 — p. 16). Chacko can certainly be seen connected with several other persons and also several acts. He was known for his "Oxford moods." Mammachi often said that he was easily one of the cleverest men in India. He came back to Ayemenem to take care of the Paradise Pickle factory. He had his own ideas of business. He was interested in Communism. Though he was not a card-holding member of the Party, he had been converted early and remained a committed supporter. He fell in love with Margaret Kochamma and had a daughter Sophie Mol by her. But they were separated soon after their marriage. "She traded me in for a better man" (p. 249), he would say to Mammachi.

II

Chacko did his undergraduation at Delhi University during the euphoria of 1957, when the Communists won the State Assembly Elections. Chacko's hero E.M.S. Namboodiripad was invited by Nehru to form a government. Chacko studied his treatise on *The Peaceful Transition to Communism* "with an obsessive diligence and an ardent fan's unquestioning approval" (p. 67). Every morning Pappachi, his father derided his argumentative Marxist son by reading out newspaper reports of *riots*, strikes and incidents of police brutality that convulsed Kerala. " 'So, Karl Marx!' Pappachi would sneer when Chacko came to the table. 'What shall we do with these bloody students now? The stupid goons are agitating against our People's Government. Shall we annihilate them? Surely students aren't people anymore?' " (p. 67). Certainly Pappachi was sarcastic and looked down upon the party as one which could be inhuman when dealing with agitators. Students or not was not the concern of the party and it wouldn't even believe that students were "people".

Chacko finished his BA and left for Oxford to do another degree where he met his future wife Margaret Kochamma. She was working as a waitress at a Cafe. Chacko walked into the Cafe one morning. He saw Margaret and almost fell in love with her at the first sight itself. She stole a glance at Chacko, who looked at her and smiled. It was an insanely friendly smile. Chacko visited the Cafe quite often and he and Margaret exchanged secret smiles. They began to go out together and he also began to smuggle her into his rooms. "Margaret Kochamma's tiny, ordered life relinquished itself to... truly baroque bedlam with the quiet gasp of a warm body entering a chilly sea" (p. 245).

For Chacko, Margaret Kochamma was the first female friend he had ever had. At the same time she was not just the first woman that he had slept with, but his first real companion. Her self-sufficiency was something that Chacko took special note of.

That Margaret didn't cling to him attracted him. "He loved the way she would sit up naked in his bed, her long white back swivelled away from him" (p. 246). He also liked the way she wobbled to work every morning on her bicycle. He even rejoiced at her occasional outbursts of exasperation at his decadence. Chacko adored Margaret for adoring him!

Chacko was completely oblivious of his family members. His mother used to write to him regularly, with detailed descriptions of her quarrels with her husband and her worries about Ammu's future. He hardly ever read a whole letter. Sometimes he never opened the letter even let alone writing back. He had no pressing reason to keep in touch with his parents. The Rhodes scholarship at Oxford gave him enough money for subsistence. Also, he was deeply in love with Margaret that he had no space in his heart for anyone else.

It was Chacko who stopped Pappachi from beating his mother. This made Mammachi love him more. His younger sister's sudden beauty was another thing that he took note of. He went back to Oxford very soon for the long-backed white girl was waiting for him.

He did badly in his examinations and the winter after he came down from Balliol he married Margaret Kochamma. Of course it was solemnized without the family's consent or knowledge. Marriage made him more impoverished. He was no more getting any scholarship and he had to pay the rent and meet all other expenses. Eventually Chacko got a job with a meagre salary. Everything had taken a bad turn and Margaret was pregnant also. He soon lost his wife for she found a better partner in Joe, a biologist who was updating the third edition of a Dictionary of Biology. Before the marriage broke Chacko had written to Mammachi telling her of his marriage and asking for money to be sent to him in England. But the money sent to him was never sufficient for him. When everything was almost over he returned to India where he found a job easily. He became a lecturer at the Madras Christian College and after Pappachi died, he returned to Ayemenem with his Bharat bottle-sealing machine.

We find here the development of a Communist sympathiser into a student abroad, a lover, a husband and a lecturer. Something that is striking about him is his disorderly life and the way Margaret Kochamma who was almost leading an orderly life getting attracted to him. But of course, he was in for a disappointment because fate soon began to show her unkindness to him in a couple of ways. Margaret parted ways, he was impoverished and he had to return to India and finally to his own ancestral house at Ayemenem. He was planning to lead a new life and the idea was to give a face lift to the family business.

III

Chacko needed his mother's adoration. Indeed he demanded it, "yet he despised her for it and punished her in secret ways. He began to cultivate his corpulence and general physical dilapidation. He wore cheap, printed Terylene bush shirts over his white mundus and the ugliest plastic sandals that were available in the market" (p. 248). Whenever Mammachi had guests or relatives he would appear before them in his most ugly dress. His special targets were Baby Kochamma's guests — Catholic bishops or visiting clergy — who often dropped by for a snack. In their presence Chacko would take off his sandals and air a revolting, pus-filled diabetic boil on his foot. The Bharat bottle-sealing machine was bought by Chacko by commuting his Pension and Provident Fund. Up to the time Chacko arrived, the factory had been a small profitable enterprise. Mammachi ran it like a large kitchen. Chacko registered it as a partnership and informed Mammachi that she would be the sleeping partner. He invested a lot of money in canning machines, cauldrons, cookers etc. and expanded the labour force. Very soon the financial problems began to stare at him and Chacko raised bank loans by mortgaging the family's rice-fields around the Ayemenem house. For Chacko it was his own factory and nobody else's. The factory which did not have a name earlier got a name once Chacko arrived in Ayemenem. He christened the factory which was earlier known as Sosha's Tender Mango or Sosha's Banana Jam as "Paradise Pickles & Preserves". He began to design and print labels at Comrade Pillai's press. Originally he wanted to call it "Zeus Pickles & Preserves" but everybody thought that it was too obscure a name.

The name "Parashuram Pickles" was rejected because of too much local relevance. A billboard was painted and installed on the plymouth's roof rack which again was Chacko's idea.

Chacko was a self proclaimed Marxist. "He would call pretty women who worked in the factory to his room, and on the pretext of lecturing them on labour rights and trade union law, flirt with them outrageously. He would call them Comrade, and insist that they call him Comrade back (which made them giggle). Much to their embarrassment and Mammachi's dismay, he forced them to sit at table with him and drink tea" (p. 65). He even took a group of them to attend Trade Union classes that were held in Alleppey. They went by bus and returned by boat happy, with glass bangles and flowers in their hair. As Buchen maintains "the novel is not defined but a discovered form. Its length, direction, content, etc., are not prescribed. There is no subject too sacred or gross for it to treat" (1974 p. 102). Thus, Chacko can afford to lead a life as he likes to! Ammu thought that it was an Oxford avatar of the old *zamindar* mentality — a landlord forcing his attentions on women who depended on him for their livelihood.

Once a month a parcel would arrive by VPP for Chacko which contained a balsa aeromodelling kit. Chacko used to assemble the aircraft with its tiny fuel tank and motorized propellor. He took it to the field to fly. But it never flew for more than a minute. Month after Chacko's constructed planes crashed in the paddy fields. His room was cluttered with broken wooden planes.

Chacko's room was also stacked from floor to ceiling with books. He had read them all and quoted long passages from them for no apparent reason. Mammachi loved to tell the story of Chacko, that is, how one of the dons at Oxford had said that in his opinion Chacko was brilliant, and made of prime ministerial material. But Ammu objected to his statement. According to her going to Oxford didn't make a person clever. She believed that cleverness would not make a good Prime Minister. Her question was that if a person could not even run a pickle factory profitably, how was he going to run a whole country. She was of the firm opinion that all Indian mothers were obsessed with their sons and were, therefore, poor judges of their abilities. Of course, Chacko had his own comments to offer. According to him one wouldn't go to Oxford. He would only read at Oxford and after reading at Oxford he would come down. Ammu then added that the sad but entirely predictable fate of Chacko's airplanes was an impartial measures of his abilities.

Chacko used to be critical of Ammu for being too strict to her children. He often would request her not to be a stickler for rules. Once when the children played with their spit Ammu scolded them. On hearing this Chacko had told her that she couldn't dictate what Rahel did with her own spit. Ammu wanted Chacko to mind his own business.

He was also a very good eater. Roast chicken, finger chips, sweet corn, chicken soup, parathas, ice cream, chocolate sauce etc. were some of the items which were his favourites. He often said that his ambition was to die of overeating. Mammachi thought that it was a sure sign of suppressed unhappiness. But he said it was sheer greed.

Chacko had more problems than he had before. The evening he went to receive his former wife and daughter, he was in his narrow bed in the hotel where he thought sleepily about the problems Pillai was creating for him. He wanted to pre-empt Pillai by organizing his workers into a private labour union. He would like to hold elections for them also. That would give them the privilege to vote. "They could take turns at being elected representatives. He smiled at the idea of holding round-table negotiations with Comrade Sumathi, or, better still, Comrade Lucykutty, who had much the nicer hair" (p. 122).

Thus, we find that ever since Chacko returned from Madras to Ayemenem he tried to lead an enterprising life. He had his own ideas about business and this naturally made him have the family business take a new look with all kinds of reformations he implemented. He thought that he was a Marxist which never prevented him from dealing freely with his women workers. One of the things that he enjoyed was the monthly VPP that he received and the assembling of the parts of the aeroplane. He was a voracious reader who liked to quote from great works even out of context. He often was critical of his sister Ammu who often pestered her children. Of course, he had a name as a good eater also.

As noted earlier, Chacko had started developing serious problems with his business. The trouble maker was none other than Comrade K.N.M. Pillai. Let us discuss in some details the problems Chacko confronted.

IV

Chacko had come to realize that there was some kind of discontentment among his workers. One day he went to Comrade Pillai to get a first hand knowledge of the state of affairs. The visit was especially relevant in the context of the massive rally the workers had taken out. Pillai informed Chacko that Velutha, the Paravan was going to cause trouble for him and so he should be shown the door. Chacko was totally puzzled to hear this from Pillai. Chacko "had expected to encounter antagonism, even confrontation, and instead was being offered sly, misguided collusion" (p. 278). Chacko tried to tell Pillai that he had no objection in Velutha being a card-holder in the party and in his eyes he was a sensible fellow and so he had great trust in him.

Pillai's reply was that as a person he might be okay; but other workers were not happy with him and were approaching him with complaints. The benefits that were given to Velutha, according to Pillai, were seen as partiality by the other workers. The main reason was Caste-issue. Velutha was just a Paravan whatever else — a carpenter, electrician etc. — he was. Chacko was a little impatient and said that Velutha was invaluable and the factory was practically run by him. He believed that sending away Paravans would not solve problems.

Chacko had addressed Pillai as "My Dear Fellow" which he did not like. He replied : "Rome was not built in a day. Keep it in mind, Comrade, that this is not your Oxford college. For you what is a nonsense, for Masses it is something different" (p. 279). He added that the proper forum to air workers' grievances was through the Union. Since Chacko was himself a Comrade there was a unique situation. Chacko replied that he was going to formally organize them into a union and they would elect their own representatives. But Pillai still believed that they should launch their own struggle.

Nobody ever learned the nature of the role that Comrade Pillai played in the events that followed. Even Chacko was in the dark mainly because he was numbed by the loss of his daughter. "Like a child touched by tragedy who grows up suddenly and abandons his playthings, Chacko dumped his toys. Pickle Baron dreams and the People's War joined the racks of broken airplanes in his glass-paned cupboard"(p. 281). After Paradise Pickles closed down, rice fields continued to be sold to pay off the bank loans and to keep the family in food and clothes. When later Chacko emigrated to Canada, the family's only income came from the rubber estate that adjoined the Ayemenem house and also the few coconut trees in the compound. After everybody else had died, left, or been returned, Baby Kochamma and Kochu Maria made their living depending on this.

In a way it was Pillai who played a crucial role for the collapse of Chacko's business. Probably Chacko was not good at judging a person like Pillai who like any other crooked politician decided to take rest only after everything disintegrated. It was something heartening to see Chacko standing by Velutha who had been a dedicated worker. But the last nail to the coffin came in the form of the tragedy that struck the family — the death of Sophie Mol and the related events like Ammu's affair with Velutha, Velutha's premature death and sending away of Ammu from Ayemenem house. Chacko himself had to leave the country ultimately, which was the most logical thing for him to do. What remains to be discussed is the tragic visit of his former wife Margaret Kochamma and Sophie Mol's death which precipitated the tragedy in the family. As Edel put it "novelists have sought almost from the first to become a camera. And not a static instrument but one possessing the movement through space and time which the motion picture camera has achieved in our century" (1974-p. 177). The novelist is doing exactly the same in the development of Chacko's character.

V

When Chacko heard about the accident in which Joe, Margaret Kochamma's second husband had died, he invited her and his daughter to Ayemenem. When Chacko wrote inviting her to Ayemenem, she couldn't resist her temptation to join him. She thought there was nobody in the world she would spend her Christmas with. She also felt that Sophie Mol also would take it as a welcome change.

Chacko left for Cochin in the Plymouth car along with Rahel, Estha, Ammu and Baby Kochamma. They had booked rooms at Hotel Sea Queen and the next day early morning they would proceed to Cochin Airport to pick up Chacko's former wife and Sophie Mol. Chacko was restless the night previous to the arrival of Margaret Kochamma and Sophie Mol. He took his wallet out of the pocket, and looked at the photograph of Sophie Mol that Margaret Kochamma had sent him two years ago. He wondered what his daughter looked like. She was nine years old and when he saw her last she was red and wrinkled. "Fierce bands of love tightened around his chest until he could barely breathe. He lay awake and counted the hours for them to leave for the airport" (p. 122).

The next day morning Chacko, who usually wore a mundu, was wearing a funny tight suit and a shining smile. They reached the airport and soon Sophie Mol's plane appeared in the skyblue Bombay — Cochin sky. She walked down the runway, the smell of London in her hair. On Margaret Kochamma's direction, Sophie Mol said 'how d' you do' to everyone and 'thank you' to Chacko when he offered her roses. Chacko introduced everyone to Margaret Kochamma and Margaret Kochamma to others. Anybody could see that Chacko was a proud and happy man to have had a wife like Margaret. But there was an air of sadness around her, the thought of car-crash in which her second husband Joe was killed still lingering in her mind.

When there was no railing left between them, Chacko kissed Margaret Kochamma, and then picked Sophie Mol up, which Sophie didn't appreciate. On the way back from the airport Margaret

Kochamma sat in front with Chacko because she used to be his wife. Sophie Mol sat between them.

Though Mammachi did not like Margaret Kochamma she never showed her dislike for her outwardly. On her reaching Ayemenem house she apparently showed her happiness expressing her regret for not being able to see her properly because of her blindness. "The Townspeople (in her fairy frock) saw Mammachi draw Sophie Mol close to her eyes to look at her. To read her like a cheque. To check her like a bank note. Mammachi (with her better eye) saw redbrown hair (N..... Nalmost blond), the curve of two fatfreckled cheeks (Nnnn... almost rosy), bluegreyblue eyes" (p. 174).

Chacko had moved out of his room and slept in Pappachi's study so that Sophie Mol and Margaret Kochamma could have his room. Chacko used to drift past the bedroom window of Margaret Kochamma like an anxious, stealthy whale intending to peep into see whether his wife and daughter were awake and needed anything. But he often lost courage which prevented him from looking in. The presence of Margaret Kochamma at home had even made a difference in him. "For the first time in years, Chacko watched her (Kalyani, Comrade Pillai's wife) without the faintest stirring of sexual desire. He had a wife.. at home. With arm freckles and back freckles. With a blue dress and legs underneath" (p. 270).

Certainly Chacko's is a well drawn out character in the novel. One can only sympathise with him when one goes through the chronology of events after his marriage especially the last part when Margaret Kochamma and his daughter Sophie Mol came to Ayemenem. To be sure, Sophie Mol loved Joe more than Chacko even though he had deep love for her. Margaret Kochamma was in a dilemma as to whether she should look at him as a husband again or not. The last blow, for Chacko came in the form of Sophie Mol's death which was in all sense an invited tragedy as he was responsible for bringing them to Ayemenem. The feeling of guilt should be very active in him as he had failed to keep track of the movements of Sophie Mol which ultimately led to her tragic end.

VI

In short, Chacko's is a great fall from a student at Delhi University, a Rhodes Scholar at Oxford and a businessman with great ideas and a lot more. Chacko, the ambitious man failed at crucial moments. He couldn't come out with flying colours from oxford to begin with. He was an ardent supporter of Communist Party and he had his own dreams about the party. But things didn't go as he wanted them to. As a lover and a husband he was a failure. The initial success as a lover was only the beginning of a shattered dream. His Margaret found him not to be a good match and she shifted her loyalty only to live with Joe.

On the business front also he proved to be a failure. It was the story of mortgage that was there for him to tell. The politics of Comrade Pillai was something that he couldn't bear. The closure of the factory coincided with the death of his daughter, Sophie Mol which was the greatest of a series of tragedies. Chacko was a failure in his dealings with the other members of his family too. He didn't have a very high opinion about his father. He even objected to his father beating his mother. It was on one of his visits to Ayemenem that he strode into the room, caught Pappachi's vase-hand and twisted it around him when he found him beating his mother. The relation with Ammu, his only sister was also not all fine. He had played a crucial role in driving her out of the house when she was found guilty for having illicit relations with Velutha. The fact that his daughter had informed him that even though he was her real Father, she loved him less than Joe was something that should have made Chacko very sad. A disintegrated family and so many personal losses were all left when he finally migrated to Canada. The fact that Margaret Kochamma wouldn't let him put his arm around her to comfort her on Sophie Mol's death gives us enough indication that the estrangement between Chacko and Margaret is not an old story.

At the sametime one positive thing about him is that he was successful in establishing a relatively better relation with Estha and Rahel, the twins. Many a time it was Chacko who came to their help whenever they were humiliated, especially by their mother, in front of others.

Chacko's attitude to life and his life itself can be summed up from the following remarks he makes when he exchanges pleasantries with the twins : " 'We're Prisoners of War', ... 'Our dreams have been doctored. We belong nowhere. We sail unanchored on troubled seas. We may never be allowed ashore. Our sorrows will never be sad enough. Our joys never happy enough. Our dreams never big enough. Our lives never important enough. To matter!" (p. 53). He was always aware of the fact that everything we are and ever will be are just a twinkle in the eyes of the Earth Woman's Life, as he himself puts it. "Later, in the light of all that happened, *twinkle* seemed completely the wrong word to describe the expression in the Earth Woman's eye. Twinkle was a word with crinkled, happy edges" (p. 54). As Schulz remarks "each one's story is complete and meaningful in itself, offering up no more than an ironical commentary on its counterpart" (1974 — p. 152).

8

The Bushy Eyebrowed Waitress

I

One of the notable phenomenon of twentieth-century fiction, according to Friedman is "the extent to which it has become extended" (1974 — p. 121). Forster gave the term "novel" one meaning when he defined it as a prose work in fiction of a certain extent. But many novels have moved beyond "certain" to become "indefinite". "For since the novel has become psychological and open, the novelist who would terminate the stream of his fiction finds that it has no necessary ending, that it goes on multiplying perspectives and possibilities" [see Friedman (1974 — p. 121)]. Roy's novel certainly has the multiplying perspective and one character who especially comes to our mind in this context is Margaret Kochamma, the "Bushy Eyebrowed Waitress" who is the Ex-wife of Chacko. She is one born and brought up outside the Ayemenem family and still playing an important role. Margaret Kochamma was almost a rebel who escaped from her parents to assert herself. But somehow she was made to lead a life which was rather tough. Unexpectedly, Chacko entered her life but it was a honeymoon which lasted for a very brief spell.

Margaret Kochamma's life was one of misery and turbulence and whenever she wanted to escape from one bondage she found herself inextricably trapped in another one. A series of misfortunes awaited her one after the other and finally we find her alone getting separated from her first husband, losing her second husband

and her daughter. At every stage she somehow thought that she would overcome the misfortunes that came her way but fresh problems awaited her which ultimately made her realize that life was nothing very simple.

The greatest tragedy in her life was certainly the death of her daughter Sophie Mol. She took with her to her grave the picture of her little daughter's body laid out on the chaise longue in the drawing room of the Ayemenem house. "Even from a distance it was obvious that she was dead. Not ill or asleep. It was something to do with the way she lay. The angle of her limbs. Something to do with Death's authority. Its terrible stillness.... A spongy mermaid who had forgotten how to swim. A silver thimble clenched, for luck, in her little fist" (p. 251).

Margaret Kochamma could never forgive herself for taking Sophie Mol to Ayemenem. She also was not able to forgive herself for leaving her there alone over the week end while she and Chacko went to Cochin to confirm their return tickets.

Now let us look at in some detail the tragic circumstances which led her to live a long life when she lost her near and dear ones. As Martin (1974) has observed "tragedy deals with the dreams and aspirations of man attempting to transcend the human and immediate but constantly being forced down by the limitations of the world" (p. 80). As we will come to realize, Margaret Kochamma was constantly being forced down by the limitations of the world in the novel.

II

Margaret Kochamma met Chacko for the first time in a Cafe where she was working. Without any provocation Chacko began to tell her the story of a man who had twin sons. She didn't show any keenness to listen to the story but he didn't mind that. The story said that the two sons were Pete and Stuart, one an optimist and the other a pessimist. On their thirteenth birthday their father gave Stuart an expensive watch, a carpentry set and a bicycle. Pete's room was filled with horse dung. Stuart did not want the carpentry set and didn't like the watch. The bicycle had the wrong kind of tyres. So he grumbled all morning. When his father went to the optimist's room he could hear the sound of frantic shovelling and heavy breathing. Horse dung was flying all over the room. He explained to his father that if there was so much shit around, there had to be a pony somewhere. Chacko began to laugh a fat man's infectious laugh. Though Margaret Kochamma had missed most of the joke she smiled and then began to laugh at his laugh. Their laughs fed each other and climbed to a hysterical pitch. Meanwhile, another customer had arrived unnoticed, and waited to be served.

Margaret Kochamma was reproached by the employer but she had not forgotten to steal a glance at Chacko. That evening, after work, she thought about what had happened and was uncomfortable with herself. "She was not usually frivolous, and didn't think it right to have shared such uncontrolled laughter with a complete stranger. It seemed such an over-familiar, intimate thing to have done. She wondered what had made her laugh so much. She knew it wasn't the joke. She thought of Chacko's laugh, and a smile stayed in her eyes for a long time" (p. 244).

Chacko continued to visit the Cafe. He always came with his friendly smile. Even when it was not Margaret Kochamma who served him, he sought her out with his eyes and they exchanged secret smiles. Margaret Kochamma learned that Chacko was a Rhodes Scholar from India who read classics and rowed for Balliol. Until the day she married him she never believed that she would ever consent to be his wife. He began to invite her to his room which always remained filthy. "Books, empty wine bottles, dirty underwear and cigarette butts littered the floor. Cupboards were dangerous to open because clothes and books and shoes would cascade down and some of his books were heavy enough to inflict real damage" (pp. 244-45).

She discovered that underneath the Rumpled Porcupine a tortured Marxist was at war with an impossible, incurable Romantic. Chacko who broke the wine glass and lost the ring made love to her with a passion that took her breath away. She had always considered herself to be an interesting, thick-waisted, thick-ankled girl who was not bad-looking and not very special. But when she was with Chacko horizons began to expand. "Being with Chacko made Margaret Kochamma feel as though her soul had escaped from the narrow confines of her island country into the vast, extravagant spaces of his. He made her feel as though the world belonged to them — as though it lay before them like an opened frog on a dissecting table, begging to be examined" (p. 245).

Chacko was grateful to her for not wanting to look after him, for not offering to tidy his room and also for not being his cloying mother. He grew to depend on Margaret Kochamma for not depending on him. She neither knew anything about his family nor asked anything about it. After marriage they decided that he should move into Margaret Kochamma's flat displacing the other waitress in the other Cafe until he found himself a job.

Within a year of the marriage things began to take a different shape. "It no longer amused her that while she went to work, the flat remained in the same filthy mess that she had left it in" (p. 247). Eventually Margaret decided to part from him. Kaminsky's view that "the writer who is interested in people, places and things is imitating or at least extrapolating from what he takes to be the real world" (1974-p. 214) appears to be true as regards Margaret Kochamma for we don't fail to meet such people around us.

Margaret was drawn to Chacko probably without her own knowledge. Being a rebel something unconventional was expected from her and Chacko also being a little different from others it was natural that they decided to live together as husband and wife. But it didn't take long for her to realize that he was not the right person she was looking for. May be the most significant factor which contributed to the strain in the relation might be the fact that Chacko was no more financially well off. As for Chacko, he never thought that the marriage would break. He continued to love Margaret and he was even ready to forget his father, mother and sister for the sake of his newly wed wife. But strange are the ways of the world and Margaret Kochamma decided to find comfort in Joe, the biologist.

III

Joe was an old school friend of her brother's. Margaret Kochamma found herself drawn towards him like a plant in a dark room towards a wedge of light. Chacko, meanwhile, had returned to his native place and Margaret Kochamma wrote regularly to Chacko giving him news of Sophie Mol. She assured him that Joe made a wonderful, caring father and that Sophie Mol loved him dearly. This gladdened and saddened Chacko in equal measure.

Margaret Kochamma was quite happy with Joe. She thought of Chacko fondly but she never had any regrets. It was impossible for her to believe that she had hurt Chacko as deeply as she had for she always thought that she was an ordinary woman and he an extraordinary man. Since Chacko did not exhibit any serious symptoms of grief she thought that he also would have taken the whole affair as a mistake. She remembered how he left sadly and quietly when she told him about Joe.

Margaret Kochamma promptly wrote letters even after their separation and for her their relationship became a comfortable, committed friendship. She enrolled herself in a teacher training course and got a job as a junior school teacher in Clapham. "She was in the staff room when she was told about Joe's accident. The news was delivered by a young policeman who wore a grave expression and carried his helmet in his hands. He had looked strangely comical, like a bad actor auditioning for a solemn part in a play. Margaret Kochamma remembered that her first instinct when she saw him had been to smile" (p. 250).

Margaret Kochamma made a bold attempt to face the tragedy with equanimity. She did so for her own sake and for the sake of her daughter. She didn't even take a day's off from her job and also ensured that Sophie Mol's routine went unaffected. She tried to conceal her anguish under the mask of a school teacher. But when she received the invitation from Chacko she persuaded herself that a trip to India would be the best thing for Sophie Mol. She knew that her friends and colleagues would take her running back to her first husband soon after her second husband's death as very odd. But she broke her term deposit and bought two airline tickets. London — Bombay — Cochin.

Life with Joe was a kind of intermission for Margaret. It lasted for a very brief period and perhaps it was Sophie Mol who was more attached to him than Margaret Kochamma herself. It is quite unbelievable in normal circumstances for one to realize that

Margaret Kochamma would readily accept the invitation from her Ex-husband to join him at Ayemenem. Though she was aware of the fact that her colleagues might think bad about it, she herself took it as a routine kind of thing. This is the only explanation that can be given for the decision of Margaret Kochamma to take a flight to Cochin. May be no one knows the ways of women!

Next we shall consider the most critical phase in Margaret Kochamma's life, that is, her Ayemenem days where she lost her daughter Sophie Mol in the boat tragedy.

IV

Margaret Kochamma and Sophie Mol were well received at the Cochin airport. Sophie Mol "the thimble-drinker" and "coffincart wheeler" was "hatted, bell-bottomed and Loved from the Beginning" (p. 135). Ammu watched them with her handbag, Chacko with his roses and Baby Kochamma with her sticking out neckmole. Margaret Kochamma smiled and wagged her rose at Chacko. "*Ex-wife, Chacko*! Her lips formed the words, though her voice never spoke them" (p. 142).

The days preceding the death of Sophie Mol were uneventful for Margaret Kochamma. Sophie Mol found herself quite comfortable in the company of the twins Rahel and Estha. "The Fond smiles stayed on Sophie Mol, like a spotlight, thinking perhaps, that the sweet cousins were playing hide-and-seek, like sweet cousins often do" (p. 186). Probably Sophie Mol's happiness might have contributed to the happiness of Margaret Kochamma in a non-trivial way. Also, for the first time since Joe died, he was not the first thing that she thought about when she woke, a clear indication that she was slowly returning to Chacko.

But the tragedy struck Ayemenem house quite unexpectedly. Margaret Kochamma and Chacko returned from Cochin to see the deadbody of Sophie Mol laid out on the chaise longue. "When Margaret Kochamma saw her little daughter's body, shock swelled in her like phantom applause in an empty auditorium. It overflowed in a wave of vomit and left her mute and empty eyed" (p. 263). In fact, for her it was two deaths in a row. She had come to Ayemenem to heal her wounded world. But she had lost all of it instead. She shattered like glass.

The next few days were shrouded for Margaret Kochamma. "Long, dim hours of thick, furry-tongued serenity (medically administered by Dr. Verghese Verghese), lacerated by sharp, steely slashes of hysteria, as keen and cutting as the edge of a new razor blade" (p. 263). She was only vaguely conscious of Chacko. He tried to be gentle when he was by her side but otherwise he was blowing like an enraged wind through the Ayemenem house. There was nothing of the amused Rumpled Porcupine she had met at Oxford Cafe left in him.

She tried to remember the funeral in the yellow church and also the sounds of doors being battered down and the frightened women's voices. She remembered her irrational rage at the twins who had been spared by fate. Somehow she believed that Estha was responsible for Sophie Mol's death. But she never knew that it was the same Estha who had broken rules and rowed Sophie Mol and Rahel across the river in the afternoons in a little boat. She also never knew that it was "Estha who had made the back verandah of the History House their home away from home, furnished with a grass mat and most of their toys — a catapult, an inflatable goose, a Qantas koala with loosened button eyes. And finally, on that dreadful night, Estha who had decided that though it was dark and raining, the Time Had Come for them to run away, because Ammu didn't want them any more" (p. 264).

Margaret Kochamma had slapped Estha three or four times whenever she was awake from the drug-induced sleep. She was calmed down and led away by someone. Later she did apologize but, it was too late because by the time the letter arrived Estha had been returned and Ammu had left. Only Rahel was there in Ayemenem to receive the latter. The apology ran like this : "*I can't imagine what came over me.... I can only put it down to the effect of the tranquillizers. I had no right to behave the way I did, and want you to know that I am ashamed and terribly, terribly sorry*" (p. 264). But Margaret Kochamma never thought about Velutha. She never remembered her, not even what he looked like. "It is unreasonable to expect a person to remember what she didn't know had happened" (p. 265).

On the whole, Margaret might have come to realize that her colleagues were more than right when they told her that anything could happen to anyone and so it was best to be prepared. She had come to Ayemenem to sacrifice her Sophie Mol, who was the seeker of small wisdoms : "*Where do old birds go to die? Why don't dead ones fall like stones from the sky*?" (p. 16). She could never forgive herself the blunder that she had committed. Sophie Mol, her daughter who came to Ayemenem to recover from the shock of the death of her dad shocked Ayemenem by never surfacing alive when the boat capsized. Margaret Kochamma continued to believe that she was responsible for the killing and she had no way of escape from the tragic memory.

V

Margaret Kochamma, the bushy waitress is thus an unforgettable character in the novel. Chacko found himself fortunate when he got Margaret Kochamma as his wife. But he was in for a disappointment. Even before she gave birth to her husband's child, she lost interest in him.

She was terribly wrong in her calculations. She expected that life would be more enjoyable than ever once she started living with Joe. The accident took away his life and she was left for herself alongwith her daughter. Somehow she wanted at least a semblance of relief from the tragedy which chased her as a shadow. The letter from Chacko inviting her to his place came as a big relief for her and her daughter and so she was highly pleased and happy to immediately book a ticket to Cochin.

Things continued to be unpleasant for her. Hardly had she spent a fortnight at Ayemenem, Chacko's native place, when a bigger tragedy in the form of Sophie Mol's death struck her. She was literally reduced to nothingness. She didn't have someone to talk to even. The loss of her daughter made her hysteric and it was without her own knowledge that she slapped Estha whenever she got up from the drug induced sleep. She expressed her regrets for being cruel to the boy. In short, Margaret Kochamma would remain in our mind as a woman who dreamed of great things in her life and ended up by losing everything she possessed and also everything she gained eventually.

9

The Ex-Nun

I

Forster (1927) distinguishes between "flat" characters, who are relatively unchanging and one-dimensional, and "round" characters, who develop during the narrative and may well surprise us with their actions. "Round" characters are complex, are seen from many sides and in many contexts, and in general are supposed to mirror the psychological depth we attribute to actual human beings. "Flat" characters, like the conventionally recognized stereotypes we call character "types", are none of these things and often have a single dominant interest or characteristic. Baby Kochamma, "the Ex-Nun" in *The God of Small Things* surprises us with her actions and in this sense she is certainly a round character.

The first reference to her name appears in page two of the novel. She was really Navomi, Navomi Ipe, the daughter of Rev. Ipe. But everybody called her Baby and she became Baby Kochamma "when she was old enough to be an aunt" (p. 2). Baby Kochamma was both adventurous and enterprising. She fell in love with a priest at the age of eighteen and became a Roman Catholic defying her father's wishes. For sometime she was in a convent where she became restless. Later her father sent her to Rochester in America from where she returned with a diploma in ornamental gardening. But after half a century "the weed that people call communist patcha (because it flourished in Kerala like communism) smothered the more exotic plants" (p. 27).

The dish antenna which she installed on the roof of the Ayemenem house was her new love. She found herself locked in a noisy Television silence. She was one who didn't trust anyone. The arrival of the twins to the Ayemenem house made her a little miserable. She disliked their mother also. A series of events had rocked the Ayemenem house and she did play a very important role in making matters bad to worse.

II

Baby Kochamma was one who lived her life backwards. As a young woman she had renounced the material world and as an old one she embraced the very same world. She fell in love with an Irish monk, Father Mulligan who was in Kerala to study Hindu Scriptures. Every Thursday morning Father Mulligan came to Ayemenem house to visit Rev. Ipe, who was a priest of the Mar Thoma Church. On these mornings she used to be busy with force-bathing a poor village child. The sexually excited Baby Kochamma would keep ready her questions for every week : "'"All things are lawful for me, but all things are not expedient. Father, how *can* all things be lawful unto Him? I mean I can understand if *some* things are lawful for Him, but — "'" (p. 23). The father was young too and he was aware that the explanations he gave for the bogus doubts were at odds "with the thrilling promise he held out in his effulgent emerald eyes" (p. 24).

Father Mulligan returned to Madras and Baby Kochamma had to invest all her hope in faith. On the hope that she would get enough opportunities to meet Mulligan she entered a convent in Madras. "She pictured them together, in dark sepulchral rooms with heavy velvet drapes, discussing Theology. That was all she wanted. All she ever dared to hope for. Just to be near him" (p. 24). But soon she realized that it was all an exercise in futility. She couldn't get anywhere near Father Mulligan as the senior sisters stood as an obstacle. She became lonelier than ever.

Within a year of her joining the convent her father began to receive puzzling letters from her. "*My dearest Papa, I am well and happy in the service of Our Lady. But Koh-i-noor appears to be unhappy and homesick. My dearest Papa, Today Koh-i-noor vomited after lunch and is running a temperature. My dearest Papa, convent food does not seem to suit Koh-i-noor... Koh-i-noor is upset because her family seems to neither understand nor care about her wellbeing...*" (p. 25). Later it was revealed that "Koh-i-noor" was none other than Baby Kochamma herself which eventually made Rev. John Ipe to go to Madras and bring her back.

She was glad to return to Ayemenem but declined to reconvert which means she remained a Roman Catholic for the rest of her life. By now, Rev. Ipe was more than sure that she was no more "marriageable". She was sent abroad to do a course in Ornamental Gardening. When she returned "there was no trace of the slim, attractive girl that she had been. In her years at Rochester, Baby Kochamma had grown extremely large.... obese. Even timid little Chellappen Tailor at Chungam Bridge insisted on charging bush-shirt rates for her sari-blouses" (p. 26). In the old days it was an altogether different story. Whenever anybody visited Ayemenem, Baby Kochamma made it a point to call attention to their large feet. "She would ask to try on their slippers and say, 'Look how big for me they are!' Then she would walk around the house in them, lifting her sari a little so that everybody could marvel at her tiny feet" (p. 20).

To keep her busy, her father gave Baby Kochamma charge of the front garden of the Ayemenem house, where she raised a fierce, bitter garden. It was a circular, sloping patch of ground, with a steep gravel driveway looping around it. Baby Kochamma turned it into a lush maze of dwarf hedges, rocks and gargoyles. "The flower she loved most was the anthurium. Anthurium *andraeanum*. She had a collection of them, the 'Rubrum' the 'Honeymoon' and a host of Japanese varieties. Their single succulent spathes ranged from shades of mottled black to blood red and glistening orange. Their prominent, stippled spadices always yellow" (p. 26).

She spent her afternoons in the garden. She was often found in sari and gumboots. She tamed twisting vines and nurtured bristling cacti like a lion-tamer. She, it seems, waged war on the weather and tried to grow edelweiss and chinese guava.

In short, Baby Kochamma's life was one of disappointment

and despair. She couldn't fulfil her dream of uniting with Father Mulligan. The short break that she had at Rochester also didn't help her much in changing her attitude to life. Gardening was only a diversion for her and she could never take this to her heart as was proved later. Ultimately she did abandon the garden though after a gap of fifty years. Next, weshall see what her attitude was to Ammu and the twins.

III

Baby Kochamma was never kind to either Estha and Rahel or Ammu. She never liked the twins. She was keen for them to realize that they (like herself) lived on sufferance in the Ayemenem house, their maternal grandmother's house, where they really had no right to be. As for Ammu, Baby Kochamma saw her quarrelling with a fate that she herself felt she had graciously accepted. It was the fate of the wretched manless woman.

When it was known that Margaret Kochamma and Sophie Mol would arrive soon at Ayemenem house, Baby Kochamma made life miserable for Estha and Rahel. She was busy teaching English. Whenever they erred they were made to write "impositions". She never trusted them and believed that they were capable of anything. She thought that they were a single unit. The extend to which Baby Kochamma disliked the twins was clear from the way she reacted when Chacko introduced the twins to Sophie Mol. When he introduced Estha as his nephew Esthappan, she immediately said he was "Elvis Presley" for revenge. Later she had expressed her dissatisfaction to Ammu about the way the children behaved: "They're sly. They're uncouth. Deceitful. They're growing wild. You can't manage them" (p. 149).

Perhaps there was some logic in Baby Kochamma being a little unkind to the twins and their mother. "They all crossed into forbidden territory. They all tampered with the laws that lay down who should be loved and how. And how much. The laws that make grandmothers grandmothers, uncles uncles, mothers mothers, cousins cousins, jam jam, and jelly jelly" (p. 31). It was a time when the unthinkable became thinkable and also the impossible became possible.

As regards Ammu, Baby Kochamma was particularly uncomfortable. She fully agreed with the commonly held view that a married daughter had no position in her parent's home. Apart from being married, Ammu was divorced from a love marriage from intercommunity.

In short, Baby Kochamma never saw eye to eye with Ammu and her children. It was as though they were enemies even before they were born. Since they had a feeling that they were unwanted guests in the Ayemenem house they couldn't put up a fight with Baby Kochamma. The only alternative before them was to silently suffer. Things took a worse shape following the incidents in which Sophie Mol got killed and Ammu was publicly humiliated for establishing an illegitimate relation with Velutha who was an untouchable.

IV

Sophie Mol's arrival changed the whole course of life at Ayemenem. Baby Kochamma also played her own role in making matters bad to worse. It was at about nine o'clock in the morning two weeks after Sophie Mol's arrival that Baby Kochamma and Mammachi got the news of a white child's body floating down Meenachal river. Estha and Rahel were found missing also. Earlier that morning Sophie Mol, Estha and Rahel had not appeared for their morning glass of milk. Baby Kochamma and Mammachi were under the impression that they might have gone for a swim. Baby Kochamma sent Kochu Maria to enquire about their whereabouts. But she returned without the children. Nobody was able to remember when they had actually seen the children. They hadn't been uppermost on anybody's mind and naturally they could have been missing all night. Later Sophie Mol's body was brought to the Ayemenem house which coincided with the unlocking of Ammu's room.

Baby Kochamma played her 'real' role in the "Ammu-Velutha" episode. Walking past the kitchen she heard a commotion in which Mammachi was found spitting into the rain, "THOO! THOO! THOO! and Vellya Paapen lying in the slush, wet, weeping, grovelling. Offering to kill his son. To tear him limb from limb" (p. 256). It was Kochu Maria who shouted Vellya Paapen's story to Baby Kochamma in the din. She immediately realized that the situation was of immense potential and made a lot of meaning to her. She saw it as God's way of punishing Ammu for her sin. She also found it an opportunity to take revenge upon Velutha for insulting her by addressing her as "Modalali Mariakutty" at the march in which Velutha and others took part. She had not forgotten how the marchers had forcefully made her to hold the flag and made her say "Inquilab Zindabad". That was why Baby Kochamma told Mammachi "It must be true... She is quite capable of it. And so is he. Vellya Paapen would not lie about something like this" (p. 257). She made Vellya Paapen repeat his story, the story of Ammu's affairs with Velutha, stopping him every now and then for details — "Whose boat? How often? How long had it been going on?" (p. 257) etc. Her solution was that before it went any further Velutha should go. She did not want them to be completely ruined. What surprised her most was that Ammu could stand the Paravan smell!

Baby Kochamma went into action. She somehow tricked Ammu into her bedroom where she was locked up. Velutha was sent for and they wanted to ensure that before Chacko returned Velutha should leave Ayemenem. The reason was that Chacko's attitude was unpredictable. Velutha had no idea what had happened. On his way back from Kottayam one of the factory workers who he met him at the bus stop told him that Mammachi wanted to meet him. Velutha was completely in the dark about his father's visit to Ayemenem. He went straight to Ayemenem house.

"When Velutha arrived, Mammachi lost her bearings and spewed her blind venom, her crass, insufferable insults, at a panel in the sliding-folding door until Baby Kochamma tactfully swivelled her around and aimed her rage in the right direction, at Velutha standing very still in the gloom" (pp. 283-284). Even though Baby Kochamma did not say anything she stayed close to Mammachi and used her hands to modulate Mammachi's fury. Mammachi was completely unaware of her manipulations.

Thus, Baby Kochamma was successful in teaching her "enemies" a lesson. She could settle scores with Velutha who had, she thought, joined hands with his fellow processionists in publicly humiliating her by addressing her as "Modalali". There was no love lost between her and Ammu and she was waiting for an opportunity to strike. The Velutha episode came as very handy to her and she made use of the opportunity by joining hands with Mammachi. Ultimately she could destroy all those who disliked her — Ammu, Velutha, Rahel and Estha by either eliminating them or leaving them as mental wrecks. Baby Kochamma was at her best in the police station related activities where she tried to checkmate both Ammu and Velutha.

V

After Velutha was given a heavy dose, Baby Kochamma rushed to Kottayam police station. She told the Inspector of the circumstances that led to the sudden dismissal of Velutha, a factory worker. She told him that he had tried to force himself on her niece, a divorcee with two children a few days ago. She distorted the facts completely. She never thought that Ammu would later invite shame upon herself and that she would go to the police station and set the record straight. She told the Inspector that the matter was not reported earlier as theirs was a respectable family with a name. She made a detailed description of how Velutha went to their house the previous evening and threatened them. She even gave a chance to the Inspector to imagine the horrors that could be visited by a sex-crazed Paravan on three women alone in a house. He had told them that according to the Labour Laws they had no grounds on which they could dismiss him. She was careful not to tell the Inspector about how Mammachi had lost control and how she had gone up to Velutha and spat right into his face. The things she had said to him and the names she had called him were not there in her version of the story. "Instead she described to Inspector Thomas Mathew how it was not just *what* Velutha had said that had made her come to the police, but the *way* he said it. His complete lack of remorse, which was what had shocked her most. As though he was actually *proud* of what he had done" (pp. 260-61).

Baby Kochamma also told the Inspector about Velutha's background which included his education in a school started by his grandfather. On hearing these, the Inspector told Baby Kochamma : "You people... first...spoil these people, carry them about on your head like trophies, then when they misbehave you come running to us for help" (p. 261). She remained quiet for sometime only to resume her story. She told the Inspector that in the last few weeks she had noticed some presaging signs, some insolence and some rudeness in Velutha. She also told him that she had seen him in the march on the way to Cochin and the rumours that he was or had been a Naxalite, which worried the Inspector a little. Baby Kochamma was assured the full co-operation of the Kottayam police. The Inspector assured her that Velutha would be caught before the evening that day. Baby Kochamma soon returned to Ayemenem.

But the unexpected happened when Ammu went to Kottayam police station after Sophie Mol's funeral. She told the Inspector that there had been a terrible mistake and she disowned whatever Baby Kochamma had told the Inspector. But he chose to misbehave with her and sent her back by insulting and humiliating her.

Baby Kochamma made a second visit to Inspector Thomas Mathew. She enquired about the missing children Estha and Rahel. From the way the Inspector reacted Baby Kochamma was able to see that she was dealing with a different person. He was no more an accommodating police officer of the previous meeting. He told her that the police were saddled with the death in custody of a technically innocent man (Velutha). He told her that technically and as per law he was an innocent man. But there was no *case*. When Baby Kochamma suggested that he should treat it as attempted rape he said that the rape-victim's complaint was not there. The Inspector put a choice before her. Either the rape-victim should file a complaint or the children must identify the Paravan as their abductor in the presence of a police witness. He threatened her that or else he would charge her with lodging a false FIR which was a criminal offence. Baby Kochamma began to sweat. She told the Inspector that the children would do as they were told if she could have a few moments alone with them.

Baby Kochamma told the children in a hoarse and unfamiliar voice that they were responsible for the death of Sophie Mol. "'It's a terrible thing to take a person's life.... It's the worst thing that anyone can ever do. Even *God* doesn't forgive that'" (p. 316). She almost threatened them that all the three might be required to go to jail. "When she had stamped out every ray of hope, destroyed their lives completely, like a fairy godmother she presented them with a solution" (p. 317). They were asked to say "yes" to the question that the Inspector would ask them. To save the life of Ammu and their own, the children had to agree to the proposal. "Baby Kochamma beamed. Relief worked like a laxative" (p. 319). As the Inspector said that only one of them would do, Baby Kochamma chose Estha, the practical of the two.

When Baby Kochamma heard about Ammu's visit to the police station, she was terrified. She never did even dream that Ammu would publicly admit to her relationship with Velutha. She thought so because it was equal to destroying herself and her children. Ammu's reaction stunned her. "The ground fell away from under her feet. She knew she had an ally in Inspector Thomas Mathew. But how long would that last? What if he were transferred and the case reopened? It was possible — considering the shouting, sloganeering crowd of Party workers that Comrade K.N.M. Pillai had managed to assemble outside the gate. That prevented the labourers from coming to work, and left vast quantities of mangoes, bananas, pineapple, garlic and ginger rotting slowly on the premises of Paradise Pickles" (p. 321).

Baby Kochamma had a way out. Somehow she wanted to ensure that Ammu was sent out of Ayemenem house. This she made possible by making Chacko believe that it was Ammu who was responsible for Sophie Mol's death. It was her idea that Ammu should be made to pack her bags and leave and that Estha should be returned. She was displaying the very same stubborn nature which she showed when she was a young girl who defied her father's wishes and became a Roman Catholic. As if she had nothing to do with the sowing and reaping she had remarked "As ye sow, so shall you reap." That is Baby Kochamma, the Baby Kochamma who was offended by the fact that Father Mulligan, her lover, had eventually renounced his vows, not for her but for other vows.

This is the most crucial phase in the life of Baby Kochamma in the novel. She wanted to avenge the insults she suffered at the hands of a few workers and got an easy prey in Velutha who was being trapped by her by the misrepresentation of facts. Though it contributed to her losing peace of mind, somehow she got Velutha killed by the policemen. Ammu also was always there in the 'hit list' of Baby Kochamma. She disliked her for reasons best known to herself. She didn't want a divorcee to be there in her ancestral house. Naturally her children also were most unwelcome in the house. Velutha's affairs with Ammu easily helped her to see that all these were 'punished' in some way or other. Her conspiracy yielded fruit. Ammu was sent away, Estha was returned and later Rahel also was sent to the convent.

But Baby Kochamma never got peace of mind. In her later years she lived alone in Ayemenem house in the company of Kochu Maria. She lived like a women suffering from neurosis unsure of herself and what she was doing.

VI

It was an entirely different Baby Kochamma that we see in her later years. After abandoning the wonderful garden she had developed she totally diverted her interest to a new area. She began to preside over the world in her drawing room on satellite TV. It was an overnight development. "And in Ayemenem, where once the loudest sound had been a musical bus horn, now whole wars, famines, picturesque massacres and Bill Clinton could be summoned up like servants" (p. 27). Baby Kochamma watched American NBA league games, one day cricket and all the tennis tournaments. She along with the servant entered all the contests, availed themselves of all the discounts that were advertised and had won a T-shirt and a Thermos flask a couple of times. Baby Kochamma inherited Mammachi's violin and violin stand, the Ooty cupboards, the plastic basket chairs, the Delhi beds, the dressing table from Vienna with cracked ivory knobs and the rosewood dining table that Velutha made.

She was frightened by the BBC famines and Television wars. "Her old fears of the Revolution and the Marxist-Leninist menace had been rekindled by new television worries about the growing numbers of desperate and dispossessed people. She viewed ethnic cleansing, famine and genocide as direct threats to her furniture" (p. 28). She did not trust the twins. She thought that they were capable of anything. "They might even steal their present back," she thought. She kept her doors and windows locked. The windows were used by her for special purpose, that is, for a breath of fresh air, to pay for the milk or to let out a trapped wasp. "She suspected that these days, even the innocent and the round-eyed could be crockery crooks, or cream-bun cravers, or thieving diabetics cruising Ayemenem for imported insulin" (p. 29).

Baby Kochamma continued to live like a young woman even at the age of eighty-three. Her hair, dyed jet black was arranged across her scalp like unspoiled thread. The dye had stained the skin of her forehead a pale grey, giving her a shadowy second hairline. She had started wearing make up. "Lipstick. Kohl. A sly touch of rouge. And because the house was locked and dark, and because she only believed in 40-watt bulbs, her lipstick mouth had shifted slightly off her real mouth (p. 21). Even at this old age she continued to wear a lot of jewellery, all that she had. They included winking rings, diamond earrings, gold bangles and a beautifully crafted flat gold chain that she touched from time to time, reassuring herself that it was there and she was the proud possessor of it. She behaved like a young bride who couldn't believe her good fortune. Elsewhere in the novel also we have instances where Baby Kochamma made her appearance t oblivious of her old age. She attended the funeral service of Sophie Mol wearing an expensive sari. For a moment she even forgot to be sad during the funeral service! "Rahel watched a small black bat climb up Baby Kochamma's expensive funeral sari with gently clinging curled claws. When it reached the place between her sari and her blouse, her roll of sadness, her bare midriff, Baby Kochamma screamed and hit the air with her hymnbook. The singing stopped for a "Whatisit? Whathappened?' and for a furrywhirring and sariflapping" (p. 6).

Baby Kochamma behaved rather strangely even in her eighties. She could never reconcile herself to Father Mulligan's separation from her. She would pick up her diary which came with its own pen. She would make a fresh entry every day. This was a routine affair. What she used to write was "I love you I love you." Every page in the dairy had an identical entry and she had a case full of diaries with similar entries. They all began with the same words " I love you I love you." Father Mulligan's death didn't make any change in this habit. The death did not alter his availability in her eyes. "She possessed him in death in a way that she never had while he was alive. At least her memory of him was *hers*. Wholly hers. Savagely, fiercely, hers. Not to be shared with Faith, far less with competing *co-nuns*, and *co-sadhus* or whatever it was they called themselves. *Co-swamis* (p. 298). Father Mulligan's rejection of Baby Kochamma was neutralized by death. He embraced her and just her in her memory. He embraced her in the way a man embraces a woman. She did even a stranger thing. On Father Mulligan's death, she stripped him of his ridiculous saffron robes and reclothed him in the Coca-Cola cassock she loved so much. "She reconverted him into the high-stepping camel that came to lunch on Thursdays" (p. 298). Every night, night after night, year after year, in diary after diary, she wrote : "I love you I love you."

In sum, in her old age, Baby Kochamma continued to lead the life of a young woman. One would agree with Rahel in her view that Baby Kochamma was living life backwards. With her make ups and expensive saris she proved beyond doubt that she had successfully overcome the feeling that she was pretty old. Her craze for television also would certainly make one feel that her mental age was not eighty-three. That she continued to make entries in her diary about her love for Father Mulligan would certainly puzzle one. The final phase of her life continued with her discomfort with Estha and Rahel.

VII

Twenty-three years after the death of Sophie Mol, Rahel came back to Ayemenem house. Baby Kochamma had written to her stating that Estha had been re-returned. She came back to Ayemenem not to see her. "Neither niece nor baby grand aunt laboured under any illusions on that account" (p. 2). Baby Kochamma showed Rahel the letter their father sent when he had sent Estha back to Ayemenem after twenty-three years.

Baby Kochamma told Rahel that Estha had lost his mind and didn't recognize people. Infact, Baby Kochamma regretted having written to Rahel about Estha's return. She wrote a letter because she had nothing else to do. She couldn't take care of him for the rest of her life. He wasn't her responsibility. Rahel did not have any immediate responses to what Baby Kochamma had told her about Estha. "The silence sat between grand-niece and baby grand aunt like a third person. A stranger. Swollen. Noxious" (p. 21). In Rahel she noticed the same eerie stealth, the ability to keep very still and very quiet that Estha seemed to have mastered.

She asked Rahel about her future plans. She wanted to know how long Rahel would be staying at Ayemenem house. "Rahel tried to say something. It came out jagged.... She walked to the window and opened it. For a Breath of Fresh Air" (p. 29). Estha had been disturbing her like anything. When he appeared at the kitchen door wet Baby Kochamma would tell Rahel. "Here he comes.... Now watch. He won't say anything. He'll walk *straight* to his room. Just watch!" (p. 90). He would also wash his clothes and the fact that Estha was over clean was something that did not escape the notice of Baby Kochamma. He wouldn't utter even a word which was still another concern for her. Rahel and Estha remaining in the same room for a long time also made Baby Kochamma uneasy.

Thus, even after a gap of twenty-three years Baby Kochamma continued to be what she was in her attitude to Rahel and Estha. The fact that she and her servant Kochu Maria were the only occupants of Ayemenem house did not influence her in any way in the way she approached the twins. She somehow wanted to ensure that Rahel would leave Ayemenem at an early date probably taking Estha also with her. It was not her concern to bother about the future life of Estha because she thought that she was in no way bound to take care of him. After all, it was she herself who made life miserable for Estha and Rahel and also for Ammu. Since Ammu had an early death she somehow escaped from the torture of life that would have awaited her. But for Estha and Rahel it was a different story. They were destined to live a longer life and they continued to suffer which was certainly something they would never wish.

VIII

Baby Kochamma gets the unique distinction in the novel of living backwards. A rebel by nature she started her real journey of life by falling in love with the Irish priest. The priest himself was tempted but even before the real damage was done he "escaped" from her hands. Baby Kochamma literally chased him but without success. Her conversion to Catholicism and becoming a nun did not cut any ice. Father Mulligan remained inaccessible to her. Life began to become a burden for her. Soon her father came to know about it and he brought her back to Ayemenem house only to send her back to Rochester for studies.

She came back to her ancestral house after two years and her father put her in charge of developing a garden in the house. She was very good at it and even people from Kottayam visited Ayemenem to see it. She was most uncomfortable with Ammu and her twin children. She disliked Ammu because she thought that a divorced daughter had no place in her house. She somehow believed that the children were capable of anything. Naturally all the three had problems with Baby Kochamma.

When Ammu was involved in the sex scandal it was Baby Kochamma who added fuel to fire and she was instrumental in sending Ammu away from Ayemenem house. In a way Velutha's death also could be attributed to her. She misrepresented facts and the police got hold of him and was tortured to death. She was avenging the insult that she received at the hands of the workers. Again it was Baby Kochamma who was instrumental in "returning" Estha to his father. Rahel also had to move away from Ayemenem house.

The most intriguing thing about Baby Kochamma is that she was living as a young woman even at the age of eighty-three. She was fond of make ups and found pleasure in wearing expensive saris. TV was her new love and she spent hours together before TV watching football tournaments, English films and other programmes. She had a good lieutenant in Kochu Maria who remained ever loyal to her. The fact that she continued to write "I love you" in her diary is another thing that could be treated as something abnormal.

Even when she was in her early eighties-there was absolutely no change in her attitude to Rahel and Estha. She was practically alone in Ayemenem house and still she was too eager to see that

Rahel and Estha left their ancestral house. The fact that they had come after a gap of twenty-three years never bothered her. She was of the firm view that she was in no way bound to look after the "abnormal" Estha. What one sees in her is the young rebel who wanted to love the Irish priest and lead a comfortable life with him.

10

The Modalali or the Blind Mother Widow with a Violin

I

Mammachi, "the Modalali" and sister-in-law of Baby Kochamma was almost blind and always wore dark glasses, when she went out of the house. She lived in her first batch of professional pickles. Her ambition in life was to master the art of perfect preservation. She had great love for her son, Chacko more so for preventing Pappachi, her husband beating her. He had become "the repository of all her womanly feelings. Her Man. Her only Love" (p. 168). At the same time she hated Margaret Kochamma. She hated her for being her daughter-in-law. She also hated her for leaving him and would have hated her even more if she had stayed.

She was a "dutiful" mother who was aware that grown up children would have their own needs and problems. That was why she had a separate entrance built for Chacko's room so that he could have his "man's needs". She was arrogant and never bothered about the consequences of her thoughtless behaviour. Whenever anything serious happened in the factory, it was always to Mammachi and not to Chacko that the news was brought. That was because she perfectly fitted into the conventional scheme of things.

She was at her worst and most unpredictable manner when Velutha was brought to Ayemenem house in connection with the affair he had with Ammu, her daughter. She insulted and humiliated him in a way which in normal circumstances a young man wouldn't tolerate. But Velutha being an untouchable and a man with immense patience did not lose his control. Mammachi would have died a sad death losing all the glory that the Ayemenem house traditionally had.

II

Mammachi started making pickles commercially when Pappachi, her husband, retired from Government service and came to live in Ayemenem. "The Kottayam Bible Society was having a fair and asked Mammachi to make some of her famous banana jam and tender mango pickle. It sold quickly, and Mammachi found that she had more orders than she could cope with. Thrilled with her success, she decided to persist with the pickles and jam, and soon found herself busy all year round" (p. 47). Her conical corneas made her practically blind. But this did not in any way affect her pickle making.

When Pappachi died she pasted in the family photograph album, the clipping from the *Indian Express* that reported Pappachi's death. At the funeral, Mammachi cried and her contact lenses slid around in her eyes. "Ammu told the twins that Mammachi was crying more because she was used to him than because he loved him. She was used to having him slouching around the pickle factory and was used to being beaten from time to time" (p. 50). She also said that human beings were creatures of habit and it was amazing the kind of things they could get used to. According to her beatings with brass vases were the least of them.

After the funeral of Pappachi, Mammachi asked Rahel to help her to locate and remove her contact lenses with the little orange pipette that came in its own case. Rahel had asked Mammachi whether she could inherit the pippette after Mammachi died. Ammu immediately punished her for being insensitive in her behaviour.

Mammachi had a very high opinion about her son Chacko. She often said that Chacko was easily one of the cleverest men in India. However, Ammu never was in agreement with this view of

Mammachi. Up to the time Chacko arrived, the factory had been a small but profitable enterprise which she ran like a large kitchen. Chacko got it registered and made Mammachi the sleeping partner. Also, Mammachi's factory got a name "Paradise Pickles & Preserves" after Chacko's arrival.

Mammachi used to remember the time when, in her girlhood, Paravans were expected to crawl backwards with a broom, sweeping away their footprints so that Brahmins or Syrian Christians would not defile themselves by accidentally stepping into a Paravan's footprint. In her time, Paravans like other untouchables, were not allowed to walk on public roads, not allowed to cover their upper bodies and not allowed to carry umbrellas. "They had to put their hands over their mouths when they spoke, to divert their polluted breath away from those whom they addressed" (p. 74).

It was Mammachi who first noticed little Velutha's remarkable facility with his hands. Mammachi persuaded Vellya Paapen to send him to the Untouchable's school that her father-in-law, Punnyan Kunju, had founded. She often said that if only he hadn't been a Paravan, he might have become an engineer. It was Velutha who designed and built the sliding-folding door for Mammachi. Mammachi paid Velutha less than she would a touchable carpenter but more than she would a Paravan. She didn't encourage him to enter the house except when she needed something mended or installed. "She thought that he ought to be grateful that he was allowed on the factory premises at all, and allowed to touch things that Touchables touched. She said that it was a big step for a Paravan" (p. 77).

Mammachi showed her obstinacy when it came to restlessness among the workers in the factory. When Punnachen the accountant, who read Mammachi the papers every morning, brought news that there had been talk among the workers of demanding a raise, Mammachi would be furious. "Tell them to read the papers. There's a famine on. There are no jobs. People are starving to death. They should be grateful they have any work *at all*" (pp. 121-22). Whenever anything serious happened in the factory, it was always to Mammachi and not to Chacko that the news was brought. "She was the Modalali. She played her part. Her responses, however, harsh, were straightforward and predictable. Chacko, on the other hand, though he was the Man of the House, though he said, '*My* Pickle, *my* jam, *my* curry powders', was so busy trying on different costumes that he blurred the battle lines" (p. 122).

Thus, we find that Mammachi began her pickle business without external help and that her husband never helped her in her endeavour. He found pleasure in beating her and it was her son Chacko who put an end to this daily practice. The complexion of the business changed once Chacko returned from Delhi. Velutha was treated in a way that suited an untouchable though she made use of his skill in carpentry. It also remained a fact that she was rather stern in her dealings with the workers. Still more would be there to say about Mammachi, the blind mother widow with a violin.

III

Mammachi held a gleaming violin under her chin. "Her opaque fifties sunglasses were black and slanty-eyed, with rhinestones on the corners of the frames. Her sari was starched and perfumed. Off-white and gold. Her diamond earrings shone in her ears like tiny chandeliers. Her ruby rings were loose. Her pale, fine skin was creased like cream on cooling milk and dusted with tiny red moles. She was beautiful. Old, unusual, regal" (p. 166).

When she was young she had collected all her falling hair in a small embroidered purse that she kept on her dressing table. When there was enough of it, she made it into a netted bun which she kept hidden in a locker with her jewellery. "When her hair began to thin and silver to give it body, she wore her jet-black bun pinned to her small, silver head.... At night, when she took off her bun, she allowed her grand-children to plait her remaining hair into a tight, oiled, grey rat's tail with a rubber band at the end. One plaited her hair, while the other counted her uncountable moles. They took turns" (p. 166). She had raised crescent shaped ridges on her scalp which were carefully hidden by her scanty hair. They were scars of old beatings from an old marriage. "She played *Lentement* — a movement from the Suite I in D/G of Handel's *Water Music*. Behind her slanted sunglasses, her useless eyes were closed, but she could see the music as it left her violin and lifted into the afternoon like smoke" (pp. 166-67).

Her mind wandered back over the years to her first batch of professional pickles as she played. It looked wonderfully beautiful for her. Bottled and sealed pickles standing on a table near the head of her bed were the first thing she would touch when she woke up. Once when she woke up a little after midnight her anxious fingers came away with a film of oil. There was oil everywhere and the pickle bottles stood in a pool of oil. The pickled mangoes had absorbed oil and expanded making the bottle leak. She consulted *Homescale Preservations*, the book that Chacko bought her. But even that failed to offer any solution. "Then she dictated a letter to Annamma Chandy's brother-in-law, who was the Regional Manager of Padma Pickles in Bombay. He suggested that she increase the proportion of preservative that she used. And the salt" (p. 167). Even though that had helped, the problem was not completely solved. Paradise Pickles' Bottles continued to leak a little. On long journeys their labels became oily and transparent and also the pickles were a little salty. Mammachi wondered whether she would ever master the art of preservation.

Thus, we find a Mammachi who would keep the netted bun in a locker unnoticed by anyone, a Mammachi who would touch the bottles of pickles when she got up and also a Mammachi who ever worried about the oily pickle bottles for which she couldn't find a lasting solution. Another feather in the character would be revealed if one looked at her attitude to her daughter-in-law Margaret Kochamma, her own son Chacko, Sophie Mol and the twins.

IV

Mammachi was known for her vanity and whenever she was invited to a wedding in Kottayam she would spend the whole time whispering to whoever she went with, " 'The bride's maternal grandfather was my father's carpenter. Kunjukutty Eapen? His great grandmother's sister was just a midwife in Trivandrum. My husband's family used to own this whole hill' " (p. 168).

She despised Margaret Kochamma even though she had never met her before. To her mind she was a shopkeeper's daughter.

Even if she were the heir to the throne of England she would not like her. That was because more than her working-class background, she hated Margaret Kochamma for being Chacko's wife. She also hated her for leaving him. But she would have hated her even more if she had stayed also.

Mammachi had always been kind to Chacko. When he finished his assignment at Oxford he had written to his mother for money. Though she was devastated she secretly pawned her jewellery and arranged for money to be sent to him in England. Mammachi also joyfully welcomed him back into her life later. She fed him, sewed for him and saw to it that there were fresh flowers in his room every day. Mammachi was aware of Chacko's libertine relationships with the women in the factory. But that never disturbed her. When Baby Kochamma brought it to her notice she would just say he couldn't help having a man's needs. Neither Mammachi nor Baby Kochamma saw any contradiction between Chacko's Marxist mind and feudal libido. Mammachi had a separate entrance built for Chacko's room which was at the eastern end of the house, so that "the objects of his 'Needs' wouldn't have to go traipsing *through* the house" (p. 169). Mammachi gave the servant girls money to keep them happy. They took it because they had young children, old parents and husbands who spent all their earnings in toddy bars to look after. The arrangement suited Mammachi, because in her mind, a fee *clarified* things. Disjuncted sex from love. Needs from Feelings" (p. 169).

Mammachi did not like Margaret Kochamma resuming her sexual relationship with Chacko. While she was in Ayemenem Mammachi managed her unmanageable feelings by slipping money into the pockets of the dresses that Margaret Kochamma left in the laundry bin. She never returned the money as she never found it. Aniyan, the Dhobi would empty the pockets. Eventhough Mammachi knew this, Margaret Kochamma's silence was taken as acceptance of payment for the favours Mammachi imagined she bestowed on her son. Thus she had the satisfaction of regarding Margaret Kochamma as just another prostitute.

When Sophie Mol arrived at Ayemenem house alongwith her mother Margaret Kochamma, Estha and Rahel and others, Mammachi was very eager to see Sophie Mol. "'Where is she?...

'Where is my Sophie Mol? Come here and let me see you!'" (p. 173). She said 'hello' to Margaret Kochamma also. But she was neither rude nor polite. She was apologetic that she was blind and so couldn't see them all. She regretted that Margaret had lost her second husband. "She sounded only a little sorry. Not very sorry" (p. 173). Even after her cornea transplant, Mammachi could only see light and shadow. If somebody was standing in the doorway, she could not say who it was. To read a cheque or a receipt or a bank note she had to keep it very close to her eyes. She would then wheel it from word to word. "The Towns people (in her fairy frock) saw Mammachi draw Sophie Mol close to her eyes to look at her. To read her like a cheque. To check her like a bank note. Mammachi (with her better eye) saw redbrown hair (N.... Nalmost blond), the curve of two fatfreckled cheeks (Nnnn.... almost rosy), bluegreyblue eyes" (p. 174). Mammachi discovered that Sophie Mol had Pappachi's nose. Later as a mark of showing happiness Mammachi played a *Welcome Home, Our Sophie Mol* melody on her violin. But Chacko couldn't stand her chocolate sound for long and so he requested Mammachi to stop it which she did.

Mammachi had her own fears about insanity in the family. She said that madness ran in their family and it came on people suddenly and caught them unawares. "There was Pathil Ammai, who at the age of sixty-five began to take her clothes off and run naked along the river, singing to the fish. There was Thampi Chachen, who searched his shit every morning with a knitting needle for a gold tooth he had swallowed years ago. And Dr. Muthachen, who had to be removed from his own wedding in a sack" (p. 223). The future generation would perhaps say that there was Ammu Ipe who married a Bengali, went quite mad and died young in a cheap lodge somewhere. When Chacko said that the high incidence of insanity among Syrian Christians was the price they paid for Inbreeding, Mammachi disagreed.

To put it briefly, Mammachi, the old woman disliked her daughter-in-law for her own reasons. Chacko remained to be her pet and even when he didn't send letters to her she was very prompt in sending him money when he was in dire need of it. When he was back to Ayemenem she took care to see that a special door was arranged for him to meet 'man's needs.' She was happy to handover the charge of the factory to her son though ultimately the business declined. She had great love for Sophie Mol and her only regret was that she was only able to "feel" her and not see her properly. She also had fears that madness was a fellow traveller of Ayemenem house. Yet another Mammachi appears in the scene where she pushes down Vellya Paapen in connection with the affair his son Velutha had with Ammu.

V

Vellya Pappen appeared at the kitchen door of ayemenem house one rainy afternoon. He was drunk and all the efforts of Kochu Maria to drive him away failed since he insisted that he would not go away unless he got an audience with Mammachi. Mammachi arrived in the kitchen in her petticoat and pale pink dressing gown with rickrack edging only to be shocked by an extraordinary action of Vellya Paapen. He climbed up the kitchen steps and offered his mortgaged eye. "He held it out in the palm of his hand. He said he didn't deserve it and wanted her to have it back. His left eyelid drooped over his empty socket in an immutable, monstrous wink. As though everything that he was about to say was part of an elaborate prank" (p. 254).

Without knowing that it was his eye Mammachi stretched out her hands, touched the glass eye and recoiled from its slippery once she realized that she had touched the hard and slimy glass eye. Mammachi was angry like anything and shouted at Vellya Paapen for being near her in drunken condition. She soaped away the sodden Paravan's eye-juices and smelled her hands when she had finished it. After a while Vellya Paapen recounted how kind the Ayemenem family had been to him and specially mentioned how Mammachi had paid for his eye and how she had organized for Velutha to be educated and given a job. Mammachi was rather flattered to hear the story. But she never dreamt about what he was going to tell her. Vellya Paapen began to cry and started telling her what he had seen. That was the story of "the little boat that crossed the river night after night, and who was in it. The story of a man and woman, standing together in the moonlight. Skin to skin" (p. 255). That was Velutha and Ammu. The whole village had heard about the affair. "His son and her daughter. They had made the unthinkable thinkable and the impossible really happen" (p. 256).

Very soon Mammachi forgot herself and what she was doing. She pushed Vellya Paapen with all her strength. He stumbled backwards, down the kitchen steps and lay sprawled in the wet mud. She spat into the rain and shouted "drunken dog", "drunken Paravan." Very soon her rage at the old one-eyed Paravan was redirected into a contempt for her daughter and what she had done. "She thought of her naked, coupling in the mud with a man who was nothing but a filthy *coolie.* She imagined it in vivid detail a Paravan's coarse black hand on her daughter's breast. His mouth on hers. His black hips jerking between her parted legs. The sound of their breathing. His particular Paravan smell. *Like animals*, Mammachi thought and nearly vomited. *Like a dog with a bitch on heat*" (pp. 257-58). Her tolerance of 'Men's needs' as far as her son was concerned, became the fuel for her unmanageable fury at her daughter. She thought that Ammu had defiled generations of breeding and brought the family to its knees. Mammachi lost control and eventually Ammu was locked up in her room before they sent for Velutha.

Vellya Paapen literally shocked Mammachi. As far as she was concerned the impossible had become possible and the unreal had become real. She wanted to punish Vellya Paapen for the crimes his son had committed. But on second thoughts she came to realize that it was her own daughter who never enjoyed privileges that her son Chacko enjoyed to be blamed for all the developments. She took the whole thing as an insult on the Ayemenem family. For the same reason the minimum she could do was to lock up Ammu in her room. Baby Kochamma who was always with her gave her all the necessary support in her endeavour. In the final phase we witness Mammachi humiliating Velutha with all her might.

VI

When Velutha arrived Mammachi lost all her control. She spewed her blind venom, her crass, insufferable insults at a panel in the sliding-folding door until Baby Kochamma tactfully swivelled her around and aimed her rage in the right direction, at Velutha standing very still in the gloom. "Mammachi continued her tirade, her eyes empty, her face twisted and ugly, her anger propelling her towards Velutha until she was shouting right into his face and he could feel the spray of her spit and smell the stale tea on her breath" (p. 284). It was a mystery to everybody how Mammachi could use such a foul language. She threatened Velutha saying that if he was found on her property she would kill him. Mammachi spat into his face which made Velutha stunned. He never tried to retaliate. What he said quietly was "we'll see about that". (p. 284).

What followed was Velutha's capture by the police and torturing him to death. In hatching the conspiracy it was Baby Kochamma who played the lead role. The same morning Sophie Mol's death also was announced. This time the culprits were Estha and Rahel. Thus, Ammu and her children suddenly became the three 'sinners' in Ayemenem house. Soon Ammu was asked to leave the house. Estha was returned to his father and later Rahel also left Ayemenem house. Mammachi, being a senior member of the family saw that everything went well and as per her designs. When Estha and Rahel returned after twenty-three years Mammachi was no more alive. She had successfully finished her role by banishing the three unwanted and undesirable elements in the Ayemenem family.

VII

Mammachi to whom her first batch of professional pickles was more than a weakness would be remembered for the inept handling of the "Velutha-Ammu episode". For a moment she completely forgot the fact that Ammu was none other than her daughter. From a feminist point of view one would even say that she was marginalising a fellow woman. She saw to it that every arrangements were made for Chacko to meet the "man's needs." Chacko got separated from his wife and she didn't want him to lead a "bachelor's life". Ammu also had been married but unlike Chacko it was her decision to get separated from her drunken husband. Chacko had a daughter who was in the custody of his wife. Ammu also had issues and they remained with her. If Chacko who was single would have "man's needs", by the same logic Ammu also would have "woman's needs". But in a patriarchal society that was something beyond the comprehension of Mammachi, Baby Kochamma and others. That is one of the intriguing things about Mammachi.

Mammachi also despised Margaret Kochamma for having left Chacko. More than that probably the fact that she was not able to lead a peaceful married life with her husband might have made her an impatient woman. She would not like a couple living a happy life for this reason. One would only consider as strange Mammachi keeping money in the pockets only to feel relieved at the thought that Margaret Kochamma was as good as a whore. But that Margaret Kochamma never knew about it was something that Mammachi had no knowledge about.

Mammachi's rage at Vallya Paapen is unjustifiable. The only fault that could be attributed to him was that he was a little drunk. That shouldn't make an old lady like Mammachi push him down in the muddy water. Vallya Pappen was more than an obedient servant and he was even ready to award capital punishment to his defiant son. But that did not in anyway help Mammachi and her behaviour was far from mature. Baby Kochamma had also played a non-trivial role in precipitating the tragedy because she had some old scores to settle.

Her verbal attack on Velutha was another instance where Mammachi behaved like an immature woman. Though Velutha showed restraint which was something one would never expect from a young man like him, Mammachi continued to provoke him which yielded no immediate result. Velutha who remained rather cool walked away as if nothing special had taken place. In this respect Velutha's behaviour was like that of a matured man. Her fellow women at Ayemenem house were shocked to hear the kind of abusive language Mammachi used against Velutha.

That Mammachi showed great love to Sophie Mol and was not ready to part with her love when it came to Estha and Rahel would again be significant. She had separate yardsticks when it came to her son's child and daughter's children. She never cared to think of the effects it would make on the minds of young children.

She was arrogant and had her own way in matters of workers also. When they had any complaints she never showed any concern or interest. Rather she chose to insult or threaten them. She was happy when Chacko returned from Delhi and took over the management of the company. But very soon he proved that he was not a fit person to run a factory. To clear the bank loans he had to mortgage the family property.

In short, Mammachi would be remembered as the one who was directly responsible for the tragedy that awaited the Ayemenem house. She was one who was never destined to lead a peaceful life and to "compensate" she made life miserable for her daughter and grandchildren. She was the Modalali who was harsh to everyone barring her own son Chacko and grand-daughter Sophie Mol, who had a premature death.

11

The Imperial Entomologist

I

The Imperial Entomologist in the novel is Pappachi, Mammachi's husband and father of Chacko and Ammu. It was before Independence that he worked as the Imperial Entomologist. When the British left, his designation was changed to Joint Director, Entomology. He retired as the Director or from a position that was equivalent to the Director. His life's greatest setback was that the moth that he had discovered had not been named after him.

He had other setbacks also in his life. His wife Mammachi was one whom he didn't like. This made him beat her on a daily basis. Naturally, his family life was a ruined one. He found his consolation in the skyblue Plymouth which he bought from an old English man in Munnar. It was a common sight for the people of Ayemenem to see Pappachi coasting importantly down the narrow road in his wide car, looking outwardly elegant but sweating freely inside his woollen suits.

His greatest disappointment might have come on his death. During his life time he never allowed his wife or anyone else in the family to use his skyblue Plymouth or even sit in it. The car was his revenge. But once he died Mammachi took possession of it which he wouldn't have allowed if at all there was any way out.

The *Indian Express* reported his death as follows: "Noted

entomologist, Shri Benaan John Ipe, son of late Rev. E. John Ipe of Ayemenem (popularly known as *Punnyan Kunju*), suffered a massive heart attack and passed away at the Kottayam General Hospital last night. He developed chest pains at around 1.05 a.m. and was rushed to hospital. The end came at 2.45 a.m. Shri Ipe had been keeping indifferent health since last six months. He is survived by his wife Soshamma and two children" (p. 50). Pappachi's greatest setback has to do with the naming of the moth.

II

While working as Joint Director, Entomology, a moth fell into his drink one evening while he was sitting in the verandah of a rest house after a long day in the field. He picked it out and saw its unusually dense dorsal tufts. After having a closer look, he mounted it with great excitement. He measured it and the next morning placed it in the sun for a few hours for the alcohol to evaporate. Then he caught the first train back to Delhi. "To taxonomic attention and, he hoped, fame" (p. 49). After six months of anxiety Pappachi received the information that his moth had finally been identified as a slightly unusual race of a wellknown species that belonged to the tropical family Lymantriidae.

There was a taxonomic reshuffle twelve years later and lepidopterists decided that Pappachi's moth was a separate species and genus unknown to science. This was a real blow to Pappachi. As he had already retired and moved to Ayemenem, it was too late for him to assert his claim to the discovery. A junior officer who was the Acting Director of the Department of Entomology took away the credit. The moth was named after him. He was an officer whom Pappachi disliked.

Pappachi's moth was held responsible for his black moods and bouts of temper in the years to come. But the fact was that he had been ill-humoured long before he discovered the moth. The moth continued to haunt him and the Ayemenem family. "Its pernicious ghost — grey, furry and with unusually dense dorsal tufts — haunted every house that he ever lived in. It tormented him and his children and his children's children" (p. 49).

Pappachi wore a well-pressed three-piece suit and his gold

pocket watch until the day he died. Even the stifling heat did not alter his way of life. On his dressing table, next to his cologne and silver hairbrush, he kept a picture of himself as a youngman, with his hair slicked down. It was in Vienna that he had done the six-month diploma course which qualified him to apply for the post of Imperial Entomologist.

Pappachi was a photogenic man, dapper and carefully groomed, with a little man's largeish head. "He had an incipient second chin that would have been emphasized had he looked down or nodded" (p. 51). In the photograph he had taken care to hold his head high enough to hide his double chin, yet not so high as to appear haughty. "His light brown eyes were polite, yet maleficent, as though he was making an effort to be civil to the photographer while plotting to murder his wife. He had a little fleshy knob on the centre of his upper lip that dropped down over his lower lip in a sort of effeminate pout — the kind that children who suck their thumb's develop. He had an elongated dimple on his chin which only served to underline the threat of a lurking manic violence. A sort of contained cruelty. He wore khaki jodhpurs though he had never ridden a horse in his life. His riding boots reflected the photographer's studio lights. An ivory handled riding crop lay neatly across his lap" (p. 51).

There was a watchful stillness to the photograph that lent an underlying chill to the warm room in which it hung. The photograph spoke it all. Pappachi was one who liked to hold his head high though he was not very proud. He liked to be polite but was known for his maleficent nature. It might be the case he had an innate desire to murder his wife which never materialised. A sort of cruelty was stamped on him and the photograph appeared to tell the world that he was one who believed in violence. One wouldn't miss the references to violence he inflicted upon his wife, in the novel.

III

Once Pappachi came back to Ayemenem after retirement, he had trouble coping with the ignominy of retirement. The thought that he was seventeen years older than Mammachi disturbed him like anything. He realized that he was an old man when his wife was still in her prime. This shocked him more than anything else. Pappachi never helped his wife with the pickle making. That was mainly because he thought pickle making not a suitable job for a high-ranking ex-government official.

He had always been jealous. For the same reason he resented his wife getting sudden attention from different quarters. "He slouched around the compound in his immaculately tailored suits, weaving sullen circles around mounds of red chillies and freshly powdered yellow turmeric, watching Mammachi supervise the buying, the weighing, the salting and drying, of limes and tender mangoes" (p. 47). Every night he beat her with a flower vase. Beatings were nothing new to Mammachi. But the frequency with which they took place was something which she found to be unusual.

On earlier occasion also Pappachi's jealousy had stood in the way of Mammachi outshining others. She had spent a few months in Vienna with him and she took her first lessons on the violin during those few months. When Mammachi's teacher Launsky-Tieffenthal told Pappachi that his wife was exceptionally talented and of potentially concert class, Pappachi ensured that the lessons were discontinued. The abrupt end to the violin lessons could only be attributed to Pappachi's jealous nature.

Pappachi often turned out to be violent towards Mammachi. One night he broke the bow of her violin and threw it in the river. The day Chacko put an end to this obnoxious practice Pappachi sat in the verandah and stared stonily out at the ornamental garden, ignoring the plates of food that Kochu Maria brought him. He expressed his real anger late at night. He went into his study and brought out his favourite mahogany rocking chair. He smashed it into little bits putting it down in the middle of the driveway. A plumber's monkey wrench came handy for him to perform this feat. He left it there in the moonlight, a heap of varnished wicker and splintered wood. Pappachi never touched Mammachi again. But he also never cared to speak to her as long as he lived. Baby Kochamma or Kochu Maria were used as intermediaries when he needed anything.

Pappachi also would tell the world that he was neglected by his wife. In the evenings he would sit on the verandah and sew buttons that weren't missing onto his shirts to create such an impression. He did this whenever he expected visitors at Ayemenem house. This action ultimately helped in corroding Ayemenem's view of working wives.

Ammu considered Pappachi as an incurable British CCP, which was a short form for *chhi-chhi-poch* and in Hindi meant shit-wiper. Chacko believed that the correct word for people like Pappachi was *Anglophile*, which in his case meant "bring mind into certain state". Chacko would explain that Pappachi's mind had been brought into a state which made him like the English.

Thus we find that Pappachi was never a good husband to his wife or a good father to his children. Though not very arrogant he did not like his wife to come to limelight. He believed in his own dignity and that made him not help his wife in pickle making. The fact that he put a sudden end to his wife's violin lesson again would corroborate this point. That his children Chacko and Ammu did not have a very high opinion about him was made clear from the observations he made about them. Pappachi had one more face which he unveiled in his dealings with visitors.

IV

Ammu had watched her father Pappachi weave his hideous web when she was in her growing years. He was very charming and urbane with his visitors. He stopped just short of fawning on them if they happened to be white. He was very generous to others and was never reluctant to donate money for public causes. To orphanages and leprosy clinics he donated liberally. He wanted others to describe him as a sophisticated, generous and moral man. In other words, he worked hard on his public profile.

But it was altogether a different story when it came to his wife and children. "Alone with his wife and children he turned into a monstrous, suspicious bully, with a streak of vicious cunning. They were beaten, humiliated and then made to suffer the envy of friends and relations for having such a wonderful husband and father" (p. 180). Once Pappachi had beaten Ammu and her mother and driven them out of their home. As a result they had to endure cold winter night in Delhi hiding in the mehindi hedge around their house. They did so in order to escape the notice of the people from good families.

On another occasion Ammu who was only nine had watched Pappachi's natty silhouette in the lit windows as he flitted from room to room. He tore down curtains, kicked furniture and smashed a table lamp not satisfied with having beaten his wife and daughter. Chacko escaped the fury as he was away at school. Pappachi had been sitting in his mahogany rocking chair all along, rocking himself silently in the dark. Meanwhile, Ammu had crept back into the drawing room and the lights were suddenly switched on. When Pappachi caught her, he didn't say a word. He flogged her with his ivory-handled riding crop which he had held across his lap in his studio photograph. Ammu did not cry inspite of his persistent beatings. When he finished it, he made her bring him Mammachi's pinking shears from her sewing cupboard. "While Ammu watched, the Imperial Entomologist shred her new gum boots with her mother's pinking shears... The scissors made snicking scissor-sounds. Ammu ignored her mother's drawn, frightened face that appeared at the window. It took ten minutes for her beloved gumboots to be completely shredded. When the last strip of rubber had rippled to the floor, her father looked at her with cold, flat eyes, and rocked and rocked and rocked. Surrounded by a sea of twisting, rubber snakes" (p. 181).

How cruel Pappachi could be to his wife and children wouldn't need further explanation. He behaved to them as if they were his born enemies. His attitude to them belied the fact that they were really his wife and children. As far as Mammachi and her children were concerned, they were passive sufferers who failed to raise even a small finger against the cruelty meted out to them. An end to this came when Pappachi returned to Ayemenem and one day Chacko, his own son ensured that this was not repeated in the house.

However, the Imperial Entomologist continued to live in his room even after his mortal life in the Ayemenem house.

V

In Pappachi's study, "mounted butterflies and moths had disintegrated into small heaps of iridescent dust that powdered the bottom of their glass display cases, leaving the pins that had impaled them naked. Cruel. The room was rank with fungus and disuse and an old neon-green hula hoop hung from a wooden peg on the wall" (p. 155).

On the top shelf, the leather binding on Pappachi's set of *The Insect Wealth of India* had lifted off each book and buckled like corrugated asbestos. "Silverfish tunnelled through the pages, burrowing arbitrarily from species to species turning organized information into yellow lace" (p. 155).

The Imperial Entomologist was a researcher in the true sense of the word. Though a disappointed man probably he continued with his readings and observations even after he returned to Ayemenem from Delhi after his retirement. He had his own collection of books and as an academician and researcher he was unparalleled. But he could not make a mark in these capacities and what remained of him was a cruel husband and a cruel father.

VI

Pappachi, the entomologist, would certainly appear as a crucial link in the hierarchy of Ayemenem family. What made him desperate could be a question which partly he and partly his wife could answer. He had disappointments in his life and may be it was the case that his wife and children never cared to understand him. His life at Delhi might have given him opportunities to have a tough time. He wouldn't have gone well with his subordinates and one of his juniors getting the credit for whatever he discovered was something that he couldn't stand. Naturally, this continued to torment him.

It was his wife who was instrumental in making his life still more miserable on his return to Ayemenem house. Whereas he continued to be a failure on almost all fronts his wife was a great success in her endeavours. She began to carve out a name for herself in the business field as she proved out to be triumphant in her pickle business. The only way to 'stunt' her growth was by beating her. That was why he made it a practice to beat her as a routine. He never bothered to think that his children were being made a casualty as they also were suffering along with their mother at least in their earlier years.

He further wanted to take revenge upon his wife by not allowing to use or even sit in his Plymouth car. But ultimately he was proved wrong. The same car that he kept as a mark of revenge passed on to his wife, whom he hated, after his death. At the same time it remained a fact that Ayemenem house could not get rid of him completely even after he died. The books and specimens continued to haunt the house and several years after his death his own grandchildren got amble chances to "see" the kind of academician and researcher their grandfather was.

12

The Untouchable

I

Velutha, Vellya Paapen's son could be taken as the representative of the untouchables in the novel. The untouchables were made to suffer humiliations at the hands of the caste Hindus and Christians. Velutha, the young rebel in the novel was a carpenter who was a master craftsman with a German sensibility. He was a committed party worker who actively took part in the activities of the party. He was also a rebel and within him there was a volcano ready to burst any time.

After returning to Ayemenem Ammu slowly got drawn to Velutha, the bare-bodied Paravan. She couldn't control her sexual desires and being a young man Velutha positively responded to her advances completely oblivious of the fact that she was a 'forbidden fruit' for a person like him who was an untouchable. But the daring Velutha saw Ammu only as a woman and their affair marked the turning point in the novel.

When his life was in danger the Marxist Party never stood by him. The spokesman of the party even told the police that he was not an active member. The Ayemenem family also was in the forefront to destroy him completely. Mammachi and Baby Kochamma plotted against him and the latter misrepresented the facts to the Kottayam police. The drowning of Sophie Mol added fuel to the fire. The police got hold him and tortured him in all possible ways. Once he died in the police custody Estha was made to tell a lie to ensure that the real culprits went scot-free.

Thus ended a life dedicated to a cause and which was a symbol of the bold and the daring.

II

Velutha's father was a toddy tapper by profession. While shaping a block of granite with a hammer a chip had flown into his left eye slicing through it. So one of his identification marks was his left eye. He was an old world Paravan and had seen the Paravans crawling backwards with a broom sweeping away their footprints. His gratitude to Mammachi and her family for all that they had done for him was as wide and deep as a river in spate. When he had his accident with the stone chip, Mammachi organized and paid for his glass eye. "He hadn't worked off his debt..., and though he knew he wasn't expected to, that he wouldn't ever be able to — he felt that his eye was not his own. His gratitude widened his smile and bent his back" (p. 76).

Apart from Velutha, Vellya Paapen had an elder son also. He was Kuttappan paralysed from his chest downwards : "Day after day, month after month, while his brother was away and his father went to work, Kuttappan lay flat on his back and watched his youth saunter past without stopping to say hello" (p. 206). Kuttappan lay alone with only a black hen for company. He lost his mother Chella who died a "coughing, spitting, aching, phlegmy death" (p. 206). It was a terrible experience for him to watch his mother's death. He had no sensation in his feet at all and occasionally he poked at them with a stick. He often wondered how long he would take to die. Unlike Velutha, Kuttappan was "a good, safe Paravan." He could neither read nor write. "Insanity hovered close at hand, like an eager waiter at an expensive restaurant (lighting cigarettes, refilling glasses). Kuttappan thought with envy of mad men who could walk. He had no doubts about the equity of the deal; his sanity, for serviceable legs" (p. 207).

A fifth "untouchable" about whom we find a reference in the novel is Velutha's grandfather Kelan. He along with a number of Paravans, Pelayas and Pulayas had embraced Christianity only to regret later. They had joined the Anglican church to escape untouchability. But it was a sort of jump from frying pan into the fire. Though they got a little food and money, they were known as Rice-Christians. They had separate churches, with separate services and separate priests. A separate Pariah Bishop was also there. To their disappointment they found that they were not entitled to government benefits like job reservations or bank loans at low interest rates. That was because officially they were Christians and therefore casteless. "It was a little like having to sweep away your footprints without a broom. Or worse, not being *allowed* to leave footprints at all" (p. 74).

That was Velutha's background as an untouchable grandson of a grandfather who was converted to Christianity. The legacy that he received from his father Vellya Paapen and Chella was one of humiliation by the caste Hindus and Christians. His brother Kuttappan was the worst sufferer as he was leading a life which was in every sense one equivalent to death. But Velutha was one who somehow tried to come out of the shell that was made ready for him by his ancestors. But as would be seen later, it all turned out to be a shattered shell where the inmate never had a choice other than getting destroyed. As an untouchable boy he had been in the habit of going to the Ayemenem house with his father to deliver coconuts plucked from the trees in the compound. These Paravans were never allowed to enter the house. They were not allowed to touch anything that the touchables touched. But Velutha at a later stage dared to touch the forbidden. But before that it would be worthwhile to know Velutha, the carpenter.

III

Even at a very young age of eleven, Velutha was like a little magician. He could make intricate toys, tiny windmills and minute jewel boxes out of palm reeds. He could also carve perfect boats out of tapioca stems. He used to bring these curiosities to Ammu who was three years elder to him. Being an untouchable he would hold them out on his palm so that she wouldn't have to touch them to take them. This was what he was taught. He called her Ammukutty — Little Ammu though he was younger than she was. This was certainly more than a privilege for an untouchable boy.

When he was fourteen, Johann Klein, a carpenter from Bavaria came to Kottayam. He spent three years with the Christian Mission Society and conducted a workshop for the carpenters who were locally available. Velutha worked with Klein till dusk at Kottayam where he went every afternoon. By the time he was sixteen, he finished his school and became an excellent carpenter. He had a distinctly German sensibility and had his own set of carpentry tools. "He built Mammachi a Bauhaus dining table with twelve dining chairs in rosewood and a traditional Bavarian chaise longue in lighter jack. For Baby Kochamma's annual Nativity plays he made her a stack of wire-framed angels' wings that fitted onto children's backs like knapsacks, cardboard clouds for the Angel Gabriel to appear between, and a dismantleable manger for Christ to be born in" (p. 75).

Velutha had a way with machines apart from his skills in carpentry. He repaired radios, clocks, water-pumps and a variety of other contrivances and also looked after the plumbing and the electrical gadgets in the house. He was in all sense an expert and knew more about the machines in the factory than anyone else. It was Velutha who reassembled and set up the Bharat bottle-sealing machine which Chacko brought from Madras. He also maintained the new canning machine and the automatic pineapple slicer. His other activities included oiling the water pump and the small diesel generator and building the aluminium sheet-lined, easy-to-clean cutting surfaces and the ground-level furnaces for boiling fruit. In short, he was a real master craftsman, 'Jack of all trades and master of all trades.'

Mammachi had rehired Velutha as the factory carpenter. He was put in charge of general maintenance. Naturally, it caused a great deal of resentment among the other factory workers who belonged to the upper castes. They argued that Paravans were not meant to be carpenters. They further asserted that prodigal Paravans were not meant to be rehired.

Thus, Velutha, we find, was unparalleled as a carpenter, as a mechanic and also as an "engineer". He was even referred to as "Dr. Velutha" by Baby Kochamma when her garden cherub's silver were dried up inextricably and Velutha fixed its bladder for her. He never had the feeling that he was an untouchable especially when it came to his profession. With full confidence he easily surpassed his fellow workers which made a peaceful co-existence impossible. But he did not attach much importance to what others said or thought about him. Otherwise he would never have become a trade unionist.

IV

Though Velutha was an untouchable in the eyes of his fellow workers, he was more than conscious about his duties to the working class. Velutha participated in the march organized by the Travancore-Cochin Marxist Labour Union as part of a secretariat march to be organized by their colleagues in Trivandrum. This would be followed by a presentation of the charter of people's demand to Comrade E.M.S. The main demand was to have an hours' lunch break for the paddy workers in between a nonstop eleven and a half hours of work from seven o'clock in the morning to half past six in the evening. Another demand was to increase the women labourers' wages from Re. 1.25 to Rs. 3 and men labourers' from Rs. 2.50 to Rs. 4.50 a day. A third demand was that the untouchables shouldn't be addressed by their caste names. They didn't want "to be addressed as Achoo *Parayan*, or Kelan *Paravan*, or Kuttan *Pulayan*, but just as Achoo, or Kelan, or Kuttan" (p. 69).

Velutha was a problem for Comrade Pillai as a trade unionist. Of all the workers at Paradise Pickles, he was the only card-holding member of the Party. Other workers had complaints about him basically to do with caste issues. The fact that he was able to outshine others in all respects would also have come as a contributing factor to their resentment. Though Velutha had stood by Comrade Pillai both as a party worker and a trade unionist, he had been most unkind to him in his hours of turmoil. When Velutha approached Comrade Pillai to find a way out, Pillai told to his face that party was not constituted to support worker's indiscipline in their private life.

The fact that Velutha had taken part in the workers' march had created ripples in Ammu and others in the Ayemenem family. When Chacko, Baby Kochamma, Ammu and the twins were on their way to see the movie *The Sound of Music*, Rahel suddenly got a glimpse of Velutha. She became restless when he marched with a red flag "in a white shirt and mundu with angry veins in his neck" (p. 71). Velutha wearing a shirt was an unusual sight for Rahel. When she called him he freezed for a moment and listened with his flag and she continued to call him "Velutha, Ividay! Velutha" (please come here); but he disappeared deftly. Ammu for reasons best known to her snubbed and even slapped Rahel in anger asking her to behave herself. Rahel was totally puzzled to see her mother reacting so strongly for a thing which she thought was trivial.

For some reason Velutha was reluctant to admit to Rahel when he met her the next day that he had taken part in the march. When Rahel told him that she saw him the previous day Velutha wanted to know where she had seen him. Rahel got a little angry and her reaction was as follows : "'Liar'.... 'Liar and pretender. I did see you. You were a communist and had a shirt and a flag. *And* you ignored me'" (p. 177). Velutha responded with an "aiyyo kashtam" (the pity of it!) and tried to argue that it would be his twin brother Urumban who he had lost long back. But Rahel knew pretty well that Velutha didn't have a twin brother.

Thus, we find that more than an untouchable and a professional carpenter he was a hard-core trade unionist and a sincere party worker. That he had emerged as the daring trade unionist who had succeeded in shedding his identity as an untouchable by being in his white shirt and mundu fighting for the rights of the oppressed is the important thing that shouldn't be missed. At the sametime he had his own problems to admit at least to the members of the Ayemenem family that he had performed his role as a trade unionist. Long years of suffering of his ancestors would certainly make its mark on him and perhaps he wanted to ensure that he had made a slow beginning.

Far from being a trade unionist Estha had proved himself to be a rebel also. He had given sufficient proof to his father as to what he was going to be when he grew up.

V

Karl (1972) has observed that "the rebel is not a criminal and not a force for evil, although he may commit anti social acts. He is fundamentally, a person for whom society does not offer a testing ground : he seeks his philosophy in himself, not in God or his environment. He is, at best, true to himself no matter what the consequences and often they are unfavorable" (p. 9). Velutha too was never a criminal. He had never been a party to evil. But he did commit what society would call anti-social act. Society was never kind to him and like a true rebel he sought his philosophy in himself. He was always true to himself and acted never bothering about the consequences.

Vellya Paapen had his own fears when Velutha grew into a young man. He couldn't say what it was that frightened him. More than what he said it was the way he said that worried him more. Similarly, what he did did not disturb him but the way he did it he found disquieting. There was a difference in the way he walked. He started offering suggestions even without being asked for the same. Sometimes he even disregarded suggestions without apparently being a rebel. Vellya Paapen thought that these qualities were all right or even desirable in touchables. In a Paravan this kind of a behaviour could certainly be insolence.

Whenever Vellya Paapen cautioned him Velutha thought that his father had some kind of a grudge against him. "Vellya Paapen's good intentions quickly degenerated into nagging and bickering and a general air of unpleasantness between father and son. Much to his mother's dismay, Velutha began to avoid going home. He worked late. He caught fish in the river and cooked it on an open fire. He slept outdoors, on the banks of the river" (pp. 76-77).

Things took a different shape and one day he disappeared. For full four years nobody knew where he was. A rumour was spread that he was working on a building site for the Department of Welfare and Housing in Trivandrum. There was also news that he had become a Naxalite. Some went to the extent of saying that he had been arrested. But some others claimed that they had seen him in Quilon. But the fact remained that Velutha had become rebellious.

When Chella, Velutha's mother died there was no way of informing him about it. Later when another tragedy struck the home when Kuttappan fell off a coconut tree and damaged his spine Velutha continued to be not available. He heard about the incident only a year after it. Even though he reappeared in Ayemenem he never revealed where he had been and so his rendezvous and what he did there were shrouded in mystery.

Very soon he grew dangerously and as a rebel he had within him a volcano ready to burst anytime. His father, more than anyone else, was fully aware of this and he feared for him more than ever. But he said nothing or rather he was dumb to tell his son anything. But soon terror took hold of him when he saw what his untouchable son had touched. Even after this incident Velutha, the rebel remained relatively cool. When Mammachi humiliated him in all possible ways and threatened that she would castrate him like a pariah dog and would also kill him his only answer was "we'll see about that" (p. 284).

To put it briefly, Velutha lived a rebel's life and died as a rebel. At a time when the untouchables were not allowed to touch those belonging to the upper strata of the society what Velutha did was something unique in the normal circumstances. He never gave up his courage and even when he realized that his life was in danger he never turned panicky. Like a true hero he was accepting death and it was a heroic death at the hands of the Kottayam police.

Velutha lived the life of a lover also. The important thing was that he ventured into an area which was often considered to be the privilege of the rich and higher ups. That again takes Velutha to heroic heights.

VI

It was Ammu who made Velutha a lover. She would watch him hidden from him. Velutha was able to know what she expected from him. The day it all began Velutha glanced up and caught Ammu's gaze, holding her daughter in her arms. "Centuries telescoped into one evanescent moment... In that brief moment Velutha looked up and saw things that he hadn't seen before. Things that had been out of bounds so far...." (p. 176). For the first time he realized that Rahel's mother was a mother. He also realized that "she had deep dimples when she smiled and that they stayed on long after her smile left her eyes. He saw that her brown arms were round and firm and perfect. He saw that when he gave her gifts they no longer needed to be offered flat on the palms of his hands so that she wouldn't have to touch him... He saw too that he was not necessarily the only giver of gifts. That *she* had gifts to give him too" (pp. 176-77).

Velutha floated on his back in the middle of the river. He flipped over and began to swim. He swam against the current. When he saw her the detonation almost drowned him. He began to swim towards her. He had almost reached the bank when Ammu looked up and saw him. "He wore a thin white cloth around his loins, looped between his dark legs. He shook the water from his hair. She could see his smile in the dark. His white, sudden smile that he had carried with him from boyhood into manhood. His only luggage" (p. 334).

He stood before Ammu with the river dripping form him. When Velutha saw Ammu watching him his heart hammered. Ammu approached him and laid the length of her body against his. He stood there unmoved. He didn't even touch her. He was shivering partly with cold, partly with terror and partly with aching desire. In spite of his fear Velutha's body was prepared to take the bait. His body wanted her urgently. He asked himself what the worst thing was that could happen. His conclusion was that he could lose everything — his job, his family, his livelihood and everything.

Then the curtain was raised to the inevitable drama. "She unbuttoned her shirt. They stood there. Skin to skin. Her brownness against his blackness. Her softness against his hardness. Her nut-brown breasts... against his smooth ebony chest.... she pulled his head down towards her and kissed his mouth. A cloudy kiss. A kiss that demanded a kiss-back. He kissed her back" (pp. 335-336). That was not all. Velutha and Ammu continued the drama. "Ammu, naked... crouched over Velutha, her mouth on his... She slid further down, introducing herself to the rest of him. His neck. His nipples. His chocolate stomach. She sipped the last of the river from the hollow of his navel. She pressed the heat of his erection against her eyelids. She tasted him, salty, in her mouth. He sat up and drew her back to him. She felt his belly tighten under her, hard as a board... He took her nipple in his mouth and cradled her other breast in his calloused palm... Once he was inside her, fear was derailed and biology took over. The cost of living climbed to unaffordable heights; though later, Baby

Kochamma would say it was a Small Price to Pay" (p. 336). Velutha did pay the price and it was not a small one. Vellya Paapen had seen night after night, a little boat being rowed across the river. He had also seen it return at dawn. The only thing that he thought he would do was to rush to Ayemenem house and report the matter to Mammachi.

One would perhaps see parallels in Lawrence Durrel's novels where the novelist would not divorce sex from love. In a sense it might be difficult to call Velutha a lover. It was purely sexual relation that Ammu had with Velutha at her initiative. But it shouldn't be forgotten that Ammu was "Ammukutty' to Velutha when they were young. In their childhood they did know quite intimately and the fact that Velutha became a well built man with strong muscles was enough provocation for Ammu, the sex starved woman separated from her husband.

Vellya Paapen's report to Mammachi about the Velutha-Ammu affair marked the beginning of Velutha's end. He was asked to appear before Mammachi and the rest of the incidents expose the rich and the privileged.

VII

It was a fellow worker of the factory who told Velutha that Mammachi wanted to see him. He had no idea about the new developments and was completely unaware of his father's drunken visit to the Ayemenem house. He was also in the dark about the fact that poor paralysed Kuttappan had been talking to his father continuously for two hours, trying to calm him down, all the time listening to the footsteps so that he could shout a warning to his unsuspecting brother.

The daring Velutha straight away went to the Ayemenem house to listen with utmost patience Mammachi's tirade. The audacious Velutha was decent to the core and suffered the insults passively. He felt that the count down had begun. His only worry was that he would never see Ammu again. He had also apprehensions about Ammu being hurt by her people.

It was to Pillai's house that Velutha went from there to explain his position which often slipped into incoherence. Pillai was more worried about the reaction of the people which made him say :

"This is a little village : People talk. I listen to what they say. It's not as though I don't know what's been going on" (p. 287). That justice is going to be denied to Velutha is made clear through these statements. He told Velutha that the party was not constituted to support indiscipline. He also made it clear that individual's interest was subordinate to the organization's interest. Velutha told himself that he had only one more night to go before a long sleep.

It was Sophie Mol's death which came as the last nail in Velutha's coffin. He was falsely implicated though everyone knew that hers was an accidental death. It was Baby Kochamma who made Estha depose before the police that Velutha had a hand in kidnapping them which ultimately led to the death of Sophie Mol. She also told the police that he had threatened them at their house.

Though Velutha was almost innocent in the affair that he had with Ammu, every body — the touchables — made that he was a true villain who should be stoned to death. The members of the Ayemenem Family, Comrade Pillai and to crown it all, the police played their respective roles wonderfully well to finish off Velutha, the untouchable.

The way he was tortured to death would perhaps be one of the breathtaking descriptions in any fiction. It would also certainly remind one of the concentration camps where mostly innocent people were tortured to death.

VIII

The police who were to protect the life and property of the citizens went to Velutha's house and woke him up with their boots. The rest of the descriptions are heart-rending. There was the thud of wood on flesh. "Boot on bone. On teeth. The muffled grunt when a stomach is Kicked in. The muted crunch of skull on cement. The gurgle of blood on a man's breath when his lung is torn by the jagged end of a broken rib" (p. 308).

The semi-unconscious Velutha was not able to move. But the torture continued. "His skull was fractured in three places. His nose and both his cheekbones were smashed, leaving his face pulpy, undefined. The blow to his mouth had split open his upper lip and broken six teeth. Four of his ribs were splintered, one had pierced his left lung, which was what made him bleed from his mouth" (p. 310).

"His lower intestine was ruptured and haemorrhaged, the blood collected in his abdominal cavity. His spine was damaged in two places, the concussion had paralysed his right arm and resulted in a loss of control over his bladder and rectum. Both his knee caps were shattered" (p. 310). Still the police brought out the handcuffs! To add insult to injury one of them even flicked at his penis with his stick and remarked : '"Come on, show us your special secrets. Show us how big it gets when you blow it up"' (p. 311).

Since Velutha was not able to walk, he was dragged by the police. When Estha entered the police lock up he could not see anything. But he could hear the sound of rasping and laboured breathing. Someone switched on the light and Velutha appeared on the scummy, slippery floor. "A mangled genie invoked by a modern lamp. He was naked, his soiled *mundu* had come undone. Blood spilled from his skull like a secret. His face was swollen and his head looked like a pumpkin, too large and heavy for the slender stem it grew from" (pp. 319-320).

When one of the policemen prodded Velutha with his foot, there was no response. Inspector Thomas Mathew raked his jeep key across the sole of Velutha's foot. Swollen eyes opened, wandered and then focussed through a film of blood on a beloved child. Someone switched off the light and Velutha disappeared. The police knew that it was death in custody of a technically innocent man. To save their face they had to concoct their own story. Meanwhile, Velutha's body was dumped in the '*themmady kuzhi*' — the pauper's pit — where the police routinely dump their dead. That marked the end of the life of an untouchable, a trade unionist, a rebel, a carpenter and to cap it all a lover.

Velutha was tortured to death in the most inhuman way. Apart from the police, Baby Kochamma and Comrade Pillai wouldn't be able to escape from the responsibility they had in killing an innocent human being. It was ironic that when he was about to breath his last, Estha his beloved friend appeared before his eyes. The same Estha was made to depose before the police in which he had to give evidence against Velutha.

IX

Velutha certainly stands out as a very tall figure in the novel. It was his desire to 'relive' as a touchable that triggered the tragedy. But he was never a coward and dared to speak out even when he knew that his life was in danger. The daring Velutha could have very well murdered at least a couple of his enemies who were in his 'hit list'. But even when he knew that his end was imminent he continued to remain a Gandhian, an apostle of non-violence.

In his profession he was unbeatable and even in his 'affairs' with Ammu he was unique in his own way. He was a good friend for those who loved him and Estha and Rahel were the ones who discovered the real friend in him. He was ready to go to any extent to entertain them. This made the children dear to him which resulted in an unbreakable bond.

His loyalty to the party was unquestionable and as a trade unionist he was committed to protect the rights of his fellow workers at any cost. In this respect he would be described as a foil to Comrade Pillai who believed that he was the true representative of the party in the real sense of the term.

On the whole, one can very well see that Velutha is a creatio. unparalleled. His place would certainly be nearer to a Shakespearean hero — a Macbeth, a Hamlet, an Othello, an Antony or perhaps all of them together. Like a true tragic hero he rises to meteoric heights and as fate would have it he had a tragic end not very much because like the Shakespearean tragic hero he had any tragic flaw. More than that it was the circumstances and the society which made Velutha die a miserable death in the hands of the protectors of law.

Velutha raises certain questions which our society should answer. A carpenter with a German sensibility continued to be ill-treated for the only reason that he was an untouchable. The party which should stand to protect the interests of the workers fails in its duty. The higher ups in the society, we find, are able to do all kinds of damage to those who are in the lower strata of the society. In this sense Velutha is not a mere character. He stands as a representative of a group of people who have been traditionally ill-treated and will continue to be treated so. What is expected is a strong social response to ensure that all the people in the society are equal and some are not more equal as George Orwell prefers to put it.

13

The Chameleon

I

"Though his part in the whole thing had by no means been a small one, Comrade Pillai didn't hold himself in any way personally responsible for what had happened. He dismissed the whole business as the Inevitable Consequence of Necessary politics. The old omelette and eggs thing. But then, Comrade K.N.M. Pillai was essentially a political man. A professional omeletteer. He walked through the world like a chameleon. Never revealing himself, never appearing not to. Emerging through chaos unscathed" (p. 14).

Pillai's attitude would remind one of a passage in Fo (1992) where Maniac says : "Are the people calling for true justice? Instead of that we'll give them a justice that is just a bit less unjust. And if the workers start shouting 'Enough of this brutual exploitation', and start complaining that they're tired of dying in the factories, then we give them a little more protection on the job... and step up the compensation rates for their widows.. They want revolution....? We give them reforms... reforms by the bucketful... we'll drown them with reforms... or rather we'll drown them with *promises* of reforms, because we're never going to give them reforms either!" (pp. 195-96).

Comrade Pillai was a specialist in creating chaos and escaping unhurt. He represented a political movement which saw its regeneration. He was an ambitious politician who perfectly knew how to make meaningful movements as in a chess-board. He was well-versed in guiding and misguiding the factory workers basically keeping in mind his own vested interests. He never revealed his inner motives. Without coming out openly he knew how to create a hell out of heaven.

He was one who found pleasure in quoting chairman Mao in Malayalam : "Revolution is not a dinner party. Revolution is an insurrection, an act of violence in which one class overthrows another" (p. 280). Pillai also did play not an insignificant role in overthrowing and also destroying Velutha, who represented a class, that is, the oppressed.

II

Rahel had somehow thought that Comrade Pillai had been born middle aged with a receding hairline. He had practised vegetarianism and consequently his gums were startlingly pink. For Rahel "he was the kind of man whom it was hard to imagine had once been a boy. Or a baby" (p. 130). In his late thirtees he was an unathletic, sallow little man. "His legs were already spindly and his taut, distended belly, like his tiny mother's goitre, was completely at odds with the rest of his thin, narrow body and alert face" (p. 272). His neat pencil moustache divided his upper lip horizontally into half and ended exactly in line with the ends of his mouth. His hair was oiled and combed back off his forehead.

That much about his physical appearance. Something could be said about his room also. His SSLC, BA and MA certificates were framed and hung on one of the walls. On another wall was a framed photograph of Comrade Pillai garlanding Comrade E.M.S. Nambodiripad. There was a microphone on a stand, shining in the foreground. There was a rotating fan by the bed. In his room there was a placard which said work is struggle struggle is work. He was one who found pleasure in his knowledge of things that were international. He also took pride in telling others that his son Lenin was a genius. He also boasted that his son was standing first in class and that he would be getting double-promotion. He showed his vanity by saying that his wife understood English very well. But she didn't speak!

He was one who liked to outshine others. When Chacko once visited him at his house Pillai thought that "his straitened circumstances (his small, hot house, his grunting mother, his obvious proximity to the toiling masses) gave him a power over Chacko that in those revolutionary times no amount of Oxford education could match" (p. 275).

Pillai hated asking questions unless they were personal ones. He thought that questions signified a vulgar display of ignorance. He used 'I suppose' to disguise questions as statements. He disliked being addressed as "My Dear Fellow!" It sounded to him like an insult in good English which made it a double-insult. Once when Chacko addressed him in this manner he had almost expressed his displeasure at the way he addressed him.

Thus, Pillai would be described as a politician who knew how and where to strike. He was an ardent follower of the communist leader EMS and found pleasure in telling the world that his loyalty to the party was unquestionable. The fact that he wanted his son to recite lines from Shakespeare's *Julius Ceasar* and also the fact that he took pride in telling others that his wife would understand English would be taken as instances to prove that he was certainly not a down to earth communist.

Pillai was highly ambitious as a politician and he made careful movements to ensure that he would reach the corridors of power by hook or crook. He never had any prick of conscience in adopting any method to achieve this aim for he believed that the end would justify the means.

III

Pillai's political ambitions had been given an unexpected boost in early 1969. Comrade J. Kattukaran and Comrade Guhan Menon, two local party members had been expelled from the party as they were suspected to have connections with Naxalites. Comrade Menon was the prospective candidate for the by-elections for the Kottayam Legislative Assembly due next March. The expulsion of Comrade Menon created a vacuum in the party and a number of hopeful leaders made an all out effort to grab the unexpected position. Comrade Pillai also was in the fore-front to secure the party ticket.

As an aspiring politician, it was essential for Pillai to be seen in his chosen constituency as a man of influence. He made use of every opportunity to prove to the fellow workers and potential voters that he was influential. Once when Chacko paid a visit to him he struggled like anything to ensure that the people around would have a high impression about him. Pothachen and Mathukutty were two villagers who had asked him to use his connections at the Kottayam hospital to secure nursing jobs for their daughters. He sent for these people and made them wait outside for an appointment with him. The idea was that if they waited for sometime an impression would be created that he was very influential and that anyone would get a job with his recommendation. "The more people that were seen waiting to meet him, the busier he would appear, the better the impression he would make. And if the waiting people saw that the factory Modalali himself had come to see him, on *his* turf, he knew it would give off all sorts of useful signals" (p. 273).

Thus, when Lata, his elder brother's daughter from Kottayam arrived with Pothachen and Mathukutty, they were made to wait outside with the doors left ajar. When Pillai spoke next, he spoke in Malayalam and made sure that it was loud enough for his audience outside to hear. He said that the proper forum to air workers' grievances was through the Union and "when Modalali himself is a Comrade, it is a shameful matter for them not to be unionized and join the Party Struggle" (p. 280).

Comrade Pillai's political ambition made him crooked. It should be so also. One would remember in this context what Saleem told the children in Rushdie's (1981) novel : "Politics, children : at the best of times a bad dirty business. We should have avoided it, I should never have dreamed of purpose, I am coming to the conclusion that privacy, the small individual lives of men, are preferable to all this inflated macrocosmic activity" (p. 435). Though Pillai claimed himself to be a communist he was not able to prove himself so. On the other hand, he was one who believed that his son should get good English education and that his wife should speak English or at least understand English. He was making preparations to ensure that he did get a berth in the next Assembly elections.

As a trade union leader he was at his worst and was easily a master plotter. He did everything he could to spoil Chacko and his factory. For this he had his own links and he knew how to make best use of them.

IV

Chacko's Paradise Pickles factory gave Pillai a lot of opportunity to become a local leader. He had begun to watch the goings-on at the factory with the keenness of a substitute at a soccer match. "To bring in a new labour union, however, small, in what he hoped would be his future constituency, would be an excellent beginning for a journey to the Legislative Assembly" (p. 120).

In the evenings, after the factory shift was over Pillai way laid the workers of Paradise Pickles and led them into his printing press. He would make speeches in Malayalam which touched upon local and international issues. It was in the line of Maoist rhetoric. " 'People of the World', he would chirrup, be courageous, *dare* to fight, *defy* difficulties and advance wave upon wave. Then the whole world will belong to the People. Monsters of all kinds shall be destroyed" (p. 120). He wanted them to demand yearly bonus, Provident fund, accident insurance, etc. These speeches were in part rehearsal of the speech he would make as the local Member of the Legislative Assembly.

He continued to plot against Pillai though he never came out openly against him. Whenever he referred to him in speeches he was careful enough not to refer to particular persons. "He never referred to him by name, but always as 'the Management'. As though Chacko was many people" (p. 121). In a way this helped Comrade Pillai to keep his conscience clear about his own private business dealings with Chacko. He made a lot of money, which he badly needed, by getting the contract for printing the Paradise Pickles labels. Chacko would tell himself that Chacko-the-client and Chacko-the-Management were two different people. He also thought that Chacko-the-Comrade was quite different from these two.

Pillai stayed in constant touch with the workers. He made it a point to know what went on at the factory. He sometimes ridiculed the workers for accepting the wages, when their own government, the People's Government, was in power. Pillai had virtually waged a war against Chacko. Once he slowly came to know about Pillai's machinations he was compelled to declare : "I am going to formally organize them into a union. They will elect their own representatives" (p. 280). But Pillai challenged Chacko and said that he could not stage their revolution for them. According to him Chacko could only create awareness and educate them. They should launch their own struggle. Also, they should overcome their fears.

Pillai was cunning enough to bag the contract for the synthetic cooking vinegar labels. Once he achieved this "he deftly banished Chacko from the fighting ranks of the Overthrowers to the treacherous ranks of the To Be Overthrown" (p. 280). Nobody knew the exact nature of Comrade Pillai's role in the events that followed. Even Chacko failed to learn the whole story. It was not entirely Pillai's fault that "he lived in a society where a man's death could be more profitable than his life had ever been" (p. 281).

This man was Velutha and though Pillai did not plan the course of events he did slip "his ready fingers into History's waiting glove" (p. 281). Velutha's last visit to him after his confrontation with Mammachi and Baby Kochamma and what had passed between them remained a secret. But everybody would have guessed that Pillai had played his role very well in the whole episode.

V

Of all the workers at Paradise Pickles, Velutha was the only card-holding member of the party. That gave Pillai an ally he would rather have done without. He knew that all the other touchable workers in the factory resented Velutha for reasons of their own. Pillai was waiting to get a suitable opportunity to strike.

Pillai wanted to discuss the 'Velutha issue' with Chacko and it was taken up rather unexpectedly. When Chacko told him that Velutha had taken part in the worker's march "his mind hummed like the table fan. He wondered whether to make use of the opening that was being offered to him, or to leave it for another day. He decided to use it...." (p. 277). When Pillai said that

Velutha was a good worker and highly intelligent Chacko also fully agreed with him saying that he was an excellent carpenter with an engineer's mind. But Pillai immediately corrected him saying that he was talking about Velutha, the party worker.

Then came a warning from Pillai. He made it clear to Chacko that Velutha the Paravan was going to cause trouble for him. " 'Take it from me.... get him a job somewhere else. Send him off' " (p. 278). He further said that Velutha might be okay as a person. The problem was that other workers were not happy with him. They were going to him with complaints. He concluded by saying that the caste issues were very deep-rooted. Pillai's true colour came out when he told Chacko that even Kalyani, his wife and the mistress of his house would never allow Paravans into her house. That he was a hen-pecked husband was clear from his statements "*I* cannot persuade her. My own wife. Of course inside the house she is Boss" (p. 278).

Pillai's problem was that Velutha was given extra benefits by the management. The other workers were resenting it and they even saw it as a partiality. For them he was just a Paravan whatever job he did. So he cautioned him again : "'It is a conditioning they have from birth. This I myself have told them is wrong. But frankly speaking, Comrade, Change is one thing. Acceptance is another. You should be cautious. Better for him you send him off...'" (p. 279). Chacko was not willing to agree to this demand of Pillai and he described it as pure nonsense. Pillai was a little angry on hearing this. He said "'That may be ... But Rome was not built in a day. Keep it in mind, Comrade, that this is not your Oxford college. For you what is a nonsense for Masses it is something different'" (p. 279).

Pillai was certainly on the winning side as far as the Velutha issue was concerned. It turned out to be a war which ended before it began. "Victory was gifted to him wrapped and be-ribboned, on a silver tray. Only then, when it was too late, and Paradise Pickles slumped softly to the floor without so much as a murmur or even the pretence of resistance — did Comrade Pillai realize that what he really needed was the process of war more than the outcome of victory" (pp. 280-81).

Thus, Pillai was a hypocrite in the true sense of the word. On the one hand he would swear by the ideals of the party. But when it came to action it was just the opposite. His attitude is more than clear when Velutha whom he described as a good and intelligent party worker approached him when his life was almost in danger. Pillai was trying to convince him that individual interest was not very important when party interests were at stake.

VI

Velutha approached Pillai with a request to help him after he was humiliated by Mammachi and Baby Kochamma. Whatever Velutha told him did not make any effect on him. The only point Pillai tried to stress was that Party was not constituted to support worker's indiscipline. "Velutha watched Comrade Pillai's body fade from the door. His disembodied, piping voice stayed on and sent out slogans. Pennants fluttering in an empty doorway.

It is not in the Party's interests to take up such matters.

Individuals' interest is subordinate to the organization's interest.

Violating Party Discipline means violating Party Unity

The voice went on. Sentences disaggregated into phrases.

Words.

Progress of the Revolution

Annihilation of the Class Enemy

Comprador capitalist

Spring-thunder.

And there it was again. Another religion turned against itself. Another edifice constructed by the human mind, decimated by human nature" (p. 287).

The last thing he did was to shut the door and return to his wife. Velutha's fate was sealed then and there. When Baby Kochamma falsely implicated Velutha and made a request to the Police Inspector to take action against him, the first thing he did was to send a jeep to bring Comrade Pillai. It was important for him to know whether the Paravan had any political support. "The two men had a conversation. Brief, cryptic, to the point. As though they had exchanged numbers and not words. No explanations seemed necessary. They were not friends, Comrade Pillai and Inspector Thomas Mathew, and they didn't trust each other. But they understood each other perfectly" (p. 262).

Comrade Pillai told Inspector Thomas Mathew that he was acquainted with Velutha, but never mentioned that he was a member of the Communist Party or that he had knocked on his door late the previous night, which made him the last person to have seen Velutha before he disappeared. Pillai also did not refute the allegation of attempted rape in Baby Kochamma's FIR. The only thing that Pillai tried to emphasise was that Velutha did not enjoy the patronage or the protection of the Communist Party. It was a clear betrayal of a worker who was loyal to the core to the Party. The Inspector got a clear signal and ultimately Velutha had to find his solace in the pauper's pit where the police routinely dumped the dead.

VII

Thus, Pillai would appear to the reader to be the real villain in the novel. The novel could be looked upon as having an angle where it could be described as a political satire. The two persons who took pride in claiming that they were communists were Chacko and Pillai. Chacko was able to prove towards the end of the novel that he was rather sincere about whatever he said.

But Pillai was altogether a different person. He had his own axes to grind and he made every movement in his political chessboard very carefully. Ultimately his ambition was to become a Member of the Legislative Assembly.

To attain his goal organizing workers was only a means. But somehow he made them believe that he was sincere as a trade union or party leader. That was what helped him to take his workers for a ride.

He was a true 'Pillai' who looked down upon Velutha, a Paravan. His wife also had her own reservations about the entry of Velutha to their house. He even took pride in telling Chacko that she didn't like a Paravan's presence in her house.

The attitude of Pillai to issues and persons would not be

complete without a discussion of the relation he had with Rahel and Estha. When the twins were in their younger days Comrade Pillai used to show interest in them.

It was he who had introduced Kathakali to Estha and Rahel. He would take them and his own son Lenin for all night-performances at the temple. They would sit till dawn and he would explain to them the language and gesture of Kathakali : "It was he who had introduced them to Raudra Bhima — crazed, bloodthirsty Bhima in search of death and vengeance. "'He is searching for the beast that lives in him', Comrade Pillai had told them — frightened, wide-eyed children — when the ordinarily good-natured Bhima began to bay and snarl"' (p. 236).

But when Estha and Rahel had come back to Ayemenem after a long gap of about twenty-three years it was a different Pillai who was before them. When he enquired in his piping voice whether they continued to have interest in Indian culture and expressed great happiness at it, he was more than sarcastic. The twins could easily see what was going on in his mind. Still they were neither rude nor polite to him and walked away without saying anything.

Estha sometimes walked past his printing press which was once the Ayemenem office of the Communist Party "where midnight study meetings were held, and pamphlets with rousing lyrics of Marxist Party songs were printed and distributed" (p. 13). The flag that fluttered on the roof had grown limp. Pillai used to come out of his house and greet him. But Estha would walk past, not rude, not politie, just quiet. He was unable to tell whether Estha recognized him after all those years or not.

Again it was Comrade Pillai who was the first person in Ayemenem to hear of Rahel's return. "The news didn't perturb him as much as excite his curiosity" (p. 14). Whereas Estha was almost a stranger to him Rahel was not. He knew her well and he had watched her grow up. He began to wonder what had brought her back after all those years.

On their first meeting after she came back to Ayemenem Pillai had reintroduced himself as Comrade Uncle to her. She said that she did remember him. But "neither question nor answer was meant as anything more than a polite preamble to conversation. Both she and he knew that there are things that can be forgotten. And things that cannot — that sit on dusty shelves like stuffed birds with baleful, sideways staring eyes" (p. 128-29).

Pillai asked Rahel a series of questions the answers of which were brimming with irony. When Pillai asked her whether she was in America she answered in the negative and said that she was in Ayemenem. Then he asked her about her husband. When she replied that he hadn't come he enquired whether any photos were available. He also asked her husband's name, details about the children they had etc. When she told him that she had no children and she had got a divorce from her husband "his voice rose to such a high register that it cracked on the question mark. He even pronounced the word as though it were a form of death" (p. 130) and described it as most unfortunate. His vanity overtook him immediately and he told Rahel that his son Lenin was in Delhi working with foreign embassy. Then he handed Rahel a Cellophane sachet with photograph of Lenin and his family. He had a wife, a child and also a new Bajaj Scooter. He also showed her a photograph in which Lenin, Estha, Sophie Mol and herself were there.

Comrade Pillai's ways and how he treated people would certainly be clear from his attitude to Rahel and Estha. He did not want to spare them even twenty-three years after the tragedy struck Ayemenem. He got a kind of sadistic pleasure from asking inconvenient questions and putting people in embarrassing situations. The Chameleon like Pillai as one would expect, might never change from the identity that he had developed over the years.

VIII

Comrade Pillai thus, would stand before the readers as a cunning politician well versed in fishing out of troubled waters. He was one who was an expert in changing even the most unfavourable circumstance to his advantage. He was more than a hypocrite who never cared about other's feelings. He did not possess any human qualities and human lives for him were "flies to wanton boys." He would happily be a party to kill them for his sport.

Rahel had known him ever since she was a young girl and she was in full control of herself even when provocation came form him. Estha, on the other hand, was beyond what was happening around him and so was not required to react to the observations Pillai made about him or his twin sister.

The ambitious Pillai left no stone unturned to grab whatever opportunities came his way. The workers who failed to see his real motives were only toys in his hands. Velutha, the loyal worker, was the one who he thought would be a problem maker. For the same reason he was too happy to tell the Inspector that Velutha was independent without any party connections.

Pillai was also known for his sexual weakness. Sometimes he would find his own wife sexy. When Velutha made his last visit to Pillai, he had just finished his "avial" (a dish) and when his wife returned to tell him that the person who had knocked the door was Velutha his immediate instinct was to touch his wife Kalyani's breast. What prevented him from doing it was the curd on his fingers!

He got immense pleasure when Chacko was in a predicament. He wonderfully managed the whole show without giving others any scope to suspect him. That was exactly the reason why even Chacko never came to know about the whole story when the Marxist Party made a siege of Paradise Pickles factory.

In short, Comrade Pillai certainly would stand out in the novel as a spokesman of the unscrupulous politicians around us who would never bother about ethics and niceties to be followed in life. Ironically enough some kind of "poetic injustice" would be discernible for the readers who fail to see the guilty punished at a time when even innocents were put on trial.

14

Politeness, Obedience, Loyalty.....

I

Very often a distinction is made between the novels where events get greater focus and novels where characters get greater attention. These two kinds are likely to be blended also. There are some novelists who address themselves to the contemporary social and political issues. In *The God of Small Things* it can undoubtedly be said that Roy is quite successful as a writer whose eyes and ears are fully open to see and hear what goes on around her.

The novelist is very critical of the functioning of some of the government departments in the novel. The sharpest attack is on the police department. The police who generally should be polite, obedient, loyal, intelligent, courteous and efficient are found innocent of these qualities. Their treatment of the helpless people can simply be described as cruel and their action may be described as heartless.

Apart from Police some other governmental agencies also come under attack in the novel. The PWD, the Airport Authority etc. are only some of the agencies the novelist criticises in the novel. She is also critical of the kind of education that is given in the Convents.

II

The novelist is certainly sharpest in her criticism of the police. The indifference of the government in maintaining hygienic condition in the police station is highlighted in more than one place in the novel. How foul smelling the station premises can be is clear from the description "anticipating the sharp, smoky stink of old urine that permeated the walls and furniture, they clamped their nostrils shut well before the smell began" (p. 7). After the funeral of Sophie Mol Ammu went to the Kottayam police station with Estha and Rahel and their immediate reaction is described in these words.

How insecure women are in the hands of the protectors of law is clear from the way Inspector Thomas Mathew treats Ammu. Thomas Mathew with his sly and greedy eyes stared at Ammu's breast as he spoke. He did not stop there. He called her 'veshya' and tapped her breast with his baton gently as though he was choosing mangoes from a basket. Ammu was helpless and she had to suffer the humiliation passively, like any other woman who would be placed in such a predicament. The irony of the situation is that there is a mute witness to whatever takes place in the police station in the name of maintaining law and order. That was the red and blue board which said :

Politeness
Obedience
Loyalty
Intelligence
Courtesy
Efficiency.

There is an account in the novel of Ammu dreaming of the night previous to her death. The theme is police atrocity. "She had woken up at night to escape from a familiar, recurrent dream in which policemen approached her with snicking scissors, wanting to hack off her hair" (p. 161). The Kottayam police did that in Kottayam to prostitutes whom they had caught in the *bazaar*. They branded them as prostitutes and new policemen would easily identify them. Ammu used to notice them in the market, "the women with vacant eyes and forcibly shaved heads in the land where long, oiled hair was only for the morally upright" (p. 161).

The police atrocity was at its worst when Velutha was taken to custody. They almost changed the human being Velutha into a pulp. His ribs were broken, skull fractured, nose and cheek bones smashed, half a dozen teeth broken, lower intestine was ruptured and haemorrhaged and almost all his vital organs knew the 'taste' of the boots of the policemen. They did all this without sufficient evidence against Velutha for having committed any crime.

We have also instances in the novel where the police prove themselves to be master manipulators. To finish off Velutha they sent for Comrade Pillai from whom they wanted a statement disowning Velutha. This they easily got and that served as a green signal to torture him to death. Also, when the police saw that their position was untenable once Ammu made the confession, they made Estha, the innocent boy tell a lie that Velutha had a role in abducting them. All these show how an important government department worked in the state.

Thus, the protectors of law who find pleasure in taking Coca-cola, torturing to death the innocents and humiliating and seducing women are severally attacked by the novelist. The police department could never escape from controversy irrespective of the combinations of political parties which ruled the state. But more than political interference unethical work culture gets highlighted in the novel.

III

Another government department which is attacked in the novel is Public Works Department. In the very first page of the novel there is a reference to small fish appearing in the puddles that fill the PWD potholes on the highways. The state highways have been notorious for their poor maintenance and during the rainy reason which lasts for about four months the road journey in the state has always been a problem. It is quite natural that this becomes an issue in the novel.

The novelist is also critical of the zebra crossing. Estha and Rahel, according to her, believed that if they were killed on a zebra crossing, the government would pay for their funerals. They had the definite impression that zebra crossings were meant for people to get killed. "Free funerals. Of course there were no zebra crossings to get killed on in Ayemenem, or, for that matter, even in Kottayam, which was the nearest town, but they'd seen some from the car window when they went to Cochin, which was a two hour drive away" (p. 4).

A reference to the poor maintenance of the PWD roads appears in the later part of the novel also. Ammu fell dead in a lodge in Alleppey and her body was taken to the electric crematorium in a van. Ammu's body was reported to have jiggled and slid off the stretcher over the jarring bumps and potholes on the road. Her head even hit an iron bolt on the floor. So roads remained the same whether in Ayemenem, Cochin or Alleppey.

Even the crematorium is not free from attack in the novel. It is compared to a railway station, the common feature being rotten, run-down air. Unlike the railway station there were no trains and no crowds to make the crematorium busy. "Nobody except beggars, derelicts and the police-custody dead were cremated there. People who died with nobody to lie at the back of them and talk to them" (p. 162).

Airport is the next target of the novelist's attack. It is compared to a local bus depot. The building was noted for the birdshit and there were spitstains on the kangeroos — all this in a state which claimed itself to be God's own land. "*Oho! Going to the dogs India is*" (p. 140). That is what the novelist tells herself as an aside about the whole thing. There is also an indication that the airport premises have established a notoriety as a nerve centre of eaves droppers.

There is in the novel the story of an electrocuted elephant. Obviously it is the indifference of the Electricity Board that is criticized here. More than that the engineers of the Municipality also are not spared. They "sawed off the tusks and shared them unofficially. Unequally" (pp. 219-20), it is reported. Killing elephants to take possession of ivory has often been in the news and the novelist reacts to this through this incident.

The novelist's effort to highlight some of these problems would remind one of Raymond Williams and his celebrated work *The*

Long Revolution (1966) which ends with a plea that art should not be seen as a "separate order" but as a means of social communication (p. 39). Apart from developing her characters and narrating the story through these characters, Roy has certainly aimed at a sort of social communication in the novel in which she is completely successful.

The novel is perhaps noted for its criticism of the system of education that prevails in the country. Both Rahel and Estha suffered at the hands of the school authorities for different reasons. While Rahel was expelled from the school a couple of times for reasons which Rahel felt to be ridiculous, Estha also did not get good treatment at the hands of the school authorities. He was stamped as one who did not participate in group activities though they never said what they meant by it.

Thus, we find a number of government departments and other agencies being sharply criticized in the novel. Whereas, the PWD is under attack for shirking from their responsibilities, zero crossing is described as a death trap. The corrupt officials who make money using devious means are not spared. The airport authorities are taken to task for the poor maintenance of the airports and school authorities are criticized for being unkind to their students.

IV

In a series of essays beginning with "The Art of Fiction" and the introductory essays to his collected novels, Henry James articulates his sense of the importance of the novel as an art form. He tries to remove the novel from the threat of simplistic evaluation as either moral instruction or light entertainment. He says that a novel cannot express "a conscious moral purpose." "A novel" he argues, "is in its broadest definition a personal, a direct impression of life : that, to begin with constitutes its value" [Quoted from Kreshner (1997)].

One can never make a simplistic evaluation of the novel under discussion. There is no moral instruction or light entertainment and what remains of it is a personal and direct impression of life. Thus, the roads lying in poor condition or airport remaining shabby are all looked at from a purely personal point of view. That there will be an improvement in the situation described here is something one cannot say for certain. Even though the drawbacks of certain educational institutions are highlighted, there is no guarantee that the schools are going to improve. Probably the novelist never expects the situation to change.

In her essay "Modern Fiction" (1919) Virginia Woolf affirms that "life is not a series of gig lamps symmetrically arranged, but a luminous halo, a semi-transparent envelope surrounding us from the beginning of consciousness to the end." It is the modern novelist's task to "record the atoms as they fall upon the mind," however, foggy or apparently chaotic the result may be [Quoted from Kershner (1997, pp. 15-16)].

Roy in her novel is doing exactly the same. When the police is mercilessly attacked she is describing a chaotic situation where the protectors of individual's rights move in the opposite direction. The officials who should be upright in their dealings are shown in poor light. The airports which should be noted for their cleanliness are far from being so. So it is on the whole a completely chaotic situation that is portrayed by the novelist. Since the novelist's task is to record the things as they fall upon her mind, she does the same thing in the novel.

15

Unadulterated Effluents

I

Ian Watt (1957) sees as the basic characteristic of the novel its use of "formal realism." By this term he means to point to a group of "narrative procedures" that includes the abandoning of traditional plots and "purple patches" of rhetoric and the stress on developing individual characters and situations so that time, place, person and even causation are given a new particularity. He develops the idea that the rise of the novel is bound up intimately with the rise of the middle class and middle class individualism, with all the accompaniments of that social movement : the growth of capitalism.... the growing influence of the commercial and industrial segments of society....

The present novel fits in very well to this classification. The rise of the middle-class and middle-class individualism get greater focus and the influence of the commercial and industrial segments of society is very much evident. That is why we have descriptions like "unadulterated factory effluents" in the novel. The contemporary society is beautifully portrayed in the novel where several issues are discussed by the novelist.

The ecological problem is only one among the several issues dealt with in the novel. Untouchability, snobbery, urbanization, the effect of the Gulf money, cultural decadence, marginalization of women and homosexuality are some of the other problems which get highlighted.

II

Untouchability is certainly a major theme in the novel. Velutha who can be considered the central figure is made to suffer for the only reason that he is an untouchable. There is a reference in the novel to a village school that Estha's great-grandfather built for untouchable children. Being a Paravan he and his father never got an entry to the Ayemenem house. There is also a reference to the Paravans crawling on their back.

The police are referred to as making a distinction between what is touchable and what is not. The theme of untouchability recurs as the activities of the police are discussed in the novel. Thus, we have descriptions like "the policemen stopped and fanned out. They didn't really need to, but they liked these Touchable games", "then together, on their knees and elbows, they crept towards the house. Like Film-policemen. Softly, softly through the grass. Batons in their hands. Machine-guns in their minds. Responsibility for the Touchable future on their thin but able shoulders" (p. 307). A further evidence we get towards the end of the novel : "The Touchable policemen didn't tear out his hair or burn him alive. They didn't hack off his genitals and stuff them in his mouth. They didn't rape him. Or behead him" (p. 309).

Comrade Pillai who often claimed to have stood by Marxist ideology which lays stress on equality never hesitated to treat Velutha, an ardent supporter of the party as an outcaste. When he had problems with his own workers taking exception to the special treatment given to Velutha his reaction to Chacko was as follows : "He may be very well okay as a person. But other workers are not happy with him. Already they are coming to me with complaints.... you see, Comrade, from local stand point, these caste issues are very deep-rooted"' (p. 278). Even his wife never allowed Paravans into her house. And Pillai couldn't ever persuade her also.

Thus, when we look at the contemporary life as portrayed in the novel, it is certainly untouchability that gets prime importance. The whole tragedy was triggered as Ammu had relations with Velutha, an untouchable. He remains in the novel as a representative of a section in the society who continued to suffer at the hands of the privileged and the uptrodden for centuries.

Another dominant theme that gets focus in the novel is environmental problems. E.M. Forster who is often referred to as a reluctant traditionalist has admitted "oh dear, yes — the novel tells a story". But felt that its most fundamental aspect "could be something different — melody, or perception of the truth...."(1927-p. 45). What is attempted in the present novel is a truthful account of the ills of the society.

III

The first reference to environmental problems we get in the very first chapter of the novel. Estha used to walk "along the river that smelled of shit, and pesticides bought with World Bank loans. Most of the fish had died. The ones that survived suffered from fin-rot and had broken out in boils" (p. 13). The novelist is here critical of the hands behind polluting the river and the policy of the government buying pesticides with World Bank, both of which will ultimately contribute in making the life of the people miserable.

Another reference to the polluted river we get in the fifth chapter of the novel where God's own country gets the notoriety of children defecating directly onto the riverbed. "The river would rouse itself to accept the day's offerings and sludge off to the sea, leaving wavy lines of thick white scum in its wake" (p. 125).

On warm days the smell of shit would lift off the river and hover over Ayemenem like a hat according to the novelist. To screen off the slum and prevent it from encroaching on Kari Saipu's estate a tall wall was built. But nothing could be done about the foul smell that permeated. Thus, it was a smelly paradise. The five-star hotel people called it 'God's own country' in their brochures because they knew that "smelliness, like other people's poverty, was merely a matter of getting used to. A question of discipline. Of Rigour and Air-conditioning. Nothing more" (p. 126).

When Rahel returned to the river after a gap of so many

years what greeted her was a river "with a ghastly skull's smile, with holes where teeth had been and a limp hand raised from a hospital bed" (p. 124). In spite of the fact that it was June and raining, the river was no more than a swollen drain : "A thin ribbon of thick water that lapped wearily at the mud banks on either side, sequinned with the occasional silver slant of a dead fish. It was choked with a succulent weed, whose furred brown roots waved like thin tentacles under water" (p. 124). The clean mothers washed clothes and pots in unadulterated factory effluents!

Van Ghent (1956) has claimed that "the subject matter of novels is human relationships in which are shown the directions of men's souls." Her interest in Gestalt psychology leads to her vision of the novel as a psychologically convincing "world" : she believes that good novels have "integral structure" and also have individual character and each is judged by "the cogency and illuminative quality of the view of life that it affords" (pp. 3,6,7). Certainly Roy's novel is a good novel in the sense in which Van Ghent uses the term. What strikes us most here is the view of life that Roy has when she discusses the environmental problems.

The impact of the Gulf money on the people of Kerala is yet another factor which dominates the discussion of the contemporary society in the novel. In Kerala there is a unique situation where in every other family there will be a person working in the Gulf countries which naturally has a tremendous impact on the social life.

IV

In the opening chapter of the novel we find Estha walking past "the new, freshly baked, iced, Gulf-money houses built by nurses, masons, wire-benders and bank clerks who worked hard and unhappily in faraway places" (p. 13). The money that flowed from the Gulf countries have totally changed the complexion of the houses. The irony of the situation is that all those who were working abroad lived an unhappy life where as their dependents lived a rather happy life in their native place.

In the sixth chapter also there is a discussion on Gulf

related matters. When the Bombay-Kochin flight landed at Cochin airport the families of the Foreign Returnees had come to meet them. They were all there in the Arrivals Lounge : "the deaf ammoomas, the cantankerous, arthritic appoopans, the pining wives, scheming uncles, children with the runs. The fiancees to be reassessed. The teacher's husband still waiting for his Saudi visa. The teacher's husband's sisters waiting for their dowries. The wire-bender's pregnant wife" (p. 138). The families of the Returnees had come from allover Kerala to meet them. Some of them had camped at the airport overnight, and had brought their food with them, tapioca chips and "chakka velaichathu." This would certainly be a common sight in the airports in Kerala and one need not look for more pieces of evidence to establish that the effect of Gulf continued to be tremendous in Kerala.

What awaited the Foreign Returnees would be desperation : "When long bus journeys, and overnight stays at the airport, were met by love and a lick of shame, small cracks appeared, which would grow and grow, and before they knew it, the Foreign Returnees would be trapped outside the History House and have their dreams redreamed" (pp. 140-41).

But apparently they all looked fresh and all right. They were in wash'n' wear suits and rainbow sunglasses. "With an end to grinding poverty in their Aristocrat suitcases. With cement roofs for their thatched houses, and geysers for their parents' bathrooms. With sewage systems and septic tanks. Maxis and high heels. Puff sleeves and lipstick. Mixy-grinders and automatic flashes for their cameras. With keys to count, and cupboards to lock" (p. 140).

Booth (1961) sees the genre of novel as an imitation of the real world, in the rich sense in which Aristotle uses the term 'imitation'. Roy's novel can be easily described as a novel which imitates the real world. The contemporary society appears in the novel in a rather realistic way and the influence of the Gulf money on the social life of the people of Kerala can only be described as something more than near to reality. People have changed their life styles and they bid goodbye to conventional houses only to enjoy a totally new life.

A related issue that should be taken up for discussion along with the influence of Gulf money on the people of Kerala is urbanization. Barthes (1968) is of the view that "a text consists not of a line of words, releasing a single 'theological' meaning (the 'message' of the Author-God), but of a multi-dimensional space in which are married and contested several writings, none of which is original" (pp. 52-53). Roy's novel can perhaps be interpreted as subscribing to the view expressed by Barthes in the sense that there is a multi-dimensional space. Thus, urbanization is only one of the dimensions that the novel lays focus on.

V

In the opening chapter of the novel there is reference to Baby Kochamma abandoning her ornamental garden. The reason for the dumping was a new love. She had installed a dish antenna on the roof of Ayemenem house. This is certainly a symbol of urbanization. Wars, famines, massacres, Bill Clinton etc. could be summoned up like servants. In Kerala dish antennas have become a very common sight and generally the phenomenon is considered as a symbol of urbanization.

In Ayemenem house the pieces of furniture include Ooty cupboards, plastic basket chairs, Delhi beds and dressing table from Vienna. This means that the Ayemenem house has been urbanized. Baby Kochamma had her paint-flaking fridge in which she had put the dozen or so bottles of insulin that Rahel brought her in the cheese and butter compartments.

In the second chapter we find Chacko, Rahel and others staying at Hotel Sea Queen on their way to the airport. That they have chosen a posh hotel for the stay is an indication that the villagers are no more leading a rustic life. They prefer an urban life with all its comforts and privileges. John Stevenson (1984) has discussed how the "laboring classes" and the middle class were engaged in non-agricultural manufacturing and production. Urbanization was a fall out to this. Major cities had expanded into metropolises and smaller cities had grown at the expense of the countryside. In Roy's novel also such a situation is very much noticeable. Ayemenem village had grown into a town and the people migrate to Cochin, the nearby metropolis.

The references to high heels, puff sleeves and lipstick and other modern comforts in the houses of the Foreign Returnees also can be taken as instances of urbanization in the Ayemenem village. Naipaul (1967) in what critics have termed the "Naipaui fallacy" has implied that colonization has an overwhelming cultural experience that it leaves the colonized permanently disabled, attempting to mimic the metropolitan culture that has swamped them where they stand on the periphery. India too had a story of colonization to tell and Kerala being a state of this country cannot excape from what Naipaul calls the disabled attempting to mimic the metropolitan culture.

Also, there is in the novel reference to the use of inexpensive perfume used by elderly women in Ayemenem house. A big cake with 'Welcome Home, Our Sophie Mol' written on it awaited Sophie Mol's arrival which again is a further piece of evidence in favour of urbanization. That pornographic magazines have reached Ayemenem village is significant and can only be seen as part of this.

Another important step towards urbanization was the renovation of Kari Saipu's house. "It had become the centre piece of an elaborate complex, crisscrossed with artificial canals and connecting bridges..... The old colonial bungalow with its deep verandah and Doric columns, was surrounded by smaller, old, wooden houses — ancestral homes — that the hotel chain had bought from old families and transplanted in the Heart of Darkness. Toy Histories for rich tourists to play in... 'Heritage', the hotel was called" (p. 126).

The craze for English can also be taken as something which is part of urbanization. Comrade Pillai had his son Lenin repeat the lines from Shakespeare's *Julius Ceasar* which would certainly be out of place in a village context. Also his observation that his wife would understand whatever was said in English could also be viewed as the effect of urbanization in the Ayemenem village. The irony of it all lay in the fact that Lenin who was only six year old shouted the lines without faltering even once without understanding even a word of it! Craze for English medium and teaching young children of three or four in this medium has become a routine affair.

In short, urbanization is one of the major themes of the novel and most of the characters are victims to it. It plays a major role in the social life of Ayemenem which was only a small village earlier. That Coco-Cola had found a place even in police stations speaks volumes about how fast urbanization is taking place. Villages become towns and towns become metropolis in no time. Sometimes one would even find it difficult to draw the dividing line between a village and a town, a town and a small city and a small city and a metropolis.

Something which has very much to do with urbanization might be cultural decadence. The novel has evidence to show that cultural life has suffered a set back in and around the village of Ayemenem.

VI

What would perhaps come immediately to one's mind when one talks of cultural decadence is the level to which Kathakali, an important art form of Kerala had fallen. Instead of Kathakali there was 'truncated Kathakali'. In the name of giving some regional flavour, the tourists of 'Heritage' were treated to this performance. The hotel people explained to the dancers that they were to perform 'small attention spans'. What ultimately happened was that ancient stories were collapsed and amputated and six-hour classics were slashed to twenty-minute cameos.

Whatever had happened to Kathakali had happened to Kathakali artist as well. He was also 'truncated' in certain sense of the term. He had become unviable, unfeasible and condemned goods. Their children derided him "They long to be everything that he is not. He has watched them grow up to become clerks and bus conductors. Class IV non-gazetted officers. With unions of their own" (p. 230). This fate awaited a man whose body was his soul and his only instrument. "From the age of three it has been planed and polished, pared down, harnessed wholly to the task of story-telling. He has magic in him, this man within the painted mask and swirling skirts" (p. 230).

The situation was such that he left dangling somewhere

between heaven and earth. He was not able to do what they were doing. He failed to slide down the aisles of buses, counting change and selling tickets. "He cannot answer bells that summon him. He cannot stoop behind trays of tea nad Marie biscuits" (p. 230). In despair he would turn to tourism, enter the market and hawk the only thing he owned, the stories that his body could tell.

But "in the Heart of Darkness they mock him with their lolling nakedness and their imported attention spans. He checks his rage and dances for them. He collects his fee. He gets drunk. Or smokes a joint. Good Kerala grass. It makes him laugh. Then he stops by the Ayemenem Temple, he and the others with him, and they dance to ask pardon of the gods" (p. 231). Sometimes the Kathakali artist would be stoned all because of the tattered and darned skirt, crowns with hollows and bald velvet blouse. As an irony of fate the Kathakali man would go back and beat his wife after taking off his make-up. Even Kunti, the soft one with breasts would do the same thing.

Youth Festivals have been very much part of the Kerala cultural scene. The competition takes place more between the parents of the participants than between the participants themselves. In the novel there is an indirect reference to the deterioration taking place in the largest cultural event in the state. Latha, the niece of Comrade Pillai who won the first prize for elocution at the youth Festival in Trivandrum was asked to do the recitation for Chacko. She complied without hesitation. Sir Walter Scott's poem "Lochinvar" was recited and at first Chacko even thought that it was a Malayalam translation of 'Lochinvar'. "The words ran into each other. The last syllable of one word attached itself to the first syllable of the next. It was rendered at remarkable speed" (p. 271). If this was the way one who got the first prize at the state level competition performed one can easily imagine the standard of the youth festivals being conducted with great fanfare.

Another major instance of cultural decadence would be seen in the attitude of the different people to marriage and sex. Baby Kochamma loved Father Mulligan, a priest with no success. Pappachi found pleasure in beating his wife as daily affair. Chacko had affairs with a number of women workers. Ammu narrowly escaped from the hands of the English manager of her husband's company. She was drawn to Velutha to have sexual relations. Margaret Kochamma gave up her first husband and went after another one. Rahel's married life also lasted for a very brief period. All these show that marriage as an institution falls from its old grace which ultimately shows how the old culture gives place to new.

In short, the contemporary cultural scene as portrayed in the novel is far from satisfactory. As the novelist remarks in the sixth chapter of the novel the feeling one gets is that India (and of course Kerala) is going to the dogs. Basically all these have also to do with the social and economic life of the people. In the main money plays a very important role. The influence of the electronic media also may be playing a role to make matters worse.

Several other aspects of the contemporary society gets delineated in the novel. Next, we shall have a cursory glance at some of the other issues which are focussed in the novel. To begin with marginalisation of women, will be considered.

VII

The first evidence of marginalization of women we get in the second chapter of the novel. Pappachi, Ammu's father had thought that college education was an unnecessary expense for a girl. For the same reason she was never sent to a college.

Kalyani, Pillai's wife referred to her husband as *addeham* which is an honorofic form of 'he', whereas, when he addressed her there was no respectful form of 'she'. He called her *edi*, which was approximately 'Hey, you!'

When Chacko called on Pillai at his house to discuss his business matters he smiled and nodded a greeting to Chacko, but did not acknowledge the presence of his wife or his mother who were there.

More importantly there was a commonly held view that a married daughter had no position in her parent's house. Thus, Baby Kochamma strongly believed that Ammu had no place in the Ayemenem house. Ammu did as much work in the factory as Chacko but he always referred to the factory as "my pineapples, my pickles" because legally Ammu, as a daughter had no claim to the property. This made Ammu use the term "wonderful male Chauvinist society" to refer to the society where she lived.

Mammachi had kept ready a back door for Chacko to meet his 'man's needs'. She even encouraged it by paying money to the women labourers with whom Chacko had an affair. But when it came to Ammu, her own daughter it was an entirely different set of rules. When it was discovered that she had an affair with Velutha, Mammachi, Baby Kochamma and Chacko joined hands to push Ammu out of the house. Clearly this is a kind of marginalization of the second sex.

As de Beauvoir (1982) put it "women lack concrete means for organizing themselves into a unit which can stand face to face with the correlative unit. They have no past, no history, no religion of their own, and they have no such solidarity of work and interest as that of the proletariat..... They live dispersed among the males, attached through residence, house work, economic condition, and social standing to certain men — fathers or husbands — more firmly than they are to other women" (p. 19). This situation is reflected in the novel at least in the treatment of some of the women characters.

The other issues which get focussed in the novel include among others the state of affairs of religion. The novelist, we find, is critical of religious leaders and she takes every opportunity to denounce their ways which she finds unacceptable to her.

VIII

There are several instances in the novel where religion comes under attack. In the opening chapter there is a reference to the sad priests who dust out "their curly beards with goldringed fingers as though hidden spiders had spun sudden cobwebs in them" (p. 6). May be, it is not clear to the novelist (and of course, also to the readers) why the priest should wear gold rings.

Nazreth Convent appears in the novel as a notorious institution. Rahel was backlisted in the school at the age of eleven, when she was caught outside her Housemistress's garden gate decorating a knob of fresh cowdung with small flowers. In that Christian institution, "breasts were not acknowledged" and were not supposed to exist. When Rahel admitted that she had collided with her seniors to find out whether breasts would hurt she was shown the door. If breasts did not exist where was the question of their hurting?

Baby Kochamma had fallen in love with Father Mulligan, who was a handsome young Irish monk. He was studying Hindu scriptures in order to criticize it. Missionary work has often been criticized and there were even complaints that missionary work often leads to converting people belonging to other religions. Probably the novelist is fully aware of the trend that has been there. Father Mulligan was drawn to the "kissable mouth and blazing coal-black eyes" of Baby Kochamma.

The novel also describes how senior sisters monopolized in asking questions to the priests. Indirectly Roy criticises whatever unholy things take place in the name of religion. In the second page of the novel itself the novelist criticizes the orthodox Bishops who "frequently visited the Ayemenem house for donations" (p. 2). Visiting houses for donations is a typical Kerala feature and it is a very common sight to see the political parties vying with one another to fill their coffers. Here the only difference is that it is religious leaders instead of political leaders.

The refusal to bury Ammu's body in the church cemetery is another instance where the contemporary religious leaders are exposed. The bone of contention was that Ammu had an affair with Velutha, who was an untouchable. Christianity was intolerant to such actions which the novelist perhaps chooses to disagree with.

In short, contemporary religion does not occupy an enviable position in the eyes of the novelist. For the same reason she takes every opportunity to criticize it rather mercilessly.

The novel helps quite a lot to know about the human relationship in the contemporary society. When the different characters are considered individually what comes to one's mind is that the human relations are attached no significance in the society portrayed in the novel.

IX

Roy's society is one of ex-wife, ex-nun, depravity, strained relations and so on. Rahel and Estha who were twins thought alike and did not have much problems when it came to the relations between them. But the children did have problems in the relations with their mother. In other words there was no peaceful existence between the mother and the children.

Rahel was stamped as a deprived child and this should be taken as an evidence to show that all was not well with others in their relation with her. She had to grow up as a neglected child. Even when she grew up, there was no one to arrange her marriage.

Estha, at least a couple of times, was more like a football than a human being. He was returned to his father after the incident in which Sophie Mol got killed. He was re-returned about twenty-three years later. He also suffered quite a lot due to depravity.

We also hear about 'biological father' and 'real father' in the novel. To Sophie Mol Chacko was only a biological father and she loved only her other father. Margaret Kochamma became his Ex-wife very soon after his marriage, she herself being one who did not attach much importance to the institution of marriage. The same was the case with Rahel whose married life also did not last for long.

Mammachi, somehow, could not maintain a good relation with Pappachi, her husband. She was not very good to her daughter either. Chacko was never a good brother to Ammu and her relation with him was strained and she always thought him to be a male "chauvinistic pig". Baby Kochamma was envious of Ammu and so naturally she never did love her.

Initially even Sophie Mol did not love the twins but as she knew them closer there was a perceptible change. But her life was for a very brief period and the good relation did not have a lasting effect.

But Velutha loved the twins and Sophie Mol. He was very good to them and they returned their love. But this was something against the relation in the mainstream and they were not at liberty to show their love publicly. Still the intensity in the love between them was something that had no parallel in the novel.

In short, it is a world of contradictions. Human relations, somehow, never get any importance in the society which Roy portrays. The characters have their own problems and as a rule they are not allowed to establish good relations by the invisible hand of fate.

Roy's society, it can be seen is a sex-starved one. Both homosexuality and heterosexuality are described in the novel in some detail. A large number of characters in the novel get themselves involved in sexual affairs which appear to be unnatural or illegal.

X

The only instance of homosexuality reported in the novel is the one between the Orangedrink Lemondrink Man and Estha. Infact, Estha was totally innocent and he was falling a prey into the hands of the other man. It was his strange behaviour in Abhilash Talkies that made the man take him to a private place where he was made to be a party to unnatural sex. On the whole the incident would tell one how sex-starved the society could be and also would hint at the fact that children might be quite insecure even in places like cinema theatres.

A good number of people in the novel got themselves involved in sexual affairs. They included both major and minor characters. Hollic, the Manager of the English Company where Ammu's husband worked was said to have a number of illegitimate children. Chacko was notorious for his sexual weakness and his mother had done everything to make him have women of his choice.

Baby Kochamma had great desire to have sexual relations with Father Mulligan and the latter also was not free from the temptation. The senior nuns also did not lag behind when it came to sexual adventures as per the indications in the novel.

Estha and Rahel had sex in a unique way though it would appear strange for a twin brother to have sexual relation with his twin sister. But several indications one would get in the novel to prove this point.

The most important sexual relations described in the novel is the one between Ammu and Velutha. It was Ammu who was the initiator and once he received the message he never thought of withdrawing from the scene. Thus, the untouchable had sexual relations with a touchable and this lasted for several days. When it was discovered that the impossible had become possible the protagonists were made to pay the price. Velutha was almost instantly put to death and Ammu had to accept a gradual death.

To put it briefly, sex plays a very important part in the novel. For Estha and Rahel it did not create any physical problems even though their mind was never free from it. But for others it was the factor which directly contributed to the end of everything that they wished to enjoy.

Roy's novel touches upon several other issues that would certainly be of relevance. She talks about snobbery, health conditions, the system of education, violence, alcoholism, consumerim and a lot of other things in the novel. In the next section a passing glance would be made on some of these issues.

XI

Roy's society is noted for snobbery, among other things. Baby Kochamma would perhaps be the single representative in the novel who was specially known for her snobbery. She was sporting on an expensive funeral sari at the church when Sophie Mol died. Even at the age of 83, she had her hair dyed jetblack. She had started wearing make up and lipstick which was noticed by Rahel.

The poor conditions of health in the society was of concern to the novelist and we get evidence in this direction in a couple of places in the novel. There is a description of the Cochin Harbour Terminus where gaunt children, blonde with malnutrition sold smutty magazines and food they couldn't afford to eat themselves. Also "a blind man without eyelids and eyes as blue as faded jeans, his skin pitted with smallpox scars, chatted to a leper without fingers, taking dexterous drags from scavenged cigarette stubs that lay beside him in a heap" (p. 301).

Also, there were 'Hollow people. Homeless. Hungry. Still touched by last year's famine. Their revolution postponed for the Time Being by Comrade E.M.S. Namboodiripad (*Soviet Stooge, Running Dog*). The former apple of Pecking's eye" (p. 301). That is how the deprived and the unhealthy are described by the novelist.

Some glimpses of the contemporary educational scene also is revealed before us in the novel. Ammu got admission to the College of Architecture where the staff was impressed by the 'size' and not the skill. There was nursery school for the untouchables and craze for English medium schools which also would be cited as evidence to show that this sector also was not free from drawbacks.

The political scene had come up for discussion even earlier and among other things what would perhaps be notable in the novel is the indication that vote-bank politics is very active in the contemporary society which Roy tried to portray in the novel.

There are several other issues like alcoholism, violence, consumerism etc. which all form part of the major and minor areas of interest in the novel. But a society with healthy people and a society without snobs and a society without corruption and unrealistic planning in the flied of education would be something that everyone might wish for. This would not mean that other issues should altogether be ignored.

XII

To sum up, contemporary society stands in the novel with its pitfalls. It would be remembered for untouchability, certainly a canker in a civilized society. It is difficult to believe that even schools were started exclusively for the untouchables.

The second major problem highlighted is environmental problems. Very often people would forget about their surroundings to make life miserable for themselves and for their future generations. One gets enough evidence in the novel to prove this point.

The influence of the Gulf money especially in Kerala has been tremendous and it is natural for the novelist to give some details about the impact the new way of life has made on the people.

Urbanization would perhaps be described as the fall out of Gulf money. Villages slowly get transformed into towns and sometimes it is even difficult to demarcate the two. So great is the process of urbanization that continues to rule the state of Kerala.

Cultural decadence is another area where Kerala has started making its contributions probably along with other states. The conventional art disappears replacing it with "new styles of architecture" and people even would fail to know what they are doing.

Marginalization of women also finds a place as a theme in the novel and it is a major issue which should be examined with the seriousness it deserves.

Religion is another institution which has never been free from controversies. Even the priests and nuns fail to escape from attack. More than anything else sex becomes the main villain. The Convent life where students are not given any freedom also gets highlighted in the novel.

Family relation is another area where the novel has its focus. It is a society where people don't see eye to eye. There are mutual suspicion and jealousy as the over ruling feeling at least for some of the characters.

Sexuality is an important theme in the novel. Several characters get involved in sex-related issues which is certainly not to be overlooked. A number of other issues also are there which all help us to give an over all view of the contemporary society.

16

'Themmadykuzhi' and Other Stories

I

Roy's novel is remarkable for the innovations in language. Different techniques are made use of in the novel which ultimately add to its beauty. As Karl (1972) has rightly pointed out "language is not in itself a criterion of greatness" (p. 13). When we read Tolstoy in English, we can recognize his genius although his language is not what we read. Nevertheless, language, whether in translation or not, indicates how seriously the writer wants to be taken. Language which embellishes, communicates and strives for visionary effects usually complements to content of a writer who is attempting more than the ordinary.

Certainly Roy attempts more than the ordinary in the novel and for this she uses a language that communicates and strives for visionary effects. Roy, we find, writes in an English that is her own variety. One would perhaps remember R.K. Narayan who has observed that "the time has come for us to consider seriously the question of a Bharat brand of English. So far English has had a comparatively confined existence in our country chiefly in the halls of learning, justice, or administration. Now the time is ripe for it to come to the dusty street, market place, and under the banyan tree" (1974- p. 57). Probably, Roy is doing exactly what Narayan has said — going for a Bharat brand of English or a brand of English that very often deviates from the standard conventions. She must have thought she needs such a variety of English to communicate to the world the culture she represents. Inaugurating a conference on "Makers of Indian English" organized jointly by Dhvanyaloka and Indian Institute of Advanced studies in June, 1998 Mulkraj Anand has observed that "Indian English is the only language which brings us close to world cultures". That means our variety of English will help us in a non-trivial way move closer to world cultures also.

In this chapter an attempt is made to have a close look at the use of language by Roy in the novel. So many things strike one when one reads her novel. They include use of words and sentences from regional language, use of capital letters, use of italics, subjectless sentences, faulty spellings, topicalization, deviation from normal word order, single word 'sentences', change of parts of speech, clustering of adjectives, nouns etc. and a variety of other techniques. Some of these will be discussed in some detail in the following discussion.

II

What can perhaps be called an innovative approach in the novel is Roy's use of Malayalam, the regional language of Kerala which is her native state. The first Malayalam word that is used in the novel is *veshyas* which means 'prostitutes'. Ammu went back to Kottayam police station after Sophie Mol's funeral and told the Inspector that there had been a mistake. Immediately the Inspector retorted saying that the police would not take statements from *veshyas*. Whereas Roy does not give the meaning of the word she does so when the second word appears in the novel in the first chapter itself. Reverend Ipe was known as *Punnyan Kunju* which means 'little blessed one'.

She makes use of a Malayalam phrase *Ruchi lokathinde Rajavu* which according to her is the literal translation of 'Emperors of the Realm of Taste' (p. 46). This was the unsolicited contribution of Comrade Pillai as part of the marketing of the products of Paradise Pickles and Preserves. This appears in the second chapter of the novel. In the same chapter the word *mundu* 'dhoti' is used but not in italics.

The next utterance of Malayalam is through the mouth of

Muralidharan who was a level-crossing lunatic. He counted the numbers *onner, runder, moonner,* which means 'one', 'two' and 'three'. Then there is the Malayalam slogan uttered by the workers in the procession *Thozhilali Ekta Zindabad* for which Roy gives the Malayalam equivalent 'workers of the world unite' (p. 66). Later in the chapter some caste names like *parayan, paravan, pulayan* etc., are given which will normally have the English equivalents 'Paraya', 'Parava' and Pulaya'. We hear a couple of Malayalam words in the conversation of Chacko later in the chapter : 'Thanks, Keto!'....'*Valarey* thanks!' (p. 70). But the novelist doesn't give the English equivalents which are 'do you hear' and 'quite' respectively. In the very next page the word *ividay* 'here' also is used without giving the meaning of the word. The word *Modalali* ('landlord') appears in the same chapter of the novel, which is repeated a couple of times later.

Kochu Maria snubs her dog by saying *poda patti* 'go dog' in the third chapter of the novel. The Malayalam equivalent of these words are not given. In the fourth chapter the Orangedrink Lemondrink Man addresses Estha as *Eda Cherukka* ('Ay! Fellow') for which also the Malayalam equivalent is not given by the novelist. In chapter five also a couple of words like *Aiyyo* (an interjection), *orkunnilley* ('don't you remember?') and *oower* ('yes') are used without giving the English equivalents. Some of these words get repeated later also. In the same chapter Chacko says *Aiyyo Paavam* ('poor fellow') about Estha and the corresponding English words are not given. *Orkunnundo* (the negative of *orkunnilley*) appears at the end of the chapter without the English equivalent form.

The late film star Adoor Basi appears in the sixth chapter of the novel and makes the remark *Ende Deivomay! Eee Sadhanangal* ('My God', 'these things') at the airport, again without the corresponding English words given. *Kochu Thomban* with the equivalent English form 'Little Tusker' appears at the end of the chapter. The word *veshyas* reappears in the seventh chapter also.

Once Chacko comes with Sophie Mol in the eight chapter everyone whispered '*Chacko Saar Vannu* ('Mr. Chacko has come'). The English equivalent is not given. Words and phrases like *ickilee* ('tickle') *aiyyo kashtam* ('how sad') *kando* ('can you see?'), *sundarikutty* ('beautiful girl') and *Kushumbi* ('jealous girl') appear in the same chapter, the English equivalent of which given only for some. The word *chenda* ('drum') is not italicized when it appears in the ninth chapter.

In the tenth chapter lines from folk songs appear in several places. Lines like *Enda da korangacha, chandi ithra thenjadu* (Hey Mr. Monkey man, why's your bum so red?), *pandyill thooran poyappol nerakkamuthiri nerangi njan* ('I went for a shit to Madras, and scraped it till it bled') and the chorus of the boatsong *Theeyome, Thithome, Tharaka, Thithome, Theem* etc. appear in this chapter. Also the lines *pa pera-pera-pera-perakka* ('Mr. gugga-gug-gug-guava'), *Ende parambil thooralley* ('don't shit here in my compound'), *Chetende parambil thoorikko* ('you can shit next door in my brother's compound') and *pa pera-pera-pera-perakka* (Mr. gugga-gug-gug-guava) occur almost with their English equivalents. In the same chapter *Aiyyo, Mon! Mol* ('oh! dear son, daughter') and the line *Thaiy thaiy thaka thaiy thaiy thome* (the boat chorus) appear.

A couple of lines from the popular song from the film "*Chemmeen*" appear in the eleventh chapter which has the title of the novel : *Pandoru mukkuvan muthinu poyi* ('once a fisherman went to sea'), *Padinjaran kattathu mungi poyi* ('The west wind blew and swallowed his boat'), *Arayathi pennu pizhachu poyi* ('His wife on the shore went astray'), *Avaney kadalamma kondu poyi* ('so Mother Ocean rose and took him away') (pp. 219-20).

In chapter 12, the word *chenda* reappears. Also there are words like *kochu* ('small') and *vellya* ('big'). The titles of the Kathakali performances like *Karna shabadam* ('Karna's oath') and *Duryodhana Vadham* ('the death of Duryodhana') appear in the same chapter. In chapter 13 ('The Pessimist and the Optimist') also the boat chorus and reference to *modalali* reappear.

In the next chapter there are words like *addeham* (respectful 'he') and *edi* ('hey, you'). Comrade Pillai later asks Chacko : *Oru kaaryam parayattey*? ('can I tell you something'). The word *keto* also follows but the English equivalents are not given. *Allya edi* ('isn't it?') appears later. There is a popular song which was there in the first standard Malayalam Reader which also appears in the novel.

Koo-koo kookum theevandi
Kooki paadum theevandi
Rapakal odum theevandi
Thalannu nilkum theevandi (p. 285)

The second word in the second line is actually *paayum* ('will run') in the popular song which is replaced by *paadum* ('will sing') in the song which appears in the 14th chapter.

In chapters 15 and 17 the novelist does not make use of words from Malayalam. But in the next chapter words like *madiyo* ('enough') and *madi aayirikkum* (must be enough) appear. The word *meeshas* ('moustaches') find a place in the 19th chapter. In chapter 20 it is a Tamil phrase *Rombo maduram* ('very sweet') which probably takes the place of a Malayalam phrase. In the last chapter *Chappu Thamburan* ('Lord Rubbish') is the phrase that the novelist makes use of and no more Malayalam words are used in the novel.

The moot question is what exactly does Roy achieve by her extensive use of Malayalam words, phrases, lines from folk songs, film songs etc. Probably she must have forgotten the fact that she is writing an 'all-English' novel. Also, she must have found it difficult to sever off the cultural context in which she lived. Probably she may have thought that if she substitutes these words and phrases with their English counterparts she will fail to evoke the required result. More importantly, she becomes totally successful in writing a novel in English in a typical Kerala background and to achieve this her use of Malayalam words, phrases etc. helps her quite a lot.

III

Another technique that Roy adopts in her novel is her extensive use of italicized words, phrases and sentences. The first italicized word in the novel appears on page three. Rahel here remembers the taste of the tomato sandwiches — *Estha's* sandwiches, that *Estha* ate. Being a two-egg twin Rahel can feel whatever Estha does and by using italics the novelist probably tries to establish here that both Estha and Rahel are twins with joint identities. The words *them*, *they* and *they'd* also are italicized probably to convey the very same sense.

The priest's funeral song at Sophie Mol's burial and epitaph on her tombstone are given in italics to make them stand apart from the rest of the narration. There is also an observation "Her funeral killed her" followed by *Dus to dus to dus to dus to dus* in italics which again stand apart from the main theme. In the same chapter Inspector Thomas Mathew taps Ammu's breasts and the words *tap, tap* follow. May be the novelist wants to infuse greater meaning in the action and more so in the words. The Malayalam word *veshya* is italicized as is the case with the word *illegitimate* both of which are words which would echo and re-echo in the minds of a person. When Ammu and her children were returning to Ayemenem the conductor's *Where to*? means more than what it implies ordinarily and so it gets italicized.

Later in the novel there is a description of Estha as a student. He is an *average student*, doing *satisfactory work*. The entry in the annual progress report *Does not participate in Group Activities* is also italicized because all these pierce into the personality of Estha. Later in the chapter there is a reference to Khubchand, Estha's friend urinating *inside* and *allowed* to exist. Again the novelist wants the words to convey senses more than the ordinary. Sophie Mol who is described as the seeker of small wisdoms asks a few questions all of which are given in italics. Again the questions are far from the routine ones like *why don't dead ones fall like stones from the sky*?

The word *depravity* and its meaning in the Oxford Dictionary, *perverted quality : Moral perversion, The innate corruption of human nature due to original* .... are given in italics. This word has great significance in the life of Rahel and naturally it should stand apart from the main narration. Rahel is described as an extremely polite child but the teachers looked at her *as though she didn't know how to be a girl*. The italicized part makes a lot of sense as far as Rahel is concerned.

The title of Larry Mc Caslin's doctoral thesis *Energy Efficiency in Vernacular Architecture* is given in italics for obvious reasons. But *There goes a jazz tune* given in Italics stands for

Rahel (p. 18). Again, the words *meant* and *personal* are italicized when Ammu's look and desperation are discussed. The word *recognize* is italicized when it is said that Estha has lost this capability. The word *should* is italicized when a question why Baby Kochamma should take care of Estha is asked. The word 'should' gets all the force here. About Baby Kochamma it is said that *she's living her life backwards*. This again is a very important and forceful statement and hence given in italics. The name *Punnyan Kunju* is in italics more so because that is basically a Malayalam name.

Baby Kochamma asks doubts to Father Mulligan. She says that she can understand if *some* things are lawful for God but cannot understand how *all* things be lawful. The words *some* and *all* are italicized obviously because more meanings than the ordinary are attached to it.

The whole letter that Baby Kochamma writes is given in italics. The statement *I have seen jewels one of which is my Koh-i-noor*, from her grandfather's will appears in italics. The word *Koh-i-noor* has a very special significance in this context. The word *her* also is italicized where it refers to Baby Kochamma. Baby Kochamma's thought that *they might even steal their present back* is also found italicized. The reference here is to the twins.

Sophie Mol's arrival at Ayemenem house is an important event. There is even a *What will Sophie Mol Think*? week. The idea is certainly to give emphasis to her visit. Chacko was a Rhodes scholar and it was his habit to utter long sentences which are given in italics.

Sometimes Roy creates a comic situation with her italicized words. *For example*, Baby Kochamma wanted the twins to be particularly careful about their prer *Nun* seaayshun. Italics is also used in the novel to present words or sentences in the reverse order. *For example*, the name of the book *The Adventures of Susie Squirrel* is read aloud as *ehT SerutnevdA fo eisuS lerriuqS*.

E.M.S. Namboodiripad is referred to as *Running Dog, Soviet Stooge* which is given in italics probably to indicate that it was quoted. There is a reference in the novel where Rahel is haunted by something terrible. What comes to her mind is given in italics : *A Sourmetal smell, like steel bus-rails, and the smell of the bus conductor's hands from holding them. A young man with an oldman's mouth* (p. 72).

We get several instances where individual words are italicized with the purpose of giving emphasis. Thus, Vellya Paapen reports to Mammachi what he had seen. "It was not *what* he said, but the *way* he said it. Not *what* he did, but the *way* he did it" (p. 76). Very strong feelings of the speakers are also given within italics. Thus, when Baby Kochamma heard about Ammu's relation with Velutha "she said (among other things) — '*How could she stand the smell? Haven't you noticed, they have a particular smell, these Paravans*?" (p. 78).

When Ammu gives instructions to Estha, whatever goes on in his mind as if in a stream of consciousness is given in italics :

Finish the drink
Watch the picture
Think of all the poor people
Lucky rich boy with porketmunny. No worries.

Also there are certain words which are deliberately misspelt and such words also are italicized. *An example* is the word *infinnate*.

There are also long passages from old notebooks given in italics. *For example*, there is Estha's story called *Little Ammu* Which runs as follows : *On Saturday we went to a bookshop in Kottayam to buy Ammu a present because her birthday is in 17th of November. We bote her a diary. We hid it in the coberd and then it began to be night. Then we said do you want to see your present she said yes I would like to see it. and we wrote on the paper For a Little Ammu with Love from Estha and Rahel and we gave it to Ammu....* (p. 158)

In short, Roy makes use of italicization as a very strong tool in the novel. The technique serves a variety of purposes of which some are certainly innovative. The conventional method of italicizing for laying emphasis on words, phrases and sentences is used by the novelist. Sometimes she italicizes to make ironic statements. Some other times she uses this technique to make comic effects. Many a time in the novel words, phrases, parts of songs etc., which are in Malayalam are italicized. Names of books, films, firms, newspapers, dictionary, treatise, theatre, pickle products etc. are found italicized. There are also letters which are given in italics. Dictionary meanings given in detail are also italicized. Whatever, the twins write as 'impositions' are also italicized. There are slogans, quotations, dialogues from plays, misspelt words etc. which are italicized. Sometimes this technique is used whenever a character wants to express strong feelings. Lessons and excerpts from notebooks are also italicized in the novel. As Robbe-Grillet has maintained "what constitutes the novelist's strength is precisely that he invents, quite freely without a mode...." (1965-p. 32). Roy is doing exactly this when she makes use of different techniques in her novel.

IV

The use of upper case letters is largely used as a technique in the novel. As in the case of italicization, the main idea probably is to emphasise certain things that the novelist thinks are different from the ordinary. It is found that certain words are given completely in upper case letters and in some other cases only the first letter all of which in normal usage are written in small case letters.

In the opening chapter itself we get so many instances where the novelist adopts this technique. Sophie Mol "showed Rahel *T*wo *T*hings" (p. 5). Thing One was the newly painted high dome. Thing *T*wo that Sophie Mol showed Rahel was the bat baby. Obviously Sophie Mol was dead and so she wouldn't be able to do what she was doing. May be the novelist wants to convey this. The epitaph written on Sophie Mol's funeral has the words *A S*unbeam *L*ent *T*o *U*s *T*oo *B*riefly (all given in italics and the first letter of the words in upper case letters).

Estha has been sent to his father after Sophie Mol's death and after about twenty-three years he was sent back to Ayemenem house. This is referred to as 're-*R*eturning' The term occurs several times in the novel consistently having the second *r* in upper case letter. 'Re-returning' is certainly used in a particular sense and that is what makes the novelist give a special status to this letter.

Sophie Mol's death did create a vacuum in the Ayemenem house and several times there are references in the novel to the '*L*oss of Sophie Mol' with the *l* in *l*oss given in upper case letters. Again, the death of Sophie Mol is a turning point in the novel and this might be the reason why the word is given special focus with *l* in upper case letter.

There is a reference to Rahel drifting into marriage with a *S*itting *D*own sense in the novel (p. 18). We find *s* and *d* in upper case letters. Again the words are used in a specialized sense and not in the literal sense. Her marriage broke because "*W*orse *T*hings had happened" (p. 19). Here again *w* and *t* are in upper case letters and may be these words have a lot of things to convey than they appear to do.

After Sophie Mol's death, the police found Velutha. Baby Kochamma's reaction was 'As ye sow, so shall ye reap' (p. 31). Then there is the authorial comment "As though *she* had had nothing to do with the *S*owing and the *R*eaping" (p. 31). The letters *S* and *R* should normally be 'small case' but these words are pregnant with meaning telling a whole lot of stories. It is in this sense that the words get a focus that is far from the ordinary.

Baby Kochamma never trusted the twins. "She deemed them *C*apable of *A*nything. *A*nything at all" (p. 29). The first letters in the three words are given in upper case letters obviously with the idea of adding strength to these words. Similarly, Rahel would walk to the window *F*or a *B*reath of *F*resh *A*ir. It should be suffocating for her to remain in the house with Baby Kochamma and she was badly in need of fresh air almost as if she would perish if she failed to get it. The initial letters in these words are in upper case with the purpose of making this point forceful. Baby Kochamma considered twins "*H*alf - *H*indu - *H*ybrids" which showed her strong dislike for the twins.

When she was at Ayemenem Ammu used to play radio. People avoided her and "everybody agreed that it was best to just *L*et *H*er *B*e. Here the upper case letters make the words strong enough to create a feeling that others were totally indifferent to her and never cared about her existence. Ammu had her own fears about Estha, who she thought, would grow up to be "a

*M*ale *C*hauvinist *P*ig". The ill-treatment she got at the hands of men would have perhaps made her make such a strong statement with the first sound of the key words given in upper case letters.

When Sophie Mol returned to Ayemenem Rahel asked Chacko whether he loved Sophie Mol *M*ost in the *W*orld. She was one who suffered a lot of psychological problems and she never received love as much as she wanted from her near ones. Probably she thought that once Chacko loved Sophie Mol the most, she would never stand a chance to receive any love from him.

In short, Roy has successfully made use of the technique of substituting the small case letters with upper case letters with very clear purpose in her mind. The psychological imbalance some of her characters have can perhaps be described only by using such techniques. We have the feeling that some of the words of which certain letters are given in upper case letters pierce through us to reach the target that is before the novelist. As in the case of her using the technique of italics, this also certainly clicks.

V

Roy makes extensive use of brackets in her novel which appears to be a technique adopted by her for the effective narration of the story. She starts making use of this device from the second page of the novel itself.

Being the twin sister of Estha, Rahel remembers, "for instance (though she hadn't been there), what the Orangedrink Lemondrink Man did to Estha...." (p. 2). Whatever comes within the bracket is a very important piece of information and the novelist chooses to put it with in brackets probably because she thinks that it will be more forceful if only it is presented in this manner.

In the next page there is a description of the bus journey when Ammu was pregnant : "Estha and Rahel's father had to hold their mother's stomach (with them in it) to prevent it from wobbling" (p. 3). That the twins were in Ammu's stomach is very crucial especially when the whole thing is looked at from the eyes of Rahel and Estha. Here again the novelist prefers to describe it by giving the piece of information in brackets.

When Sophie Mol's funeral is described there is a reference to "an old lady masquerading as a distant relative (whom nobody recognized), but who often surfaced next to bodies at funerals (a funeral junkie? a latent necrophiliac?) put cologne on a wad of cotton wool..." (pp. 4-5). Whatever is given within brackets appears to be an aside or authorial comment which is very significant from the point of view of the narration of the story.

A similar reading we get in the statement "It's true (and must be said) that it would have been easier to notice...." (p. 5) also. It is the invisible author who makes her own observations on certain situations and also on the action of certain characters which is no doubt an effective technique made use of by the novelist.

When Sophie Mol's coffin was lowered into the ground Rahel "heard (on Sophie Mol's behalf), the soft sound of the red mud and the hard sounds of the orange laterate that spoiled the shining coffin polish" (p. 7). Here again the author wants to comment on the actual feeling of Rahel when the coffin is lowered.

Two weeks after the funeral Estha was returned to his father who had "remarried, stopped drinking (more or less), and suffered occasional relapses" (p. 9). What is given in brackets again shows that the author has her own comments to make on the issue. Estha had been a quiet child and so "no one could pin point with any degree of accuracy exactly when (the year, if not the month or day) he had stopped talking" (p. 10). Here also the author wants to put forth her own view point when she narrates Estha's story.

In short, Roy makes use of brackets as an effective tool in the novel mainly as a device to offer authorial comments. She makes us know what goes on in the mind of a particular character, as a sort of stream of consciousness, by making use of the brackets almost throughout the novel.

VI

Roy makes use of a technique in the novel where she goes for sentences which very often do not have subject. She even goes to the extent of using just a word in the place of a full fledged sentence. As is wellknown, in normal writing subject cannot be dropped in an English sentence. But Roy takes a lot of liberty in her use of this language.

Rahel never returned to Ayemenem when she was busy with her studies. Following this there are sentences like "Not when Mammachi died" and "Not when Chacko emigrated to Canada" both of which don't have subjects. Similarly there is a sentence "with a Sitting Down Sense" which appears in connection with Rahel's marriage in the novel.

Baby Kochamma regrets for having written to Rahel when Estha was "re-Returned". There was some kind of silence between Baby Kochamma and Rahel. It was like "a stranger. Swollen. Noxious" (p. 21). Here again instead of full sentence we find that only a nounphrase and an adjective are used.

Clubbing of adjectives and other word classes is another favourite device of the novelist which is adopted almost through out the novel. Thus, we have sentences like "The baby clutched his index finger while he conducted his insane, broken, envious, torchlit study" (p. 117), "he felt the shaming churning leaving turning sickness in his stomach" (p. 113). What is interesting here is that there are no commas used in the second sentence where the adjectives are to be separated as per the conventions of the language. There is a reversal of the situation where the novelist uses full stops to demarcate adjectives when they are not absolutely necessary as in the following : "Wild. Sick. Sad." (p. 159).

The repetition of determiners also appears in several places in the novel. *For example,* we have a description "one corner for cooking, one for clothes, one for bedding rolls, one for dying in" (pp. 206-07).

There is also a long passage in the novel where the preposition 'past' is repeated more than a dozen times : Estha walked among the giant cement pickle vats to find a place to think in —

"past floating yellow limes in brine....
past green mangoes, cut and stuffed with turmeric
past glass casks of vienegar with corks.
past shelves of pectin and preservatives.
past trays of bitter gourd....
past gunny bags bulging with garlic....
past mounds of fresh green peppercorns.
past a heap of banana peels on the floor....
past the label cupboard full of labels.
past the glue.
past the glue-brush.
past an iron tub of empty bottles....
past the lemon squash." (pp. 193-194)

Thus Estha does not miss all these when he goes for the walk and the repetition of the preposition has a tremendous effect on the narration.

The novel is also noted for Roy's use of words which are coined to serve special purposes. Thus, instead of 'led' she uses 'shepherded' (p. 120) and talks about Ammu's 'moonwalking' Estha (p. 108). She describes "iron railing that separated Meeters from the Met and Greeters from the *Gret*" (p. 142). Similarly she also talks about "a medieval executioner peering through the tilted eye-slits of his peaked black-hood at the *executionee*" (p. 223). Another coinage we have in the sentence "Until Ammu shook her and told her to *stoppit* and she *stoppited* (p. 300). We have also words like "bottomful" (p. 107) used as the opposite of "bottomless". Similarly the word "exit" is changed into past tense to get the word *exited* (p. 101). There are also expressions like *moonwalked* (p. 108). "The *pickling....* stopped" (p. 171) is another instance where the novelist takes liberties with words.

Compounding of words is another important characteristic of the novel. Thus, there are so many instances where Roy makes use of such words. We have examples like "Ammu's trying-not-to-cry mouth" (p. 300), "Chacko-the-Management", "Chacko-the-Comrade" (p. 121) "clear-as-glass kiss" (p. 221), "bottomless-bottomless feeling" (p. 323), "God-knows-what" (p. 253) "Love-in-Tokyo" (p. 307), "part-Time Happiness" (p. 89) "Clear-as-glass Kiss" (p. 221) etc. which are very significant.

Another technique that Roy makes use of in the novel is changing of the word-classes. *For example*, *sequinned* in the sense of 'decorate' is normally used as an adjective. But she uses it as a verb in "a thin-ribbon of thick water that lapped wearily at the mud banks on either side *sequinned* with the occasional silver slant of a dead fish" (p. 124). Similarly in the sentence "but alone with his wife and children he turned into a monstrous, suspicious bully, with a streak of vicious *cunning*" (p. 180), 'cunning' which is an adjective is used as a noun. In the sentence "the flat, foolish pallathi, the silver paral, the wily, whiskered koori, the sometimes karimeen" (p. 203) the adverb *sometimes* is used as an adjective.

Still another device that is largely used in the novel is a syntactic technique often referred to as topicalization : Thus we have *examples* like "'Heritage', the hotel was called" (p. 126) "Levin he called himself now" (p. 128), "Poor old Vellya Paapen, had he known them that History would choose him for its deputy..." (p. 199) etc. scattered across the novel. Another *example* that can be cited is "stopped talking altogether that is" (p. 10) which should have been "That is (he) has altogether stopped talking."

The novel also is noted for a phenomenon in which words run into each other. Plenty of *examples* can be cited where the novelist makes use of this method. Some of these are "whatisyourname" (p. 127), "okaythen" (p. 130), "Flatfeet" (p. 139), "lefrightlef" (p. 141), "Finethankyou" (p. 145), "bluegreyblue eyes" (p. 147), "carsmile" (p. 153), "mydearjudges" (p. 271), "whateveritis" (p. 279), "deadlypurposed" (p. 304) etc. which are only some of the very many words used in this way.

Another device in which the last syllable of one word is attached to the first syllable of the next word is found used in the novel. Thus, we have the *example* "Locusts Stand I" (p. 159). When Rahel tells Comrade Pillai that she had been divorced his reaction is "Mo-Stunfortunate" (p. 130) where also we find the consonant cluster in the first word attached to the first syllable of the second word. "Hello, all" becoming "Hello Wall" (p. 143) is another *example*. Similarly, the syllables which normally go together are deliberately separated as in "while Chacko got the bags, at the dirty -- curtained window *Lay Ter* became Now" (p. 147). There is also a reference to "Bluegreyblue eyes snapped open, A Wake, A Live, A Lert" (p. 238) where again we find that the syllables which should go together are separated deliberately. As Fieldler observes "to speak to the people... means to speak in the language of the people rather than in some artificial tongue invented by academicians precisely for the purpose of creating an elitist or hermetic art" (1974-p. 197). Probably Roy is trying to speak in the language of the people by making use of all these innovations.

In short, subjectless sentences, clubbing of words like adjectives, determiners, new coinages, compounding of words, change of word classes, topicalization, words running into other words, syllables getting attached to nearby syllables, syllables getting separated are only some of the innovative techniques Roy makes extensive use of in the novel. Certainly there are other techniques also which are to be discussed.

VII

Roy makes fun of the Indian pronunciation of English for which we get plenty of *examples* in the novel. When Rahel told Comrade Pillai that she was divorced he pronounced the word as "die-vorced" (p. 130). The word 'pronunciation' to Baby Kochamma is "Prer Nun Sea ayshun" (p. 154). This version of 'pronunciation' is filled with irony as Baby Kochamma is an 'Ex-Nun'.

Another device in the novel is use of certain words which are deliberately spelt wrong. Thus, 'America' is *Amayrica* (p. 129), 'hello' is *Hell-oh* (with a comic effect), 'always' is *Orlways* (p. 154), 'anxious' is *angshios* (p. 158), 'fatal' is *fatle* (p. 158), 'cainster' is *cannister* (p. 229), 'infinite' is *infinnate* (p. 301), 'very' is *verrrry* (p. 323), 'minute' is *mint* (p. 134), 'kangaroos' is *kangeroos* (p. 140) and 'exactly' is *eggzackly* (p. 324).

At least a couple of times in the novel we find Roy beginning the sentence with a co-reference pronoun with the antecedent appearing later in the sentence. This again is quite unconventional. The sentence "*They* looked cheerful in the photographs, *Lenin and his wife* (p. 131) can be cited as an *example*.

Another important innovative device that is largely made use of in the novel is reversal of the order of letters in certain words, phrases and sentences. Thus, 'welcome to the Spice Coast of India' becomes *emoclew ot eht ecips tsaoc fo aidnI* (p. 139) 'The Adventures of Susie Squirrel' becomes ehT SerutnevdA fo eisuS lerriuqS, 'One Spring morning Susie Squirrel Woke up' becomes *eno gnirps gninrom eisuS lerriuqS ekow pu* (p. 60) and 'satan in their eyes' becomes *natas ni rieht seye* (p. 302). At the Kottayam police station Estha had read aloud the words 'Politeness', 'Obedience', 'Loyalty', 'Intelligence' 'Courtesy' and 'Efficiency'. They appear as 'ssenetiloP', 'ecneidebO' 'ytlayoL', 'ecnegilletnI', 'ysetruoC' and 'ycneiciffE' respectively (p. 313).

Deviation from rules of grammar and usage is another characteristic of Roy's language in the novel. In the very first paragraph of the book she describes how the black crows in Ayemenem in the month of May "gorge on bright mangoes in still, dusty green trees" (p. 1). "Gorge" is a word which is usually used in a derogatory sense to mean 'to fill oneself completely with (food) or 'eat in a greedy way.' The idiomatic expression is 'gorge oneself on/with'; but we find that Roy does not use the 'self' form with the word. In the very same page she describes the nights as clear but suffused with 'sloth and sullen expectation'. In fact, "sloth" is normally used only as a noun in the sense of 'unwillingness to work' or 'laziness'. At the sametime 'sullen' is an adjective which means 'dark and unpleasant' or 'gloomy'. The novelist links a noun and adjective with a conjunction 'and' which is quite unconventional for an ordinary user of the language. Her description of the pepper vines which 'snake up' electric poles is still another instance of taking liberty with language. 'snake through' is an idiomatic expression, 'snake up' is rarely used by the native speakers of the language. We have an instance in the novel where she conjoins verbs which are transitive and intransitive which is a very rare phenomenon in the language : "Ammu resting under the skin of her dream, *observed* them and *ached* with their love for them" (p. 218). Similarly, there is a sentence "Not finding words with which to tell her that for them there *was* no Each, no Other" (p. 225) which again is a deviant sentence.

There are also any number of instances where "Single word sentences" appear. After saying that Rahel and Estha are no longer what they were or ever thought They'd be, there is the word "ever" after the full stop. Another full stop follows the word also (p. 3). In the police station the Inspector "tapped her breasts with his baton. Gently. *Tap, tap*" (p. 8). The word gently appears as if it were a full sentence here. Thus goes another description : "Rain. Rushing, inky water. And a smell. Swicksweet. Like old roses on a breeze". (p. 32). Here again "rain" and "Sicksweet" appear as if they were full sentences. Another instance we get in "Ammu realized that the slightly feverish glitter in her bridegroom's eyes had not been love or even excitement at the prospect of carnal bliss, but approximately eight large pegs of whisky. Straight. Neat." (p. 39). The words "straight" and "neat" appear flanked by full stops.

Repetitions of negatives also mark the language of Roy. Thus, we have passages like the following in the novel. "No milestones marked its progress. No trees grew along it. No dappled shadows shaded it. No mists rolled over it. No birds circled it. No twists, no turns... Not to know. Not to know what each day held in store for her. Not to know where she might be,... Not to know which way her road might turn and what lay beyond the bend" (p. 224).

The novel is also noted for uses of words like "bum" which is a slang. Words which are popular only in Indian and Pakistani English like *ayah* are also made use of by the novelist. There are also expressions which make a comic effect like "hugely pregnant" in the novel. The novelist also sometimes clubs together two words with opposite meanings. Thus, we have the oxymoron *sicksweet* (p. 6). Ammu makes a *fierce whisper* (p. 100) to Estha to remain slient which again can perhaps be classified as words with opposite meanings.

Thus, we find that the novel abounds in innovations in language use. Roy takes liberty with words, phrases and sentences and makes them deviate from the conventional ways in which they are used in the language. We have words which are wrongly pronounced, words which are wrongly spelt and also instances where co-reference pronoun begin the sentence followed by their antecedents. There are also cases where the sentences deviate from the normal rules of grammar and "one word sentences" which are effectively made use of by the novelist. Repetition of negatives is another technique which she uses. Also, there are a few cases of words which are not used in the standard usage. Words which are opposite in meaning are clubbed together which becomes another technique. Roy makes use of some other techniques also which are considered in the following section.

VIII

The novel is marked for its extensive use of similes. An examination of some of these will reveal the wide range of comparisons the novelist makes.

When Rahel met Comrade Pillai after a long gap he received her with a volley of questions. The things that cannot be forgotten "sit on duty shelves *like* stuffed birds with baleful, sideways staring eyes" (p. 129). The image here is that of stuffed birds with staring eyes. Pillai's nipples are described as peeping at Rahel "over the top of the boundary wall *like* a sad St. Bernard's eyes". Next, Pillai's smile is compared to a searchlight : "Comrade Pillai's smile broadened as he turned all his attention *like* a searchlight on Rahel" (p. 130).

The younger days of Lenin is described and once he was taken to a doctor. His dress is compared to that of a taxi : "Lenin, dressed *like* a taxi — yellow shirt, black stretchlon shorts" (p. 132) The nurse who appeared and disappeared through the tattered-curtained doctor's door has "shiny black hairpins, *like* straightened snakes" (p. 133). Pillai is later described as one who "was *like* a flasher in a hedge" (p. 134). There is a description of a photograph taken in the younger days of

Lenin, Rahel and Estha who "looked *like* frightened animals that had been caught in the headlights of a car" (p. 134) in it. Sophie Mol's eyes are described as looking "*like* pink-veined flesh petals" (p. 135).

Estha's puff is crisp and surprised. "*Like* well — whipped eggwhite" (p. 137). There are also descriptions like "Red betel spit stains spattered their kangaroo stomachs *like* fresh wounds" (p. 138), "Rahel looked *like* an Airport Fairy with appalling taste," "the smallest one stretched its neck *like* people in English films who loosen their ties after office", "she gnawed it with her front teeth *like* a rodent" (p. 139) "and the air port itself : More *like* the local bus depot" (p. 140), "one hand in her mother's. The other swinging *like* a soldiers" (p. 141), "a column of shining black ants walked across a windowsill, their bottoms titted upwards *like* a line of mincing chorus girls in a Busby Berkeley musical" (p. 155) etc. in the novel which are only some among the varieties of similies used in the novel.

The novel is also rich in its use of sentences beginning with "as though". Thus, we have instances like "Comrade Pillai lowered his voice *as though* there were people listening, though there was no one about" (p. 131), "*as though* standing side ways was a sin" (p. 135), "they looked *as though* if you pressed them they might say 'Ma-ma' in empty battery voices" (p. 138), "*as though* they hadn't been made to rehearse it all week long" (p. 154), "It was *as though* Ammu believed that if she refused to acknowledge the passage of time, if she willed it to stand still in the lives of her twins, it would. *As though* sheer will power was enough to suspend her children's childhoods until she would afford to have them living with her" (p. 159), "when she smiled her dimples looked *as though* they hurt" (p. 160), "'you must always check it', she whispered hoarsely, *as though* phlegm was an Arithmetic answer sheet that had to be revised before it was handed in" (p. 160), "*as though* meaning had slunk out of things" (p. 225), "although you know that one day you will die, you live *as though* you won't" (p. 229), "he looked *as though* he was laughing at himself", "Margaret Kochamma's mother was looking away, out of the photograph, *as though* she would rather not have been there".

(p. 240), "dense clumps of yellow bamboo dropped into the river *as though* grieving in advance for what they knew was going to happen' (p. 291) and hundreds of other uses of this structure in the novel where she makes a contrast between something unlikely or impossible and something that is before her.

In short, the novelist using sentences with similies and sentences with *as though* in them successfully drives home rather effectively the points that she wants to make. The only thing that surprises one is the abundance of such sentences in the novel as if the sentences with *as though* or *like* in them were her favourites. What is remarkable about her similies is that they are vivid and far from earthy. The object of comparison are as diverse as "a werewolf", "a joke" (p. 296), "an angular, arthritic hen settling stiffling on her clutch of eggs" (p. 295), "calves" (p. 301), "sunken treasure dredged up from the ocean bed" (p. 307), "flat chalk on a blackboard" (p. 339) etc.

IX

The novel is also remarkable for the use of words which indicate different colours. Infact, the reference to colours we get from the very first page of the novel. In the opening paragraph there is a description of the ripe "*red* bananas" (p. 1). In the next page there is a sentence "hopeful *yellow* bullfrogs cruised the scummy pond for mates". It continues till the penultimate page of the novel where there is a reference to Sophie Mol touching Velutha "like jet-streaks in a *blue* church sky" (p. 339).

Some of the other instances where we get references to different colours are : "beyond the circle of folding chairs was a beach littered with broken *blue* glass bottles", "the silent waves brought new *blue* bottles to be broken," "on a rock, out at sea, in a shaft of *purple* light," "the sea was *black*, the spume vomit *green,*" "a thin red cow with a protruding pelvic bone" (p. 216), "the *black* sea smoothed" (p. 218), "the *blue* cross — stitch darkness" (p. 219), "blue cross-stitch afternoon" (p. 220), "the *brown* of the backs of their hands was the exact *brown* of their mother's stomach skin" (p. 221), "the bedroom with *blue* curtains'' (p. 224), ''a pianist killing the piano kings. Even the *black* ones'' (p. 225), ''Rahel sat down.... resting her back against.... a *white* pillar,'' (p. 229) ''mustard instead of *red*'' (p. 276), ''*red* varnish'' (p. 288), ''*white* mundu'' (p. 289), ''*black* as the night'' (p. 289), ''*yellow* moon in it'' (p. 293), ''*yello*-rimmed *red* sunglasses'' (p. 301), ''like a dead *green* snake'' (pp. 305-306), ''yellow maps'' (p. 306), ''moss *green*'' (p. 307), ''*black* suit'' (p. 318) and so on.

Invariably there are references to all the colours. The objects described varies form 'glass bottles', 'sea', 'cow', 'skin', 'curtains', 'piano keys', 'doorwood', 'pillar', 'face', 'eyes', 'dress', 'walls' 'plate', 'blouse', 'mundu', 'pepper', 'water', 'varnish', 'garbage', 'boot', 'sock', 'snake', 'suit', 'bamboo', and a number of others. Sometimes instead of objects there are descriptions of ''light'', ''darkness'', ''afternoon'', ''night'', ''music'', etc. The effect of the use of these words which denote colour are tremendous and the references we find across the novel which ultimately add to the beauty of the narration.

X

Finally, it will be in the fitness of things to show how Roy successfully makes certain descriptions which are significant for their minute details.

The opening page itself abounds in such descriptions as the following show : ''The river shrinks with black crows gorge on bright mangoes in still, dustgreen trees. Red bananas ripen. Jack fruits burst. Dissolute bluebottles hum vacuously in the fruity air. Then they stun themselves against clear window panes and die, fatly baffled in the sun.'' In the same page there is a beautiful description of rain in Ayemenem : ''It was raining when Rahel came back to Ayemenem. Slanting silver ropes slammed into loose earth, ploughing it up like gunfire.''

Another description of June rain in Ayemenem goes as follows : ''Heaven opened and the water hammered down, reviving the reluctant old well, greenmossing the pigless pigsty, carpet bombing still, tea-coloured puddles the way memory bombs still, tea-coloured minds. The grass looked wetgreen and pleased.

Happy earthworms frolicked purple in the slush. Green nettles nodded. Trees bent" (p. 10).

There is a description of the History House in the second chapter of the novel which again is notable for its vividness : "With cool stone floors and dim walls and billowing shipshaped shadows. Plump, translucent lizards lived behind old pictures, and waxy, crumbling ancestors with tough toe-nails and breath that smelled of yellow maps gossiped in sibilant, papery whispers." (p. 53).

The description of the wheeling kites is also remarkable for the minute details : "Steelshrill police whistles pierced holes in the Noise Umbrella. Through the jagged umbrella holes Rahel could see pieces of red sky. And in the red sky, hot red kites wheeled, looking for rats. In their hooded yellow eyes there was a road and red flags marching. And a white shirt over a black back with a birthmark" (p. 79).

When Rahel is on her way to Cochin beautiful pictures are unveiled through her eyes : "The sun shone through the Plymouth window directly down at Rahel.... The sky was orange, and the coconut trees were sea anemones waving their tentacles, hoping to trap and eat an unsuspecting cloud. A transparent spotted snake with a forked tongue floated across the sky. Then a transparent Roman soldier on a spotted horse" (pp. 82-83).

We get an account of Pappachi's study in chapter seven of the novel which again is remarkable for the minute details : "In Pappachi's study, mounted butterflies and moths had disintegrated into small heaps of iridescent dust that powdered the bottom of their glass display cases, leaving the pins that had impaled them naked. Cruel. The room was rank with fungus and disuse. An old neon-green hula hoop hung from a wooden peg on the wall, a huge saint's discarded halo. A column of shining black ants walked across a windowsill, their bottoms tilted upwards, like a line of mincing chorus girls in a Bushy Berkeley musical. Silhouetted against the sun. Buffed and beautiful" (p. 155).

Chapter nine begins with beautiful descriptions where Rahel's memories go back to her Washington days : "The green-for-the day had seeped from the trees. Dark palm leaves were splayed like drooping combs against the monsoon sky. The orange sun slid through their bent grasping teeth.

A squadron of fruit bats sped across the gloom.

In the abandoned ornamental garden, Rahel, watched by lolling dwarves and a forsaken cherub, squatted by the stagnant pond and watched toads hop from stone to scummy stone. Beautiful Ugly Toads.

Slimy. Warty. Croaking" (p. 187).

When the Ayemenem house loses its glory it is a pathetic picture that the novelist draws which again is noted for its vividness : "On the roof of the abandoned factory, the lonely drummer drummed. A gauze door slammed. A mouse rushed across the factory floor. Cobwebs sealed old pickle vats. Empty, all but one — in which a small heap of congealed white dust lay. Bone dust from a Bar Nowl. Long dead. Pickledowl" (p. 328).

In short, Roy is at her best in her descriptions which are notable for their vividness. She has a special skill in going into the minute details which makes these descriptions all the more effective.

XI

To sum up, the novel is perhaps more important for the innovativeness in the use of language than for anything else. The different techniques she uses in the novel may not have many parallels in the world of fiction.

Her use of words, phrases and even sentences of Malayalam is specially significant because not many a writer will choose to take such a liberty. Italicisation also comes as a handy tool for her and this is also made use of very effectively with different objectives in her mind. The use of upper case letters is another device that has been extensively used again with very specific purpose in mind. The use of brackets also is more a technique in the novel than a routine use as in the case of other writers of the genre.

She makes use of sentences without subject which again should be taken as something very special. The use of clusters, of adjectives, nouns, verbs, determiners etc. is another device in which she is very comfortable. The novel also abounds in the use of words coined by the novelist for which we have any number of examples. Compounding is another device made use of by the novelist. Changing the word class also is a well used technique in the novel.

Topicalization, a grammatic technique is largely used in the novel by Roy. Words running into another and syllables getting attached to the other syllables are some of the other techniques she makes use of.

In pronunciation and spelling also the novelist takes a lot of liberties. The technique of a co-reference pronoun starting a sentence and words written in the reverse order are some of the other innovative use of the language. Very often the novelist deviates from the conventional language use. Another important feature might be her use of single words which very often stand for the whole sentence. Repetition of negatives, use of slang etc. are also certain other features. Her obsession with colour and vividness in the use of her language in general are some other points which are discussed.

17

Living Backwards

I

Any discussion of a novel should involve characterization, plot and style of the author. Perhaps something that is equally important is the structural problems. Allott (1959) maintains that "the conception of artistic structure has taken more than a century to lay hold of the popular imagination" (p. 162). Roy's novel is especially important when one considers the artistic structure.

Sophie Mol's visit to Ayemenem in the month of December in 1969 is to be taken as the base year from the point of view of the development of the plot of the novel. She was in Aymenem for just two weeks at the end of which she was drowned. The same day Velutha was tortured to death by the police which was the consequence of a false implication.

In this chapter an attempt is made to show how the plot is developed and how the story of five generations is effectively linked in the novel. For most of the time it is a kind of "living backwards" and also perhaps "living forwards."

II

The novel begins with an account of Rahel's visit to Ayemenem twenty-three years after the death of Sophie Mol. Baby Kochamma her baby grand aunt is the only person left in the house. Estha, meanwhile, had been sent back to Ayemenem by his father and Rahel has come to Ayemenem to meet him. The fact that Rahel and Estha are born together is indicated here. The kind of special relations they have also gets revealed along with this.

Then there is an account of how the twins were born. Ammu, their mother and Baba, their father are also introduced. Then there is a sudden shift where there is a reference to Sophie Mol's funeral. Margaret Kochamma, her mother, Chacko, her biological father and Mammachi the grandfather of Estha and Rahel are also introduced here. Inspector Thomas Mathew of Kottayam police station appears soon. Before that Velutha also makes his appearance.

There is a short reference to Estha's return to his father two weeks after the death of Sophie Mol.

Again the action passes on to the point where the novel begins, *i.e.*, twenty-three years after the death of Sophie Mol.

Next, we get an account of Estha, the quiet child. The details of his education once he was sent back to his father follows. There is a reference to Khubchand, his friend in this part of the narration.

There is a sudden shift to describe Estha twenty-three years after the death of Sophie Mol. The name of K.N.M. Pillai is mentioned and his son Lenin's name also appears in this connection. Kalyani, Pillai's wife is referred to here. Kochu Maria, Baby Kochamma's cook makes her appearance. Some reference is made to Mammachi's and Ammu's death and Chacko's life in Canada.

Again it is the 'backward' story where we get an account of Rahel's education, love-affair and marriage to Larry McCaslin and the divorce.

Then it is back to Estha and Rahel's return to Ayemenem and the life of Baby Kochamma. Like the story Baby Kochamma also lives "backwards". Her life from her younger days and her love with Father Mulligan is then described. John Ipe who is her father is also introduced along with her mother Aleyooty Ammachi. There is almost a continuous life history of Baby Kochamma up to the point where the novel starts where we meet Rahel in Ayemenem.

Again we are taken back to Sophie Mol's funeral, Velutha's tragedy, and Estha's return to his father.

The chapter is concluded giving an account of Sophie Mol's visit and its significance. We also get hints about the violation of "love laws."

III

The second chapter begins with an account of Chacko and others proceeding to Cochin in connection with the visit of Sophie Mol in a Plymouth car, which was the property of Pappachi, Chacko's father.

Some background information about Chacko (being a Rhodes Scholar, etc.) we get next. This is followed by an account of Ammu's early life which includes her marriage and the problems created by Mr. Hollick, the English Manager of the company where her husband worked.

Then it is back to the Plymouth car. Soon there is an account of their way back from the airport.

There is a sudden shift here when we get an account of Mammachi's pickle making. This is followed by a detailed account of Pappachi's discovery of the new moth and his disappointment followed by his death.

Then again it is back to the Plymouth where Chacko tells the twins about Kari Saipu's house. This is followed by an account of Chacko's old days when he used to receive a parcel once a month. Chacko's managing the factory is also discussed.

It is back to the car. Then there is an account of how Baby Kochamma taught English to the twins. Miss Mitten, her Australian friend also makes her appearance here.

The journey continues and they see Muraleedharan, the level-crossing lunatic.

Then we get an account of Chacko, the self-proclaimed Marxist. Also, why communism was successful in the state of Kerala is discussed. The political situation in Kerala is described at some length.

There is an account of the worker's march which Chacko and the others witness from the car.

From here we are taken to New York where Rahel remembers her American days.

We are immediately back to Cochin and then there is an account of the early life of Velutha with main focus on untouchability. Vellya Paapen, Velutha's father also makes his appearance here. There is a passing reference to Chella, his mother and also to Kuttappan, his other son.

There is a sudden shift to the incident which took place in which Vellya Paapen was a witness — Ammu's affairs with Velutha.

This is followed by some background information about Vellya Paapen's family which is suddenly followed by the journey in the Plymouth car. There is a mention of Vellya Paapen followed by an account of the life of the twins at Ayemenem house. Then it is back to the Plymouth car.

IV

The third chapter begins with an account of Ayemenem house which is presently occupied by Baby Kochamma and Kochu Maria. Estha and Rahel make their appearance and enough indications are given here about the incestuous relations of Estha and Rahel. Estha's room which once belonged to Ammu and had kept secrets is also described.

V

In the fourth chapter the main focus is on the incident in which Estha was made to do certain things by the homesexual the Orangedrink Lemondrink Man. Ammu, Estha, Rahel and Baby Kochamma are in the Abhilash Talkies to see *The Sound of Music*. After the film, they return to the hotel room to join Chacko.

Then we are told about the political ambitions of Comrade Pillai. The way he treated Velutha, the untouchable is also mentioned. There is also a reference to Mammachi's handling of the factory affairs. When the chapter concludes the limelight is on Chacko who is planning to pre-empt Comrade Pillai.

VI

In the next chapter it is again the story of Rahel twenty-three years later. She meets Comrade Pillai who asks her a number of questions. The scene passes on to Lenins's childhood when she along with him, Estha and Sophie Mol posed for a photograph. The chapter ends with a reference to Sophie Mol's arrival.

VII

The next chapter also begins with details of Sophie Mol's arrival at Cochin. Chacko and others receive her and Margaret Kochamma and they all exchange pleasantries. Estha and Rahel are made to sing in English in obedient voices.

VIII

Chapter seven brings us back to Rahel's visit to Ayemenem after twenty-three years of Sophie Mol's death. Rahel is busy with searching old notebooks which brings back to her mind old memories.

Then there is a reference to Ammu's last visit to Ayemenem with presents for her daughter. Her death is reported subsequently. Ammu and Chacko were there for her cremation.

The chapter concludes where it began. We find Rahel with her notebooks carrying old memories.

IX

The next chapter begins with an account of Ayemenem house as it stood when Sophie Mol came from England. Mammachi remembers her old 'pickle days'. The details of Chacko's younger days when Mammachi had a separate entrance built for his room also are given.

The arrival of Chacko with Sophie Mol and others is announced next. Everybody welcomes her and she is introduced to everyone.

Then some details are given about Velutha and Ammu's affairs with him. Later he is seen in the company of Estha and Rahel.

Then we find Kochu Maria and Sophie Mol together. She takes her hands and inhales them which embarrasses Sophie Mol. This is followed by an account of Ammu's childhood when her father did not care much for her.

The scene again shifts to Sophie Mol and Chacko. Velutha and Rahel appear which is followed by a scene where Kochu Maria distributes pieces of cake. The scene changes to Velutha and Rahel. We find Ammu calling her to have her nap. Sophie Mol, Margaret Kochamma, Mammachi, Baby Kochamma are all seen together. The chapter ends with Sophie Mol moving away from Kochu Maria and trying to establish a friendship with Rahel.

X

Chapter nine also begins with an account of Rahel twenty-three years after the death of Sophie Mol. Rahel is found immersed in Washington thoughts. There is an account of her visit to Velutha's house along with Estha and Sophie Mol. All of them visited him in Saris. Subsequently there is a description of the day three days before the death of Sophie Mol. The chapter ends with Rahel back in the earthly remains of Paradise Pickles and Preserves.

XI

In the next chapter it is Sophie Mol again. While Kochu Maria distributes cake Estha walks out past green mangoes cut and stuffed, past a heap of banana peels on the floor, etc. The Orangedrink Lemondrink Man is very much there in his mind. Then we find him along with Rahel who asks him why he is rowing the jam. His answer is "'India's a Free Country'" (p. 197).

Next there is a description of Vellya Paapen who claims to be the last human being to have set eyes on Kari Saipu's house. There is an account of this house as it appears to Vellya Paapen.

Again we are in the midst of Rahel and Estha, the latter sitting under the magnosteen tree. There is also reference to Rahel going for her afternoon nap on thc instruction of Ammu.

The scene passes on to a description of the old days when

Estha and Rahel used to go to Velutha's house in the boat which Ammu would use to cross the river. Velutha and Vellya Paapen were not at home and the voice that they heard was that of Kuttappen, Velutha's elder brother. Later Velutha also appeared on the scene. He set the boat for Estha and Rahel. The chapter ends with a reference to Rahel's apprehensions about her being caught by her mother for going away skipping her afternoon nap.

XII

Chapter eleven has as its title the title of the novel itself. It begins with Ammu dreaming of Velutha. What goes on here is almost a continuation of what happened in the previous chapter. Estha wonders whether he should wake her up. The story of the Malayalam film *Chemmen* is briefly narrated here, may be with some parallels in Ammu's own life. Then there is a brief mention of the electrocuted elephant. Ammu notices her children covered in a fine dust. Later we find her undressing and putting a red toothbrush under her breast to see if it would stay. Then there is a reference to the high incidence of insanity in the family and among Syrian Christians. We have reference to Ammu's old days and also Rahel returning to the room years later.

XIII

The next chapter begins with the sound of drum mushroomed over the Ayemenem temple. Rahel is found near the temple elephant, after twenty-three years. There is a long account of the decadence of Kathakali and the pathetic condition of the Kathakali artists. Some details are also given about a couple of stories of that evening's performance. Estha also is there and later at the end of the performance they meet Pillai who expresses surprise to see that they are still interested in Kathakali.

XIV

Chapter thirteen takes us back to 'Sophie Mol days". Chacko moves out of his room and sleeps in Pappachi's study so that Sophie Mol and Margaret Kochamma can have his room.

Next we get a pretty long account of Margaret Kochamma's

early life, her love affairs with Chacko, her marriage, divorce, her meeting with Joe who became her second husband and his death. There is also a reference to Chacko's invitation to Ayemenem followed by an account of Margaret Kochamma's strong feelings for leaving Sophie Mol alone and going to Cochin to confirm their return tickets.

Next we find Mammachi and Baby Kochamma getting news of Sophie Mol's death. Ammu is locked into her bedroom in connection with the 'Velutha episode.' There is a detailed account of Vellya Paapen's report to Mammachi about the same and how she loses control.

In a short paragraph we are told how the fisherman traced the body of Sophie Mol.

Then we are taken to the Kottayam police station where Baby Kochamma complains to the Police Inspector about Velutha's 'excesses'. The Inspector sends for Comrade Pillai.

Back in Ayemenem Margaret Kochamma slaps Estha when she gets up from her drug-induced sleep. There is a reference to her writing an apologetic letter. But only Rahel was there in Aymenem to receive it. Then there is a brief reference to the fact that Margaret Kochamma knew nothing about Velutha.

Towards the end Sophie Mol is 'back to life' and searches for things to be given away to the twins as presents. The chapter concludes with Sophie Mol becoming a memory.

XV

The next chapter opens with Chacko's visit to Pillai. There is a description of Pillai's wife also. Lenin, his son and Latha his niece from Kottayam also make their appearance. The first one recites a few line from Shakespeare while the latter recites a poem. Chacko discusses with Pillai the layout for the new label that he wants Pillai to print. The discussion then focusses on Velutha and his role as a worker.

Then there is an account of how victory was gifted to Pillai "wrapped and be-ribboned, on a silver tray" (p. 281). The closure of Paradise Pickles, Chacko's emigration to Canada, etc. are also discussed. There is a reference to Velutha's last visit to Pillai.

Next, there is a detailed account of Velutha making his appearance at the Ayemenem house. He is insulted at the hands of Mammachi and suffers humiliation passively. He straight away goes to Pillai in the hope that he will come to his rescue from the unenviable position in which he found himself.

Velutha comes to Pillai's house and he snubs Velutha saying that worker's indiscipline cannot be tolerated. He reminds him that violating party discipline means violating party unity. He shuts the door and returns to his wife. Velutha realizes that his end is very near.

XVI

In the short chapter 'The Crossing' Velutha makes his appearance wet sitting on the topmost of thirteen stone steps that lead into the water. He has become a lonely man : "He held his mundu spread above his head to dry. The wind lifted it like a sail. He was suddenly happy. *Things will get worse*, he thought to himself, *Then better*. He was walking swiftly now, towards the Heart of Darkness. As lonely as a wolf" (p. 290).

XVII

In the chapter 'A Few Hours Later' we find the twins and Sophie Mol in a boat. How Sophie Mol gets drowned is described in some detail in the chapter. Early morning at four o'clock the twins "exhausted, distraught and covered in mud, made their way through the swamp and approached the History House" (p. 293). They fail to notice Velutha lying asleep in the shadows. "As lonely as a wolf. A brown leaf on his black back" (p. 294).

XVIII

Chapter seventeen again takes us back to Estha twenty-three years later. We are also told that four years after Chacko left for Canada Baby Kochamma had had the Plymouth car washed regularly.

Kochu Maria and Baby Kochamma are then introduced the latter busy with her diary writing. Then we get some details about Father Mulligan's death.

Rahel is found lying on Estha's bed. Estha remembers his mother's mouth "that had kissed his hand through the barred train window. First class, on the Madras Mail' (p. 300). Rahel remembers Chacko's marching orders to Ammu after the Velutha episode. Then there is an account of Estha's return to his father. The chapter ends with another reference to Sophie Mol's death, Velutha being charged with kidnapping and murder, Communist Party siege of Paradise Pickles and Preserves and the policemen picking "their way through the wet undergrowth, clumping into the Heart of Darkness" (p. 303).

XIX

The chapter 'The History House' takes us to the Kottayam police station. The police are after Velutha and they torture him in the most impossible way. At the end of the operation he is not able to walk. As mute witness a pair of two egg twins are there who are totally helpless. This again is a twenty-three year old story.

XX

In the ante-penultimate chapter also we have the Kottayam police station where the words 'Politeness', 'Obedience', 'Loyalty', 'Intelligence', 'Courtesy' and 'Efficiency' have taken the reverse order at least in the eyes of Estha. Baby Kochamma makes the children tell a lie to ensure that the police will not have any problem in connection with the custodial death of Velutha. Estha is taken to the lock up where he finds Velutha almost dead. Then there is an account of Baby Kochamma returning to Ayemenem, and removal of Velutha's body to Pauper's pit. The chapter concludes with Baby Kochamma joining hands with Chacko to drive away Ammu from the house.

XXI

The penultimate chapter gives an account of Estha's train journey to his father in the Madras Mail. This is almost a continuation of the action of the earlier chapter. On the platform "Rahel doubled over and screamed and screamed" (p. 326).

Again it is the story after twenty-three years. Estha and

Rahel are found together again. "Once again they broke the Love Laws. That lay down who should be loved. And how. And how much" (p. 328).

In the short section that follows we are taken to Sophie Mol again. Rahel and Ammu also are there. Ammu longs for Velutha. "Ached for him with the whole of her biology" (p. 330).

XXII

In the concluding chapter we find Ammu wearing Chacko's old shirts over a long white petticoat. She is found restless. She moves quickly through the darkness to reach Velutha. Then there is a detailed description of Velutha having physical relation with Ammu. Thirteen nights follow this one. "They knew that there was nowhere for them to go. They had nothing. No future. So they stuck to the small things" (p. 338). The last part of the novel talks about the night on the day Sophie Mol arrives in Ayemenem. Velutha "took her face in his hands and drew it towards his. He closed his eyes and smelled her skin. Ammu laughed.

Yes, Margaret, she thought. *We do it to each other too.*

She kissed his closed eyes and stood up. Velutha with his back against the mangosteen tree watched her walk away.

She had a dry rose in her hair.

She turned to say it once again : '*Naaley*'

Tomorrow" (p. 340)

That is how *The God of Small Things* comes to an end.

XXIII

To sum up, the novel begins with Rahel's visit to Ayemenem house twenty-three years after the death of Sophie Mol and ends with a day in the life of Ammu when she has an affair with Velutha which is to be followed by thirteen similar days.

Roy's approach is rather cinematic for the scenes change one after the other. From Rahel's visit to Ayemenem the scene changes to the birth of the twins, Sophie Mol's funeral seven years later, Estha's return to his father a week later, and again to Rahel's visit. Then again we hear about the younger days of Estha followed by Rahel's visit twenty-three years after the death of Sophie Mol. Some incidents which take place in between like Mammachi's and Ammu's death and Chacko's migration to Canada are also described. It is back to Rahel's education, her marriage etc. followed by Rahel's return again. Baby Kochamma's past years is described followed by Sophie Mol's death twenty-three years before Rahel's visit to Ayemenem.

The interesting thing about the opening chapter is that almost the whole story is told and all the major characters are introduced.

The pattern is almost repeated in the second chapter also. A significant revelation made here is about Ammu's affairs with Velutha which is a turning point in the novel. In the third chapter the whole focus is on Ayemenem house and the scene does not pass on to anywhere else. In the next chapter also there is cinematic effect where there are quick succession of scenes. The following chapter also is a repetition of the earlier one in this respect.

In chapter six it is only about Sophie Mol's arrival. In the next chapter also different scenes are made available. Chapter eight mainly discusses Sophie Mol's arrival but with a minor distration — Ammu's affairs with Velutha. The next chapter also has multiple scenes. In chapter ten again the scene shifts from one to the other. In the next chapter it is mainly about Ammu of course with some reference to her earlier days. In the following chapter there is only a single scene — Rahel and Estha in the temple to watch Kathakali performance. In Chapter thirteen also the focus shifts from one action to another at different periods. Next, the main focus is Pillai's house and Chacko and Velutha visit him at different times. In the following chapter we find only Velutha. The same is the case with the next chapter where we meet the twins and Sophie Mol in the boat. In chapter seventeen different scenes are enacted one after the other. The focus of the next chapter is Kottayam police station. In the following chapter also the main focus is on the police station. In the chapter twenty-one we are taken back to Estha's return to his father after the death of Sophie Mol followed by Rahel's return to Ayemenem twenty-three years later and then back to Sophie Mol. The main focus of the concluding chapter is on the sexual relations Ammu has with Velutha which is unique for its vivid descriptions.

To put it briefly, two factors are of importance as regards how the novelist approaches his work : his own temperament and the nature of his subject. " 'Every great artist necessarily creates his own form', says Tolstoy in a statement which reads like a corollary to Jame's pronouncement about form and substance" (quoted from Allot 1959 — p. 164). Roy also creates her own form which probably she finds fit to narrate the life history of five generations with special focus on one incident- the incident in which a young girl gets drowned.

The structure of the novel is certainly not defective as Flaubert thought *The Pickwick Papers* was "Some bits are magnificent; but what a defective structure! All the English writers are like that. Walter Scott apart, they lack composition. This is intolerable for us Latins" (Quoted from Allot (1959 — p. 168).

Probably the problem with the plot of this novel is that it does not involve a hero's journey and trial. Several other major and minor characters do appear in the play and all of them in some sense or other get linked to the main plot. Also, the same novel will have several readings : "A psychologist may find that a particular novel's main plot involves the painful but necessary loss of innocence for the protagonist, an anthropologist may note that the story embodies a mythic pattern of journey, trial and renewal for the protagonist, a sociologist may be struck by the fact that the protagonist's movement from the country to the city shapes his or her experience; a Marxist historian may feel that the narrative fundamentally celebrates the rise of a member of the petite bourgeoise at the expense of the lower classes" (see Kershner 1997 — p. 110). Interestingly enough almost all these issues we find discussed in the novel and the development of the plot some how doesn't get affected and the novel becomes highly readable.

18

What Happened to Our Man of the Masses?

I

There are three major ways of telling a story. First is the narrative or epic in which the author relates himself the whole adventure in the manner of Cervantes in his *Don Quixote* and of Fielding in his *Tom Jones*. The author, like the muse, is supposed to know everything and can reveal the secret springs of acti . He can be concise, or diffuse as the story requires it.

Another mode is that of memoirs where the subject of the adventures relates his own story. Smollet in his *Roderic Random* and Goldsmith in his *Vicar of Wakefield* have adopted this mode. It has the advantage of the warmth and interest of a person and has a greater air of truth, as it seems to account for the communication to the public.

A third way is that of the epistolary correspondence, carried on between the characters of the novel. This is the form made use of by Richardson and many others. It gives the feelings of the moment as the writers felt them at the moment. It makes the whole work dramatic since all the characters speak in their persons. According to Thomas Hardy ''the advantages of telling a story (Passing over the disadvantages) are that, hearing what one side has to say'', one is ''led constantly to the imagination of what the other side must be feeling, and at last are anxious to know if the other side does really feel'' what one imagines. (Quoted from Allot 1959 — p. 260).

Much of the importance attributed to the point of view in the novel grew from ideas developed by Henry James in his introductions to his novels, which were collected under the title *The Art of Novel* (1934).

We usually sub-divide the third-person point of view into either omniscient or limited. In *Omniscient* ("all-knowing") point of view, the narrator is capable of going into the minds of a variety of characters or of speaking about "future" events in the novel. Booth (1961) uses the term *privilege* to refer to a narrator's ability to know what could not be known by naturalistic means; complete privilege is omniscience.

The omniscient narrator may be *intrusive* or *editorial* interrupting the novel's action to express opinions about the book's events and characters. An *impersonal* or *objective* narrator, on the other hand, withholds comment on the action. According to Kreshner (1997) "a majority of twentieth century authors are *impersonal*, on the grounds that this convention is supposed to be more realistic. Some go so far as to sacrifice any insight into the characters' thoughts and feelings" (p. 119). A third-person narrator that is not omniscient is said to be *limited* — limited to the perceptions and thoughts of one character or rarely several characters. Kreshner (1997) is of the view that "narration that is strictly limited to a single character, especially if that character is the protagonist, has much the same effect as first-person narration, with the difference that the language of the narration need not be appropriate to the character" (p. 120).

II

Roy in the present novel is the omniscient narrator who is intrusive. An attempt is made here to show how effectively she 'intrudes' in the narration of the story.

From the opening chapter of the novel we find the narrator intruding. In the funeral of Sophie Mol there is a description of an old lady masquerading as a distant relative. The author comments that she is a "funeral junkie" (a person who habitually takes the drug HEROIN and is dependent on it) or "a latent necrophiliac" (a person who suffers from necrophilia — sexual interest in dead bodies) (p. 5).

After Ammu died Rahel spent her holidays largely ignored by Chacko and Mamachi, who, according to the author had "grown soft with sorrow, slumped in their bereavement like a pair of drunks in a toddy bar" (p. 15).

Sophie Mol, the author comments is "the seeker of small wisdoms : *Where do old birds go to die? Why don't dead ones fall like stones from the sky?* The harbinger of harsh reality : *You're both whole wags and I'm a half one*. The guru of gore : *I've seen a man in an accident with his eyeball swinging on the end of a nerve, like a yo-yo"* (p. 16).

Rahel who was blacklisted in Nazareth Convent was expelled after repeated complaints from senior girls. She was accused of hiding behind doors and deliberately colliding with her seniors. The author comments that they were quite right in doing so. Later when the teachers whispered to each other that it was as though she didn't know how to be a girl, the author reacts by saying "they weren't far off the mark" (p. 17).

Later the author comments that the size of the charcoal still-life sketches of Rahel were "enormous" (p. 17) which made the staff feel impressed. This helped her to get admission in a College of Architecture in Delhi.

When Rahel returned to Ayemenem after twenty-three years, Baby Kochamma regretted having written to her about Estha's return. Then we listen to the authorial comments : "But then, what else could she have done? Had him on her hands for the rest of her life? Why *should* she? He wasn't her responsibility. Or was he?" (p. 21). Rahel thought that she was living her life backwards. Then the author offers her own views : "It was a curiously apt observation. Baby Kochamma *had* lived her life backwards" (p. 22).

Ammu, Estha and Rahel are described as transgressors who broke rules. They all crossed into forbidden territory and tampered with the laws that lay down who should be loved and how. Then comes the author's remark : "It was a time when uncles became fathers, mothers lovers, and cousins died and had funerals. It was a time when the unthinkable became thinkable and the impossible really happened" (p. 31).

Baby Kochamma had been teaching English to Rahel and Estha. She was very particular about their pronunciation of English. In this connection also we get an anthorial comment on the way Baby Kochamma pronounces it : "Prer Nun sea ayshun" (p. 36).

Chacko had explained to Estha and Rahel that history was like an old house at night — with all the lamps lit and ancestors whispering inside. Then he gave them a sense of historical perspective "though perspective was something which, in the weeks to follow, Chacko himself would sorely lack" (p. 53). The part within the inverted commas comes as a remark by the novelist.

It was Chacko who christened the factory Paradise Pickles and Preserves. He had wanted to call it Zeus Pickles and Preserves which was vetoed. Then comes the author's comment : "Comrade Pillai's suggestion — Parashuram Pickles — was vetoed for the opposite reason : too *much* local relevance" (p. 58).

Chacko used to call the women workers in the factory 'Comrade' and he wanted them to call him back Comrade "which made them giggle" (p. 65). The part that is quoted is again the observation made by the novelist.

"As the marchers approached, Ammu put up her window. Estha his. Rahel hers". Then comes the comment "Effortfully, because the black knob on the handle had fallen off" (p. 65).

Comrade E.M.S. Namboodiripad is reported to have expelled the Naxalites from his party and gone on with the business of harnessing anger for parliamentary purposes. The author refers to him as "*Running Dog. Soviet stooge*" (p. 69).

When Rahel declared that she had seen Velutha among the marchers Ammu was angry with her. Then she saw that "Ammu had a film of perspiration on her forehead and upper lip, and that her eyes had become hard, like marbles. Like Pappachi's in the Vienna studio photograph" (pp. 71-72). Then the author exclaims : "How Pappachi's Moth whispered in his children's veins!"

Velutha had a way with machines. Mammachi often said

that if only he hadn't been a Paravan, he might have become an engineer. According to the novelist she said it "with impenetrable Touchable logic" (p. 75).

Estha and Rahel had never been shy of each other. But they had never been old enough to know what shyness was. When they met again after twenty-three years Estha was in the room and Rahel at the door. Then the author expresses her doubts : *Had he seen her? Was he really mad? Did he know that she was there*? (p. 92).

In the Abhilash Talkies when Baby Kochamma went to the toilet Rahel studied her enormous legs. Then there is the following observation from the novelist : "Years later during a history lesson being read out in school — *The Emperor Babur had a wheatish complexion and pillar-like thighs* — this scene would flash before her. Baby Kochamma balanced like a big bird over a public pot. Blue veins like lumpy knitting running up her translucent shins. Fat knees dimpled. Hair on them. Poor little tiny feet to carry such a load!" (p. 95).

After the incident in which he had an unpleasant experience with the Orangedrink Lemondrink Man "Estha held his Other Hand carefully (upwards, as though he was holding an imagined orange). He slid past the Audience (their legs moving thisway andthat), past Baby Kochamma, past Rahel (still tilted back), past Ammu (still annoyed)" (p. 105). Whatever is given within brackets appears as comments from the author.

How the back verandah of the History House had been enclosed and converted into the airy hotel kitchen is described in chapter five. According to the author the History House was a place "where a posse of Touchable policemen converged, where an inflatable goose was burst" (p. 127).

There was a photograph of Sophie Mol, the twins and Lenin in which Sophie Mol had turned her eyelids out so that her eyes looked like pink-veined flesh petals which are "grey in a black and white photograph" (p. 135). She had hijacked Mammachi's thimble "the day she arrived, and vowed to spend her holidays drinking only from a thimble". The part with in the inverted commas come as comments from the writer.

The Foreign Returnees in wash'n' wear suits and rainbow sunglasses were waiting in the Airport. The author takes exception to their dress. "*Look at the way they dressed! Surely they had more suitable airport wear! Why did Malayalees have such awful teeth?*" (p. 140). Later she also comments : "*Oho! Going to the dogs India is*" (p. 140).

In chapter ten we find Estha walking past green mangoes... gunny bags... etc. The author remarks that the green mangoes, etc. "needed no attention for a while" (p. 193).

There is a description in the novel how Ammu looked a little critically at her round, heavy behind. The author remarks that "Chacko-of-Oxford would no doubt have put it" as "not big *per se*" (p. 223).

When Chacko and Margaret met first the former had told the latter the story of a twins. The writer remarks that for some reason — "natural prudence perhaps, and an instinctive reticence with foreigners" — (p. 242) she did not evince keen interest in the story.

There is a reference to an incident in which Chacko "stopped Pappachi from hitting. Mammachi with the brass vase, and a rocking chair was murdered in the moonlight" (p. 246) the part within the inverted commas being a comment by the novelist.

Margaret Kochamma is often referred to as Ex-wife and atleast once in the novel it comes in the form of an authorial comment. "He had a wife *(Ex-wife,* Chacko!) at home" (p. 270).

Another comment is made by the author in connection with the Velutha episode : *With the smell of her skin in the air that he breathed. Her body on his. He might never see her again. Where was she? What had they done to her? Had they hurt her?* (pp. 285-286).

Baby Kochamma had somehow forced Estha and Rahel to tell the police that Velutha was the man who had abducted them. When she continues to argue with the twins there comes an authorial comment : "*Then what happened*" (p. 317)?

Another comment has to do with Velutha affair : *If he touched her, he couldn't talk to her, if he loved her he couldn't leave, if he spoke he couldn't listen, if he fought he couldn't win*" (p. 330).

In short, Roy effectively makes use of authorial comment as she narrates the story. These comments help us to know the characters more closely. Sometimes this technique is used to expose some of the characters. She makes use of irony also in these comments. At times she criticises the contemporary society through the remarks that she makes.

Next we shall consider how Roy uses the technique of stream of consciousness in the novel.

III

An important aspect of point of view is the degree of access we have to the mind of the book's central consciousness. In third-person narration one of the most common ways of presenting experience is through the indirect free style. This refers to the way in which direct experience is conventionally paraphrased. Instead of "She turned away in dismay and thought, 'How beastly he is", a novelist writes in indirect free style, "She turned away in dismay. How beastly he was!."

Stream of consciousness writing is a further step into a character's consciousness, in which we are presented directly with what purports to be the running thoughts of a character, as in Mr. Bloom's breakfast in Joyce (1986) : "The tea was drawn. He filled his own moustache cup, sham crown Derby, smiling. Silly Milly's birthday gift. Only five she was then. No, wait : four" (p. 51).

A passage like this is often called *interior monologue*. It can work within a novel somewhat as a *soliloqui* works in a play.

In Roy's novel we get many instances where she makes use of the stream of consciousness technique.

Baby Kochamma was one who hated the twins. She deemed them capable of anything, anything at all. She thought that *they might eve steal their present back* and also *she might steal her present back* (p. 29). These come as interior monologues.

Chacko had explained to the twins that the whole of human civilization began only two hours before in Earthwoman's life.

He also said that it was an awe-inspiring and humbling thought which made Rahel think "*humbling along without a care in the world*" (p. 54).

Mammachi had said that what her grandchildren suffered from was far more worse than inbreeding. But Rahel was not sure what she suffered from : "*It is a far, far better thing that I do, than I have ever done*, she would say to herself sadly" (p. 61).

Her co-passenger's madness comforted Rahel. "It drew her closer into New York's deranged womb. Away from the other, more terrible thing that haunted her." This is followed by what went in the mind of Rahel : *A sourmetal smell, like steel bus-rails, and the smell of the bus conductor's hands from holding them. A young man with an old man's mouth* (p. 72).

Rahel and Estha had never been shy of each other's bodies and "they had never been old enough (together) to know what shyness was." "What a funny word *old* was on its own, Rahel thought, and said it to herself : *Old*" (p. 92). It is the word "old" that comes to her "conscious stream" here.

Baby Kochamma was surprised to see Rahel taking a lot of time in the toilet in the Abhilash Talkies. What went on in Rahel's mind was :

Rubadub dub....
Three women in a tub,
Tarry a while said Slow (p. 96)

After the Orangedrink Lemondrink Man incident, Estha was totally upset and began to behave in a strange way. When Ammu asked him what the matter was what went on in his mind was :

Finish the drink.

Watch the picture.

Think of all the poor people.

Lucky rich boy with porketmunny. No worries. (p. 107).

Pillai had his own views about the Ayemenem family. When he heard from Rahel that she was divorced, his immediate reaction which came in the form of a thought was : *One was mad. The other die-vorced. Probably barren* (p. 130). When he asked about Estha, Rahel's reaction was "he was fine" which was followed by the following thought : *Fine. Flat and honey-coloured. He washes his clothes with crumpling soap* (p. 131).

When a foreign object was lodged in her nostril when she was young, one day Rahel happened to be at the doctor with Lenin (also with the same complaint). When she sat there waiting for her turn to be called what went on in her mind was *Please God, please make it come out* (p. 133).

When Rahel thanked her mother for providing her with new frock and knickers Ammu said "You're welcome, my sweet-heart." This continued to linger in the mind of Rahel which she repeats : "*You're welcome, my sweetheart*" (p. 136).

On their way across the airport car park, hotweather crept into the clothes of the children. When the twins said that their crisp knickers wouldn't hit them Sopie Mol remarked that they were lucky. In their mind the response was *Lucky rich boy with Porketmunny. And a grandmother's factory to inherit. No worries* (p. 150).

There is a long stream of thought of Rahel presented in chapter nine of the novel. "*Around now... if this were Washington, I would be on my way to work. The bus ride. The streetlights. The gas fumes. The shapes of people's breath on the bulletproof glass of my cabin. The clatter of coins pushed towards me in the metal tray. The smell of money on my fingers. The punctual drunk with sober eyes who arrives exactly at 10 p.m. : 'Hey, you! Black bitch! Suck my dick*!" (p. 187).

Velutha also appears in the novel making interior monologues a couple of times. There was a time, when he tried to hate Rahel as *she's one of them .... Just another one of them*. But he couldn't hate her. *She had deep dimples when she smiled. Her eyes were always somewhere else* (p. 214).

When it was decided that Estha should be returned to his father, what Ammu whispered in her mind was *May be they're right. May be a boy does need a Baba* (p. 302).

Estha and Rahel were taken to the police station and the sight of Baby Kochamma made them suddenly sober. What they thought was : *why had she come? Where was Ammu? Was she still locked up* (p. 315)?

Thus, we find that interior monologue is used as an effective technique in the novel which helps considerably to know what exactly goes on in some of the important characters. It is mostly Rahel who, we find, makes these monologues than anybody else.

IV

In Roy's novel, as discussed in detail, it is not a simple narration. She takes every opportunity to intrude when she tells the story. One important thing she achieves through this 'interference' is that she can be ironic whenever she wants to be. She, at times, becomes critical of the ills of the society and at others times she tries to expose some of the characters who wants others to believe that they are fault less.

It can be said that the differences in mood and tempo brought out by a novelist's handling of 'story', 'plot' and "time" are emphasized further by his choice of narrative method. In Roy's case also it is certainly true. Roy has always been very much alive to the importance of selecting the angle of vision from which she will best be able to illuminate and interpret her material and, most important of all, make it seem authentic.

The narrative, is the most common method and has the advantage of flexibility because of the author's assumed omniscience. What makes the narration of the novel all the more effective is the use of the technique of interior monologue at several points in the novel. By using this technique Roy displays the genuine novelists's gift of realizing diverse experience outside her own immediate modes of thinking and feeling and of adding to its authenticity by solidity of detail. The author's temperament and sensibility are felt with great vividness in the novel. Roy is able to illuminate for us the 'eternal moment' of intense experience and the narrative technique she has adopted helps her quite a lot to make the story telling as effective as she wanted it to be. Her sense of hidden forms of violence and treachery (especially in her portrayal of the police and Pillai) beneath the superficial amenities of social intercourse gives her work its shapeliness and energy. The title of this chapter 'What Happened to Our Man of the Masses' is only one of the instances where the novelist reveals her intentions to the reader by describing Chacko in his "suit and well-fed tie leading Margaret Kochamma and Sophie Mol triumphantly up the steps like a pair of tennis trophies that he had .... won" (p. 173).

19

The God of Small Things

I

"Somehow, by not mentioning his name, she knew that she had drawn him into the tousled intimacy of that blue cross-stitch afternoon and the song from the tangerine transistor. By not mentioning his name, she sensed that a pact had been forged between her Dream and the World. And that the midwives of that pact, were, or would be, her sawdust coated two-egg twins.

She knew who he was — the God of Loss, the God of small Things. Of *course* she did" (p. 220).

The passage quoted is from the chapter "The God of Small Things" and obviously the "she" is Ammu and the 'God of Small Things' is Velutha. Ammu had a dream in which a one-armed man had embraced her. "*If he touched her, he couldn't talk to her, if he loved her he couldn't leave, if he spoke he couldn't listen, if he fought he couldn't win*" (p. 217). Then a series of questions are asked : "Who was he, the one-armed man? Who could he have been? The God of Loss? The God of Small Things? The God of Goose Bumps and Sudden Smiles? Of Sourmetal Smells — like steel bus-rails and the smell of the bus conductor's hands from holding them" (p. 217).

Thus, we find that Velutha, a very important character in the novel is 'The God' in *The God of Small Things*! Roy talks about 'small' and even 'things' recur in the novel and these terms have meanings far from the ordinary when she uses them across the novel.

II

In the opening page of the novel itself Roy makes use of the word "small" when she says "... small fish appear in the puddle" (p. 1). The first reference to 'small things' is made in connection with what Rahel remembers of Estha's experience at Abhilash Talkies and Estha's sandwiches on the Madras Mail "...these are only the small things" (p. 3). As far as young children are concerned these are certainly not silly or small things and are big or serious things.

Thus, throughout the novel, trivial things become serious and serious things become non-trivial. Sophie Mol is reported to have showed Rahel two things : newly painted high dome and the bat baby. She is described as seeker of "small wisdoms." But "where do old birds go to die?" cannot be a 'small wisdom'.

We have reference to 'Small God' and 'Big God' in the novel where Rahel's marriage to Larry McCaslin is discussed : "That Big God howled like a hot wind, and demanded obeisance. Then small God (cosy and contained, private and limited) came away cauterized, laughing nimbly at his own temerity" (p. 19). One more reference we get in the same page of the novel : "So small God laughed a hollow laugh, and skipped away cheerfully."

Certainly a distinction is made between small things and big things in the novel. This is made more than clear when we get a description of Sophie Mol's arrival. Chacko greets Margaret Kochamma and Sophie Mol most cordially and the authorial comment that follows makes clear what the title of the novel or at least part of it means : "And the Air was full of Thoughts and Things to Say. But at times like these, only the Small Things are ever said. The Big Things lurk unsaid inside" (p. 142). This is the pattern that is followed throughout the novel -- the small things become big and the big things become small.

In this sense it is logical that Velutha is the God "of Small Things." "He left no footprints in sand, no ripples in water, no image in mirrors" (p. 265). He was born on the earth with a mission. Once he completed it he slowly disappeared leaving no trace in the world where he lived. He was a human God, a God who lived in flesh and blood. His was, in a certain sense, a life of loss, not of gains. Thus, it is apt that he is repeatedly referred to as "The God of Loss" (pp. 265, 290, 312). We find that in the same breath he is referred to as "The God of Small Things" also. The title and the way he was killed reminds one of Golding's novel *Lord of the Flies* where the little ones shout "kill the beast! cut his throat! spill his blood" (1971 p. 168). But the crucial difference lies in the fact that whereas *Lord of the Flies* is evil incarnation, 'God of Small Things' is all that is good.

Ammu continued her affairs with Velutha for a full fortnight and on the first night and "even later, on the thirteen nights that followed this one, instinctively they stuck to the Small Things. The Big Things ever lurked inside. They knew that there was nowhere for them to go. They had nothing. No future. So they stuck to the small things" (p. 338).

There is a reference to *Chappu Thamburan* (Lord Rubbish) in the penultimate page of the novel which is again very significant from the point of view of the title the novel. Without admitting it to each other or themselves, Velutha and Ammu "linked their fates, their futures (their Love, their Madness, their Hope, their Infinnate Joy) to his. They checked on him every night (with growing panic as time went by) to see if he had survived the day. They fretted over his frailty. His smallness. The adequacy of his camouflage. His seemingly self-destructive pride. They grew to love his electric taste. His shambling dignity" (p. 339).

Velutha and Ammu chose *Chappu Thamburan* because they knew that they had to put their faith in fragility. "Stick to smallness. Each time they parted, they extracted only one promise from each other", to meet the next day.

Chappu Thamburan outlived Velutha and fathered future generations. He died of natural causes whereas Velutha's was an unnatural death. It means that Velutha and Ammu were wrong in their perception of Chappu Thamburan, the Lord Rubbish.

III

That is 'The God of Small Things,' the title and the novel

itself. In a sense the course events took sounds absurd and rubbish. The characters themselves, like Velutha and Ammu are reduced to nothing and the culprits are big men who are in fact, small men.

Ammu and even her children were interested in small things. Velutha was in several ways the possessor of these small things. He did possess qualities that were certainly divine especially when they are compared to those of some of the other characters in the novel. For example, her mother Mammachi was never kind to her and took every opportunity to insult and humiliate her. She was waiting for opportunities. Her father also was not very keen about her well being or what would happen of her. That was why her education became a non-issue. Whatever remembered of her father was only a cruel side where he continued to beat his wife.

Baby Kochamma also chose to remain 'monstrous' in her attitude to Ammu. It might be attributed to the problems she was made to confront with, she herself being a dream which never fructified. For the same reason she took every chance that came her way to denounce Ammu.

Chacko, her brother also more or less maintained an attitude that was far from satisfactory. He took pride in the fact that he was the sole owner of the Paradise Pickles Factory and very often made himself clear the fact that it was all his. This was what made Rahel, the feminist remark that Chacko was a 'male Chauvinist pig.''

She did not get a different kind of treatment from her husband either. Even though it was a marriage of her own choice, he was someone who she failed to put up with. He was a drunkard who never showed concern for her. A stage came when her self-respect was questioned and that made her run away from him with her twin children.

Velutha, on the other hand, was an entirely different person. Even when she was a child he was very good to her and saw everything that was divine in him. She was 'little Ammu' for him and the divine relationship continued for quite sometime.

They grew up and the relation remained the same as when

they were children. Since she got separated from her husband, she was leading the life of a spinster. It was quite logical and natural that Ammu, the young woman was attracted to Velutha, the youngman. They established a physical relationship which could perhaps be described as divine.

In a sense the sexual relationship that Ammu had with Velutha could be described as 'small things' if properly placed in the Ayemenem context. That is because, having illegitimate relations with women was something very ordinary for Chacko, the Ayemenem man. He had affairs with the women workers in the factory and his mother Mammachi saw to it that he got every opportunity to have his 'man's needs' met. Again, Baby Kochamma was one who was madly after Father Mulligan to have physical relations with him. It was more because of the restraint shown by the Father that she failed to have such relations with him.

If that is so, illegitimate sexual relations can certainly be described as "small things". It became a big thing when it came to Ammu's relation with Velutha because of other reasons. To begin with, Velutha was no more in the good books of either Mammachi or Baby Kochamma. The incident in which the former was addressed as 'Modalali' continued to echo and re-echo in her mind. Baby Kochamma also was waiting to get an opportunity to strike quite expectedly. But both these people never anticipated that Ammu would set records straight after Baby Kochamma filed a false FIR which implicated Velutha.

In short, there couldn't be a more appropriate title for the novel than "The God of Small Things" as "The God", "Small" and "Things" get well defined. Of course there are things which are small and which are big. But as already indicated, at times 'small' becomes 'big' for some and 'big' becomes 'small' for some others.

Ultimately, the novel becomes a saga of lost dreams in the sense that almost all the characters in the novel, both major and minor are made to live in a dream world only to realize soon that they are shattered. Even Ayemenem and Ayemenem house do not get isolated from the general pattern.

As de Bono (1994) has observed “brilliant new ideas are produced and we do not know how they come about. We can study and analyze the behaviour of creative people, but this will not tell us very much, because often such people are themselves unaware of what triggered the brilliant idea” (p. 4). Roy has in her maiden venture produced new ideas and we do not “know how they come about.”

Epilogue

I

The God of Small Things is at the top of the best seller list in Australia, America, Spain, France, Portugal and England. Roy earned $ 1.2 million in the U.S. before she won the Booker Prize. The manuscript was bought by Flamingo for Rs. 3.5 crore. The book was on the New York Times best seller list for ten weeks.

The Booker Committee has described Roy as "an architect in literary circle moulding language in all shapes and sizes as was never done before at least in the Indian literary context." The jury chair person comments : "The story she tells is fundamental as well as local, it is about love and death.... Her narrative crackles with riddles and yet it tells its tale quite clearly. We are all engrossed by this moving novel. The novel keeps all the promises it makes."

According to Kate Kalleway of "The Guardian", "the book — a first novel — has turned out to be a very big thing." John Updike, the American writer described it as "Tiger woodsian debut." Jason Cowley, a literary journalist and a critic who is also one of the five 1997 Booker Prize judges observes : "The God of Small Things" had a radical difference, it was unlike anyother book we read."

The Editor of "Washington Square" News weekly Ric Ornellas says : "The book has proved that Americans could be persuaded in millions to buy and read books by exotic novelists other than Marquez..."

Shomit Miller, Roy's close friend and author says that the book "uses language in a way that is rare... very rarely do you get someone who can tear apart the rules and give you something that is fresh and not pretentious." Tarun Tejpal is reported tc have told a Swedish journalist (even before the novel became popular as the best seller) : "I've just read the book that is going to win the Booker Prize."

Roy herself has remarked that *The God of the Small Things* would be her first and last book. About the novel she has said : "It tells a different story from the story the book is telling you. The book is not about what happened but about how what happened affected people." On her use of language she has remarked : "For me language is a skin on my thought and was thinking of way of telling... I wrote it.. the way an architect designs a building."

She further says : "I have to say that my book is not about history but biology and transgression. And, therefore, the fact is that you can never understand the nature of brutality until you see what has been loved being smashed. And so the book deals with both things — it deals with our ability to be brutal as well our ability to be so deeply intimate and so deeply loving."

About her childhood Roy has observed : "Well, as a child I know there was such a struggle to come to terms with the world is about to do to you. I was an unprotected child in some ways and I felt that one was always trying to anticipate the world, and therefore, was trying to be wise in some ways. Often I think if you have a sort of strange childhood two things happen. As a child you grow up very quickly but obviously the part, *i.e.*, a child remains a child. And when you become an adult there is a part of you that remains a child. So the communication between you and your childhood remains open. It isn't an effort for me to see things through that mirror. It's just all the boundaries are blurred. You make your own rules."

II

Roy's mother Mary Roy was a Syrian Christian and her father was a Bengali Hindu. In the novel Ammu, Rahel's mother is a Syrian Christian and her husband is a Bengali Hindu. As a child Roy confronted a lot of difficulties in her grandparent's house. Rahel in the novel also has a lot of problems at Ayemenem house. After Mary Roy got separated from her husband, she alongwith her brother was brought to Ayemenem. In the novel, Ammu gets separated from her husband and she brings her daughter Rahel and Estha to Ayemenem. Mary Roy who had once escaped from her house to save herself from the boredom of life ended up by getting married to a Bengali. She was forced to come back to the same place which she had deserted once. She was not expected to come back leaving behind her parents. She was an unwelcome guest in her own house. Ammu in the novel does exactly the same. She leaves for Calcutta when she realizes that there is nobody to take care of her or to show some concern. She even fears that her marriage will never materialize. She ends up marrying a Bengali but is forced to come back to the place from where she had run away. She is most unwelcome when she returned to Ayemenem house, which is her own house.

As a child Roy witnessed the handicaps of her mother. At the age of three Roy's mother asked her to be independent. According to Mary Roy even as a child Roy was not in need of a teacher. She learnt her lessons on her own. Roy has been a voracious reader and even at an early age she has read works like *The Tempest*. She left Ayemenem at the age of eighteen with a range of harsh experiences and struggles of life. She joined the school of Architecture in Delhi. She met her first husband Gerard, an architect in the school of Architecture. After her separation from Gerard she acted in a Hindi film *Marey Sahib*. She wrote scripts for the films *like The Banyan Tree, Electric Moon* and *In which Annie Gives it — Those one*. She lives with her husband Pradip Krishen who is a film producer in New Delhi.

In the novel Rahel witnesses the handicaps of her mother. She is almost independent at a very young age. She also leaves Ayemenem early in her life and joins the school of Architecture. She meets Larry McCaslin who is a researcher at the school of Architecture. Just a Roy is separated from Gerard, Rahel in the novel also gets separated. However, Rahel is portrayed as one who is a divorcee and there is no reference to her remarrying or living with a second husband in the novel as is the case with Roy.

To put it briefly, it is very difficult to look at the novel keeping away the turmoil that the novelist Roy and her mother Mary Roy have undergone in their lives.

References

Allot, Miriam, *Novelists on the Novel*, London : Routledge, 1959.

Barth, John. ''The Literature of Replenishment'', *Atlantic*, Jan., 1990.

Barthes, Roland, ''The Death of the Author'', *The Rustle of Language*, trans., Richard Howard, New York : Hill and Wang, 1968.

Bergson, Henri, *Time and Free Will : An Essay on the Immediate Data of Consciousness*, trans., F.L. Pogson, London : Allen, 1971.

Booth, Wayne, *The Rhetoric of Fiction*, Chicago : University of Chicago Press, 1961.

Bradbury, Malcom, *The Modern American Novel*, New York : Oxford University Press, 1985.

Buchen, Irvin, H. ''The Aesthetics of the supra -- novel,'' *The Theory of the Novel : New Essays* ed. John Halperin, New York : Oxford University Press, 1974.

Collins, Carvel, ''William Faulkner, The Sound and the Fury,'' *The Voice of American Forum Lectures*, Washington.

Conrad, Joseph, *The Nigger of the Narcissus*, London : Everyman, 1965.

de Beavoir, Simonne, *The Second Sex* (Le deuxieme sexe), Paris, trans. and ed. H.M. Parshley, London : Jonathan Cape, 1949.

de Bono, Edward, *Serious Creativity*, New Delhi : Indus, 1994.

Dreiser, Theodore, *Sister Carrie*, Pennsylvania : Penguin, 1981.

Edel, Leon, ''Novel and Camera'', *The Theory of the Novel : New Essays* ed. John Halperin, New York : Oxford University Press, 1974.

Faulkner, William, *The Sound and the Fury*, London : Chatto and Windus, 1966.

Fielder, Leslie A, "The Death and Rebirth of the Novel", *The Theory of the Novel : New Essays* ed. John Halperin, New York : Oxford University Press, 1974.

Fo, Daria, "Accidental Death of an Anarchist, *Plays : . 1*, London : Random, 1986.

Forster, E.M. *Aspects of the Novel*, New York : Harcourt, 1927.

Friedman, Alan Warren, "The Modern Multivalent Novel : Form and Function," *The Theory of the Novel : New Essays* ed. John Halperin, New York : Oxford University Press, 1974.

Golding, William, *Lord of the Flies*, London : Faber and Faber, 1971.

Halperin, John (ed.), *The Theory of the Novel : New Essays* New York : Oxford University Press, 1974.

Hughes, Stuart, H., *Consciousness and Society : The Reorientation of European Social Thought, 1890-1930*, New York, Knopf, 1958.

Jain, Jasbir, *Women's Writing : Text and Context*, Jaipur, Rawat Publications, 1996.

James, Henry, *The Art of Novel*, ed. R.P. Blackmur, New York : Scribner's, 1934.

Joyce, James, *Ulysses*, New York : Random, 1986.

Kaminsky, Alice, R, "On Literary Realism", *The Theory of the Novel : New Essays,* ed. John Halperin, New York : Oxford University Press, 1974.

Karl, Frederick, R. *A Reader's Guide to the Contemporary English Novel*, London : Thames and Hudson, 1972.

Kreshner, R.B. *The Twentieth Century Novel : An Introduction* Boston : Bedford Books, 1997.

Levin, David, "Nathaniel Hawthorne, The Scarlet Letter," *The Voice of America Forum Lectures*, Washington.

Martin, Robert Bernard, "Notes Toward a Comic Fiction", *The Theory of the Novel : New Essays* ed, John Halperin, New York : Oxford University Press, 1974.

Mc Hale, Brian, *Post modernist Fiction*, New York : Methuen, 1987.

Naipaul, V.S. *The Mimic Men*, New York : Macmillan, 1967.

Narayan, R.K. *Reluctant Guru*, New Delhi : Orient Paperbacks, 1974.

Richardson, Dorothy, *Pilgrimage*, Vol. 2, New York : Knopf, 1967.

Robbe -- Grillet, Allain, *For a New Novel : Essays on Fiction*, trans. R. Howard, New York : Grove Press, 1965.

Roy, Arundhati, *The God of Small Things*, New Delhi : India Ink, 1997.

Rushdie, Salmon, *Midnight's Children*, London : Picador, 1983.

Shakespeare, William, *Macbeth* ed. Bernard Lott, Moscow : Progress Publishers, 1977.

Shulz, Max, F. "Characters in the Contemporary Novel", *The Theory of the Novel : New Essays* ed. John Halperin, New York : Oxford University Press, 1974.

Stevenson, John, British Society, 1914-45, London : Penguin, 1984.

Stevenson, Randall, *Modernist Fiction : An Introduction,* New York : Harvester, 1992.

Van O' Connor, William, *Seven Modern American Novelists*, New York : Montor Book, 1964.

Van Ghent, Dorothy, *The English Novel : Form and Function*, New York : Harper, 1953.

Volpe, Edmund, L., *A Reader's Guide to William Faulkner*, London : Thames and Husdon, 1964.

Watt, Ian, The Rise of the Novel, Berkeley : University of California Press, 1957.

Welleck, Rene, *A History of Modern Criticism*, Vol. IV, London.

Williams, Raymond, *The Long Revolution*, rev. ed. New York : Harper, 1966.